IN THE MIDDLE OF
SOMEWHERE

Roan Parrish

REAMSPINNER
PRESS

Published by
DREAMSPINNER PRESS

5032 Capital Circle SW, Suite 2, PMB# 279, Tallahassee, FL 32305-7886 USA
http://www.dreamspinnerpress.com/

This is a work of fiction. Names, characters, places, and incidents either are the product of author imagination or are used fictitiously, and any resemblance to actual persons, living or dead, business establishments, events, or locales is entirely coincidental.

In the Middle of Somewhere
© 2015 Roan Parrish.

Cover Art
© 2015 AngstyG.
www.angstyg.com
Cover content is for illustrative purposes only and any person depicted on the cover is a model.

ISBN: 978-1-63476-212-0
Digital ISBN: 978-1-63476-213-7
Library of Congress Control Number: 2015906026
First Edition Juily 2015

Printed in the United States of America
∞
This paper meets the requirements of
ANSI/NISO Z39.48-1992 (Permanence of Paper).

For Anni, who wanted a story. This wouldn't exist without you.

Acknowledgments

The deepest thank you to Anni, who read every chapter as I wrote it and kept asking for more. Our conversations about this story (and many others) were always the best part of my day. Thanks for showing me what it's like not to write into the void.

To the ladies of DIRGE, the smartest readers I know. Thanks for taking the jump with me; as always, you made everything more fun.

To my early readers, some of whom read this in chunks printed on the backs of things—many thanks for your enthusiasm about this story, even when it wasn't necessarily your cup of tea. To Judith and Ellen for being such excited, opinionated readers, and for the tipsy conversations about (mostly fictional) love.

Profound thanks to the Dreamspinner team for all your hard work. From semicolons to cover design, your professionalism and support have made this journey a joy.

To my parents for being open-minded readers, for listening to me ramble on about my "secret project" for months before I would tell you what it was, and for taking me seriously when I told you.

To my wonderful sap of a sister. This may be the first story other people are seeing, but you've heard them all. Thank you for being unfailingly excited about everything I write and perpetually willing to discuss it. Loudly. In public. Over nachos and beer.

And to Dorian Gray, for alternately curling up and stretching out beside me (or on my computer) as the situation required.

Chapter 1

February

I TOSS my bag in the door of my rental car and practically throw myself in after it. Once the door is safely closed, I slump into the seat, close my eyes, and curse the entire state of Michigan. If Michigan didn't exist, then I wouldn't be sitting in a rental car at the edge of Sleeping Bear College's tiny campus, having a premature midlife crisis at thirty.

I just spent the day interviewing for a job at Sleeping Bear, a small liberal arts college I'd never even heard of until six months ago. My interview went well, my teaching demonstration went even better, and I'm pretty sure I never let my cuffs slide up to show my tattoos. I could tell they liked me, and they seemed enthusiastic about hiring someone young to help them build the department. As they talked about independent studies and dual majors, I mentally catalogued all the bear puns I could. Of course, what they'd think if they found out that I associate bears' hairy chests and lumbering gaits with large men drinking beer instead of the college, the nearby dunes, and the animal they are named for, I can't say.

I've been working my ass off to get where I am today, and all I can think is that I'm a fraud. I'm not an English professor. I'm just some queer little punk from Philadelphia who the smart kids slummed it with. Just ask my ex. Just ask my father. Ask my brothers, especially. God, what the hell am I doing here?

Sleeping Bear is the only college where I got an interview and it is in the middle of fucking nowhere—near some place called Traverse City (which is *definitely* not a city, based on anything I've ever seen). I had to drive for nearly four hours after I flew to Detroit to get here. I could have gotten closer with a connecting flight in a tiny plane, but I'll be damned if the first time I ever flew I was going to crash into one of the Great Lakes. No, overland travel was good enough for me, even if the flight, the rental car, and the suit I bought for the visit put me even deeper in the hole than I was before. At least I saved a hundred bucks getting the red-eye from Detroit to Philly tomorrow night.

I shudder when I think what my credit card bill will look like this month. Good thing I can turn the heat off in my apartment in a few weeks when it gets above forty degrees. Not like there's anyone there except me. My friends from school never want to come to my neighborhood, claiming it's more convenient to go places near campus. Richard, my ex, wouldn't be caught dead in my apartment, which he referred to as "the crack house." Asshole. And I only see my brothers and my dad at their auto shop. Still, I love Philly; I've lived there all my life. Moving—especially to the middle of nowhere—well, even the thought is freaking me out.

Now, all I want is to go back to my shitty little motel room, order a pizza, and fall asleep in front of crappy TV. I sigh and start the rental car I can't afford.

I have to admit, though, the road from the school to my motel is beautiful. All the hotels near campus are cute (read: expensive) bed and breakfast joints, so I booked in at the Motel 6 outside of town. It's down a two-lane road that seems to follow the tree line. To my left are fields and the occasional dirt road turnoff with signs I can't read in the near-dark. God, I'm starving. I haven't eaten since an ill-advised Dunkin' Donuts egg sandwich at the airport.

It's really cold so far north, but I crack the window to breathe the sweet smell of fresh air and trees anyway. It's actually really peaceful out here. Quiet. It isn't something I'm used to—quiet, I mean. Library-quiet and middle-of-the-night quiet, sure. But in the city there's always noise. This is a quiet that feels like water and trees and, well, nature, I guess, like the time my parents took us to the Jersey Shore when we were kids and I hid under the boardwalk away from the crowds, listening to the overwhelming sound of the ocean and the creak of docks.

And peace? Well, never peace. If it wasn't one of my asshole brothers starting shit with me, it was my dad flipping his lid over me being gay. Of course, later my lack of peace came in the form of Richard, my ex, who, while we were together, was apparently sleeping with every gay man at the University of Pennsylvania.

My hands tighten on the wheel as I picture Richard, his handsome face set in an expression of haughty condescension as he leveled me with one nauseating smile. "Come on, Dan," he said, like we had discussed this before, "who believes in monogamy anymore? Don't be so bourgeois." And, "It's not like we're exclusive." That, after we'd been together for two years—or so I'd thought—and I'd taken him to my brother Sam's wedding.

Anyway, I hate being called Dan.

I grit my teeth and force myself to take a deep breath. No more thinking about Richard. I promised myself.

I glance down at the scrap of paper where I scrawled the directions to my motel. I can almost taste the buttery cheese and crispy pizza crust and my stomach growls. When I look back up a second later, something darts into the road in front of me. I swerve hard to the right, but I hear a sickening whine the second before the car veers into a tree.

ALL I can see is blackness, until I realize I scrunched my eyes shut before I hit the tree. I open them slowly, expecting to look down and see that my legs are gone or something, like in one of those war movies my brother is always watching, where a bomb goes off and the soldier thinks he's fine, laughing and smiling, until the dust clears and he looks down and has no lower body. Then the pain hits. It's like the cartoon physics of awareness: we can't hurt until we see that we're supposed to.

But my legs are there, as is everything else. I do a quick stretch, but aside from some soreness where the seat belt locked in, I actually feel okay. The car, however, is another story. I can already see that I'm not driving out of here. I jam the door open and slide out, a little unsteady on my feet. And then I hear it. A terrible whining noise.

Fuck, what did I do?

The dark seems to have settled in all of a sudden and it's hard to see the road. I take a few cautious steps toward the noise, and then I see it. A dog. A brown and white dog that doesn't look much older than a puppy, though it's already pretty big. I don't know anything about dogs, have no idea what kind it is. But it's definitely hurt. It looks like maybe I broke its leg when I hit it.

"Fuck, fuck, fuck," I say. The dog is whimpering, its big brown eyes wide with pain. "Fuck, dog, I'm so sorry," I tell it, and reach out a hand to try and soothe it. As I reach for its head, though, it growls and I jerk my hand back.

"I know, dog, I'm sorry. I'm not going to hurt you. Hang on."

I rush back to the car for my phone and try to call information so I can find an emergency vet, but I can't get a signal out here at all. I put the car in neutral and try to rock it away from the tree enough so that I can look under the hood—growing up with a family auto shop means you can't help but know how to fix cars, even if you don't want to go into the family business. But there's no way. The undercarriage must've caught on the tree's roots or something.

I grab my bag and sling it over my shoulder, and go back to where the dog is lying, still whimpering. I can't leave it here. It'll get run over by a car in the dark. Or, worse, it'll just lie here all alone, terrified and in pain. The sound it's making is ripping my fucking heart out. I can't believe I did this. Christ, how did I even get here? I ease to the other side of the dog and gently run my fingertips over the soft fur on its head. It whines, but doesn't growl.

I keep petting it, talking low as I ease my arm underneath.

"Okay, dog, you're okay. Don't worry, I've got you. Everything's going to be fine." I'm saying things I haven't heard since my mother said them when I was little. Words that are meant to comfort but mean nothing.

I roll the dog into my arms and it whimpers and growls as I jostle its hurt leg. I cuddle it close to my chest to keep it immobile and try to stand without falling over and hurting it worse. I'll just walk a little ways. There has to be a gas station, or a house, or something, right? I'll just ask someone to call a vet. Hell, maybe this is what police do in a nothing town like this. Rescue dogs that get stuck in trees, or something? No, wait, that's cats. Cats get stuck in trees. Right?

I walk for what feels like forever. The dog has gone quiet, but I can feel it breathing, so at least I know it isn't dead. What it is, though, is getting heavy. I stop for a second to check if I have phone service for what feels like the millionth time. I haven't come across a single gas station and I'm not sure how much longer I can walk.

"Okay, dog; it's okay," I say again, but my voice is as shaky as my legs, and, really, it isn't the dog I'm talking to anymore. Still no service. Fuck.

Then, off to my right, I see a light. A shaky beam of light that's getting closer. Just as I pull level with the light, a man steps out of the woods. I rear away from the large form, and the dog whimpers softly. The man looks huge and the way he's shining the flashlight is blinding. My heart beats heavily in my throat. This guy could take me apart. Squaring my shoulders and setting my feet so I look as big as possible, I plan how I can set the dog down without hurting it further if I have to fight. Or run. Then a warm voice breaks the silence that stopped feeling peaceful the second I swerved.

"You okay?"

His voice is deep and a little growly. For half a second, all the puns about bears that I was making earlier dance through my head and I laugh. What comes out sounds more like a hysterical squeak, though.

"Do you mind?" I say, squinting and hoping my voice sounds more threatening than the noise I just made. He lowers the flashlight immediately and walks toward me. I take a half step back automatically. All I can really see in the dark, with the ghost of the flashlight leaving spots in my vision, are massive shoulders clad in plaid.

"Are you okay?" the man asks again, and he puts out a hand as he takes the last few slow steps to my side. I nod quickly. His hand is huge.

"I, um."

He bends down and looks in my face. I don't know what he sees there, but his posture shifts, the bulk of him softening ever so slightly.

"I didn't mean to," I try to explain when it's clear he isn't a threat. "Only, it came out of nowhere and I couldn't—" I break off as he shines the flashlight on the dog. It whines and I gather it closer to me, suddenly unsure. "I tried to find a vet, but I can't get a signal here and my car hit the tree so I couldn't drive and I—"

"You were in an accident? Are you hurt?"

"No—I mean, I'm not. I'm… but my car's fucked. Do you have a phone? Can you call a vet?"

"No vet," he says. "Nothing's open this late." It's maybe 7:00 p.m.

"Please," I say. "I can't let it die. Fuck! What the fuck am I doing here? I can't believe I—" I break off when I can tell my next words won't be anything I want a total stranger to hear.

"Come with me," the man says, and turns and walks back into the woods. What the hell?

"Um," I say. Am I actually supposed to follow a total stranger into the woods? In the dark? In the middle of nowhere? In *Michigan*? I know stereotypes about cannibals who live in the woods and eat unsuspecting tourists are just that: stereotypes. Maybe I've watched *The Hills Have Eyes* one too many times, but still. Isn't it, like, a statistical fact that most serial killers come from the Midwest?

While I was distracted by regionally profiling the man, he'd come back out of the woods and is now standing directly in front of me, close enough that I can kind of see his face. He has dark hair and eyes, and a sharp nose. That's all I can see in the dark. But he is definitely much younger than I assumed. His low voice sounded older, but he looks like he's in his midthirties. And up close, he is massive, with hugely broad shoulders, powerful arms, and broad hips—how much of that is flesh and how much is flannel remains to be seen. He's nearly a head taller than me, and I'm not short.

"You need to come with me," he says, and his voice suggests that he's considering the fact that I might be an idiot.

"Er, sure," I say, figuring that if worse comes to worst, at least I can run; I have to be faster than this guy, right? I take an experimental step toward him and, in the way it sometimes happens when you rest after an exertion, nearly fall on my face as my body takes longer to wake up than my brain. The man catches me with one easy hand under my elbow and steadies me. Shit, that was embarrassing.

"Here," he says. "Let me take the dog. You take this." He shrugs something off his shoulder and hands it to me. It takes a few seconds to process the unfamiliar shape in the dark.

"Is that a *gun*?"

"Yeah," he says.

"Why do you have a gun?" I ask warily. Though, I guess I should be reassured that he's handing it to me and not pointing it at me.

"To hunt with," he says matter-of-factly.

"Right," I say. Hunting. Michigan. *Michigan.*

He gently sets what I can only assume is a rifle on the ground next to me.

"Let me." He slides his hands under the dog. His hands are huge, covering practically my whole stomach as he worms them under my arms. "I've got him," he says.

"I don't know if it's a boy," I say. "I don't know anything about dogs. I mean, I guess I would've been able to tell by looking, but I didn't think of it. But it's really common, defaulting to male pronouns to refer to things of indeterminate gender." Christ, I'm babbling.

He cocks his head at me and walks away. I pick up the strap of the gun gingerly and take off after him, holding it as far away from the trigger as I can. With the luck I'm having today, I'd trip and end up shooting the man. Or myself. Or, shit, probably the dog.

"HAND ME the scissors," the man says. I'm petting the dog's head and surreptitiously trying not to look at the poor thing's leg, which the man has determined is, indeed, broken. His house was only about a ten-minute walk from the road.

I hand him the scissors and examine his face in the light of the lamp. I tell myself it's just because I'd rather look anywhere but at the dog's leg. He has a really good face, though. Strong, high cheekbones and a straight nose; straight, dark eyebrows, one with a white scar bisecting it, and dark brown hair that waves slightly. His eyes are lighter than I thought in the woods: a kind of whiskey brown that looks almost gold in the light. Maybe one is a little narrower than the other, but he hasn't made eye contact with me long enough for me to be sure. His mouth is set in a grim line of concentration while he works, but it's soft and generous. He hasn't smiled yet, but he probably has a nice one.

He stripped off his outer layer of flannel as he laid the dog down on the kitchen table. It was a bulky, quilted jacket, but even without it, he's huge, his shoulders and the muscles of his arms tightening his blue and gray flannel shirt. He rolled up the sleeves to reveal a white waffle-knit shirt that's too short in the sleeves, exposing thick wrists and powerful forearms. His huge hands are gentle on the dog's fur and I can't help but imagine what they'd feel like on my skin. What it would be like to be held in those hands, to be enveloped. My hand tightens in the dog's fur and I force myself to relax as it makes a sound.

"She's a girl, by the way." His voice startles me and I meet his eyes, praying that he can't read what I've been thinking about on my face. The last thing I need is for tomorrow's local paper—if they even *have* a paper in this town—to carry a story that reads, "Out of town gay man found beaten to death in cabin of unfairly handsome local straight bruiser. Police assume queer panic ensued after out of town gay made a pass at straight bruiser."

"Huh?" I say. He swallows, like he isn't used to talking.

"The dog. You were right, she isn't a boy." He pats the dog gently and scoops her up, depositing her in a nest of blankets in front of the fireplace.

"Oh," I say. "Great." I stand and follow him. I realize I'm nodding compulsively and force myself to stop. He touches a long match to the newspaper and kindling below the logs in the grate.

"Is she going to be okay, do you think?" The fire consumes the paper and there's a delicious, earthy smell as the bark on the logs starts to crackle. With the fire lit, he turns toward me.

"I think so. If she can stay off this leg tonight, I'll take her into town tomorrow. Have the vet check her out for any internal injuries."

I'm suddenly so relieved that I go a little woozy. I didn't kill anyone. I didn't hurt the poor dog beyond repair. I'm not a total fuckup.

"Whoa," he says. In one step, he's there, grabbing me by both shoulders to keep me upright. My vision is a little blurry and I blink up at him. God, he's handsome. His brows are furrowed with worry, his eyes narrowed.

"Sorry," he says, looking down. "I should've made sure you weren't hurt."

"No, I'm okay," I say, stepping out from under his hands.

"You were in a car accident. Come here." He steps behind me and puts his hands back on my shoulders, guiding me to the bathroom. When he flips the switch, I wince at the harsh light after being so long in the dark. In the mirror, I can see why he's concerned. My black hair is messy and there's a smear of blood on my cheek from the dog. A bruise is already coming out on my forehead, though I don't even remember hitting my head. I blink at my reflection. My pupils are huge, even in the bright light, leaving only a thin ring of green around them.

He's looking at me in the mirror, his light eyes fixed on mine. I can smell him behind me: wood smoke and damp wool and something lightly piney, like deodorant. Or, hey, I guess in the woods it could actually be pine. I can feel the warmth he's giving off and it reminds me of how cold I am. He turns me around by the shoulders again, like he's my rudder.

I shiver. I dropped my coat by the door, but even though it was cold out, I sweat through my shirt and suit coat while I was carrying the dog, and now they've turned cold and clammy. The tie I borrowed from my brother, Sam, and the new white shirt I bought for my interview are both streaked with blood.

"Shit." I halfheartedly swipe at the blood. As I rub a little harder, I wince, realizing that my chest is sore.

"Were you wearing your seat belt?"

"Huh?" I feel like I'm processing everything five seconds after he says it. "Oh, yeah."

He slides my suit jacket off my shoulders and starts to unbutton my shirt.

"Um," I mumble. He bats my hand away and pulls my shirt apart. When I look down, I can see a purple bruise forming in the shape of my seat belt. Well, good to know it worked, I guess. The bruise is long, disappearing into the tattoos that cover most of my torso.

"Tell me if it's particularly tender anywhere." He probes the length of the bruise gently.

"No, it's okay," I say, half because it's true and half because I can't think with his fingers on my skin. His hands are warm the way big guys' are sometimes—great circulation, I guess.

"Wasn't expecting those," he says, gesturing to my tattoos. It's funny. Anyone who meets me when I'm dressed professionally is surprised to find out I have tattoos, but anyone who knows me from my real life—at concerts, coffee shops, or just around—thinks my professional drag looks out of place.

I shrug and he gives me a cursory once-over, looking for other bruises. "Take your pants off."

"Oh, um, I—" I scooch backward, away from him. There's no way I'll be able to keep it together standing in front of this gorgeous man almost naked. "Maybe, could I just take a shower?"

He doesn't say anything, but turns the water on and grabs a towel from a shelf on the wall. It's forest green. It seems like everything about him and this house is green and brown. Earthy.

"Here, give me your clothes," he says. "I'll get you something of mine to wear."

When he leaves, I toe my dress shoes off, trying not to notice that anyone who looked could see the soles are worn almost through, but they're polished to a mirror shine—or, at least, they were before my trek in through the woods. Five-dollar-new-shoes: that's what my dad always called a shoeshine.

He knocks a minute later and hands me a pile of neatly folded sweatpants and a T-shirt. Then he hands me a drink.

"I thought you could use something to warm you up."

I sniff it. Whiskey. I down it like a shot.

"Thanks."

He backs out of the bathroom and I undress and step under the hot water with a sigh.

I can't let myself think any more about this shit show of a day—much less the fact that I'm in the shower of a total stranger who may or may not be about to axe murder me and wrap me up in this shower curtain—or I'm going to lose it. Instead, I pretend like Ginger is giving me a stern talking-to because, unlike mine, Ginger's talking-tos sometimes work. Well, first Ginger would tell me to have a fucking drink, so I'm good on that count. Then it would probably go something like this:

Me: I'm having a nervous breakdown. I have no clue what I should be doing with my life. What if my dad is right and academia is for assholes who think they're better than everyone else but never do a day's work in their lives?

Ginger: Your dad is a fucking idiot. We know this. First of all, you don't have to know what you're doing with your whole life. Just what you're doing right now. And right now, you're being a professor. Second, you don't think you're better than everyone. Third, you've worked hard your entire life.

Me: Okay, but what if Richard's right and I'm not really smart enough to do this? I mean, I wasn't smart enough to realize that he was having sex with approximately 10 percent of Philadelphia, even though everyone else knew.

Ginger: Richard is a fucking idiot. Also, he looks like a boring version of an Abercrombie and Fitch model. You hate that all-American shit. You only went out with him because you were insecure about being the only one at Penn whose parents weren't professor-types. You were flattered when he wanted to go out with you because you thought it meant you were smart. Well, you are smart, but that was stupid. You're smart enough to be a professor; that's why you're going to get this job.

Me: Fuck me, Ginge—this place is ridiculous. I'm probably the only queer within a hundred miles. There's a park near here called Gaylord, and I bet no one even thinks it's funny. Seriously, if I get this job I'll have to be celibate. Until some cute little gay undergrad catches me in a weak moment, after I haven't had sex in seventeen years, and then I'll get fired for inappropriate conduct, or put in jail for sexual harassment.

Ginger: Look, kid, you're flipping out over maybes and you're overthinking, as usual. Just see what this job is before you're so positive it has nothing to offer you. Ride the wave. Besides, you know the stats. I don't care if it's the lunch lady, your accountant, or the butch lumberjack; there have got to be homosexuals, even in that godforsaken little slice of Minnesota.

Me: Michigan.

Ginger: Whatever, pumpkin.

She's right, as usual. And, of course, her mention of butch lumberjacks brings me right back to… shit, I don't even know his name.

I MAKE my way back into the living room, holding up my borrowed sweatpants in an attempt not to trip and kill myself. The T-shirt sleeves reach past my elbows. It's like when I used to have to wear my older brothers' stuff, only worse because I wasn't concerned about looking attractive in front of my brothers, who would've told me I looked like an idiot no matter what I was wearing. Of course, it makes no sense to worry about how I look in front of this man either, since it's not like some super masculine straight guy is going to care. These clothes do have one advantage over my brothers', though: whereas my brothers' hand-me-downs smelled like stale sweat beneath industrial-strength bleach, these smell like fabric softener and cedar.

As I walk past the fire, the dog lifts her eyelids and regards me sleepily, but doesn't stir. I can hear noise coming from the kitchen.

"What's your name?" I ask the man's broad back, where he's bent over the sink, washing a plate.

The muscles in his back and shoulders tense, as if I startled him. He turns around and his eyes immediately go to my hips.

"Those things are gonna fall off you," he says. "Come here." He rummages around in a drawer next to the sink.

Be still, my fantasies, I insist as I step toward him. The last thing I need is to pop a boner in this guy's sweatpants and have him kick my ass. Not that it'd be the first time.

He squats down, gathers the excess fabric around my hips, and folds it over, then holds it together with a binder clip. I must look confused because he shrugs and mutters, "I use them for chip clips."

"Thanks," I say, and roll the T-shirt sleeves up a little so I don't look like a child.

"What's yours?"

"Huh? Oh, I'm Daniel." I stick out a hand to him in a weirdly professional gesture, as if we haven't been together for an hour, as if he didn't just binder-clip the waist of my borrowed sweatpants. But he just takes my hand in his large palm and shakes it firmly. God, his hands are so warm.

"So?" I ask again.

"Rex," he says, and ducks his head a bit shyly. Rex. King. It suits him.

"I guess I should go," I say, making a vague gesture toward the door. "Oh shit, my car—I have to call someone—and I didn't even check in to my hotel yet, so I need—" God, I'm tired.

"I took care of it," Rex says, turning back to the sink. "Here, do you want another drink? You look like you could use it." He pours another whiskey and holds it out to me.

"Thanks. What do you mean, you took care of it?" I sip this whiskey a bit slower. My head feels like it's full of cotton.

"I called someone and had your car towed. It was a rental, right?" I nod. "So, you can just pick one up at the airport. It's right near here." Relief floods me that I won't have to handle that. I can't even remember the last time someone took care of anything for me.

"Thank you," I say, and I can hear the relief in my voice. I finish the whiskey in my glass and hold it out for a refill without thinking about it. Rex gives me an amused nod and refills my glass, pours one for himself, and then gestures me into the living room.

I sink down onto Rex's green plaid couch and pull the blue flannel blanket over me. The couch dips with Rex's weight as he sits beside me and I open my eyes. In the firelight, he is a god. The flames flicker over the planes of his face and the straight lines of his eyebrows, create a shadow under his full lower lip, turn his stubble to velvet and his eyes to molten gold. I slug back the rest of my drink and put the glass down. I can't look away from him. He's regarding me calmly and I can smell him on the blanket I'm wrapped up in.

Something is happening to me. It's like there is a magnet drawing me toward him and I am in actual danger of making an idiotic move on a stranger who is, as far as I know, straight, in a cabin in the woods, when no one knows where I am. Okay, *now* is when I need to remind myself of all those stereotypes of rural cannibalistic serial killers. Remember *The Hills Have Eyes*, Daniel! *Texas Chainsaw Massacre*! Or, more realistically, I just need to focus on how much it actually hurts to get hit in the face, which is what's likely to happen if I get any closer to Rex than the other side of the couch.

I clear my throat and shake my head, trying to banish the fog that's taken over.

"Is everything you have made of plaid?"

"No," Rex says. "Some of it's just plain flannel."

I start to laugh and can't stop, even though it's not particularly funny. All of a sudden I realize what should've been obvious: I'm drunk. I've had three whiskeys after being in a car accident and I haven't eaten since breakfast. Can Rex tell?

"When was the last time you ate?" he says. Yep, I think he can tell. And I almost don't care. It's so nice and warm here, so cozy. No one I know is here to witness me potentially losing my shit in Holiday, Michigan. No one ever has to know that I hit a dog. And no one here knows that in approximately one month I will be evicted if I can't grab a whole lot of extra hours at the bar so I can afford my rent. None of it matters while I'm warm and tipsy here, in the land of flannel and wood.

Suddenly, the middle of nowhere seems like the best possible place I could be.

I MUST'VE fallen asleep for a minute, because when I wake up, Rex is standing over me holding a sandwich.

"Daniel."

I sit up a little and take the plate from him.

"Uh, yeah."

"What are you doing here?"

I look around the room, my head still spacey. No, Daniel, he means in town. Get it together.

"I had a job interview. At Sleeping Bear College." I take a bite of the sandwich and feel a little sick, the way I sometimes do if I wait too long to eat. But the second bite is heaven.

"What kind of jam is this?" I ask.

"Mixed berry."

"It's good."

"What was your interview for?"

"To teach in the English department." The words make my stomach clench with anxiety. Or maybe that's just the peanut butter.

"You're an English professor? You seem so young."

"Yeah. Well, technically, I'm still a grad student, but if I get the job, it'll start in the fall, and I'll defend my dissertation in the summer, so then I'll be a professor. It's funny you think I'm younger than usual. Most people, when they hear I'm in grad school, they're like, 'Oh, so that'll take you, what, two or three years?' And I'll say, 'No, more like seven or eight,' and they think it's crazy because they've seen TV shows where all the characters have three PhDs by the time they're twenty-three. It's unrealistic and propagates total misinformation about higher education. Drives me crazy."

"A dissertation. That's the book you write to get your degree, right?" Rex seems to actually be listening, even though I've gone off on a grad school tirade.

"Yeah. I've been working on it for five years." Alongside teaching every semester, bartending on the weekends, applying for fellowships, and, recently, applying for fifty-six jobs across the country, that is.

"What's it about?"

"Oh, it's boring; you don't want to hear about that," I tell him.

"Well, if you think I won't understand," Rex says, and his jaw tightens.

"No, no, that's not what I meant. I just—no one who isn't writing a dissertation ever actually wants to hear about them. Hell, even the people who are writing them don't really want to hear about them; they only ask so that you'll ask about theirs in return. Do you seriously want to know?"

"I asked, didn't I?"

"Um, yeah. Well, I study nineteenth and early twentieth century American literature. Basically, I'm writing about authors from that time period who use social realism to explore the different models of economic theory available. So, some of them were critiquing capitalism, but didn't offer anything in its place; some were radically anarchist; some were staunch Marxists; etc. But all of them used their writing to explore the effects of those different models."

Rex is looking into the fire.

"Sorry. I'm boring you. That was so geeky. This stuff isn't really interesting to anyone except me. I shouldn't—"

"You aren't boring me," Rex says. "Go on."

He has this low, authoritative voice that makes me forget that there's any possibility except to do what he says. So I go on. I tell him about the books, about the authors' lives; before I know it, I'm talking about literary naturalism and Marxist materialist criticism, and ranting about the job market. I never talk this much—not to anyone but Ginger.

And Rex seems interested. He doesn't seem to think I'm a total geek or a pretentious asshole. Or maybe he just feels sorry for the idiotic city boy who got himself marooned in Northern Michigan, almost killed a dog, and is currently drunk in a stranger's sweatpants in a cabin made of plaid and flannel. I trail off.

"So, do you think you'll get the job?" he asks.

"Yeah," I say, and sigh.

"What, you don't want it?"

"Well, I need *a* job," I tell him. "I need the money, for sure. And, no matter what, I can use this position as a springboard for another job if a better one comes along. And it's actually a pretty good fit for me, you know. Like, I don't want to be lecturing to three hundred unfamiliar faces at a huge university. I like how small the school is, how they're excited about building up the English department. They even want to have a creative writing graduate program eventually. They think the—how did they put it?—'natural isolation' will be a draw for writers."

"But," Rex prompts, looking at me intently.

"But…. No offense, man, but there's, like, *nothing* here. I've lived in Philly my whole life. I don't know shit about trees or animals or nature. I mean, I just never saw myself someplace so… isolated." My stomach is a knot of fear. Every word I speak hammers home how totally and completely screwed I would be living here.

I spent the last eight years in graduate school, all of it leading up to this moment—a moment, I must add, that most grad students would kill for in this crazy economy and terrible job market. But now… shit. I'm just so unsure.

"And, anyway, I don't even know if I want to *be* an English professor. Like, what good would that actually do, you know? Really? It's not useful. It's like, what, teaching a bunch of overprivileged, sheltered kids with their parents' credit cards how to construct a thesis statement or, if I'm lucky, getting to teach one senior seminar a year in the stuff I'm actually interested in, which no one will care about anyway."

I can hear my voice, but it sounds like it's coming from a million miles away. I think maybe I did hit my head. My ears are ringing and I feel like someone poured cement into my stomach. God, the idea of sitting at a desk for the rest of my life, teaching kids who don't care, talking to other professors in their fifties and sixties about the decline of the written word with the advent of texting, totally alone in this godforsaken place. My hands are fists and I shake my head to try and clear it.

"Besides, I'm probably the only gay guy in a hundred-mile radius," I blurt out, forgetting that I'm not talking to Ginger, like I was in the shower. Fuck. I can't believe I just said that. "And, uh, there's, like, no music scene here?" I look around the room, everywhere but at Rex. The dog is still snoozing in front of the fire, her front paw twitching as she dreams. I wish I were her. I wish I were asleep, in front of a fire, cozy and warm, and not having to worry about anything except whether I'll get breakfast soon.

I force myself to meet Rex's gaze. To look at him calmly and confidently, as if what I just said is no big deal. This is what I've learned over the years. You just stare, like everything is normal, make them feel like they'll be the awkward one if they say anything to you about it. Just stay calm and narrow your eyes a little like you're not scared of a fight.

But Rex isn't saying anything, isn't reacting at all. I get up, clumsily, and bring my plate and glass to the kitchen sink. I pour a quick slug of whiskey in the glass and down it, then start scrubbing the plate. *Everything's fine*, I say in my head. *Everything's fine. Everything's fine.*

When Rex comes up behind me, the soapy plate slips out of my hand and shatters in the sink. I jump backward.

"Shit! Shit, I'm sorry." I look up at him, expecting anger, maybe disgust. When he doesn't say anything, I start to pick up the pieces of broken plate, but they're slippery and I keep dropping them.

"Stop." Rex puts his hands over mine in the sink. He dries my hands with the dishtowel, then takes me by the shoulders and turns me around so I'm leaning against the wall.

"You need to calm down," he says, and his voice is a warm ocean of command. I nod, trying to calm down, but my heart is racing. What is wrong with me? It's not like people don't know I'm gay. Hell, I've always enjoyed letting idiots bro down with me and then just casually talking about my boyfriend to watch their surprise. It's obvious that Rex isn't going to hurt me; if he were, he would've done it already. I take a deep breath, his heavy hands weighing my shoulders down, anchoring me.

I look up at him, his eyes the same color as the whiskey I just drank. He steps closer, until I can feel his warmth. I open my mouth to tell him I'm fine, but what comes out is an embarrassingly shaky breath.

"Just calm down," he says. And then he kisses me.

His hand is so big that when he cups my cheek his fingers trail down my neck, warm and rough. His mouth is soft on mine, but the power of his body behind it makes it clear he's holding himself back. As one hand strokes my neck, the other cups my head, tangling in my hair. I open my eyes for a moment to make sure this is real, and his are open too, heavy-lidded and golden.

He pulls back and straightens up. He's tall enough that he had to bend down to kiss me. I wonder if that's annoying—to have to bend down all the time. Or, I guess if he were kissing someone his same height, he wouldn't have to, but that's probably pretty rare. Also, holy crap, Rex is gay! I wonder—

Then I can't think of anything else because his mouth is on mine again, and this time it's a real kiss. His hands are on my hips and my head is tilted back against the wall and he's kissing me, his tongue filling all the empty spaces. I reach up and put my arms around his neck, trying to pull him closer to me. He slides a hand up my side and around to my back, and he hooks his hand around my shoulder, locking me to him. I gasp into his mouth as he pushes his hips forward, his hardness hot against my stomach even through his jeans.

He pulls back, his mouth leaving mine with a lewd smack.

"Better?" he asks, and when he gives me his first real smile, it's the sweetest thing I've ever seen. His whole face is transformed. He has dimples and his teeth are a little crooked, one incisor slightly twisted.

I huff out a laugh and grin back.

"Better." And, actually, I am. I feel calm and boneless. Well, not exactly boneless. In fact, I'm trying to psychically communicate that he could make everything a whole lot better if he'd just release the binder clip barely holding my sweatpants up and take me on the kitchen table, but he doesn't seem to be getting the message.

He takes me by the hand and leads me back to the couch. He covers me with the flannel blanket, sinks down next to me, and flicks on the TV with one hand while he subtly adjusts himself with the other. When he looks at me out of the corner of his eye, I grin at him. He laughs and shakes his head.

"Just relax."

He's channel surfing—more channels than I would've expected to find in a log cabin. I think I finally have to admit to myself that I am helpless to control my dumb stereotypes about rural places and the people who live in them. As if he can read my mind, Rex rolls his eyes and points out the front door.

"Satellite dish."

He stops changing channels at a black-and-white movie, looking totally delighted when he turns to me and points at the screen expectantly. I have no idea what movie it is. I'm not sure I've ever even seen an entire black-and-white movie except when I took a film class in college. I don't even own a TV.

"*Gaslight*," he says, smiling. "I love this movie." He's still looking at me expectantly; I shake my head.

"I've never seen it."

"Really? Ingrid Bergman. I love her."

"So you *are* gay," I joke.

He fixes me with a smoldering look.

"Were you in doubt?"

"No," I squeak. He looks back at the screen.

"This version is the most famous, but MGM actually made it only four years after the UK film version. Then they somehow cut a deal so that the UK version wasn't allowed to be rereleased in the US. I do think this one is better than the 1940 version, though. Mostly because Ingrid Bergman's better than Diana Wynyard.

"It's great, although MGM's corniness ruins it in some parts. And, you know, the Production Code. It's Angela Lansbury's first film role."

He's speaking absently, as if I know all this, his face animated even as his eyes are glued to the screen.

"You're a film geek, huh?"

"What? No. I mean, I just like old movies," he says, looking a little uncomfortable.

"I think that's awesome," I say, desperate not to have offended him. "I never saw many movies growing up, so I guess I just never developed a taste for them. It was always sports at my house."

"Do you still follow sports?"

"Oh, no, I never did. My dad and my brothers, though. Huge sports fans. I think as long as it's got a ball, they watch it. Well, except soccer. They think soccer's for pansies. Oh, and golf, because it's not violent."

"How many brothers do you have?"

"Three. All older. You?"

"No," he says, and turns back to the TV. We watch the movie in silence for ten or fifteen minutes.

"Hey, wait, is this where the term to gaslight someone comes from?"

"Yeah," Rex says, looking back at me. "Ingrid Bergman's husband—Charles Boyer—messes with her head, trying to make her think she's going crazy."

It is so hot to watch him talk about this stuff. He's so, well, burly; he doesn't look like the kind of guy who'd be into old movies. And unlike Richard, my ex, or the people I went to grad school with, he doesn't sound like his interest is academic. There's none of the desire to impress with his knowledge, none of the analysis asserted as fact. He's just really excited about an old Ingrid Bergman movie. And I want nothing more than to kiss him again.

"I guess I always thought it had something to do with gas fumes making people hallucinate or something," I murmur.

He smiles at me. "I think that's a common mis—"

He breaks off when I launch myself into his lap. I kiss him, throwing my arms around his neck. His mouth is soft and his body is hard beneath me. When I kiss him, his hands go automatically to my back, stroking up and down my spine, sending sparks of heat through my whole body. I moan into his mouth, and he drags me down by the shoulders. I'm dizzy with lust, his scent and his warmth and his big hands making it impossible to do anything but keep kissing him.

I reach between us and fumble for his fly, but I'm pulled out of my haze by hands holding mine still.

"Hey, hey, Daniel." He takes my hands between his and puts them back on his shoulders. He kisses me softly, but it's a good-bye kiss. I can tell. A we're-done-now kiss. A pity kiss. The warmth of lust is immediately replaced with nausea. My head is pounding and I'm too hot, not to mention humiliated. I move off him with as much dignity as I can muster, considering I'm straddling someone with binder-clipped sweatpants and a too-big shirt that has fallen off one shoulder like a valley girl's sweatshirt.

On the floor, the dog has raised her head and is looking at me as if even she can tell something is wrong with me. I stare at the fire intently, wishing I could disappear into it.

"Look," Rex says, his voice gentle. "It's really late, and you've had a long day. You should get some sleep." I nod without looking at him.

He brings me a pillow from the hall closet, and another blanket, but instead of going into his room, he lingers in the doorway, looking at me.

"You know," he says, and he sounds a little shy. "You kind of look like you could be one of those old-time Hollywood leading men."

I look up at him, startled. He's looking at me intently, leaning forward, but his eyes are sad, dark.

"You'd be wasted on black and white, though. Your eyes." He makes a vague gesture toward my face, then turns away. "Good night, Daniel," he says. And then he's gone.

Chapter 2

August

THE AIR conditioning in my car died somewhere in Ohio, so it's hard to hear Ginger above the highway sounds coming in through the windows I've rolled down to avoid roasting. Fortunately, the girl's never been accused of being quiet.

"Okay," she says, "so I google-mapped this town of yours and I've gotta tell you, pumpkin, I'm a little concerned."

It's taken Ginger all summer to be able to remember that I'm moving to Michigan—not Minnesota, not Missouri—so this is progress.

"Number one: are you aware that this state is shaped like a mitten and people actually refer to it as The Mitten?"

"I am," I say. Ginger is one of the smartest people I know, but she reminds me of someone's grandmother sometimes with her insistence that the things beyond her daily routine are bizarre and shocking.

"So, you're moving to a state that people refer to by its winter wear. This state also gets a lot of snow. There is only so much geological coincidence I can bear, sweet cheeks. Also, from what I can tell, the main claim to fame of this hamlet you will soon call home is its cherries. Tart cherries."

"Yeah."

"Daniel! *Tart* cherries. Who wants a tart cherry?"

"Dunno, Ginge; I've never tried one. I'll be sure to let you know."

"Okay, fine, clearly you're not in the mood to be distracted, so get on with it. What did your dad say?"

I didn't tell my father or my brothers about getting the job at Sleeping Bear College until last night, after I finished packing. I got the call offering me the job only about a week after my visit. Bernard Ness, the chair of the job search committee, was enthusiastic and friendly and didn't even mention anything about my never checking in to my hotel the night I was there. At first, I didn't tell them because I kind of couldn't believe it had happened. This was what I'd been working toward for about the last decade of my life. It was surreal and shocking to all of a sudden have achieved it.

Then I didn't tell them because I was madly finishing up my dissertation and planning for my dissertation defense where my committee would decide whether or not to award me my PhD. That was three weeks of fifteen-hour days where I guzzled coffee all day and NyQuil at night, terrified I wouldn't be able to sleep.

The thing about my father is that he's like the world's most accomplished boxer: there's no predicting which direction the hit will come from. After I passed my defense, I thought of every angle I could—every way in which telling him "hey, I just got my PhD" could be met with something more negative than all the things he'd been saying ever since I decided to go to college and then grad school in the first place. It seemed like a pretty safe announcement. So, that night, I stopped by my dad's house, knowing I'd catch at least one of my brothers on the couch, drinking my dad's beer. And if one of them knew something, all of them knew.

My mistake was showing up a little tipsy after drinks with some of my grad school friends, on my way to meet Ginger at her tattoo shop. I'm usually able to keep it together and take whatever my dad and brothers throw at me. And I'd certainly learned long before that if they saw me get even the littlest bit upset, they were like sharks smelling blood in the water.

My dad and Brian, the youngest of my three older brothers, were watching the Phillies when I got there and they barely looked up when I came in. My other brother, Colin, came into the room a minute later and didn't acknowledge me at all. I told them about passing my defense at a commercial break. Brian looked up, confused, and said, "Didn't you do that last year?" Typical. My dad said, "Well, that's great, son. I'm glad you've gotten that out of your system. Now what?" Colin didn't say anything at all.

It was nothing, really. He even said the word "great," when I'd anticipated the possibility of something like, "Ah, so now you're a snob officially."

"Now what?" I said, and I could hear the nasty edge creeping into my voice that tries to scare people away before I fall apart. "Now I thought I'd take a few weeks off after working nonstop for the last twelve years."

Brian looked up again, taking in my suit, and said, "Whoa, Danielle, what are you all dressed up for?" My brothers had called me Danielle before they ever knew I was gay, but learning I was gay had made it more pointed.

"Don't call your brother that," my dad snapped. It wasn't out of protectiveness for me or anything, he just hates to be reminded of how I'm not the to-the-garage-born specimen of beer-swilling, sports-watching, car-fixing masculinity that he wishes I were.

Then the game came back on and they forgot I was there.

Needless to say, I didn't tell them about the job then, either. And, okay, I may have gotten a little choked up as I slammed the door and walked to Ginger's shop, but I blame it on exhaustion. The upside was that when I told Ginger about the latest installment of the Mulligan family assholism, she gave me an emergency tattoo to distract me. The fact that I woke up the next morning and saw that I'd asked her to tattoo "Let Sleeping Bears Lie" above my left hip suggests that I was feeling a bit more sentimental than I'd thought.

Which brings us to last night, when I finally told my dad I was leaving Philadelphia and moving to the middle of nowhere in Northern Michigan.

"Well?" Ginger asks again.

"He was fine with it," I say.

"Which means?" Ginger presses.

"I told him about the job and he said great, at least I wouldn't have to borrow money from him."

"Not that you ever have," Ginger chimes in, a familiar chorus.

"Not that I ever have. Then I told him it was in Michigan and he seemed confused."

"Understandable."

"I don't actually think he ever considered the fact that jobs exist outside the county of Philadelphia."

"So you never told him when you went to Michigan for the interview?"

"Nah. I think I told Sam I had an interview because I borrowed a tie, but that's it." Sam, my oldest brother, is married to Liza, a really sweet woman—god knows what she sees in him—who does things like invite me over to dinner once a month because she cares about family and stuff. Sam... goes along with it. "Anyway, he just did his handshake-shoulder-pat thing and said good luck."

"That's it?"

"Yeah. Well, no, he looked under the hood of my car and gave me twenty bucks for gas."

"Which is, like, your dad for 'I love you,' though, right?"

"Yep. Just think: some kids only get told things like, 'I love you, son,' or 'I'll miss you,' which aren't actually useful for anything, whereas I get a tune-up *and* gas money. Lucky me."

"So, lucky you," Ginger drawls, clearly changing the subject, "what about this Sleeping Bear of yours?"

"Dude, would you stop calling him that?"

"Ooh, touchy. I like it. Speaking of secret languages, that's Daniel for 'I'm invested in someone and it's freaking me out.'"

"If by 'invested in' you mean 'made a complete fool out of myself in front of,' then, yes."

"You didn't make a fool out of yourself; *he* kissed *you*."

"Yeah, to calm me down. Then I basically assaulted him." My stomach sinks and I shiver at the memory, despite it being approximately two thousand degrees in my car right now.

"Whatever; he obviously wanted you. He was just being a gentleman and not falling into bed with you when you were drunk and possibly suffering from a closed-head injury."

I snort.

"Sooooo, do you think you'll see him again?"

"Dunno. I mean, it's not like it's a bustling metropolis; I'm bound to, right?"

"Great. So, do you think you'll, like, *see him* see him?"

"I just...."

"What, pumpkin?"

"I just can't stop thinking about him, Ginge. It's idiotic. I mean, I barely know the guy. But when I woke up and he was gone, I just...." I was fucking devastated.

That morning, I woke up warm, the blanket wrapped around me, soft light coming in through the curtains. It took me a minute to remember where I was, but when I registered the cedar smell of the blanket, the whole night came rushing back. I rolled off the couch, my bruised chest and my throbbing head competing for which was most pissed off at me, determined to talk to Rex. To apologize for throwing myself at him, to thank him for not only saving the dog but kind of saving me as well.

But the house was empty. Even the dog was gone. I wandered around the cabin, feeling like some demented fairy-tale character (and cursing my stupid brain for instantly supplying about ten filthy Goldilocks and the three bears references). In the kitchen were a pot of coffee and a plate of toast that was slick with butter and cool to the touch. On the lip of the plate, where I couldn't miss it, was a Post-it with a phone number on it. I called it right away, thinking it was Rex's, but a cab company answered.

He hadn't left a note. Not even a *Nice to meet you*, or a *Try not to hit any more dogs in the future*.

"I'm just nervous about running into him, that's all. I didn't make the best first impression—you know, what with me practically killing a dog, getting drunk and sexually assaulting him, insulting his town, and all."

"I have the feeling you made a better impression than you may think," Ginger says in the know-it-all voice she generally reserves for lecturing me about people I sleep with and telling college students who wander into her shop that they should definitely not get that tattoo.

"Whatever," I say, sounding petulant even to myself. "Hey, what ever happened with that new guy you hired? The one with the Motörhead shirt."

"Changing the subject: check. Um, he's…. Well, he's…."

"Ah ha! How was he?"

"Let's just say that Motörhead isn't an inapt analogue to his approach in the bedroom," she says.

"Um, I'm not actually sure I know enough about Motörhead to understand that," I admit. "What does that mean: wham, bam, thank you, ma'am?"

"Yeah, only without the thank you."

"Yikes. Well, at least he didn't seem the type to make things awkward in the workplace."

"No. And he's only here for the month as a favor to Johnny. No big deal." Johnny taught Ginger to tattoo.

Out the window to my right are trees, trees, and more trees. I'm not sure exactly where I am, but I should be about an hour away.

"Listen, Ginge, I'm getting close; I need to go so I can look at the directions."

"Okay." She pauses. "Hey, pumpkin, listen. I think this is a good thing. This Michigan thing. This job. I'll miss the shit out of you and I'll be royally pissed if I don't hear from you at least once a week, just so we're clear, but seriously, I have a good feeling."

"God, I hope you're right."

"Of course I'm right."

"Well, I'm glad the self-esteem is coming along." I don't want to hang up. I don't want to cut off the one tie I have to the only place I've ever called home.

"Bye, babycakes."

"Later."

LYING IN bed, tossing and turning, I try not to think about how freaked out I am.

The apartment is even worse than it looked online. First of all, it's tiny. The door at the top of the stairs opens into a kitchen that's sticky with disuse. That opens into one medium-sized room that's the living room slash bedroom, and off to the side is a tiny bathroom with a shower stall and a sink. The walls are a greasy off white; the kitchen linoleum is yellowed and peeling up at the edges. The blue carpet in the other room is thick with dust and matted in places with I don't want to know what. The windows are mostly painted shut, so it's incredibly hot and stuffy. What I thought, based on the pictures, was a door to another room turned out to be a door out to a rickety fire escape that would as likely kill me as save me in the event of an actual fire. The ceiling is low, since it's really an attic room, and even at average height it feels claustrophobic. It's the first time in my life I've ever not wished to be taller.

I guess it'll only be for a year or so, until I can pay off my credit card bills, but it's still a little depressing. I don't know why, since my apartment in Philly was kind of a shithole too. It's weird, though. I'm supposed to be an adult now—a real professor with a real salary who moved to start a real job—but I'm still living in a crappy apartment, only now my concerns can be roasting and/or freezing to death instead of getting mugged.

I'd opted for an apartment that was close enough that I could walk to campus and the library. I figured if I was going to be living in the middle of nowhere, at least I could be in the center of what town there is. It's a single apartment above a hardware store with a side entrance. Carl, the man who owns it, used to live up here before he got married, but it's been empty since, so he let me have it dirt-cheap. At least I won't have to worry about living in the same place as any of my students. Since Sleeping Bear College is so small, only underclassmen live in the dorms, and the last thing I want is to end up sharing a parking lot with a student angry about a grade on a paper.

After I lugged in the stuff from my car, it only took me about an hour to unpack. I'd left my shitty furniture on the curb in Philly for someone to grab and I don't have much stuff. The bed is here, like Carl promised, and a couch, but there's no air conditioner and no way I was staying in this stuffy place without it. So I grabbed my keys and went to go find one, figuring I could stop and grab some takeout on my way back.

Outside, the sun was setting and the air was thick, at least as humid as it was back in Philly. It smelled nature-y, though, even in town. Like trees and water and lots and lots of oxygen. It wasn't even 8:00 p.m., but almost nothing was open.

The town of Holiday—seriously? it sounds like something on a postcard, or one of those Christmas towns that only exist during December—is picturesque. I'll give it that. The only thing I have to compare it to is Manayunk, a neighborhood in Philly that's gotten really gentrified in the last ten years or so and now has freshly painted storefronts and arts festivals in the summer.

The shops here are all one of a kind. On Main Street, it's touristy shops: candles with scents like "Winter Wonderland," "Morning Rain," and "Indian Summer"; expensive-looking kitchen stores with hand-carved cutting boards and Swedish-looking single-use gadgets with faces painted on them; specialty food stores selling dried fruit, tiny packets of nuts that are more packaging than food, and every conceivable type of preserves. And, every other storefront or so, shops selling Michigan paraphernalia: aprons and boxer shorts and visors and scarves; oven mitts and cookie cutters, field guides and notepads. Everything cut in the shape of the Michigan mitten (the oven mitts with hearts where Holiday would be on the map) or emblazoned with it.

Off Main Street it's a bit more normal, but still, it looks like something from a movie set—so curated and clean. The sidewalks are even and wide, separated from the streets by decorative brick, and a line of trees alternating with lamp posts, mailboxes, and the most attractive garbage cans I've ever seen, painted a dark green, as if they too are a part of nature.

I finally peeked into an Italian restaurant and immediately regretted it because it was kind of a nice place and I was sweaty, wearing jean cutoffs and a black T-shirt with the sleeves torn off from Ginger's shop, which said *Tattoo Bitch* in bold Gothic font across my chest. I asked the hostess if there was a diner or a takeout place nearby and was peppered with overly friendly questions about my favorite foods. I wandered off in the direction she had pointed, reminding myself that this was a small town and people were probably just friendly, not trying to give me the third degree.

At the diner, people stared again. I grabbed a sandwich to go and practically ran back to my apartment with it.

It's finally sinking in. I live here now. I live here in this tiny town. Everyone knows each other and I'm a stranger. They'll want to know me. Know about me. And then maybe they'll hate me.

Before, I always had the option to just disappear. Don't like the people in my classes? No problem. Hide out in the library or hop on the subway and go work somewhere else. Don't want to run into an ex in the coffee shop? Slept with the bartender at this bar? Just walk half a block and go to another one. Have an awkward encounter with someone? Who cares? I'll never see them again.

But now it all counts. There's nowhere to hide here. No blending in or fucking off. I've never felt so terrified or so exposed.

IN THE past week, I've cleaned my apartment, scraped together a quasi-professional wardrobe for teaching, finalized my syllabi for the upcoming semester, eaten at every single nonfancy restaurant in town, and answered some variation of the question "who are you" approximately eight thousand times. I ran into Carl, whose apartment I'm renting, at the diner and he was solicitous—how's the apartment, how do I like Holiday—but I got the sense that it was mostly for the benefit of everyone else in the diner who was listening when he asked me if I had a partner. Kind of like he wanted to prove that he didn't have any problem with me being gay.

Bernard Ness, the chair of the job search committee, had me over to his house for dinner. It was pleasant enough, and it's lucky we have work to talk about, since I don't think we have much else in common. He filled me in on enough departmental gossip to last a lifetime and the entire time I prayed that this would not become my life: gossiping about which of my colleagues is getting a divorce and whose forthcoming article should never have been accepted for publication.

And all week I've wondered when I'd run into him. Rex. Last night, I had a dream that I walked into the diner and he was working there, only it was one of those old-timey soda shoppes and he was wearing the whole soda jerk getup: white shirt and apron, black bow tie, dorky white hat perched on his perfect head. He made me a delicious-looking milkshake but then refused to give it to me. I know, right? You don't have to be Freud.

Classes start on Monday, so the town has begun to buzz as students get back. Still, it's nine o'clock on a Saturday night and it doesn't look like anything is going on. At least I won't have any distractions while I'm here; it'll give me time to work on turning my dissertation into a book, which, among other things, will be required of me to get tenure at Sleeping Bear. More to the point, I'll need to have a publication offer in hand if I have any hope of getting a job that isn't in the middle of nowhere.

Now, though, I'm antsy as hell. It's hot in my apartment, even with the air conditioner that I had to drive an hour to find. I spent the day making sure I knew where everything was: my classes, my office, the library, the one pizza joint that stays open after ten. I've finished all the reading and done course planning for my first week of classes. I've watched four documentaries that have been in my Netflix queue for ages. And I may or may not have googled "Rex + Michigan" to no avail.

I decide I just need to get out of the house, so I throw on shoes and grab my beat-up copy of *The Secret History*. I've read it a hundred times, but it fits perfectly in my back pocket and it's a comfort book: as long as I'm reading it, it doesn't matter where I am. Besides, the main character of the book leaves his home in California to go to college in a small town where he's never been before, so it seems particularly relevant to my life right now. I figure I'll take a walk and find a park bench to read on or something.

It really is beautiful here once it's not sweltering. I'm actually looking forward to the winter; I bet it looks like a storybook village when everything's covered with snow. The quiet freaks me out, though, so I pop in the earbuds of my beat-up iPod, saying a tiny prayer to the music gods, as I do every time I use it these days, that it'll last me just one more year.

That was my mantra all through grad school. When I first started, it was a nightmare. Everyone at Penn came from good colleges that had prepared them for the classes. I went to community college for three years, then transferred to Temple and squeezed all my remaining credits into one year since it's all I could afford. I'm pretty sure I only got into grad school at Penn because they needed to fill a quota of first generation college students or something. I was totally unprepared, but I told myself that after one year, the playing field would have evened. *One more year.* Then, when I was so exhausted from doing all my reading and writing for coursework while bartending five nights a week, I would tell myself, *Just one more year and then you'll be done with coursework and starting your dissertation.* When I felt like I would never finish writing, I told myself, *One more year; you just have to hang on for one more year.*

Now, here I am. If I can just deal with my crappy apartment for one more year, I'll have enough money for a nicer place. If my car will just keep running for one more year, I'll be able to get a new one—well, a less-used one. Et cetera. *One more year.*

I've walked farther than I meant to, away from campus, and somehow, even though I've always associated Tom Waits with the city, his voice like pavement and whiskey and heartbreak, listening to him makes me see the winding road in front of me in a new light. He's the perfect soundtrack to this deserted place, the only light now from the moon, the trees encroaching.

I'm looking up at the moon, feeling a bit smug and rather impressed by myself for, like, being in nature, when I'm knocked over from behind.

I pitch forward, barely catching myself on my right hand, and jerk my earbuds out, whipping my head around to see where the attack is coming from. I should have fucking known better than to be walking alone at night when I couldn't hear someone coming. I've known that since I was twelve years old. I can't believe I thought it was safe here just because there's nothing to fucking do. Serial killers, Daniel! Remember?

All this runs through my mind in the second it takes me to see that I am, in fact, *not* about to be serial killed. Because what knocked me over was a dog. A brown and white dog that is now licking my face and trying to put its paws on my shoulders.

"Marilyn! Marilyn, here, girl."

I know that voice. That low, commanding voice. Not as gravelly as Tom Waits, but so much more welcome.

Rex.

Chapter 3

August

HE COMES crashing through the trees and, from my current position on the ground, he looks even bigger and more imposing than I remember.

He practically skids to a stop when he sees me.

The dog—Marilyn, apparently—barks once at Rex and then sits down next to me, one paw on my knee.

My head is swimming, and it's not from being knocked over. He's here. He's really here. If I'm being honest, I've thought about him so much more than I even admitted to Ginger. In the six months since I got back from Michigan, I've imagined him a thousand times. What he might be doing, what he would say to me if he were there—even though I have no idea what he would say, since I *don't know him*. I've told myself that a hundred times too. I even got *Gaslight* from the library and watched it on my computer, pretending he was sitting next to me on my crappy couch in Philadelphia. Then I took my computer to bed and watched it a second time, pretending he was there all over again.

I don't do this. This isn't what I do. I don't moon over guys. I don't pine. I don't wonder what they're doing. I never have. I mean, sure, I've had crushes. Usually, though, I just show up and if someone's appealing, I go for it. It's always been just sex, except for my monumentally stupid time with Richard.

But now I'm sitting here on the ground like an idiot because the man I've fantasized about, dreamed of, and jerked off to is finally standing in front of me and I do not have a clue what to say.

He leans toward me, quizzical.

"Daniel?" He sounds shocked.

"Hi," I say.

We're staring at each other. It's really dark, so he mostly looks like shoulders and hair. He's wearing jeans and a dark T-shirt with a tear in the neck that's stretched tight over his muscular frame. He reaches down a hand, but rather than help me up, he pats the dog on the head.

"I guess she got you back, huh?" Rex says.

"What? Oh." I laugh, looking at the dog. "Yeah, I guess she has."

Now he reaches one huge hand down to me, his biceps stretching that poor T-shirt even more. His hand is warm, just like I remember it. He pulls me easily to my feet, so easily that he has to grab me by the shoulders to keep me from slamming into him. In this position, I can't help but think of the last time he held me like this. Up against his kitchen wall, seconds before he kissed me.

He drops his hands and looks down.

"What are you doing here?" He doesn't sound very pleased.

"Well, I got that job," I say.

"Congratulations." He's looking at the dog, not me.

"Oh, yeah, thanks." I look down too. "Oh shit." My book is lying in the dirt. It must've fallen out of my pocket when I fell. I scoop it up and brush it off, but the cover is torn and there's mud ground into the last twenty pages or so. "Shoot."

"I hope you know how it ends," Rex says, looking at the muddied book.

"Yeah, I've read it before," I say, but I feel like I've injured a friend. I've had this copy for ten years, read its corners round. I put it in my back pocket and try to shake it off. I'm not usually sentimental about shit like this. I don't know what's wrong with me. I don't have the heart to check whether my iPod survived the fall; I just stuff my earphones in my hip pocket alongside it.

"Uh, so... Marilyn?" I say, nodding to the dog. "She seems okay, huh? And she grew a lot, didn't she?"

"She's fine," Rex says, smiling fondly. "She's a good dog."

"I didn't know you were going to keep her. I hope—I mean, I hope you didn't feel obligated or anything."

"Nah, I haven't had a dog in a while. It was time. We get along pretty good. Well, I mean. We get along pretty well."

"Why Marilyn?"

"Like Marilyn Monroe—she just, um—you know, she was a little banged up, so I figured she could use a star's name. Especially one who took some hits and kept getting back up. Marilyn just needed some taking care of." He seems a little embarrassed as he explains.

"Right, of course, movies. I like it," I tell him, smiling, but actually I'm thinking, *Didn't Marilyn Monroe kill herself?*

"I had a dog called Brando for a little while when I was a kid. My mom named him. Said it was because he was ugly, so the name would balance him out. I just figured it couldn't hurt."

"Look," I say, "I wanted to thank you. That night… I was a mess. I'm not usually like that, I want you to know. So, thank you for helping me. And—" I laugh nervously. "Also, I want to apologize. I… was kind of all over you and I'm sorry if I made you uncomfortable or anything. I mean, it was so cool of you to let me stay and then I just kind of jumped on you and—anyway. So, I'm sorry."

I force myself to look up, plastering what I hope is an unconcerned expression on my face: an it-was-casual, no-problem, I'm-not-mortified expression. But the second I look into his eyes, I feel it slide off my face. He looks stern, serious. Like I've disappointed him in some way. Or I'm about to.

But beneath the stern expression is heat. It's dark and, okay, I can't see him that well, but I can feel his eyes drinking me in, sliding over my face and my body like he owns them. Me. Like there's not a force in the world that could stop him from taking whatever he wants from me. And I'll be damned if I wouldn't let him.

When he speaks, though, his voice is calm, controlled, giving away nothing.

"I kissed you, Daniel. Don't you remember?"

"Hell yeah," I say softly. My eyes are glued to his mouth.

"I think maybe you want me to kiss you again." He takes a step toward me. Ninety-eight percent of me is desperate for exactly that. But the other 2 percent is all of a sudden terrified. Terrified in a way I've never been before when it's come to guys or sex. Terrified because it feels like this may be the most important decision I ever make. More important than deciding to go to college when all my teachers thought I was trouble. More important than sticking my hand down Corey Appleton's pants in seventh grade, proving to myself that I was gay and I would fuck up anyone who gave me shit about it. More important than applying to grad school or taking this job. I can feel it in my gut.

I feel myself nodding, but I can't feel anything else. I can't smell the trees anymore, can't hear the irritating chirrup of cicadas that's been buzzing at my nerves all week. He's taken up all my senses. Every nerve in my body is tuned to his frequency, every bit of my attention focused on the man in front of me.

He takes another step forward, pushing me backward with his huge body. But instead of falling, one step puts my back up against a tree. Rex's chest is right against mine. With every breath he takes, his chest expands, pushing me against the rough bark behind me. He is heat and power and the air between us is electric.

As if in slow motion, he raises his hand. He places it at my neck, stroking my skin gently with his thumb, then in one powerful movement, he puts pressure on my jaw, tilting my head back and my mouth open and then his mouth is on mine and I'm dissolving into his kiss.

I moan when he deepens the kiss. He tastes like nighttime, something dark and fathomless and necessary. Then he pulls back. I blink quickly, trying to figure out what made him stop. He's looking at me, his mouth only a breath away from mine.

"Lie down, Marilyn," he commands, and I hear a yawn and the comfortable snuffle of a well-trained dog getting comfortable. He never breaks eye contact.

"Daniel," he says in that same voice, and I nod. Nod at whatever he's asking because whatever he wants I want it too.

He kisses me deep and hard and I pull his hips toward mine to fit us more tightly together. He moves to my neck, his stubble scraping sweetly across my throat as he kisses my neck slowly and bites the muscle there. I pull in a breath and moan, pushing my hips into his. Every scrape of his teeth sends a pulse to my groin. I've gotten hard so fast I'm overwhelmed, like all the blood drained from my head and rushed to my erection.

His mouth is soft and powerful, and I slide a hand into his hair to guide his lips back to mine. I push up on my tiptoes to get better access. Our kiss is like a conversation: getting to know each other, tilting to find each other, exploring.

I nip at Rex's full lower lip and he growls, frustrated, and grabs my ass in his hands, pulling me against him and lifting me off the ground to hold me against the tree with no effort at all. I wrap my thighs around his hips and he thrusts against me.

I've never been with someone so built, and his strength is driving me crazy. It's like I could do anything to him without hurting him and he could do *anything* to me, which makes my mind spiral to a thousand places at once.

He pushes harder against me, spreading my legs with his body until he can grind against me. He's holding my whole weight like it's nothing and as he rocks into me he brings our cocks into perfect alignment.

"Fuck," I breathe, stiffening with the effort of not coming right away. It's been too long. He eases off a little, still kissing me, and lowers me to the ground.

"I want to feel you. Can I?" he asks, and he slides one warm palm down the back of my pants, cupping the muscle, running a thick finger between my cheeks. I shiver against him and nod again, going for his pants. He stops my hands and, for a second, I think it's going to be a repeat of what happened in his cabin all over again. But he just looks at me intently and says, "Tell me I can touch you."

"You can touch me—shit!" The second the words leave my mouth, he pushes my pants and underwear down and grabs my ass with both hands.

"Your book," he says.

"Huh?"

"Your book's getting all messed up again," he says, and I look down to where my copy of *The Secret History* is once again on the ground. Note to self: try not to step on your iPod.

"'S fine," I say, reaching for him again.

He spreads me apart and kisses me with a hunger that makes me tremble as I fumble with his pants. When I finally drag his jeans and boxer briefs down, his erection springs out, hard and thick against his belly. He pushes me back against the tree and thrusts against me and, as our cocks meet skin to skin for the first time, we both moan. He's all hardness and heat and he bites his lip and looks into my eyes as he rocks against me.

"C'mere," Rex says, and he lifts me again, pulling me against his body, my back against the trunk of the tree. As he holds me steady, I thrust against him and shudder with pleasure. He groans and runs possessive hands over my lower back and hips. He spreads the globes of my ass and runs a thick finger down the crevice between them, circling my opening and making me shiver and clench up. He brings his finger up to my mouth and I suck on it. Then there's wetness at my opening, wringing tiny shudders from me. He leans in to kiss me hard, sucks on my lower lip, and strokes me open. I cry out into Rex's mouth as his finger slides inside.

"Oh god."

"Is this okay?" he asks. I nod enthusiastically, my head falling back against the tree.

"Tell me," he whispers.

"Fuck, it's good," I say, my eyes clenched tight.

"The night I met you," Rex says against my mouth, "all I could think about was getting inside you." He strokes inside of me with his thick finger, thrusting against me as he speaks. His voice is low, smoke curling around me. "Your mouth." He kisses me. "Your gorgeous ass." He flexes his wrist and fucks me with his finger. My arms fall against his shoulders, curl around his neck. I clench around his finger and he growls, rutting harder against me.

"But—" I gasp. "But you didn't want me."

"Nng," Rex groans, looking into my eyes. "I was trying to be a fucking gentleman."

"No," I huff, "now you're a fucking gentleman."

He shakes his head and drops his forehead to mine. "You," he says darkly, "talk when you're nervous."

"No," I gasp, and it's true; I usually don't. Rex quirks an eyebrow. "Only with you," I say. His smile is slow and predatory.

"Don't be nervous," he says, amused. Yeah, right, thanks. I only thought I was attacked by some murderer, like, ten minutes ago. I don't even let myself think about why I'm nervous about how it feels to have him against me, inside me.

"It's just—you know, the woods, and—there's—did you know statistically the greatest percentage of serial killers come from the Midwest?"

I can*not* believe I just said that. There's babbling because you're turned on and then there's sounding like a total psycho.

Rex is giving me a strange look.

"So, you're nervous that I might be a serial killer?"

I shake my head miserably. "No, no, I was just saying. Sorry. Ignore me."

Rex's expression softens and he runs the back of his free hand over my jaw.

"I don't want to ignore you," he says. "I just want you to be here. Are you here?" He strokes inside me again and my breathing goes all funny.

"I'm here," I say.

"Just relax, okay?"

"Easier said than—" He kisses me hard. His tongue stroking over mine shoots sparks of pleasure to my stomach and my cock. My thighs tremble and I unclench. He kisses like he talks—confidently, with authority, but so receptive to my every response. I moan into his mouth and he slips another finger inside me. When I cry out he presses even closer, his chest and shoulders dwarfing mine.

"You feel fucking amazing," Rex says. "You're pulling me inside." Fuck. The things he says. Usually I hate when guys talk during sex. It always sounds ridiculous, like bad porn. Besides, I'm used to sucking off guys behind the tires at my dad's shop or fucking them in bathrooms at concerts, not much time for conversation. But everything out of Rex's mouth turns me on even more.

The tree against my back and Rex's fingers inside me are the only things I can feel. Until Rex takes hold of both our cocks in his big hand and begins to stroke us together.

"Oh!" I cry, and Rex moans low. My head spins as jolts of pleasure shoot through my cock. I slide my hands under Rex's shirt, dig into the thick muscles there. I can imagine what his body would feel like crushing me into the mattress, and I'm not sure where that thought came from because it's not something I've ever particularly wanted before.

Rex strokes us faster, our erections now slippery with fluid, and I brace myself on his shoulders so I don't slide down the tree—and because I don't want to give up the shivery full feeling of his fingers inside me.

Everything feels liquid, and Rex's breath is coming in pants now. He bites his lip and his rhythm stutters.

"Fuck, baby, I'm so close," he says and I can only whimper in response and nod. He takes a shaky breath and his hand slows slightly. When he kisses me, it's softer and his mouth tastes sweeter. I can feel him trembling with the effort to hold back his orgasm.

He slides his fingers even deeper inside me and I feel wracked against the tree, on his hand, by his mouth and his chest and fucking voice and, god, his smell. I'm barely aware of what I'm doing, just anything to get more. More contact, more tongue, just more. Hands on his shoulders, I grind down on his fingers and cry out in pleasure.

"Oh fuck," he says, but it's like his voice is coming from a great distance, far away from the feeling of his fingers zinging pleasure through my channel and his big hand stroking us together faster now. I should be embarrassed of the broken sounds I'm making, but I can't seem to care.

Rex flexes his fingers inside me at the same time as his stroke catches the head of my cock just right and I'm spiraling into orgasm, clutching at his shoulders, his neck, anything to keep me from losing contact with his body. Warmth tingles at the base of my spine and in my balls and then it's just white-hot pleasure shooting through me.

"Oh, oh," I cry out. Heat pours out of me, making everything slippery. I gasp for breath and my hole spasms around Rex's fingers as my muscles contract, pulling a final hot spurt from me and leaving me shuddering against Rex, his fingers still inside me.

"Holy shit," Rex says. He strokes us twice more, my cock so sensitive it's almost painful, and then he's coming too, striping my chest and stomach with powerful spurts as he crushes me against the tree.

We're both breathing heavily. Rex puts his mouth back on mine and kisses me softly as he slowly slides his fingers from me. I groan, shuddering against him, and I can't help but clench up. Hands now free, he hefts me a bit higher, holding me against him.

He keeps kissing me, and then, like he can't help himself, he dips a fingertip back inside me.

"Rex!" I mumble, and wrap my arms around his neck. We kiss softly, our mouths moving together, warm and liquid. As he slides his finger inside me, my cock gives one last shivery jolt against Rex's stomach and I hiss. My head falls back against the tree and I take a deep breath. My head is spinning. Rex nuzzles into the curve where my neck meets my shoulder and I can feel his moist breath on my skin. He slips his finger free and gently lowers me to the ground.

My legs are shaking and my ass is a little tender. He must see it on my face because he pulls me against him, one arm around my waist, the other braced against the tree as he catches his breath.

His body engulfs mine so that all I can feel is his heat and all I can smell is his scent: fabric softener and pine and light, clean sweat. I can't actually remember the last time I was held like this; maybe I never have been. I hug Ginger, but she's small and it doesn't feel anything like this. Other than that.... No one. I feel like I could melt right into Rex, and I want to stay like this as long as I can.

It freaks me out—how much I want this.

"I, uh," Rex says, and with my ear pressed to his chest his low voice rumbles through me. "I didn't think I'd see you again." The feeling of comfort drains out of me, leaving me exhausted just thinking about waking up that morning, hopeful and unsure, and finding him gone, without even a note to say good-bye.

"I didn't think you wanted to," I say, and I can hear the resentment in my voice. Rex shifts backward so he can see my face. I make sure my expression is neutral.

"Not true. I just wanted to get Marilyn to the vet. And, like I said, it seemed pretty clear you'd take any job over one here. I didn't think our little town made a real good impression."

"I dunno. You were a pretty good welcome wagon," I say. "Even if you didn't say good-bye."

"Hmph," he says. His expression has shuttered. It makes him look sterner, older. "Well, you're here now. I suppose you'll be using this job as—what'd you call it? As a springboard?"

"Maybe," I say. I'm amazed that he remembers our conversation so well. He even remembers the word I used. "I'll have to see. I'm here for this year at least. Um…." I make a vague motion toward my pants, which are bunched at the bottom of the tree.

Rex lets me go and I try to go about putting my twisted underwear and pants back on with some semblance of dignity. Not that there's much room for dignity when you've just been wrung dry against a tree in the middle of the night.

"Suppose you walked?" Rex asks. I nod.

"Hey, you're not from here, are you?" I ask.

"Nope. Texas, originally," Rex says, doing a much better job of putting himself back together with dignity than I've done. "But I lived all over. Why?"

"Your accent. You don't have that nasal Michigan thing. And you say *suppose*."

"What's wrong with suppose?"

"Nothing's wrong with it. Just, usually people who say suppose are either, like, being formal or they're from the South. So I just wondered. Texas, huh? So, are you into that whole cowboy thing?" I'm babbling again, but there is just something about Rex on a horse—or a bull, or whatever the hell they have in Texas—that's incredibly hot. Rex with a whip.

"For a professor, you're kind of into stereotypes, aren't you?" Rex says, but he doesn't seem offended. "Serial killers are from the Midwest; everyone in Texas is a cowboy."

I groan. "You remember that, huh?" I was desperately hoping that, what with the orgasms and all, maybe he wouldn't have registered that part of our exchange.

"It only happened a few minutes ago, Daniel," he says, and he chucks me under the chin.

"Yeah, yeah. I don't actually think those things. I just—"

He pulls me into his chest and tips my chin up. He kisses me lightly and smiles, then strokes my stomach. I look down and see his come has dried in white streaks on my black T-shirt.

"That's pretty grim," he says.

"Oh, don't worry about it. I'm doing laundry tomorrow." Rex's eyes darken and that predatory expression is back.

"I'm not sorry about that," he says. "I mean your shirt. You sure know how to put a guy in his place."

"Oh," I say, looking down again. I forgot that my shirt says *No One Will Ever Love You.* "It's a Magnetic Fields song," I say, and I turn around to show him the back: *69 Love Songs.*

"Mmhmm." He pats my ass. "That's a band, I suppose?" he says with a playfully exaggerated drawl.

I once again slide my copy of *The Secret History* into my back pocket and feel for my iPod in the left.

I'd almost forgotten she was here, but Marilyn lets out one bark and stands up.

"Yeah, girl, time to go," Rex says, and pats her head.

I stick my fists in my pockets, trying to figure out how I can make sure I see him again.

"Hey, where am I?" I ask Rex. "I walked from that way, I think."

"You living in town?"

"Yeah. Above the hardware store."

"Carl's place?"

"Whoa, small town," I say. I'm joking, but he doesn't smile.

"If you follow the road for about a mile, you'll hit town," he says. "On your left."

"I walked for a lot more than a mile, I'm pretty sure," I say.

"Yeah, you likely looped around. This road has a horseshoe curve that you can avoid. Just stay left. I can drive you if you want. I mean, I need to go back home and get my truck, but—"

"Nah, I'm cool," I say. "It's a nice night." I need to clear my head.

"Sure," he says, rubbing the back of his neck. "Well, I guess I'll see you, Daniel."

Wait, that's it? He still doesn't want my number, or...?

"Um, yeah, I'll see you," I say. "Maybe... in town?"

"Very likely," he says.

"Okay. Well, I guess I'll just...." I gesture down the road. "Bye, Marilyn. I'm really glad you're all right." I pet between her ears and she puts out a paw.

"She wants you to shake," Rex says.

"Oh, right." I take her large paw in my hand and shake it. "Um. Good night." I turn away slowly, my face burning. He doesn't have any interest in making plans, clearly.

"Daniel." Rex's hand on my shoulder spins me around. He leans down and kisses me, short and hard. "I'm glad you're here. I'll see you." This time it sounds reassuring. He doesn't just think I'm a quick fuck against a tree.

Better.

Then he walks away, Marilyn trotting at his side.

Chapter 4

September

"BECAUSE RESTATING the prompt isn't a thesis, Malcolm. A thesis needs to make a claim. It tells the reader what you'll spend the rest of the paper demonstrating. Remember?"

Stab, throttle, smash, annihilate, disembowel. I try to calm myself down by listing words that describe what I'd like to do to Malcolm. Preppy, entitled, slickly handsome Malcolm. *Raze, liquefy, obliterate, eviscerate, pulverize, gut.* Malcolm is the sixth student to come to my Friday afternoon office hours to argue about his grade on the first short paper for my Intro to American Literature class. All six complaining students missed class the day I assigned the papers and explained very clearly what a thesis was. All six complaining students turned in papers with no thesis statements.

"But you never said we needed to make a claim," Malcolm says, scanning his paper. "I mean, like, if I'd known that was a requirement, then I totally could have done it."

"Well," I say, "this assignment is called 'Advancing a Claim.' I'd suggest, in the future, that you draft your papers with the assignment sheet in front of you. And I'd suggest making sure you find out what you miss on days when you aren't in class. Anything else I can do for you?"

"I mean, I basically made a claim. It's right here."

"As I mentioned, this is a restatement of the prompt I gave you in class, so it can't be your claim."

"But it's totally a claim."

"It's a question, Malcolm. My question. I wouldn't really assign a paper where you were supposed to make a claim I already made on the assignment sheet, would I?"

"How am I supposed to know what you'd do?" Malcolm says, sounding sincerely confused. But it's clear that his confusion masks aggression. He disliked me on sight.

"Look, I'll give you the same opportunity I gave your classmates who were unhappy with their paper grades. If you'd like to rewrite the paper and give it to me next week, I'll regrade it with a cap at a *B-*. It's up to you."

"So I can't get higher than a *B-*? No way, man!" Ooh, Malcolm's pissed now. I admit, I get a little bit of a rush out of staying perfectly calm when I know that a student would be punching me in the face if we were at a bar instead of across a desk from one another.

"Well, as of now, this is a *D* paper. Whether you choose to keep that grade or try the assignment again is completely up to you."

Malcolm gathers his things up angrily, sliding his chair back with a loud scrape on the old hardwood floor.

"Yeah, fine, next week, thanks," he mumbles, and jerks his backpack over his shoulder. He pulls my office door shut behind him. Hard. It's an old building, and, as the new kid, I clearly got stuck in the office that either: (a) was recently cleared out when some faculty member who never used it died, or (b) is a gateway to the fires of hell. As such, when Malcolm slams the door, a crack peels open in the ceiling drywall from the corner of the door to the rickety light fixture hanging precariously from the ceiling three feet away. The light fixture droops from the drywall and hangs cockeyed from a cluster of wires.

"Have a nice weekend," I mutter.

Then, as I watch, the light fixture falls to the floor in a gunshot of dented tin, frosted glass, and plaster dust.

Great.

THANK GOD it's the end of the week. After I call maintenance at the college and leave them a message about the disaster that my office has become, I order pizza and call Ginger. She's always in the shop on Friday nights but only works by appointment because she doesn't want to be implicated in people's stupid, drunken mistakes. After some sorority girl's mom came into the shop, dragging her daughter by the wrist, to ask why Ginger gave her daughter a tattoo of a cupcake on her ass with the words "sweet to the last lick" curling in a banner underneath, and didn't respond well to Ginger's assurance that the girl was very much of legal age to get a tattoo and quite insistent on this one in particular, Ginger stopped participating in Friday night walk-ins, leaving the easy cash to her employees. She answers on the first ring.

"Have you seen him again?" she says.

"Dude, come *on*," I say. She's asked me this every time we've spoken since I told her about running into him—well, about Marilyn running into me.

"Sorry, sweet cheeks. I'm just having a hell of a dry spell in the city of what is clearly *exclusively* brotherly love and I need a little pick me up."

"I'm not holding my breath, Ginge. Like I told you, he didn't even want my phone number. I think maybe he just saw it as a onetime thing."

"Come on. There are, like, thirty-seven people in your town. It's totally inevitable. Besides, he knows where you work. I think he could find you if he were trying."

Well, she's right about that.

"Sorry, sorry," she says. "I just mean that he's obviously into you, so I don't get why he's playing it so cool."

"Changing the subject for the millionth time…. What's new back home?"

"Oh, the yuzh: you've missed a bunch of good shows, everyone always asks where you are, everyone else in this city sucks, and SEPTA workers are on strike, so I can't take the subway and even though I totally support their cause—go, union!—it's basically ruining my life. Oh! And your fucking brother came into the shop yesterday."

"Brian?" Brian is the only one of my brothers I could see getting a tattoo.

"No, Colin."

"What? What did he want?"

"Not what did he want—what did he want *covered up*?"

"No!"

"Pumpkin, were you aware that your idiotic, gay-bashing, misogynist brother had a tramp stamp?"

"Impossible."

"Of a butterfly."

"No."

"Swear to god! His story was that his girlfriend made him get it last year and now they broke up and he wanted me to cover it up with a vintage car." She says "story" and "girlfriend" like they have enormous air quotes around them.

"Oh my fucking god, this is the best thing that's ever happened to me."

"He swore me to secrecy."

"Yeah, right. So, did you do it?"

"I told him that a tattoo of a car just above his ass would really give people the wrong idea about what kind of a lady he was. He got all offended and left. I guess I forgot what a total misogynist he is for, like, five seconds." I laugh. "Oops!" she says in a baby voice that is not at all sorry.

I GET up early the next morning, eager to get to my office and get my course prep for the next few weeks done so that I don't have to work tomorrow. I hate Sundays. They're depressing enough without having to work on them. Besides, structural issues aside, I've grown to really like my office. I've never had one before. In grad school I'd work at the library or in a coffee shop. And I was always trying to get reading done behind the bar at work. Consequently, I'd have to air out the books before I returned them to the library because they always ended up dotted with booze. Even in my apartment in Philly, I just worked at the kitchen table. The place was really only a couch, a bed, a bathroom, and a kitchenette anyway. It's nice to have a place to work that's just mine (and *isn't* two feet from a toilet). And, interesting as it always was to read Emily Brontë or Schopenhauer against a backdrop of tipsy concertgoers, it was pretty hard to concentrate.

As I walk to Sludge to get a coffee, the early morning air has a bit of a chill. It'll be hot again by noon, but for now I can almost pretend I'm home, walking out to the middle of the Ben Franklin Bridge and watching the sunlight crest the crisp wavelets of the Delaware. Everything's still in bloom, so the early morning sun filters through the trees lining the streets.

I like Sludge's brown and white striped awning and its photographs of used coffee grounds on the brick walls. It's early enough that Marjorie—the owner of Sludge, as I learned the first time I stumbled in fiending for coffee and was treated to a twenty-minute introduction in addition—is behind the counter. She smiles broadly at me, but her smile fades when she looks down to my arms.

"Hmm, Daniel, honey, I don't understand why you kids do that to yourselves." She's looking at my tattoos. I guess I've only seen her when I was dressed to teach, wearing long sleeves. I don't get some people's assumption that you want to hear their opinion of your personal choices. And they say it like it's not rude. I would never say, "Hey, Marjorie, I hate the way you dress," or, "Oh, Marjorie, you should really have plastic surgery, because your nose would be so much better another way."

"You're such a handsome boy. Why would you want to look like a hoodlum?"

"Well, I actually am a hoodlum, Marjorie, so I was required to get them," I say with what I hope isn't too annoyed of a smile. "Can I have an egg sandwich and a triple shot in a large coffee to go?" I add, before she can comment.

"How on earth can you drink that much caffeine?" Marjorie asks.

"It's what all the hoodlums drink," I say, shrugging, and she turns away to make my drink, shaking her head.

The walk to campus only takes about fifteen minutes. Sleeping Bear College is a hodgepodge of old and new buildings. It was built on land that originally had a large estate and a smaller farmhouse. When they opened the college, they built a number of new brick buildings to house the math and science departments, one that looks kind of like a greenhouse for the art department, and, at the very back of campus, farthest from my apartment, a blocky brick monstrosity to house the library. The sidewalks connecting the buildings are clean and they must pay someone a hell of a lot of money to landscape, because there are flowers everywhere. During the week, students congregate on wooden benches around campus and eat lunch under the trees that dot the grass, which must have been original to the property because they look too old to have been planted when the college opened.

The estate was turned into the student center and the farmhouse into Snyder Hall, where the humanities classrooms are on the first and second floors and our offices are on the third. It's a cool building from the outside—weathered wood and a huge front porch where students hang out between classes. In fact, it reminds me more of a Cracker Barrel restaurant than any academic building I've ever seen. Still, it's got a relaxed vibe that I like. Inside, though, it's rickety and worn, especially the offices.

It's locked on the weekends, so I don't have to worry about running into students—another perk of my office. The building is quiet and dark, and my heels echo on the hardwood floors. The downstairs walls are white and dotted with fliers for film screenings, clubs, fundraisers, and tutors. My office is on the third floor, in the back of the building, which overlooks the parking lot.

I barely manage to avoid scattering glass everywhere as I juggle open the door with my egg sandwich in one hand and my coffee in the other. I drop my stuff on my desk, making a mental note to clean the mess up before I leave for the evening, and settle in with my course planning for the upcoming week, playing Mark Lanegan on my iPod (which, thank god, I did not squash when Marilyn knocked me over).

I'm so caught up in what I'm doing that I don't even notice anyone's in the building until the door swings open and scares the shit out of me.

"Fuck!" I say, dragging my earbuds out. I'm lucky not to find myself clutching my heart. I don't like to be startled.

And double-fuck me. The huge form in my doorway, carrying a heavy toolbox, is Rex.

For a few days after our… um, encounter, in the woods, Rex was on my mind constantly. I couldn't stop thinking about the way he smelled, about how it felt to be held like that, how he touched me. I mean, sex is great and all, but it felt different with him. He was so sure of everything he did, and it was like he knew me already—what I'd like, how I'd respond. He seemed to know things I didn't even know myself. And while he was touching me, it felt like he actually cared. I know it's stupid to read anything into someone getting off, but it felt… I dunno, personal. Then, after, it was clear I was wrong, since he didn't even ask for my phone number. But then, that kiss. No idea what to make of it.

As soon as the semester started, all thoughts of Rex and his strange hot-cold switcheroo were replaced by teaching, office hours, putting books on hold, finding the best printers on campus, course planning, grading, finding the best coffee in town, getting a school ID, making nice with/avoiding my colleagues, and so on.

Well, maybe not *all* thoughts.

At night, in the uncomfortable bed that Carl left in the apartment for me, thoughts of Rex still trickled in. Like, I still hadn't seen him completely naked. That I wondered what his come tasted like. That, although I usually topped, I was fairly desperate for him to fuck me.

Then there were the other thoughts. Idiotic, sappy, confusing thoughts that must have meant I was half-asleep. Like, I wondered how his mouth tasted in the middle of the night, just woken up from sleep. I wondered if he let Marilyn sleep in bed with him. Did he shower in the morning to get ready for the day, or at night, falling into bed clean, with the day washed away? What would it feel like to kiss his stubbled cheek?

And somehow it's those thoughts—the sappy, confusing ones—that flood through me when he appears in my office doorway. I realize that I've never seen him in the daylight before and that there's a lot of red in his brown hair and in his stubble, and a little gray in his sideburns. I wonder if there's a chance at all that giving him a hug so that I could smell him and feel his heavy arms enfold me could be seen as in any way normal, and immediately answer *no*.

"Hey," he says, sounding confused. "This is your office?"

"Yep, every last crumbling inch of it." He's still hovering in the doorway, looking around. "Um, do you want to come in? Watch the glass." He closes the door behind him and I can hear the glass crunch under his heavy footfalls. "So, do you work for the school?" I can't believe I never asked him what he did when we met in February. I guess I was too busy freaking out.

"No," he says, setting down his toolbox on the corner of my desk. "Well, yeah, I do work for them, but they don't employ me."

That clears things up.

"Um," I say, "what?"

"I mean, I'm not a janitor. I fix things. For lots of folks around town. And the school sometimes calls me to fix things for them. And I make furniture."

Does he think I'd think there was something wrong with being a janitor? Well, maybe so. A lot of professors are weird about class shit—crusading for the working classes in their lectures about Dickens but thinking anyone who does a blue-collar job is too stupid to do what they do.

"That's cool," I say. "That you can fix things, I mean. My dad has an auto shop in Philly and all my brothers work there. I'm not very good at it, though. I mean, I can do basic maintenance and fix easy stuff, but I never really got into it the way they did."

Rex visibly relaxes.

"Cars are one thing I never really learned to fix. So, your light fixture fell," he says, shifting into professional mode. His whole posture changes: his shoulders loosen and he shifts his weight from foot to foot in a wide stance as he looks up at the ceiling.

"More like it committed suicide," I say. "This student slammed the door and that's what made the crack. I think the light fixture just decided it couldn't stay in this office one day longer."

Rex turns to me, his eyes intense.

"What happened?" He looks weirdly protective, like if I told him that students complain about bad grades he'd offer to beat them up for me or something.

"Just an entitled brat pissed off because I wouldn't change his grade. First-semester freshman. Some of them are so nervous to be in college they work really hard. But some of them have never been told no before. They're convinced they'll never have to sacrifice anything. Like, they can skip class and party and still get all *A*s, you know? It wears off." Jesus, Daniel, stop rambling.

Rex nods.

"How come you don't have a bunch of books in here?" he asks, looking around at my tiny cluster of books on the floor-to-ceiling bookshelves that gape around the perimeter of my office. "Most of the professors' shelves are full. Did you not unpack yet?"

All my grad school friends had tons of books: old favorites from when they were kids, all their books from college, a ton of books for research. They thought it was weird that I didn't because almost all of them came from smarty-pants families, but I never got books as a kid. I got a library card when I was in sixth or seventh grade, but I never wanted to check books out because I shared a room with Brian and he could be counted on to destroy anything I owned at any moment. Then, later, I never had cash to spare on buying books when I could get them from the library—especially not the pricey books of literary criticism or theory that my classmates spent thirty or fifty bucks a pop for.

"I don't really have many," I say. "Could never afford it. I just get the library to order things I need. Of course, that's hard here because this library is tiny."

"What's that one about?" Rex asks, pointing.

"Oh, *The House of Mirth*? I'm teaching it in my Intro to American Lit class. It's about this woman, Lily Bart, who wants to be a member of the upper class, so she goes to all the right parties and tries to make the right friends. But then she meets this guy who she really likes—he's different than the stuffy people she usually socializes with—and kind of falls for him. Only he's not rich, so she can't let herself be with him. She tries to marry this awkward rich guy she doesn't like, but it doesn't work out. Eventually, she ends up in debt to the husband of one of her friends by mistake and has to get a job making hats. I don't want to ruin the ending, but let's just say it's not happy. Edith Wharton hates happy endings."

"Why was she so desperate to marry a rich guy?" Rex asks.

"Um, because she's terrified of being poor. Terrified of living in an ugly place and not being admired. It's really sad. A lot of people read it as Wharton's commentary on how vapid and materialistic the upper class is, but she definitely writes it as a tragedy, so she's not totally unsympathetic to Lily." I break off, aware suddenly that I sound like I'm lecturing him about the book.

"She wrote that one about the guy and the sled, right?" Rex asks.

"*Ethan Frome*, yeah," I say. Huh, maybe he wasn't just asking about the book to be polite.

Rex smiles shyly. "I liked that one. It reminded me of here—all that snow, and how isolated it can feel."

"So, do you read a lot?" I ask. Rex studies the mess on the floor.

"Oh, well, I like some of the stories," he says, looking self-conscious. "So, let me grab a broom to clean this up, and then I'll replaster the crack. I think we'll have to get you a floor lamp, because the wiring in these offices is garbage, and I don't want to try and hang a new light just to have these old wires crap out on you. I'll put in the order for it on Monday." He heads for the door.

"I can clean it up," I say, getting up.

"Daniel, sit," Rex says. "It's fine. This is my job." He turns around without another word.

"So," Rex says when he gets back, running a hand over the back of his neck. "What with the chatting and all, I didn't really think. You probably don't want me in here doing this when you're trying to do your work. They had me come by on a Saturday because they figured that's when I wouldn't be disturbing anybody."

"No, no, I don't mind. Stay."

"Well, I don't want to disturb you, banging around and all."

"No, seriously. I worked as a bartender all through college and grad school. It was at this music venue in North Philly, and I'd do all my reading for classes while the shows were going on, because that's when fewer people were at the bar, right? So, one night, I'm trying to finish the whole second half of *Moby Dick* for my seminar in the morning and the band that night is some shitty speed metal group trying to be Slayer and failing miserably. So I'm pouring drinks and trying to finish one of the greatest literary works of all time while the band is screaming unintelligibly in the background. I still hear feedback whenever someone even says the word 'whale.'"

Rex laughs and leans a hip against my desk.

"Really, stay. I'd like the company."

"Sure," he says. "I can pretty much guarantee that I won't scream, at least." He pushes off the desk to reach for his toolbox and the whole thing lurches. He's pretty heavy.

"Jesus, Daniel," he says, squatting down to look at the desk, which I've shimmed with some old copies of the school literary magazine that I found in my filing cabinet. "This thing is falling apart. Did you put these here?"

"Yeah," I say. "I stood on the desk the first day I was here to try and change the lightbulb in the ceiling fixture and the desk kind of slumped."

"And they never gave you a new one?"

"Oh, well, I never asked. I just stuck those there and they were actually the perfect height, so it's fine now."

"Yeah, as long as no one touches it," he says.

"Well, not everyone's as big as you." The words are out of my mouth before I think about it. "Um, I mean…." Heat sparks in Rex's eyes as he looks me up and down. "As heavy as you, I mean. No! As muscular, is what I meant." Jesus, Daniel.

Rex laughs, his smile wide. "I know what you mean," he says, his voice a little lower than it was a minute ago. "Here, I'll put in a work order for a new one for you."

"No, don't bother," I say.

"Why not?"

"Oh, I just—I dunno. I don't really need a new one; it's fine as it is." Rex is looking at me strangely.

"Your call," he says, shrugging. Then he starts to sweep up the glass.

It's nice to have some company while I work—just to be in the same space with someone. Rex has moved on to whatever he's doing to the crack in the ceiling, but now I'm definitely finding myself distracted because he's standing on a stepladder, and his every move causes the muscles in his back and shoulders to flex beneath the white T-shirt he's wearing. His body is gorgeous. He's not perfectly sculpted like those guys who work out at gyms all the time. He's big—heavy frame, wide hips, wider shoulders, big feet and hands. And, I can see now, an ass for days.

I'm zoning out, staring at his ass in his worn jeans, when he turns around and looks at me. There's not even any point in trying to look back at my notes and pretend I wasn't just seriously scoping him out. But he has a little smile on his lips.

"I can see your reflection in the window," he says.

"Oh, jeez." I drop my head into my arms on the desk. "Sorry," I say miserably.

"That's okay. I kind of feel like Marilyn Monroe in *The Seven Year Itch*."

"You really love Marilyn Monroe, huh?" I say.

"She was my mom's favorite."

"Oh, hey," I say, remembering. "I watched *Gaslight*. When I got back to Philly. I really liked it."

Rex grins and it almost takes my breath away. It's a smile that reaches all the way to his whiskey-colored eyes, wrinkling the skin at the corners. Whereas his face is classically handsome, with those high cheekbones, straight nose, and strong brows, his dimples make him look boyish when he smiles, that crooked incisor just catching on his lower lip, and one front tooth the slightest bit behind the other.

"But the library only had the one that was on at your house. The American one. You were talking about the British one, but they didn't have it."

"I have it," Rex says. "You could borrow it." He pauses and looks down. "Or, if you wanted to come over some time, we could watch it." He seems almost shy about asking.

"Yeah, that'd be great," I say.

"So, how has your first month been?" Rex asks, turning his attention back to the plaster.

"Um, yeah, been okay," I say. "I found coffee, there's a library, and I have Internet in my apartment, so there's that. You know what's *killing* me, though, is that nowhere has takeout or delivery after, like, nine o'clock except the pizza place. And, I mean, I love pizza, but there's only so much of it I can eat in a week."

"You don't like to cook, I guess," Rex says.

"Never really learned," I tell him. "When I was a kid, my dad would always make a huge pot of something—chili or spaghetti or something—and leave it on the stove for me and my brothers to grab. Then, when I was in school, I just didn't have the time to learn. And my stove in Philly was... well, I don't know for sure it would've exploded if I'd used it, but there was a distinct possibility." Rex smiles. "I guess I'll need to learn now, though, or I'm going to get scurvy. I think the waiters at the diner already know my name, which is embarrassing because I don't think anyone else even knows I exist."

"Oh, they know," Rex says, sounding amused.

"Huh?"

"Oh, yeah. You're the"—he speaks like he's quoting—"angry, gay professor from New York City who uses all the ten-dollar words."

I try to remember what words I've used when I've talked to people, but I can't. So, people here already think I'm both pretentious and aggressive. Great.

"I'm from Philadelphia," I say.

"Yeah, but they think you look like you're from New York. Because of how you dress."

"How I dress?"

"You look... um, edgy. Your hair and all." My hair just happens to look messy no matter what—possibly because I pull on it when I'm irritated—so I go with it.

"And I'm not angry. Well...." Thinking back, I may have expressed disappointment that certain establishments closed at 5:00 p.m. a couple of times in public.

Rex laughs.

"Daniel, this is a small town. They'll get to know you soon and stop making assumptions about you. But they go from what they hear, and every kid who works at the coffee shop whispers about the professor who swears and drinks more espresso than anyone they've ever seen. Carl tells anyone who'll listen about how he's got a gay man living in his apartment because he thinks it makes him seem, I don't know, hip or something. They're interested in you, that's all."

"Hmph." I don't know what to make of that. I suppose I should've guessed. "It's like high school or something. Everyone knowing everyone else's business."

"I suppose." Rex climbs down the stepladder and wipes his hands on his jeans. He gives me a little smile. "All set," he says. "I'll put in the order for a lamp for you on Monday. They have extras in storage, so it shouldn't be long."

"Oh, great, thanks." I wrack my brain for something to say to delay him leaving. Should I ask him to get a coffee or something?

"All right, then. I have to get home to walk Marilyn or she's like to be stir crazy." Rex puts everything back in his toolbox and rests it on my desk again. I stand up, unsure of whether I'm supposed to shake his hand or just say good-bye or what.

"Thanks," I say again, and my voice sounds disappointed even to me. I hear Ginger's voice in my head: *Just ask him for his phone number! The worst he can say is no, and at least then you'll know and you can stop obsessing over him. Because you* are*, you know. Obsessing over him.*

"Rex, can I—" He looks right at me and I feel all out of sorts. I swallow and try again. "Can I have your phone number? You know, um, so I can call you...." And that, ladies and gentlemen, is where I trail off. Could I *be* any stupider? Yeah, Rex, can I have your phone number in case you ever want to talk to a socially awkward *idiot*?

Something crosses Rex's face that I can't quite read. Oh shit, he's actually going to say no.

He searches his pockets without looking at me and doesn't seem to find whatever he's looking for.

"Um," he says, "why don't you give me yours?"

Oh god, that is a *classic* blow-off. My face heats and my ears are ringing like they do whenever I'm fucking mortified. But I rip a corner off of the syllabus on my desk and lean over to write my cell number on it. Then I write *Daniel*, in case it's one of a dozen slips of paper with phone numbers Rex never intends to call. Christ, should I put my last name in case there's another Daniel?

I hand Rex the paper and he folds it carefully and puts it in his pocket.

"Have a good night, Daniel," he says, and leaves, taking all the air in the room with him.

I'M PASSING by Sludge a few days later, debating whether an evening cappuccino would hit the spot or just make it impossible to sleep, when a sound like a gunshot drops me to the ground out of habit, my heart pounding. I peek around the tree I ducked behind but see nothing except the lush, trimmed grass and well-maintained garbage cans. Then Marjorie pushes open the door to Sludge, wrestling with the glasses she keeps on a chain around her neck.

"Paulie!" Her voice is shrill and I'm struck with the sense that I'm somehow in trouble. "Paulie, was that my car?"

Across the street, the door of a white Honda Accord opens slowly and a thin man slinks out of the car.

I can't decide whether to stay down, out of the fray, or make a break for it. I'm doing something ill-advisedly in the middle—a kind of pretend-I-dropped-something slash tying-my-shoe maneuver—when Marjorie notices me.

"Daniel? What's wrong? Why are you on the ground?"

"Oh, well," I say. "Um, just—in my shoe—or…."

That went well.

"Ah, yes, dear," she says, then turns her attention to the man walking toward us.

"Sorry, Mother," the man says. "I don't know what happened. I just tried to start the car and it… exploded."

"I said you could borrow my car, not break it, Paul," Marjorie says tartly, and the man winces. Wow, I guess even adults can still get told off by their mothers. I wouldn't know.

The man—Paul—sighs in irritation. "Well, Mark's closed for the evening, so I guess I'll have to take the car in tomorrow."

"Well, I should hope so, since you're the one who broke it."

"I didn't *break* it, Mother. Cars just do things. No one knows why. Except Mark," he says resentfully. "And god knows whether he's even telling the truth about the cars. I swear, every time I take mine in it costs me three hundred dollars." I take in his khaki pants and polo shirt and figure that he's not particularly comfortable in a garage.

"Um, hi," I say, stepping toward them. "I can take a look at it, if you want. From the sound of it, though, it's probably your spark plugs, or maybe the catalytic converter."

They're both staring at me.

"I'm Daniel," I say, offering my hand to Paul. That's what you're supposed to do in a small town, right? Be friendly and, like, tell people things about yourself?

"You're the new professor over at the college?" Paul says, trying for casual, but peering at me intently.

"I told you about him, Paul," Marjorie says, elbowing Paul, and my stomach clenches. "And I wish you would get over this tiff with Mark, dear. You're not in high school anymore."

"And you know about cars, do you?" Paul says, clearly desperate for a change of subject even though he looks skeptical.

"A bit. You want to pop the hood?"

While Paul fumbles to pop the hood, I take off my button-down shirt so I don't get it dirty and untuck my T-shirt so I don't look like an idiot.

Staring down into the guts of the Accord makes me feel like I'm ten years old again, when my dad would open up a car and line up me, Brian, Colin, and Sam in front of it to see which of us could guess the problem first. Colin, who's extremely competitive, almost always won. You wouldn't guess it, since he tends to act like a yahoo much of the time, but Colin's actually really smart. He could spot the problem before the rest of us had even started to narrow it down. Of course, later, after I'd stopped pretending that I cared about the cars, I wondered if Brian and Sam didn't sometimes let Colin win because he got so angry when he didn't.

Marjorie appears at my elbow, holding out a bundle of paper towel when I start to unconsciously wipe my hands on my pants.

"Thanks."

She just shakes her head at me and I can practically hear the word "hoodlum" rattling around in her head as she takes in my tattoos and my now-dirty hands.

"Um, it's not the cat, so that's good. The catalytic converter," I correct myself, when Marjorie and Paul exchange a look that clearly says

I've confirmed their suspicion that I don't know anything about cars. "I think it's probably a spark plug wire. If it sparks too early or too late, it messes up your ignition timing. I can't test the wires here, but if that's what it is, it shouldn't be that expensive to fix."

Marjorie's smiling and Paul's looking at me blankly. Two Sludge customers holding iced coffee concoctions have found their way over and are standing next to Marjorie, staring at me.

"Hey," I say to them. "Um, so, yeah. It's not hard to replace them," I say to Paul. "Mark—is it?—will just need to run a diagnostic to see which wire's the problem and then replace that one. I mean, if that's what's wrong," I say, not wanting to sound like a know-it-all. I could offer to try and fix it for them, but in a town with only one mechanic, it doesn't seem wise to step on his toes.

"Thank you," says Paul, holding out his hand.

"Aren't you the new professor?" one of the coffee-drinkers—a thirtysomething woman with badly bleached hair—asks confusedly.

"Yeah, hi," I say, holding out my hand to her. "I'm Daniel." She seems confused by the gesture, but then gives a limp, lingering shake.

"Wow," she says. "I'm Ellen. So you fix cars too, huh? I wonder what other tricks you've got up your sleeve."

"Oh, no, not really," I say. "My dad owns a shop in Philly, so I've just picked up some stuff."

They're all looking at me like they expect me to give them more information, but I don't have anything else to say. I can't tell if they're thinking that knowing about cars disrupts the gay stereotype or the academic stereotype more. I gather up my stuff and try to extricate myself before they can ask any more questions.

"You," Marjorie says, pointing at me. "Free coffee tomorrow."

"Oh, that's okay. I didn't really do anything."

"Don't argue; just accept it," Marjorie says, and I smile.

"See you tomorrow!" Marjorie calls after me.

Chapter 5

October

FOR THE last twenty minutes, Guy Beckenham, a skinny, mousy man with a gray mustache who specializes in medieval literature, has been flipping through what appears to be some kind of illustrated manuscript. It's either in Middle English or my upside-down reading skills have really deteriorated. Every so often he'll lean back in his chair, hands over his stomach, and grin as if whatever is going on in this medieval tome is just tickling the hell out of him.

It's Friday afternoon and I am in the last place that any academic ever wants to be, most especially on a Friday afternoon: a faculty meeting. As a graduate student, I heard faculty complain about them all the time, but I was so curious about who these people really were that I imagined there could be nothing more interesting than getting to see the inner workings of the English department—who is friends with whom, who is actually a pompous asshole and who has people's best interests at heart, what's the real reason so-and-so took a semester off, etc.

Wrong. Faculty meetings feel like some form of psychological water torture, each inconsequential point of order boring more deeply into my skull than the last. For people who are so smart about books and history and philosophy, my colleagues do not seem to understand the whole listen and then speak thing.

Certain I'm missing absolutely nothing, I let my tired mind wander to the two high points of an otherwise draining week. Number one. I was pretty sure that Rex was blowing me off on Saturday when he took my phone number instead of giving me his, but the next evening, when I was at the grocery store, he called me. It was awkward, but I was so glad he hadn't thrown my number out the window of his truck while laughing at how pathetic I am that I was willing to overlook that. Our conversation went something like this:

Me: Hello?

Rex: Daniel?

Me: Yeah.

Rex: Oh, hello, good, hi. This is Rex. From, um, from—

Me: I know who you are, Rex. Hi.

Rex: Right, of course. Well, I was wondering if you're free on Saturday night?

Me (trying not to yell "yes" into the phone instantaneously): Yeah, I think so. Why?

Rex (his suave somewhat back in place): Great. I thought, if you weren't doing anything, that maybe you'd like to come over and we could watch *Gaslight*. The 1940 version that your library didn't have?

Me (trying not to yell "yes" into the phone instantaneously, again): That sounds great, sure.

Rex: Great, great. How about eight on Saturday?

Me (determined to use any word but "great"): Great! That works.

Rex: Oh, I just wanted to let you know that I put that work order in for a new lamp. I ran into Phil—ah, the guy in charge of that—at the hardware store, so I just went ahead and let him know.

Me: Wow, that's some service. Thanks.

Rex: My pleasure. Um, okay, then. Have a good night, Daniel.

Me: Good night. Oh! Wait, um, I don't know how to get to your house.

Rex: Of course. Do you have a pen?

Me: Can you just e-mail me directions if I give you my address?

Rex: Oh. I don't have e-mail.

Me (impressed): Wow. Okay. Um….

Rex: Why don't I call you on Saturday before you come and I'll give them to you then. Okay?

Me: Yeah, sure, great.

Rex (in a ridiculously low and growly voice): Good night.

THAT'S IT. If you edit out the "okays," "greats," "ums," and "ohs," it's really only a few sentences, but I hung up the phone and wandered through the produce section with a humiliating grin on my face. I even bought apples because it seemed like something someone who got asked on a date might do. Then, of course, I told myself that it wasn't necessarily a date. That Rex might just be doing me a favor, since the Free Library of Philadelphia had failed me and the library here wasn't likely to be of more help. Or that he just wanted to hang out, as friends, and share his love of classic cinema with someone.

Still, I allowed myself. If nothing else, it made Sunday not so depressing.

On Monday, as promised, there was a floor lamp in my office. It seemed to only take 25-watt bulbs, one of which flickered with an eerie irregularity that made me constantly jerk my head around to see if someone was behind me, but at least it lent the place atmosphere.

Tuesday and Wednesday were nightmares. Like a total idiot, I'd prepped the wrong readings for my classes (I blame Rex's delectable ass in those worn blue jeans for distracting me during course planning), so I was scrambling around all day Tuesday, didn't sleep Tuesday night, and cocked up class on Wednesday as a result, proof that I was getting old, since staying up all night never used to faze me. To add insult to injury, Peggy Lasher, a very well-meaning but extremely irritating colleague of mine, decided to be buddies with me.

Peggy is the kind of person I avoided all throughout grad school. She's nice enough if she likes you, but she's incapable of letting anyone be right or achieve anything unless she's more right or has achieved something better. She's snobby and passive-aggressive—a quality I cannot abide—and just when you think she's leaving, she sees something in your office that reminds her of a story she simply *must* tell you.

She stuck her head in my door twice on Tuesday and three times on Wednesday, and when I finally told her that I really needed to concentrate she looked so offended that I found myself admitting to her that I'd done the wrong preps for class. Rather than leaving me alone, she told me a very long story about her own first year teaching here. It seemed, for a while, like it would be about a similar incident, but it quickly became clear that this wasn't an I've-done-stupid-things-too story; this was an it-seems-like-I'm-commiserating-but-I'm-actually-bragging story that ended with Peggy having *almost* made a mistake similar to mine but catching herself in time because she pays attention to detail. I wanted to take her by her unfortunate bowl-cut and use her head to open another crack in the ceiling.

Needless to say, by Thursday all I wanted was for the week to be over, especially after I spilled coffee on my stomach walking to campus and had to go around all day with a shirt that made me look like I worked in a prison cafeteria. I got to my office already out of sorts, threw my stuff on my desk, and checked my e-mail, only to find that the afternoon's faculty meeting, which I was going to have been able to miss because I had to supervise a lecture across campus, had been moved to Friday afternoon, so everyone was delighted that I'd be able to make it after all.

Which brings me to high point number two. Hands on my desk, I pushed myself back onto the two back legs of my chair in frustration, without thinking about it, then immediately froze, remembering that the last time I'd done so, the desk had scudded off its literary magazine stack and almost taken my computer to the floor with it. That time, though, all four of the desk's legs stayed firmly on the floor. Confused, I looked at it more closely and realized that the literary magazines I'd shimmed the legs with were gone, and it was resting solidly on new legs.

And I knew it could only have come from one place.

I called Rex.

"This is Rex Vale."

"Rex, this is Daniel."

"Daniel, hi." His voice warmed when he said my name.

"I, um, I—did you fix my desk?"

"Yeah, well. Couldn't have your whole office collapsing." He paused. "And you said you didn't want me to put in a work order, so…."

"No, no," I said quickly. "It's great. I just… you didn't have to do that. I wasn't expecting…." I didn't know what to say. No one had ever done anything like that for me before. "Thank you," I said, pleased to hear that I sounded genuine and not pathetically emotional. "Really, thank you. I'm sorry. I guess I should've started with that."

"Okay, now, don't worry. You're welcome."

There was a pause, but it didn't feel nearly as awkward as the ones during our last conversation, which was heartening.

"Listen," Rex said. "They say it's going to get real cold on Saturday, maybe storm, so I just want to make sure you still want to come. To my place, I mean."

"Yeah, of course I do," I say. "I mean, this is Michigan, right? I knew it had to get cold at some point."

"All right, then," Rex said. "Good-bye."

Then he hung up before I could ask for directions.

"AND YOU'RE all right with that, Daniel?" Bernard Ness is saying.

"Um, I'm sorry, Bernard, what was that?" I say. Clearly I've been nodding along with the meeting as I thought about Rex.

"You're all right with heading the committee?" Crap. Way to not repeat yourself at all, Bernard.

"Yep, yep, sounds good," I hear myself saying since I can't think of any way to admit I've been zoning out.

"Wonderful," Bernard says, and ends the meeting as I sit there, dazed.

I gather my things and make a beeline for my office to get my jacket. All I want is to go home, take a shower, and listen to music with a bottle of wine. I'm slipping on my jacket when Jay Santiago pushes my door open. Jay is maybe ten years older than me, in his early forties, and seems like a nice guy, though I don't know him well.

"The first-year personal essay committee," he says.

"Huh?"

"The committee Bernard stuck you on while you were staring out the window. It's for first-year students' personal essays. You pick a first place, second place, third place, and two runner-up essays and then they read them at an end of the year open house while their parents drink wine out of plastic cups, eat pepper jack cheese cubes, and brag about their kids to anyone who'll listen."

"Whoa, grim," I say. But it could be worse. I actually like reading students' creative writing. It's kind of cool to see who they are outside the classroom, what they think is important on their own time.

"Yeah, I did it last year, so if you need any pointers, just let me know."

"Will do," I say. "Thanks, Jay." He nods good-bye.

I WALK the long way home—well, it's two blocks longer—so I can pick up some wine and get a pizza since I have nothing edible in my house. As I walk out of the store with my box of wine, though, there's shouting coming from behind the store. It's kind of a park, I guess, a patch of grass and a bench and a few trees.

Two guys are messing with a kid sitting on the bench. He's maybe sixteen or seventeen, with longish, light brown hair and checkerboard Vans. You could ID him as a skater kid from thirty paces even if his feet weren't currently resting on a skateboard. I can't really see his face, but he's skinny, and definitely smaller than the guys messing with him. They might be the same age, but they're of the polo-shirt-and-boat-shoes variety, with lingering summer tans and muscles honed by football and fathers who expect certain things from them. I know the type.

Would I be intervening if it weren't "fag" that the polo shirts were calling the kid? I'm not sure. But I was that skinny kid and I'm sure as hell not going to watch him get the shit beat out of him the way I did, even if these guys don't look quite as hardcore as the ones who used to throw me up against crumbling brick walls and threaten me with busted bottles if I ever looked at them in the hallways.

The kid isn't reacting to the polo shirts at all. Not sure if he's scared of a fight or just knows they won't actually throw a punch, but I walk over anyway. When I get a little closer, I can see that he's smiling. It's a mischievous, self-possessed smile. It's a smile that's going to get this kid a lot of ass in a few years, or in a lot of trouble, depending on who he's smiling at. Right now, I'm banking on the latter, because the polo shirts do not seem amused.

When I'm ten feet away, the one in the salmon-colored polo shirt— seriously, kid, salmon?—throws a punch. Whatever skater said to him was too low for me to hear, but now they're both on him, pushing him down on the bench.

"Hey!" I yell. "Get the fuck off him." I pull salmon polo shirt off, bobbing to the side so the punch he throws goes wide. Both polo shirts step away and stare at me oddly, but I can't tell if they're scared of getting in trouble or are about to start in on me too.

I'm still dressed for teaching, in gray pants, a gray and black striped shirt, and the vintage black wingtips Ginger gave me as a going-away present, but my sleeves are rolled up to the elbows, showing some of my tattoos, I'm carrying a box of wine, and, as it's the end of the day, my black hair is probably a mess. I must look like some kind of drunken hipster poet or something.

"Get the fuck out of here!" I yell, pointing toward the street, before they can decide.

"Screw you, asshole," and "Fuck off," the polo shirts say, but it's halfhearted and they're already leaving, shooting the kid poisonous looks from under the stiff brims of their baseball caps.

I smirk and set my wine and my messenger bag down on the bench. It felt really fucking good to yell at those assholes, especially since I've wanted to do it to students all week.

"You okay?" I ask the kid. I lean down to look at his face. There's a red mark on one high cheekbone that will definitely be a bruise tomorrow, but he mostly just looks a little dazed. He has big brown eyes and his olive skin is spattered with freckles. He has a small, straight nose that will probably make him handsome in a few years, but now just looks cute. In fact, the only thing that keeps him from being pretty is that in contrast to his expressive eyes, his brows are straight, dark slashes that turn his otherwise sweet face serious.

"Omygod, you're the guy!"

"Uh, sorry?"

"You're the professor! The gay one from New York!"

"Holy shit. I am from fucking Philadelphia, for the love of god. And how does everyone know I'm gay? Not like I care. Just, seriously, you all gossip like a sewing circle."

"Philly, right on," he says. "I dig Kurt Vile and don't laugh but I totally love Christina Perri. And, like, cheesesteaks. Right?"

"Right, as in, you're listing things from Philadelphia? Yes."

"Cool, cool."

"So, are you okay?" I gesture to his cheek.

"Pshh. Those closet cases are just jealous because they know I'll never make out with them. I'm fine." But his lower lip is trembling a little. I sit down next to him and try not to look like a pedophile as I rest one elbow on my box of wine. I remember after I'd get in a fight all I really wanted was for someone to sit with me.

"So, Kurt Vile, huh?" I say, keeping my voice casual and tilting my head back to look up at the darkening sky. "What do you like about him?"

"Well, he's kinda hot," the kid says, testing the waters with me.

"He's not as hot in person," I tell him. "He's kind of vapid."

"No way; you've met him?" The kid's eyes go wide and his genuine enthusiasm takes five years from his age.

"Yeah. I used to work at the bar in a club. He played there all the time. Nice guy, just kind of a space cadet."

"Whoa," the kid says. I hope I didn't just sound like a music snob.

"I like Christina Perri too," I offer. "Her voice is awesome and her songs are kind of addictive, even though they're a little bubblegum. She uses interesting progressions. My best friend, Ginger, tattooed her once, said she's really cool."

"Hey," he says, turning on the bench to sit cross-legged facing me. His face is serious again. "Thanks. For getting rid of them. I mean, I coulda handled it. Probably. I just. Thanks."

"No worries," I say, and hold out my hand. "I'm Daniel."

"Leo," he says, shaking it.

"Short for Leonardo?" I ask.

"No, short for leotard," he says, rolling his eyes.

"Smartass."

"You love my ass," he says, winking, and there's that mischievous smile again.

"You must be okay if you're trying to pick up a guy twice your age. I'll leave you to your bench."

"Well, whattaya say?" He inches closer to me, clumsy and enthusiastic. "Want to make out?"

I think he's kidding, but....

"Leo," I say, breathing out through my nose and trying not to sound 876 years old. "You've got to be careful. You don't want to go around flirting with older guys. With strangers. Okay? You'll get into trouble." I am such an incredible hypocrite right now.

"Maybe I want a little trouble," he says with an eyebrow waggle.

I take him by the shoulders firmly, the bones delicate under my hands.

"You don't," I say, as seriously as I mean it. "Not that kind of trouble." Something changes in his eyes and he drops the smirk.

"Got it," he mutters, looking down at his dirty Vans. I feel like I kicked a puppy. I pat him on the shoulder and grab my bag and my wine.

"I'll see you around, okay?" I say. He brightens.

"Yeah, cool, man," he says. "I work at the record store. You should totally come by!"

"Wait, there's a record store in this town?"

"Um, well, they don't only have records. But still! On Willow, near the alley behind the library. Come *on*, please come visit me some time. I get *so* bored." He's giving me a look that's equally dangerous to the smile, only this one is puppy dog, through and through.

"Sure," I say. "I'll definitely check it out. Night." I wave at him and turn to go. Leo jumps up, nearly tripping over his skateboard. Skinny arms snake tight around my shoulders and I catch a whiff of sweat and clove cigarettes before he lets go. God, it's such a familiar smell.

"Thanks," he whispers again. Then he grabs his board and runs away.

"SEE, BABYCAKES? He wasn't blowing you off by asking for your number," Ginger says.

I'm slightly buzzed on cheap red wine—the kind of buzz that happens after one and a half glasses of wine on an empty stomach after not enough sleep—and lying on my back, staring at my ceiling as Pink Floyd pulls me so deep into my bed that I don't ever want to come out.

"Yeah, I know that *now*. But I still convinced myself of it, which made me think how dumb I would be to get involved with him."

"Clarify, please."

"Well, if it made me feel that shitty to think he didn't want me when I'd only seen him, like, three times, then it'll be that much worse when he loses interest a few weeks from now."

"Oh, that's logical," she says. "So, the more you like someone, the stupider it is to actually date them because the more it might, hypothetically, hurt if the relationship ever ends." She snorts. "Wow, you're smart. That's, like, Nobel Prize material. Daniel Mulligan's theory of dating relativity."

"Shut up," I mutter.

"Oh, come on. What's really going on?" she asks.

"Tomorrow," I say. "I think I might have an actual date."

"Aw, baby's first date!" She pauses. "Does he know you have no idea how to go on a date?"

"I can go on a date," I insist.

"You've never been on one," she says.

"What about—"

"Getting picked up at the bar where you work and blown in an alley does not a date make, pumpkin," she says sweetly.

"Fine," I mutter.

"Tell!"

So, I start to tell her about what's happened this week.

"Wait," she interrupts me. "Is that 'Shine On You Crazy Diamond'?"

"Yeah."

"Put it on speaker so I can listen too," she says. "I was just thinking I haven't played this album in way too long."

I put my crappy phone on speaker and turn up the stereo. Then I tell her about everything that's happened with Rex as *Wish You Were Here* soars in the background.

"That's awesome, babycakes," she says. "So, are you going to finally—*you* know—uuuuggghhh," she moans. "This song is so fucking good it's making me cry right now."

"Ha-ha," I say. "You totally wish I were there."

"I do!" she wails. Ginger's very sensitive, but it makes her uncomfortable. "And thinking of you maybe, actually, possibly going on a date with a nice guy… I can't do that and listen to Pink Floyd at the same time without getting emotional. I'm only human." She sings this last to the tune of the Human League song and I groan.

"Music social foul: no singing a song when another song is playing. *Double* music social foul: don't ever fucking sing anything while Pink Floyd is playing. What's wrong with you?"

"I should be shot," she says. "I should be dressed in a *Dark Side of the Moon* shirt and shot into space so I can never disrespect Pink Floyd again. And not even a concert T-shirt, but one of those ones they sell in head shops that white boys with dreads buy. But enough about me. What are you going to wear on your date?"

"I dunno. I mean, he's already seen me in a suit and jeans and a T-shirt. Oh, and half-naked. Oh! And carrying a half-dead dog. So, I don't think it really matters."

"It matters because if you look like you made an effort to look nice then he'll think you care about the date and if you don't then he'll think you think it's no big deal."

"Um. Is that true?"

"Yeah, totally true."

"Huh. So, what do I wear, then? I don't want to dress up. I'm going to his house to watch a movie."

"Mmmm." I can hear Ginger mentally flipping through my (very limited) wardrobe. "Wear the black jeans you got last year, your boots, and any shirt that doesn't have writing on it."

"Uh, okay, if you say so."

"Ooh, no. Specification: wear the maroon button-down I gave you that that guy left at the shop after puking like a tiny wuss and running outside without it."

"The sleeves are too short."

"Cuff and roll, baby, cuff and roll. It's hot. It draws attention to your forearms."

"You like my forearms?"

"No, not yours in particular. I mean, they're fine. Just, it's a sexy body part."

"I totally agree. I just didn't know girls liked them too."

"Oh, yes, Daniel. All girls like forearms. Every single one. No really, I've asked all of us and we all agree. We don't even agree about whether or not the long arm of the law should be able to reach into our vaginas, but we agree about forearms."

"Jesus fucking Christ, Ginger, have you been fighting with the pro-lifers again? They're gonna bomb your shop."

"They make me want to get pregnant just so I can get an abortion and make a YouTube video of it to send to them."

"All right, the maroon button-down and black jeans. Thanks. I'm going to ignore the thing about forearms, since I think you know what I meant."

"Yeah, fine."

"Hey, I think I accidentally kinda made a friend."

"Oh yeah, someone you work with?"

"No. I stopped him from getting beat up. Little smartass skater kid. Babyqueer. He tried to make out with me."

"Um, you didn't, did you?"

"I didn't make out with a kid, Ginger. What the fuck?"

"Just checking."

"Jesus, you think I'm a pervert."

"Well, yeah, but not in that way."

I start to giggle.

"He was skinny and smelled like cloves and he said he liked Kurt Vile."

"Oh my god," Ginger says, laughing, "it's like you have your own little *you*. I remember when you smoked cloves. And, jeez, you were scrawny."

Then she says something about the universe sending us pieces of our past selves to embrace so we can heal them and I must be drunker than I thought because I don't follow her at all.

"Aw," I mutter. "The wine's all the way over there."

AND THEN it's morning. I must have rolled over onto the phone and flipped it shut at some point because it's lodged under my left hip bone. The light's still on and my wine-stained coffee mug is perched on the windowsill, right about where my hand reaches if I stretch. My teeth feel grainy and I'm starving since I fell asleep without ever ordering pizza.

But, despite feeling a little muzzy, I'm not hungover and I'm going to see Rex tonight, so things are looking just fine.

My phone buzzes with a text.

Ginger: *You alive, kid?*

I text her back, *Alive. Wish you *were* here*, and jump in the shower.

AN HOUR later I'm showered, I've driven to Traverse City and bought a bottle of nice bourbon to bring with me to Rex's tonight, and I'm parking in the lot at the library, congratulating myself on remembering to drive since I have a bunch of books to pick up and won't be able to walk home with them. I have my laptop and I'm planning to get a ton of writing done today. Then I'll get my books and run home with enough time to shower and change and get to Rex's at nine. It's a plan.

The Sleeping Bear College Library isn't particularly expansive and it isn't particularly nice; it kind of looks like a book prison. It also doesn't have windows above the first floor. Still, I have a faculty carrel with an actual door, so I can tear my hair out in privacy. I collect a teetering stack of books and haul them to my carrel, ready to start the new section that I'm adding to chapter two.

A major part of what I need to do to get tenure is turn my dissertation into a publishable book. That means not just polishing what I've already written, but tearing it apart and rethinking central questions from a different perspective. Now, instead of having to prove to my committee that I know what I'm talking about and can make an interesting argument, I have to prove to an academic publisher that I have something to say about literature that hundreds of other academics will want to read.

After about three hours of deleting every sentence the second I write it, I begin to get into a rhythm, and I'm actually drafting some not-terrible stuff when I finally look at my watch and see that it's already 7:30. I had meant to be home by now. I scribble a quick half page of notes to myself so I'll know where I left off, gather my things, and go to check out the books I have on hold at the front desk.

ALL MY life I've had this fear—no, not really a fear. A niggling thought that my annoying brain lands on again and again. I have it when I come out of a movie theater or a concert, or when I've slept all weekend without hearing from anyone. It's this thought that just maybe, when I step outside, the world as I know it will be gone and it will have been replaced by another. It's half horror movie and half wishful thinking, but I've had it ever since I was a kid. I remember I had it the first morning I woke up after my mom died. I woke up and she was there. For a second. But then I remembered that she wasn't there anymore. That I'd woken up to a world where she didn't exist.

Now, that's exactly what has happened. When I got into my car this morning, it was a pleasantly chilly day, one that made me glad I grabbed a hoodie. I vaguely remember that when I walked into the library the wind had kicked up a bit, but it was only a few yards into the building. Now, nine hours later, it is a world of swirling, whirling winter. There has to be at least a foot of snow on the ground and more is falling heavily, gusting against the side of the library and the few cars in the parking lot. It's wet snow, creeping down my collar and into my nose.

I heave my bags of books onto my shoulders and trudge to my car. The snow is up to my shins and it soaks through my beat-up Vans and jeans immediately. I throw my bags into the backseat of my car and jump in, freezing. I'll have to kick the snow away from the back of the car so I can get out of the lot, but I figure I'll warm it up first. I turn the key in the ignition and—of course!—nothing. Crap. Thanks, car.

I figure I'll walk home and call a cab to take me to Rex's. It's only a mile and a half or so to my house from here, and it's cold, but it's not too cold. I dig out my phone to check the time and remember that it's still on silent from being in the library all day. When I flip it open to turn the volume back on I see I missed a call from Rex about two hours ago. He must have been calling to give me directions. I figure I'll call to get his address when I get home, but as I'm slipping the phone back in my pocket, it rings. It's Rex.

"Hi, Daniel," he says. "Sorry to call again, I just wanted to give you directions to my place."

"Um…," I say.

"Is it—do you not want to come anymore?" he asks, sounding wary. "I mean, I understand. The snow and all."

"No, no, it's not that. It's just. Crap, well, I'm just leaving the library to go home and I—my car won't start. So I'm just going to walk home and then get a cab to your place, but I might be a little late. There are cabs here, right? Like, do I call a number or something?"

"I'll be there in ten minutes," Rex says, and the line goes dead. Well, shit.

I pull up my hood and pop the car's to take a gander while I wait for Rex. It's probably just a dead battery since this one's old, but I might need a new starter. It's hard to see anything with the snow swirling around.

"Daniel!" Rex calls from the window of a dark-colored Chevy Silverado that's pulling up next to me.

"Hey," I say. "Sorry, man. I would've been fine walking, really."

"Don't be an idiot," he says, eyes flashing. "You don't even have a jacket. You should have waited inside."

"I wanted to see what was up with my car."

"I told you it was going to get cold, remember? Because I didn't want you to be unprepared. I know you're not used to this weather."

I'm annoyed at him for telling me what to do, but also a little weirded out because he actually seems concerned.

"Yeah, but it's October. I thought you were just making conversation. Like, 'oh, the seasons are changing.' I didn't know you meant there was going to be a freaking snowstorm. Anyway, it's no big deal. It probably just needs a jump," I say, patting the hood of my car.

Rex is looking at me with a mixture of annoyance and concern. Probably coming out in a snowstorm to pick up a guy he barely even knows wasn't high on his list of pre-date activities.

"I'll just get my stuff," I say, and duck back into the car.

When I turn around with my bags of books and my backpack, Rex is right behind me. Even in the swirling snow I can feel his heat. He closes his eyes like he's trying to get himself under control.

"Hey," he says, looking into my eyes, "Sorry if it sounded like I was lecturing you. But every year a tourist freezes to death or gets caught in a snowstorm up here because they don't know the weather."

"Okay." I nod.

He shoulders one of my bags and I follow him to the truck.

I'm soaked to the knees, so we head to my apartment so I can change and drop off all my books.

As we walk through the door of my apartment I'm suddenly struck with a familiar feeling. This apartment, like every one I've ever had, is run-down and musty, with garbage furniture, milk crate shelves, and floors that stay dirty-looking no matter how many times I wash them. I wish Rex would wait outside and never see my unmade bed, its mismatched sheets in a nest where I left them, my stove gummed with oil and dust and god knows what—not that I use it for much anyway—and my dresser with the drawers that sag out of their tracks from what must have been years of someone—Carl?—jamming them in and yanking them out, though dissatisfied with what they contained or the life that surrounded them I don't know.

It's a dump, depressing even with every light on. I've gotten used to it the last few weeks, since it's become my haven from work and from a town that seems to know what I do before I do it, but now, looking at it through a stranger's eyes, I once again see it for what it is.

"So, I'm just going to grab a shower," I tell Rex. "Do you want some…?" I glance around the kitchen. Do I have anything to offer him?

"I'm fine," Rex says.

"Wine," I say, "or water?"

He shakes his head.

"Okay, well, make yourself comfortable. I'll just be a few minutes."

I grab the Ginger-approved outfit and duck into the bathroom. I catch a glimpse of myself as I run the water, and make a mental note to buy a heavy winter coat, like, now. My lips are almost blue and my cheeks are dead white against the black of my hair, which my hood has squashed into an unattractive helmet around my head. I look tired.

"Great," I say to the Daniel in the mirror.

As I step under the mercifully hot water, I think I hear the opening notes of *Wish You Were Here* from the living room, but then the hiss of the water is all I can hear.

IT'S NOT entirely true that I've never been out on a date, though I never told Ginger about it. Richard and I went on one date before falling into the pattern that I thought was dating and he apparently thought was just getting his rocks off. It was soon after we met at a lecture on campus. Richard was a grad student in the chemistry department, done with coursework and writing his dissertation like I was. The lecture was dull and the question and answer portion that followed downright painful, and I caught him smiling at me when I accidentally rolled my eyes at some pompous nonquestion that the chair of the history department asked like he was a king bestowing a knighthood.

We chatted. He was handsome and funny and incredibly smart and so not my usual type. He was very clean and well dressed, like a perfect ivory tower Ken doll. But there was something about him that made me feel… grateful that he thought I was interesting enough to talk to. He asked me to dinner the next night and I looked up the menu online in a panic to see what I could order that wouldn't wipe out my cash for the whole month. Not much.

It was, I suppose, a good date, if a good date is interesting conversation, common tastes, and an appreciation of each other's senses of humor. But the entire time we sat there, I could tell he was half listening to me and half planning what I was useful for. There was a cold, calculating air to him that made it feel more like an interview than a date. I was dressed all wrong for the restaurant Richard had chosen, I picked a wine that was (he informed me) a terrible choice given what I ordered, and when it came time to pay and I pulled out cash for my half, he slid the check from under my hand with a subtle shake of the head, as if I were embarrassing him. He paid the check, I realized later, the way I'd seen the fathers of fellow students pay checks when they took their kids out to dinner: with absolute knowledge that the person across the table wouldn't be there if it weren't for them, and with the gratification of being able to lift that person out of their sad world of cafeteria food and ramen noodles for one special night.

A treat. That's what Richard thought he was giving me.

At the time, though, I was so distracted by trying to shove cash back in my wallet and thank him that I didn't think about it. As we left the restaurant and I told him he needn't have paid for me, he smiled indulgently and told me I could buy him a drink next time. That he wanted to see me again was a balm to my wounded ego; that he *expected* to see me again wasn't something I thought about until later.

I PULL on my black jeans and the maroon shirt that Ginger gave me, cuffing back the too-short sleeves and thinking about my best friend doing battle with the pro-lifers on South Street. Every few months they mass at the Planned Parenthood near her shop and make everybody miserable. Ginger insists that she doesn't just fight with them because she finds them ethically and politically abhorrent, but also because she thinks signs of aborted fetuses are a deterrent to getting tattooed.

I towel-dry my hair and put a little wax in it so it won't turn into a knot the second the wind blows. I look okay. A lot better now than I did when I got in the shower. There's some color in my cheeks and my eyes don't look so tired anymore. I brush my teeth, take a deep breath, and go to find Rex.

He's in a crouch, picking at the painted-over windows in the living room. When he sees me, he gets to his feet.

"You look great," he says, looking me up and down.

"Thanks. Um, should we go?"

"It's not safe to have these windows painted shut," he says. "If there was a fire… or carbon monoxide."

I laugh a little at the shitty luck of living my whole life the way I have and then dying of carbon monoxide poisoning.

"Don't worry about it," I say.

"Seriously," he says. "Carl should fix them for you."

"I'll mention it if I see him," I say, mildly irritated.

I grab my backpack with the bourbon I bought for Rex and shrug into my jacket.

"Do you have a warmer coat?" Rex asks, running a finger over the shoulder of my leather jacket.

With him standing in my apartment I'm more aware than ever of how low the ceilings are.

"Er, it's on the to-buy list," I say, tucking the cuffs of my jeans into my boots. I doubt they're going to be much help in keeping me dry, though. The leather is worn and cracked from years of puddles and rowdy concerts and the soles are worn smooth. I wonder if there's a cobbler in this town.

DESPITE IT killing my car, the snow is really beautiful. In Rex's truck it doesn't seem so formidable and the drive to his house passes in appreciative silence. The last mile or so is just the woods, dark and quiet, the laden pine boughs dipping to kiss the ground.

"I can see why *Ethan Frome* would remind you of here," I say.

"Yeah."

When we pull into Rex's driveway, his little cabin is lit up inside like some kind of real-life Thomas Kinkade painting, the snow in drifts against the rough wood exterior and the windows glowing yellow. It's beautiful, guiding us home like a lighthouse. Except, this isn't my home. I can't even imagine living someplace like this—someplace nice and clean and private. Someplace in the middle of nowhere.

Inside, it looks just like I remember. The wood makes it feel cozy and natural, and the scent of cedar seems to come from the walls themselves. The front door opens onto the living room, with the couch and armchair arranged near the fire, and the kitchen is off to the left, the bedroom and bathroom to the right. Everything is greens and blues and browns, but the cabin looks very clean. My eye catches on the blue flannel blanket neatly folded on the back of Rex's forest green and black plaid couch. I'm flooded with memories of Rex wrapping me in that blanket back in February, of pulling it up over my nose after Rex went to bed, thinking it was the closest I would ever get to him. I know how that blanket smells, how it feels against my skin.

"So," Rex says, once we've shed our snowy boots, "if you were at the library so late, you probably haven't eaten, right?"

"Um, I had some soup earlier," I say, distracted by Marilyn, who has come running to the front door to greet us. "Hi, Marilyn," I say, squatting down to pet her. "Do you think... do you think she remembers that I was the one who hurt her?" I ask. "Like, when she sees me, does she remember that I broke her leg?"

"I think she remembers that you saved her," Rex says. He steps close and takes my jacket, and then he runs his knuckles over my cheekbone. "Here, I'll make us something." He walks into the kitchen before I can say anything.

I follow Rex into the kitchen. He's wearing another dark blue and gray plaid flannel shirt that doesn't have even a centimeter of space to spare. You have to be born with the capacity for a body like Rex's. No amount of protein or time at the gym would ever make it happen for me. I wonder what it would be like to be that big. I'm not small or anything, but it doesn't feel like that long ago that I was a skinny kid getting kicked around at school. Rex's size makes him seem… I dunno, impervious. Like I could throw myself against him with everything I am and he wouldn't budge an inch.

"Can I help?" I ask as Rex pulls things out of the refrigerator and lays them out on the counter.

Rex gives me a singularly sweet smile and it transforms his whole face. There are faint lines around his whiskey-colored eyes when he smiles, the straight line of his brow softens, and he has dimples.

"I thought you didn't cook?"

"Well, not really, no. But I could help cut stuff or whatever."

"You only have macaroni and cheese," Rex says.

"Were you looking through my kitchen?" I say.

"I was looking for a glass for water," he says. "All you have to eat is macaroni and cheese and frozen burritos."

"Looking for a glass in my freezer, were you?" I mumble.

"Looking for ice," he says levelly, but I don't quite believe him.

"I have soup."

"Soup is flavored water, not food. No, just hang out," he says. I slide onto a stool on the other side of the counter. He chops, slices, salts, and does a whole bunch of other things I couldn't do if my life depended on it.

"You don't use recipes?" I ask.

"Nah. More fun to just figure it out as I go along."

"How'd you learn to cook?"

"My mom worked nights," Rex says as he slices carrots into tiny uniform matchsticks. "She was an actress—well, she wanted to be. She *wanted* to be Marilyn Monroe." I smile at him. "She was in a bunch of plays when we lived in Houston and Tulsa—that's when I was little—so I just fended for myself. Didn't really care if I ate peanut butter and jelly every night. Then, later, when we went to LA she was working as a cocktail waitress, so she was never home in the evenings. We didn't have the money for getting takeout every night and I was sick of peanut butter, so I decided I'd learn. Mostly I just experimented until I got it right. Since I had to eat anything I messed up it was a pretty good incentive to learn quick. I didn't really like it, though.

"Then, later, when I was living alone, I started watching the Food Network. That's when I fell in love with cooking, I think. I could just watch someone do something and then I could do the same thing. It was like going to cooking school for free."

Note to self: Rex talks more when he's doing something with his hands.

"I've never really watched it," I say. "My brothers would've thrown a fit."

Sam watches nothing but sports, Brian watches sports and those shows where frat boys dare each other to eat bugs and crawl through sewers, and Colin watches horror movies or war movies where people get blown to pieces. He would take one look at the Food Network and start ranting about pretentious faggots and how only girls watch cooking shows.

"I like it," Rex says quietly, and there's something about the moments when he pulls into himself that make me want to protect him.

"Well," I say, "maybe we could watch some."

Rex smiles that sweet smile again. God, that one crooked tooth catches on his lip just a little. It kills me.

"So your mom wanted to be Marilyn Monroe, huh? How'd that work out for her?"

Rex looks back to his vegetables, chopping for a minute in silence.

"She was in some movies. Small-time stuff. You know: screaming girl number three, secretary—that kind of thing. In LA, she was always dating someone who could get her a part because she was pretty, just never a big part. She was actually really good, though. We would watch all the old movies—those were the ones she really liked: Old Hollywood glamour—and she'd do the parts. She wanted to be Marilyn, but she was actually better at the dramatic parts. The really high drama death scenes and all—Helen Hayes at the end of *A Farewell to Arms*, you know?"

I don't, though I read the book.

"Anyway, she loved being in front of the camera, but she was never going to have the kind of career she wanted. Old Hollywood had been dead for more than twenty years. No one was looking for that kind of thing anymore."

"That's sad," I say. "So, what did she do?"

"Oh, along the way she realized it was never going to happen. And then she dated some guys who didn't want her acting anymore." He quiets. "Anyway, she still loved the movies, even after. Sometimes I wouldn't even be sure if she was talking or doing the dialogue from a movie."

"Sounds like you were close."

Rex nods, but his expression darkens.

"Are you still?"

"She died when I was sixteen."

I feel a rush of sympathy and I wonder if I should tell Rex that my mom died too. That I know what it's like. Only, I have no idea what his situation was, so maybe I really don't know what it's like. I hate when people presume that they know how you feel.

Rex slides two plates of food onto the table while I'm still deciding if I should say anything. "Here, let's eat," he says, obviously not wanting to talk about it. He slices some bread and puts out butter. "Do you want something besides water? Wine? Tea?" I shake my head.

He gestures for me to sit down, but I push up on my toes and kiss him on the cheek, my hand braced on his firm chest. His cheek is smooth, and I realize I haven't ever seen him clean-shaven before. I wonder if what Ginger said about putting effort into your looks for a date is true.

"Thanks," I say. "For dinner and for picking me up earlier. You didn't have to, but I—thanks." Rex covers my hand with his own where it still rests on his chest and squeezes, smiling that shy smile.

On my plate is pasta with strips of grilled chicken and vegetables in what I assume is a white wine sauce, since I saw him add wine to the pan. It smells heavenly.

"Holy shit," I say with my mouth full of pasta. "This is the best thing I've ever eaten."

Rex smiles and shakes his head, but I'm telling the truth. I guess I was hungrier than I thought too, because I barely stop to breathe for a few minutes, distracted by the food in front of me, which somehow manages to be hearty and delicate at the same time. Kind of like the man who prepared it. I glance up to find Rex looking at me, his expression unreadable. Immediately, I realize I've probably been shoveling food into my mouth like a starving orphan and I put my fork down, embarrassed.

"It's so good," I say, hoping to distract from my table manners. I usually eat while I'm reading or walking somewhere. Maybe Ginger should have listed "Don't eat like a hammerhead shark" among her dating tips.

"I'm glad you like it," Rex says. And though he's staring at my mouth, he doesn't seem disgusted at all. "I like watching you eat." Then he blushes and looks down. That should seem creepy, I tell myself, but for some reason it's just really hot.

Rex turns back to his own plate.

"No, seriously, you could be a chef or something."

"I worked as a short-order cook at a diner for a bit," Rex says. "But you have to go so fast that it kind of took the fun out of it."

Rex has finished the food on his plate and is absently eyeing mine. I'm full and warm and happy and can't eat another bite.

"I'm done," I say, pushing my plate toward him.

"You sure?"

"I'm stuffed, man. I haven't eaten that well in… ever. Please."

He pulls my plate up and starts to take a bite with my fork.

"I don't mean to be a pig," he says, pausing, and it has the ring of someone else's words being repeated.

"You're not a pig. I was the one cramming food in my face," I say, awkwardly trying to put him at ease. "Besides, you need fuel for all that." I indicate his brawn, giving him an appreciative look.

He smiles and cleans my plate.

"When we were in high school, my brothers would practically fistfight over who got the last of the food," I say. "They ate constantly. Don't know how my dad kept enough to feed them."

"You're the youngest, right?"

"Yeah. Sometimes my dad would put a plate aside for me before he called out that it was ready. Probably afraid I'd starve to death otherwise. God, I was such a runt."

"Were you?"

"Yeah, I was skinny and I didn't really have a growth spurt until my senior year of high school. Don't worry, though," I joke. "I made enough trouble for two kids."

"Oh yeah?"

"Yep. I was a little runty kid from South Philly. I did what I had to do. Pissed everyone off doing it too."

Rex regards me curiously.

"I can see it," he says, considering me. "Not the runty part, I mean. So, you got in trouble at school?"

"Not on purpose, but yeah. When I was in high school my teachers thought I was a loser. I was always mouthing off because the teachers would say stupid things or I'd get bored. There were so many people in every class that the teachers could never keep people focused on the lesson, so it was hard to concentrate. I would cut class a lot to avoid people. Got in a lot of fights. As a direct result of my big mouth, no doubt." I smile at him wryly. It's true. As a teenager I just couldn't stop myself from saying smart-assed shit to the wrong people.

"A lot of the time, they'd just assign busywork to keep the class under control, so I never did it because it was pointless. Then, when I actually did my homework, teachers acted shocked, which would piss me off. One year, I wrote an essay for my English class after I hadn't turned in much homework and the teacher accused me of plagiarizing it. The only thing that saved me was that I'd written it out longhand because I had to type it at the library, so I had the draft and everything.

"Anyway, got in trouble at school, at home. You name it. I got suspended for fighting, suspended for smoking, suspended for skipping. Then when the school'd call my dad I'd get in trouble with him."

"You get picked on?" Rex says, and I swear, a vein pulses in his temple like he wants to punish the kids who beat the crap out of me in high school. I smile at him.

"A bit. I wasn't a bad fighter; I was just small. Had to play to my other strengths."

Rex raises an eyebrow in question.

"You know, freak them out a little so they'd leave me alone."

At first that was all I'd wanted—just to be left alone so I could pay attention when Mrs. Caballeros would talk about Shakespeare and Emily Dickinson, and Mr. Seo about the Civil War. Then, later, when I was alone, I wished for a friend. A real friend. Not the kids I hung out with when we cut class, smoking while we leaned against the chain-link fence in the abandoned lot a few blocks from school, talking about nothing, fronting like we didn't want anything else.

"Your brothers didn't look out for you?" Rex asks.

I let out a bark of laughter. "Ah. No."

The dark look in Rex's eyes is back. He's a rather strange conversationalist. It's almost like he's interviewing me. Not that he doesn't seem interested; he does. His eyes never leave me when I talk. It's more like he's out of practice or something.

"Then junior year, when we did mandatory standardized testing and they found out that I wasn't stupid, they gave me all this shit about applying myself and rising above my circumstances. Just total savior bullshit, you know. Like, we treated you like crap for years because you weren't a good kid, and now that you have high test scores we suddenly believe you have a responsibility to yourself. It really turned me off school even more."

"So, how'd you end up going on to college if you didn't like school?"

"Um, I really liked learning, even though I hated school. I'd read in the library for hours. Just wander through the stacks and pull out books on whatever seemed interesting. Sometimes when I was there, there'd be free lectures downstairs and I'd go listen and just never want it to end. It was mostly adults in the audience and they were quiet and respectful and they seemed to care. I saw this guy speak once and he'd written a book about the Essex, this nineteenth-century ship that got rammed by a whale and sunk. The crew had to abandon ship and try and survive in these small boats and eventually they had to resort to cannibalism to survive. He was a really good speaker and he made it so interesting. I got his book from the library and read it and I was just amazed because this had happened, like, almost two hundred years before and was kind of a mystery in some ways and this guy had done all this research and was able to reconstruct something after the fact and then write the whole thing like an adventure story. I think that was the first time I thought, oh, learning doesn't have to be like it is in my shitty high school.

"And I loved to read, you know? Ever since I was a kid. Just not the same book for two months the way it was in school, reading it out loud torturously. I read all the time and when I was in school, I would daydream, pretend I was a character in a book. Sometimes that's how I got in trouble too, because I'd be thinking, hey, this is the scene where the scrappy hero tells off the bully, so I would. But things don't usually go the way you write the scene in your head."

Rex smiles. "I used to do that with movies sometimes," he says. I grin, picturing him as a noir detective, the collar of his overcoat turned up against the rain, brushing his strong jaw, but he doesn't elaborate, just keeps looking at me like he wants me to say more.

"Anyway, that's how I met Ginger," I say, smiling at the thought of her. "My best friend. I skipped school one day when I was seventeen. Don't remember why. I walked over to South Street, just for something to do, and I ended up looking through the window of this tattoo shop around the corner. Really old place, not fancy or anything. There was this girl in the shop tattooing an older guy. Fifties, maybe. And the guy was just crying. Not from the pain or anything, but, like, sitting there totally still with tears running down his face. I couldn't see what the tattoo was of, just their faces. I must've stood there for half an hour just watching them. I remember thinking that anything that could have that kind of an effect on someone, I wanted to know more about. Finally, the guy left and the girl looked right at me. She gestured for me to come in. Of course, I tried to play it off like I hadn't been spying on them, but she just rolled her eyes and came outside.

"She sat on the steps of the shop and just stared at me. I had no idea what to do. I wanted to ask her about the man's tattoo, but it seemed so personal. I wanted to ask a bunch of things. Eventually, after we sat in silence for two cigarettes, the girl said, 'I'm Ginger. Who are you?' I told her my name and she said, 'Okay. I'll give you a freebie because I can tell you'll be back. What do you want?' And she did. She gave me a tattoo and we talked and she was right. The second I had money, I was back."

I smile absently, thinking of Ginger. Of how she, though only four years older than me, seemed to know everything. How she gave me stern talking-tos that helped me graduate, convinced me to follow my gut and take classes at the community college. How she let me crash with her when I had nowhere to go, or when my brothers were making life unbearable.

"What was it of?" Rex asks, yanking me back to the present.

"Huh?"

"That first tattoo. The one Ginger gave you that day."

"Oh," I say, embarrassed. "It's silly."

"Tell me," Rex says gently.

I unbutton my shirt, pull my left arm out of the sleeve, and roll up the sleeve of my T-shirt to expose the flowers among the other tattoos on my left biceps.

"They're Irish primroses. They were my mom's favorite flower. It was all I could really think to get when Ginger put me on the spot. She said to pick something small, since she was doing it for free."

Rex's head jerked up when I said they *were* my mom's favorite. He rubs his thumb over the little flowers and smiles at me.

"Of course, my brother, Colin, saw it when he walked in on me in the shower about a month later and gave me hell for being a fairy with a flower tattoo." I shrug. "Anyway, we've been friends ever since."

Rex's hand is still on my shoulder.

"Um, I should—here, let me do the dishes since you cooked. Thanks again for dinner. It was amazing."

"Leave it," he says softly, still looking at my skin.

Rex traces the exposed tattoos with curious fingers, his hands warm and rough. Birds and a memento mori skull and some designs Ginger was obsessed with for a while. Rex reaches for the other sleeve of my button-down.

"Can I? May I, I mean?" he asks, and when I nod, he pulls my shirt off. He rolls the other sleeve of my T-shirt up, exposing the Philadelphia skyline, a wolf, and, running down my arm, the Ben Franklin Bridge.

Rex traces the line of the bridge down my arm and his touch makes me shiver.

"You cold?" he says. "Here, let me make a fire."

I follow him into the living room where Marilyn is lying in front of the fireplace, just like she was all those months ago when we first brought her here. Rex kindles the fire quickly and the flickering light illuminates the strong planes of his face. Only this time, instead of staring at the television, all his attention is on me.

"Can I look at you?" he asks again. I start to pull my T-shirt off, but his hands are right there, sliding underneath the hem and lifting the shirt over my head.

Rex is looking at me so intently that I can't quite meet his gaze, and I stare into the fire instead as he looks over my tattoos. He doesn't touch me, just looks at me in the firelight. I feel like he's reading me, reading the story on my skin. Of course, the downside to having a best friend who'll give you tattoos for free is that you end up with a few you wish you could erase.

Rex moves behind me to look at the ones on my back and I can feel his breath touch the nape of my neck. His big hands curve around my hips and he presses a kiss to my neck. I gasp at the sudden touch.

"You're so beautiful," he says, low.

"I guess I'm lucky you're not turned off by tattoos," I say.

I turn to face him. I don't know why, but suddenly I feel very exposed. I reach for his shirt and he lets me pull it off him. God, he's gorgeous.

"I feel like that skinny kid I was in high school next to you," I say, immediately cursing myself for speaking out loud. Ginger always says confidence is the most attractive quality. Guess I blew it with that one.

Rex grabs me by the wrists and pulls me into the warmth of his body. His eyes are blazing but he looks at me tenderly.

"No," he says. "You're so—" He shakes his head and leans in to kiss me slow and sweet, like his kiss can reassure. It's a good kiss. A great kiss. I wrap my arms around his waist to tug him closer and then somehow his mouth is gone and I'm just hugging him. Am I supposed to be hugging him? I don't think so, but I can't make myself stop. His heart is pounding under my ear like I've startled him. Then he wraps his arms around me and his heartbeat slows. The fire is crackling and the smell of wood smoke combined with Rex's scent is heady. He runs his hands up and down my back and then cups my ass and pulls my hips forward to meet the firm bulge in his jeans.

"Mmm," I mumble. Rex tips my head back and kisses me again, smiling now.

"I bet you were cute when you were a skinny kid," he says. "I can picture you looking pissed off at the world, glaring at people, only they thought it was cute because your eyes are so damn pretty."

"Um, my rage at the world was *not* cute," I insist, winking. He squeezes my ass and my knees go a little weak.

"Right there," he says. "Your eyelids flutter and your eyes go all sleepy." He runs a rough thumb over my mouth. "You go from mad to liquid so easy." His voice must be hypnotizing me or something because my eyes do *not* go all sleepy. Do they?

"I bet you ran your hands through your hair until it stuck straight up, just like you do now," he says, smoothing my hair back. "Right? You probably leaned back against the school with a cigarette in your mouth like James Dean and closed your eyes. I bet there was some guy you drove crazy."

"Like you?" I ask.

"Nah," he says, shaking his head. "You wouldn't have even looked at me twice in high school."

"I bet I would have," I say.

He looks at my face, runs fingertips over my eyebrows, my cheekbones, the bridge of my nose, mapping my features like a blind man.

"I was so shy I wouldn't have known even if you had," he murmurs. "Never talked to anyone." His accent comes out a little when he's not paying attention.

"No one?" I ask, my breath coming a little quicker as his hand drifts down to my chest and finds my nipples, his rough finger pads tracing them lightly.

"No one," he says. "Never talked in class. Never talked period. Stuttered if I tried. Didn't look at anyone. Not at any of the schools." His fingertip slides into my navel and down to trace the edge of my jeans where they've slipped below my hip bones.

"Schools?"

"We moved a lot." He presses kisses to my collarbones and my chest as he unbuttons my jeans and pushes them down. "Made it easier 'cause no one really notices the new kid anyway." His hands cup my ass, squeezing gently, and I shiver against him.

I run my hands up and down his sides, feel the huge expanse of his ribs as he inhales. Compared to his hands, the skin here and on his back is smooth and untouched. His stomach's another story. At first I didn't notice because of his dark hair, but the flickering firelight casts a scar into relief on the right side of his stomach.

"What's this from?" I ask, running my finger over the raised scar.

"Had my appendix out," he says, then kisses me again, dragging me tight against him. I grab at his waist to keep my balance.

"Daniel," he grinds out, his voice like crushed rock. "I want you so bad." I feel an answering pulse in my groin.

I nod, try to answer, but it just comes out as "Mmphfhm." Apparently Rex understands, because he takes my hand and leads me to the bedroom. It's spare but comfortable. There's an iPod and a Discman on the bedside table. I didn't know anyone still listened to Discmen. Rex's sheets are—I see just before I end up on my back on top of them—green flannel.

Rex drops his pants on the floor next to the bed and crawls on top of me. His legs are powerfully muscled, his thighs twice the size of mine, and his plain white briefs fail to contain his erection. He is, all in all, overwhelming. His size, his heat, the fucking delicious smell of him that's now mixed with a scent that must be his arousal. I cup his balls through the damp fabric and he growls, shimmying out of his underwear and dragging mine down too.

He flips me onto my stomach effortlessly and kisses the back of my neck and down my spine. When he gets to the small of my back, he licks his way back up. I shiver as the wet stripe catches the air. He nuzzles my neck and kisses my ear and I turn my head to try and catch his mouth.

"You don't know what you fucking do to me," he murmurs. I can feel his erection pulse against my ass with the beat of his heart.

My skin feels too tight but my hips and spine are loose with desire. He flexes his hips and his hardness slides between my cheeks. Rex moans and kisses the center of my back. I feel shivery and a little uncertain, realizing that I'm about to fuck Rex. Or, what seems more likely is that he's about to fuck me. I want to just lose myself in his body, his strength, but my heart starts to race, and a little voice in the back of my head is whispering things I don't want to hear. *It's not safe to be this vulnerable*, it whispers. *You can't trust someone like that. He'll think you're weak.*

I shake my head to clear it and grab the sheets, the green flannel an anchor.

Rex's heat recedes a little and I'm rolled gently onto my back. I open my eyes to see Rex leaning over me. His gaze is steady, hot with desire, but still calm. Like he's totally in control of what he's doing.

"You okay?" he asks. I nod and reach for him again. "What's up?" I shake my head. "Daniel, we don't have to do anything you don't want to do," Rex says, sinking down next to me. His weight makes the bed dip and I roll into him.

"No, no, I want to. I totally want to," I say, but my voice sounds a little shaky. "I just—it's been a long time since I…." I look away.

"Bottomed?"

I nod.

"Just tell me what you want." One big hand is stroking my back gently, but the look in his eyes is intense.

"I want to," I say. "I want you." I bite my lip. I can't stand the sound of my own voice. I sound needy and weird.

Rex pulls me on top of him and tangles our fingers together. Then we're kissing, our mouths and cocks straining together, but he won't let us touch each other. I pull at his hands and he draws mine to his mouth and kisses each before he lets them go. I reach for his balls, hold them warm and tight in my hand and then I kiss him slow, watching his eyes drift shut. I tug gently and he gasps into my mouth. I reach underneath him and stroke his ass. It's thick and strong and his whole body tightens when I squeeze, etching his muscles like stone.

Rex pulls me forward and kisses me deeply, our tongues sliding together, and I feel his finger at my entrance, just tapping there. But every tap zings a jolt through me and I shiver against him. Then the finger is gone and he cups my head, runs his hand through my messy hair and I moan into his kiss. He spreads me open with both hands and then his finger is back, slick with lube he must have reached for but I didn't even notice. He rubs the slickness into my hole while he kisses me, then slides slowly inside. I tense up, but he runs his hand down my neck, stroking my back.

"Okay?" he says, and I nod, thrusting my hips as I adjust to his finger. Our erections slide together, his hips meeting mine.

"Fuck, baby, you feel amazing," Rex groans and he slides a second finger inside me. I kiss his neck and throat. I can feel a spot he missed when he was shaving and I'm flooded with tenderness for him. I kiss the spot and shake my head at myself because apparently I'm turning into a total sap.

Rex looks at me curiously and I smile at him.

"Hi."

"Hi there," he chuckles.

I lean down slowly and kiss him on the cheek.

"You're fucking gorgeous," I tell him, and kiss his other cheek.

"Thanks," he says softly, looking at me like he's surprised to hear it. He strokes my cheek.

He rolls us over, his fingers still inside me, and puts a pillow under my hips. He kisses the inside of my knee, then the sensitive crease of my thigh. He kisses my hip bones, avoiding contact with my cock, which is now straining upward, desperate for his touch. I can feel how flushed my face is and my lips are swollen and tingly from our kisses.

"Rex," I say, and it comes out as a whisper.

"Yeah, sweetheart," he says. There's a strange ringing in my ears.

"I want you."

"Yeah?" he murmurs, and he strokes my prostate with his fingertips. My hips shoot off the pillow and he holds me down easily. He slides a third finger inside me and I cry out, heat fizzing in my spine.

"Please," I say roughly.

He slides his fingers in deeper as he reaches for a condom. My hole clenches around his thick fingers and I can see him shudder. I reach for him, but he bats my hand away, breathing heavily. He slides his fingers out of me, kissing me slow and sweet, and massages more slickness inside me.

All I can see is the tiny line of concentration between his eyebrows and the dark sweep of his lashes against his cheek as he kisses my opening with the tip of his cock. He tilts my hips up further and brushes a piece of hair off my forehead, taking a deep breath.

"Tell me," Rex growls. I can feel him, hot, against me.

I nod frantically, searching for words.

"I want—I need—please!" I groan, and he breaches my entrance. My eyelids flutter and my breathing gets shallow, but he doesn't go any farther.

"Tell me," he murmurs, licking behind my ear.

"Please, please, fuck me," I beg, and my voice is strained, my body trembling around him.

As he slides all the way inside me, I feel heat and fullness and a heartbeat of fear caught in my throat.

He's so close. I'm in his house and in his bed and he's inside me and there's nowhere to go and, just for a second, I panic. My body tightens and Rex groans. I'm breathing a little too fast and his weight is immovable.

But then he opens his eyes and looks at me, and he's here, right here. This isn't a fuck in a bathroom stall. It's not a blowjob in the alley outside the club, or jerking off one of my brothers' straight friends at work, knowing they'll come on my stomach and never look me in the eye again.

I squeeze my eyes shut and open them again and he's still right there, frozen, trembling above me.

"Breathe, Daniel."

I loop an arm around Rex's neck and pull his mouth to mine. I kiss him—just a touch of our lips—and rock my hips into his, sliding him the rest of the way inside me. He hisses and I groan as his thickness spears me open, fills me. And then, in the space of a heartbeat, we're one body, melted together as my channel adjusts to his size and he relaxes into me.

"Oh fuck, baby," he says, pulling back, and I can feel his thighs shaking with the effort not to hurt me.

"Go," I say, and pull his hips flush with mine again. We both cry out, and then I cease to exist except where we're joined. He's surging into me and I'm pushing back at him and everything is slickness and heat. Every time he fills me he brushes over the spot that makes my whole channel pulse with pleasure. I reach down to stroke myself, but Rex pushes my wrists to the mattress, his huge hand stroking me in time with his thrusts.

I'm whimpering and moaning as he works me, his other hand holding my wrists easily. My spine is liquid heat and my thighs are trembling. I can hear Rex groaning, but my entire concentration is focused on the exquisite pulse of pleasure that's begun deep in my ass, radiating through me like pebbles dropped in a pond. It's joined by a boiling heat at the base of my spine and my groin.

Rex is stroking me and with every stroke, I am closer to exploding. I pull my wrists from his grasp and grab him around the neck, needing to hold on to something.

"Don't stop," I gasp, and he bears down on me, his added weight pressing his erection even deeper. I cry out and his stomach brushes the tip of my cock and white-hot pleasure explodes inside me, tightening every muscle and blowing every nerve ending. The sounds coming out of me are tiny whimpers because every muscle has clenched down in orgasm. My eyes are shut so tight I see stars and I shudder as my erection keeps pulsing.

Rex is wild above me, his hands squeezing my hips as he thrusts deeply into me. I cry out, my prostate zinging a last pulse of pleasure through me, and Rex roars, his heat flooding the condom, searing me even through the barrier between us.

He collapses on top of me, careful to take his weight with his elbows, and kisses my throat, moaning.

I feel languid, like I couldn't possibly move. Rex gently eases himself from my body and leans to drop the condom into the trash. As his back is turned to me, I feel the prickling in my ears that means I'm in danger of tearing up. I don't know what's wrong with me. I reach out a shaky hand to touch his back, then hesitate. Maybe he doesn't like being touched when we're not fucking?

He rolls back over to face me and any hesitation I felt is gone as he drapes a heavy arm over my stomach and kisses the side of my neck. His breath is hot on my neck as his fingers draw absent designs in the puddle of my come. I'm a little gross and sticky. Rex must feel my stomach tense because he takes his hand away.

I ease over the side of the bed, biting my lip when my sore ass scrapes over the sheets. I pull my underwear on.

"I'm gonna just…." I gesture toward the door. "Can I use your bathroom?"

"Of course," he says. His eyes are warm, but he looks a little wary.

In the bathroom, I clean up, pee, and wash my hands. When I look in the mirror to see how ridiculous my hair looks, my eyes surprise me. I look scared and uncertain and vulnerable. I look like I let my guard down. And even though Ginger has told me often enough that that's not a bad thing, I don't believe her. You let your guard down and people fuck with you; you let your guard down and you get hurt. That's what I know. So what the hell am I supposed to do now?

Rex is facing the door when I walk back in and I can see him relax at the sight of me.

I hesitate a foot from the bed.

"Um, do you want me to take off?" I ask, trying to sound neutral and failing.

"You don't have a car," Rex says evenly.

"Oh, right."

"I can take you home if you want," Rex says, "but I wish you'd stay."

"Yeah?"

He smiles. "Yeah."

He reaches for my hand and I let him take it. He pulls me on top of him, sliding my underwear back off, and I let him. I let him settle me next to him too, where he cradles my neck in his hand and strokes my hip with the other.

"Do we need to take Marilyn out?" I ask.

"She's fine."

"Should we do something to the fire?"

"It'll die out."

"Do you want me to—?"

"I want you here, in this fucking bed," Rex says, and he pulls me closer against him, palming my ass with one big hand and turning off the bedside lamp with the other. I slide my hand under his shoulder for balance and lean my cheek on his chest. He rests his chin on my head. "Just stay," he murmurs. He traces the cleft of my ass with his finger, slipping in the lube that's still there. He slides his finger back inside me, just as he did that night in the woods. I huff out a breath.

"I just want to be inside you," he says softly. He's already falling asleep. I sigh, not letting myself think about the fact that I've never slept beside a lover before—not unless I'd passed out drunk, anyway. I try to match my breathing to Rex's, feel his rib cage rise and fall, carrying me off to sleep like a ship held safe in port.

Chapter 6

October

I WAKE up wrapped in a cocoon of delicious warmth, with a bone-deep feeling of satisfaction and comfort, so I know I can't be at home. I'm not sure what's causing it until I open my eyes and see that I'm basically lying on top of Rex, holding on to him like I'm a squid and he's the whale I'm trying to snuggle the life out of. My face is nuzzled into his neck, my arms are wrapped around him, and my leg is slung over his hip in a way that would be borderline obscene if we weren't sleeping.

It's the way I used to wake up wrapped around this stuffed lion that I slept with as a kid. Sam won it at a school carnival for some girl, but when he found the girl to give it to her, she was making out with a guy on the basketball team behind the water ice stand, so he called her a slut and threw the lion on the couch when he got home. That was right before my mom died and I slept with it for years.

One of Rex's arms is holding me and the other's stretched under his pillow, his biceps round and strong even in slumber. I allow myself a few moments to look at him—the pulse beating in the vulnerable hollow of his throat, the scar under his right eyebrow that's only visible when his eyes are closed, the perfect teardrop indentation above his upper lip—before I convince myself that I need to extricate myself from the death grip I have on him before he wakes up and thinks I'm some kind of desperate limpet.

I start to inch off of him slowly, but he makes a small sound and pulls me closer. He's not even really awake. I kiss the underside of his chin—the only place my mouth can reach now—and he makes a soft mew of what might be satisfaction or just sleep, and puts his other arm around me.

I feel the first tinglings of panic—the kind of claustrophobia that comes when you know you need to sit very still—and I pull away a little.

"Daniel?" Rex murmurs softly. "Y'okay?"

"Yeah," I say, pushing myself off him and rolling away. "I'll be right back." I retreat to the bathroom and splash some water on my face. I wonder if I should get out of Rex's hair before he wakes up, but that doesn't feel quite right. Besides, I hated it when I woke up alone the morning after we met. And it's cold in the bathroom. I walk back to Rex's room and look at the man spread out before me on the bed. He looks so young when he's asleep, his face slack, his body relaxed, all that powerful muscle rendered merely decorative.

I slide back into bed beside Rex's warmth, thinking I'll just sleep for a few more minutes. The next thing I know, I wake up to Rex's warm hand on my waist, his thumb stroking my hip bone.

"This is new," he says, "right?" He's looking at "Let Sleeping Bears Lie" inked above my hip and I groan in embarrassment.

"Yeah."

"It wasn't there when I clipped your pants," he says.

I can't believe he remembers a glimpse of my hip from eight months ago; I can't believe he even noticed it the first place.

He presses warm lips to the words and licks my hip bone, then drags his teeth lightly over it. My breath catches. There's something about Rex's laser focus that makes me incredibly hot. It's like the air between us is thinner than usual and I'm more aware of him.

He runs his hand over my stomach and ribs, just stroking, then slides up and kisses my neck and my jaw. My skin feels hot and tingly everywhere he touches. When he kisses the inside of my biceps, I shudder. It's so weird. I barely know Rex, but he may be the only person who's ever touched me in that spot. Definitely the only person who's ever kissed me there.

"You're so sensitive," Rex growls.

"No," I say. "I mean, I never was." But my breathing's gone all funny and my heart is pounding. I pull Rex down and kiss him as hard as I can. He kisses me back, but when I clutch at his back and try to pull him on top of me, he eases back to those gentle touches again. He strokes along the veins on the inside of my forearm and sucks gently at the skin under my ear; he traces my ribs and places soft kisses along my collarbone.

I feel strange. Shaky and out of control. No one's ever touched me like this. Paid this much attention. Am I supposed to reciprocate? I've never touched anyone the way he's touching me, either. Never traced patterns on someone's skin or run my fingertips over the swell of muscle and the dip of bone. Never felt where hair changed from soft to rough or skin from thin to callused.

It's like Rex is mapping my body, each stroke of his hand and touch of his lips learning me better.

There are unfamiliar sounds clawing their way out of my throat. Vulnerable sounds. What if he gets up and leaves? What if he doesn't? And now, I realize, in the moments it's taken me to ponder this, Rex has stopped touching me and started staring at me.

"Do you want me to stop?" Rex asks abruptly.

I stare up at him and it's as if I'm watching this play out like reading a scene in a book. I just keep wondering what's going to happen next. And by the time my brain can process that I have to *make* something happen next, Rex has swung his legs over the side of the bed and is giving me a sweet but hesitant smile.

"No worries," he says. "I didn't mean to be so touchy-feely. I'm just gonna shower."

I hear the water turn on and pull the pillow over my head. What the fuck is wrong with me? Unlike my inability to answer Rex, I can think of about a hundred answers to that question. Like, I barely know this guy, so why am I so goddamned worried about what he thinks of me? Like, I should've left last night after we fucked and I don't get why I didn't. Like, I've never had a real relationship, so why would I start now? Especially when I finally have a job that's going to make it possible to pay off all my debt and not live paycheck to paycheck, checking my bank balance every time I have to buy groceries. Especially when, in order to keep that job, I need to spend all my time proving to the people who hired me that they didn't bet on a losing horse.

And the biggest thing wrong with me: why, even now, does my whole body feel pulled toward Rex when I was just touching him a minute ago?

Before I can let myself think about it, I walk to the bathroom and knock on the door.

"Yeah," Rex says over the shower.

I open the door slowly and there he is, the sharp lines of shoulder and leg softened by steam and glass.

"Can I?" I ask, gesturing to the shower.

"Course," he says. "You don't have to ask." But of *course* I have to ask. You don't just get in the shower with someone.

The water's a little hotter than I like and I can feel my skin turning pink almost immediately. Rex puts a hand on my hip and draws me toward him. I go to kiss him, but he stops me with a hand on my palm. He pulls us tight together, his body hot and slick from the water. He wraps his arms around my shoulders and runs a hand up and down my spine, making me squirm closer to him.

"Look," he says. "It's been a while since I've done all this. I know I can be a little…. I just like touching you, but I didn't mean to overstep. Okay?"

He's looking right into my eyes and he's so big and solid that I find myself telling him the truth.

"I've never done this before."

He pulls back like I scalded him.

"Wait, you mean last night was your first—"

"No! No, no. I mean *this*. The kiss and shower together and sleep over thing. I've never done that."

He looks puzzled.

"You've never dated someone before?"

I sigh, relieved he's supplied the word.

"Well. No. Well—I went out on a date once, but it didn't go so well. So, I don't know how it goes, really, or if I'm any good at it." I look down and watch the water swirling down Rex's drain. It's easier to talk in here, like the sound of the water takes the edge of fear off my voice.

Rex regards me, frowning slightly.

"Well, here's how it goes," he says. "I'm going to take you to breakfast. Then we're going to jump your car. Then I'm going to ask you out on a date. Are you free Thursday night?"

"I thought asking me out on a date was going to come after jumping my car?"

"Just getting my ducks in a row," he says, and squeezes my shoulder. "What do you say, dinner on Thursday night?"

I nod and take a deep breath. I can do this, right? It's just dinner.

"I CAN'T do this," I tell Ginger.

It's late and I should be in bed, but I've missed a dozen calls from her since Sunday, no doubt wanting to know how my night with Rex went, so I picked up when she called.

"Dandelion!" she says. "Tell me everything. Don't leave anything out. Can't do what?"

"I'm supposed to meet Rex for dinner tomorrow," I tell her. "And it's definitely a date."

"No, no, no," she says, irritated. "You don't get to skip right to the telling me your problems part. You have to start with something like, 'Oh, Ginger, let me tell you all about my date instead of ignoring your calls for four days,' or, 'Ginger, let me tell you how good the lumberjack is in bed.' Got it?"

"Mmhmm."

"Excellent. So, how was your date on Saturday night?"

"It was good."

"Seriously? That's what I get from you?"

"Do you think I'm a pessimist?" I ask her, staring at the pile of papers I'm only halfway through grading.

"Yes," she says. "Well, I think you're a pessimist where you're concerned. You tend to be pretty realistic about other people's shit. Why? Did he tell you you're a pessimist? Because you know how I feel about dudes who tell you who you are on a first date. Control freak abusers."

"No, he didn't say anything about it. I just—I keep doing this thing where I think a nice thought about Rex and then my brain thinks, like, 'It's never going to work.'"

"Well, sweetie, that voice in your head is the same one that said you could never go to college. It's the same one that told you not to bother applying to grad school because they'd never want you. It's the same one that told you all the other students thought you were stupid when you first started."

"They did think I was stupid when I started."

"Well, they were asshole snobs. And, anyway, you proved to them it wasn't true. So you just have to prove it to this voice too."

"I don't know how to do this. What do I talk about? What if we actually hate each other?"

"Um, Daniel. You don't hate each other. You had a date the other night and, even though you apparently *refuse* to tell me about it, it went well enough that you're having another one tomorrow. And I *know* you didn't ask him, so he must have liked you enough that he at least wants to see you again."

"I could have been the one to ask him," I grumble.

"Um, sure, pumpkin; whatever you say." She pauses, then her voice changes. "Come oooooon, *please* tell me about the date?"

"He rescued me from a snowstorm and cooked me dinner and I spent the night, and then he took me out to breakfast. And he said he used to be really shy, but I totally didn't get that from him until breakfast when we went to the diner and he was really tongue-tied ordering. It was kinda sweet."

"It's October."

"Uh. Yeah."

"How was there a snowstorm in October?"

"Right! Michigan, man. Fucking Michigan."

"Oh. Right. So, wow, you spent the night? Were you drunk?"

"No. Bitch."

"Hunh," she says, like that explained something. "Okay, so how was it? The sex, I mean, obviously."

"Dude, it was really good. He's... I dunno, magnetic or something."

She's quiet for a while and my mind drifts to Rex's big hands on me. The way he pulled me close to him in the shower after I told him I'd have dinner with him, his strong hips flexing into mine, our erections sliding together in the steamy heat. The way he grabbed my ass, grinding us together, his chest hair scraping my nipples. The way he bit down on my throat like I was a kitten trying to wander away, and pulled me up into him, hard. The way he kissed me, tongue everywhere, hands everywhere, our cocks straining together until we both grabbed them at the same time, jerking white heat on our stomachs and chests and leaning against each other as the water washed it all away.

"Earth to Daniel," Ginger is nearly shouting into the phone.

"What!"

"Oh my god, you're thinking about having sex with him *right* now."

"Guilty," I laugh.

"Fuck, that's so hot," she says.

"What?"

"Sweet cheeks, you've fucked the lead singers of bands on international tours and never said anything more than, 'He looked taller onstage,' or, 'Yeah, nice guy.' If you're sitting there right now fantasizing about sex you had with the lumberjack to the point where you don't hear me *yelling* your name, then I *know* it was hot. God, I'm so jealous. I want a lumberjack."

"He's not a lumberjack. And you should be."

"Uuunnghhh," she groans.

"Hey, any highlights from the shop lately?"

"Oh my god, *yes*. You remember that really tall, skinny guy who had me do the vertebrae tattoo down his spine?"

"Yeah, the one you kept calling Skeletor, thinking you were funny until Megan told you Skeletor is actually big and blue and muscular?"

"Yeah," she mumbles. "*Anyway*, he came back in and he wants me to do his whole skeleton. Like, every bone, little by little."

"That's awesome," I tell her. Ginger likes large-scale projects and she loves doing realistic black and gray. "Did you start?"

"Yeah, I did his left arm. It's gonna be sick. Not sure when he'll have the cash for more, but I'm totally into it."

"Sweet. Hey, my brother hasn't come back in, has he?"

"No," she scoffs. "Definitely scared him away. Asshole. Have you talked to them recently?"

"It may shock you to know that none of them have sent so much as a text message since I left."

"Sorry, babycakes."

"No surprise," I say. And it's not, really. It's not like I've been thinking about my dad and my brothers much or anything. I mean, most of my contact with them in the last few years has been cursory and everything before that was them messing with me, since they found out I was gay. No. Before they found out. Still, I hadn't even realized I was hoping maybe now that we had some space between us, they'd.... What— miss me? Nah. But... wonder if I was okay? Maybe.

"Listen," Ginger says, "it's their fucking loss, you hear me? You just don't worry about them. You just do your teaching and write your book and forget about them. Go on your date. Talk about whatever you want. Oh, and ask lots of questions. And don't swear."

"What?"

"Just, you know, don't swear too much. It's not polite on a date."

"What are you, a fucking matchmaker?"

"Just, don't say 'fuck' every five seconds, okay, asshole? It's crude. And it shows you don't have respect for your date."

"Girl, you're crazy." But I like when she tells me shit like that. It feels like the kind of scolding that someone who cares about you gives.

"Where are you going for dinner?"

"Some Italian place near campus. I mean, this town only has, like, four restaurants."

"Don't wear a white shirt, in case you get sauce on it."

"Dude, I don't even own a white shirt." Not since the one I bought for my interview got covered in Marilyn's blood, anyway.

"Oh, right. Well, you know what I mean. When I went to La Dolce with that Andrew guy last year, I wore my white jacket—you know, the cloth biker-style one?—and I sprayed tomato sauce all over it. Looked like I'd been in a shoot-out. Not a good look. Just saying."

"God, I forgot about Andrew. He was such a tool."

"True that. Anyway: learn from my mistakes, young Jedi."

"No white. Check."

"Hey, D?"

"Hmm."

"I can tell you like the lumberjack. Just... be yourself, huh? Like, your actual self. The way you are with me. Not the way you are with your brothers. Or with Richard."

"And how am I with them?" It comes out snippier than I meant it.

"You're just really... guarded. Quick to throw down. You know."

"Whatever," I mutter.

"I'm serious. It may not work out with him, sure. And that's fine. Just... give him a chance."

"Message received," I tell her with a sigh.

"I adore you," she says in the voice I can never resist.

"Yeah, yeah, yeah. Go draw on someone."

"Bye, babycakes."

MY CONVERSATION with Ginger has been on my mind all day, so when I run home to change before meeting Rex, I call the auto shop. It's about 5:00 p.m., so they'll probably all be there. I'll just say a quick hello, check in; no big deal.

"Pat's," a gruff voice says on the eighth ring.

"Luther?" I say. "It's Daniel."

"Oh, hey, kid. How's tricks?"

"Pretty good," I say. "Weird to be out of the city and all. How's Maria and the kids?"

"Oh, good, good, you know."

"Great. Hey, listen, are any of them around?"

"Yep, here's Sam. Bye, kid."

"Daniel?" Sam sounds a little surprised to hear from me, but not unfriendly. We don't really have anything in common, but he always gave me the least shit. Most likely just because he's the oldest and didn't want to waste his time.

"How's it going, bro?" I ask.

"Not bad," he says, and starts talking about some new car he's working on. It's like I never left. My brothers all do this. They know I don't care about cars but they don't have anything else to say. So I let him talk while I pull on jeans and change my shirt.

"Liza good? She still working at the florist?"

"Yup. She's fine. Bugging me about kids."

"Do you want kids?"

"Eh, you know. We'll see. Anyway, kid, gotta run. Here's Pop."

"Daniel?" My dad says it in the same voice as Sam, like he's surprised to hear from me, even though it's been over a month since I left. "How's the car running?" I roll my eyes, forcing myself to remember what Ginger said: that this is my dad's way of making sure I'm okay.

"Battery died when we had a snowstorm," I say.

"In October?"

"Pretty far north here, Pop," I say patiently.

"Hmm. Well, it could be—"

I cut him off, forestalling what would otherwise be a twenty-minute disquisition on what the other problems with the car might be.

"It's okay, Dad. It was just the battery. I jumped it and it's fine now."

"All right, then."

"How's business?" This is the only thing I ever ask my dad about because it's the only question he'll ever really answer.

"Busy right now," he says. "Folks trying to get everything shipshape before winter. And god bless the Streets Department for never paving a damned pothole until it's screwed the alignment on half the cars in the city. It'll slow down, though. Always does."

He pauses and I can hear the familiar soundscape of the garage: the grind of hydraulics, the hiss of the power washer, the clank of metal dropped on concrete. As if in sympathy, the ghost smells of oil, lube, and hot metal tickle my sinuses.

"So," my dad continues, "you need something?"

"What? No. Just wanted to check in. See how you guys are."

"Oh," my dad says. "Well, that's fine. Uh, here's your brother, then. Bye, son."

"Brian?" I ask.

"No, it's me. What's going on?"

"Hey, Colin," I say. "How's it going?"

"Uh, fine. What did you need?"

"Damn, Colin, I don't need anything. I just wanted to say hey. Christ." And just like that, my temper's fried. Something about Colin triggers it every time. Sam treats me like a dumb kid sometimes and Brian's almost always an idiot, teasing me about everything from my sexuality to the way I talk. But Colin's nasty. He's not teasing when he gives me shit. I don't remember him being like that when we were kids, but I guess I don't remember a whole lot from then, anyway. I just know that he looks at me like I disgust him and he speaks to me as little as possible.

"Well, hey, then. I'm gonna get back to work."

And shit, that pisses me off.

"Oh, yeah, got to go get some hearts and flowers tattooed to match your manly butterfly?" I say, unable to stop myself. Ooh, Ginger is going to kill me.

"Fuck you, you little bitch," he says, his voice ice cold, and the line goes dead.

Damn.

I splash some water on my face and force myself not to think about what Colin said. I should've known better than to tease him and expect anything else. Colin teases; Colin does not get teased.

I finish getting ready and grab my jacket. After the snowstorm, which was apparently a fluke, the weather settled back into something more familiar for October. Good thing, too, since I'm at least a paycheck away from buying a coat.

As I'm walking to the restaurant, my phone buzzes with a text. It's Colin. As the only other time I can remember him texting me was last Thanksgiving to tell me to get more beer, I know it's not going to be good.

Keep yr fucking mouth shut. I shake my head. I'm just about to text Ginger to apologize in advance in case Colin gives her shit for telling me when another text from him comes through. *I'm fucking serious, you little shit.* Apparently Colin didn't get Ginger's memo about cursing. I don't text back. Figure I'll let him sweat a little. Asshole.

Rex already has a table when I get to the restaurant. He starts to stand up from the circular booth and I put my hand out to shake at the same time, resulting in an awkward collision where Rex grabs my shoulder to keep me from knocking into the table, and I kind of slither into the booth.

"Hey," I say.

He smiles at me. That slow, warm smile that wrinkles his eyes and shows that twisted tooth.

"Hey."

"Daniel?" Standing next to our booth is an unfamiliar man of about forty or forty-five. He's on the short side, with pumped-up arms to compensate, a blond crew cut, and nearly invisible blond eyebrows over light blue eyes.

"Uh, yeah."

He sticks out a beefy hand and I can see the grease ground deep into his nail beds.

"Hey, tiger, it *was* the spark plugs!" His voice is deafening, and his clap on the back almost slams me into the edge of the table.

"Um, Mark?" I guess.

"Can't lie, bud, woulda never thought a gay teacher'd know about cars." He chuckles, the kind of well-meaning, jovial chuckle that lets me know there's no threat behind his words. "Oh, uh, hey, Rex," he says, his grin fading. Rex looks stormy, his brows furrowed and his chin out. "Didn't mean nothing. I'll leave you gents to it, then."

"What the...." I say, shaking my head.

"Spark plugs?" Rex asks, relaxing again.

"Oh, um, outside Sludge the other day, I helped Marjorie with her car. Her son tried to start it and it backfired. The car, I mean."

The waiter comes over and I'm pretty sure I've seen her around campus. Small goddamned town. Rex asks me to choose the wine and I try really hard not to have flashbacks to Richard telling me I ordered the wrong one. Apparently, I'm still distracted by that and the whole Colin thing because when Rex orders the special pasta I realize I didn't hear her tell us the specials at all, and I just order the first thing my eye lands on—chicken marsala, which I don't much care for.

Rex has just asked me how my day was when my goddamned phone buzzes again.

"Shit," I say, "sorry." I go to turn it to silent, but catch the text from Colin before I do. *Not a fucking word, Daniel.* Jesus Christ, Colin!

"What's wrong?" Rex asks.

I shake my head. "Just my fucking brother," I say. Then I remember Ginger's admonition, realizing I've said, like, four words and half of them have been swear words. I guess I really do swear a lot.

I tell Rex about what happened with Colin and what Ginger told me. Then I find myself telling him about talking to him today.

"Colin's just mean, man. He's an asshole. 'What do you need?' Like I'm inconveniencing him by calling to say hi for the first time since I left. Not like he does anything other than fucking work anyway—oh shit, I'm not supposed to be swearing on a date."

Rex looks amused. "Says who?"

"Ginger," I mutter. Can't believe I said that out loud.

Rex's eyes go dark and he puts his hand on my thigh.

"So," he says in that growl that raises the hairs on my arms, "you told Ginger you were going on a date with me, huh?"

"Um. Yeah."

"Do you tell Ginger everything?"

"Um. No," I say, completely lost in his eyes. He focuses on me like nothing I've ever experienced, like he's reading every blink and breath.

He leans back, as if satisfied, and I fiddle with my phone. Colin might actually hate me. It's a thought I've had before, but I always figured it was regular brotherly friction. The fact that it can still happen when we're three states apart means he may actually, *actually* hate me.

"Fuck him," I mutter, and I swear—not for the first time—that I won't care what he thinks about me ever again. I won't care the next time he calls me Danielle. I won't care the next time he looks at me like I'm trash or laughs when I hurt myself. I won't care the next time I see him around town and he pretends he doesn't notice me. I just won't care.

"Here you go, gentlemen," the waiter says. "Artichoke ravioli and the chicken marsala." She puts our plates down and pours the wine.

"That was the pasta special?" I say. "I didn't even hear her say them or I totally would have gotten that too."

"Do you want some?" Rex offers.

"Sure, want a bite of mine?" He nods.

"That's really good," Rex says.

I duck my head. "I actually don't like marsala that much. I don't know why I ordered it," I say.

"I don't like artichokes," Rex says, and I burst out laughing. I guess we were both a little distracted.

"Wanna switch?" I say, and Rex has the plate out of my hand before he even nods. Damn, he can eat.

He's wearing a plain black button-down and the dark color sets off the red in his brown hair. His table manners are perfect.

"Colin's the one who first found out I was gay," I find myself saying while Rex is distracted by the food.

"Did you tell him?"

"Oh fuck no," I say. "I mean, uh, no. He walked in on me, um, sucking off this guy behind the auto shop." It was one of the worst moments of my life. I was sixteen. Actually, it wasn't long before I met Ginger. Buddy—the guy—picked up the occasional shift at the shop and was a friend of Colin's from high school. I'd caught him looking at me a few times when I'd come through with a message for my dad or to borrow a car. I'm not even sure if he was gay, but apparently he could tell I was. He was kind of handsome, I suppose, in a blond football-player-gone-to-seed way, but I didn't care about that. I just wanted to know if the pull I felt toward guys was real or if there was just something wrong with me and that's why I didn't care about girls at all.

There was someone at the auto shop that I'd had a stupid crush on for what felt like forever. His name was Truman and he was about as straight as they come. He was far too old for me, married, and would probably have detached my head from my shoulders if he so much as suspected any heat in the way I looked at him in his coveralls. He was a big, muscular black guy in his late-thirties who always wore a red bandana over his hair and had the cleanest fingernails I'd ever seen on a mechanic. He wore a signet ring on his right hand and a wedding ring on his left and he had a deep chuckle when he was amused and an incongruously high laugh when he was delighted—which I only ever heard in reaction to a victory by the Cleveland Browns (his hometown team) and his twin daughters.

Anyway, I'd taken Buddy out behind the shop expressly *because* I was concerned that Truman would be getting to work soon. He was the only one who came from the south and used the alley behind the shop. I never found out why Colin came through there that day.

Suddenly, Colin was there and he was screaming at Buddy, "Get the fuck off of my little brother, you fucking pervert." I was afraid Colin was going to kill him. Smash his head into the cement wall. At the same moment, though, I registered that Colin coming to my defense, calling me his little brother, was the most intimate thing he'd done in years. I stood up and grabbed at Colin, yelling that it wasn't Buddy's fault. Buddy ran off down the alley and never came back to the shop. I'm not sure what ever happened to him. The second he was gone, Colin rounded on me. He looked like he was going to puke.

"You.... You...." Colin couldn't even find words bad enough for what he wanted to say to me. I was terrified of him, but with Colin, you never let him know you were scared or he'd eat you alive.

"Um, so, I'm gay," I said. I was going for levity, but my voice was scratchy and thin.

"Don't you ever fucking say that!" Colin said, his voice low and intense, his nostrils flared. He came toward me like a bull, head lowered.

"It's not a big deal—" I started to say, but that was all I got out before Colin hit me in the stomach. Then the mouth. I slid down the pocked concrete wall and retched on the ground, the vomit stinging my bloodied mouth. Colin turned and stalked back through the alley the way he'd come. So much for brotherly intimacy.

"He hit the guy so hard he knocked two of his teeth out," I say to Rex. "And got in a couple hits on me. I told my dad and my other brothers I was gay later that night so they didn't hear it from Colin. My dad's not religious, but I think he was praying the ground would open up and swallow him so he didn't have to say anything."

Rex makes a strangled sound in the back of his throat and I look over to see that he's squeezed his wine glass so hard the stem broke in his hand.

"Shit!" I say. "Are you okay?"

"I'm sorry," Rex says, shaking his head. "I apologize," he says to the waiter when she comes over to clean up the spilled wine and take away his broken glass.

He turns to me. "Listen," he says. "Can we get out of here?"

"I—sure," I say. "Did you want—" But he's already standing up and throwing money onto the table. I fumble for my wallet as I stand, but he's put down more than enough, and I jog after him.

His back is to me when I get out of the restaurant, shrugging my jacket on. His hand is on the back of his neck.

"Hey," I say. "Did you cut yourself?" He shakes his head. I step in front of him, trying to look at his face, but his chin is on his chest. I reach out and squeeze his arm. "Are you okay?" I ask again. He nods, but still doesn't look up.

"C'mere," I tell him, and I tug on his shirt and start walking toward my apartment.

When I unlock the door, I sit him down at the kitchen table, since the only other place to sit is on my unmade bed. Got to add new sheets to my ever-expanding list of things I need to live in Michigan and interact with other human beings.

I look at his hand and see that he really didn't cut himself. I've never seen someone break a glass like that, except in cartoons.

I pull up a chair in front of his and sit, leaning close to him.

"Rex, what's going on?" I say.

He finally looks at me and his eyes look more uncertain than I've ever seen them. His jaw is clenched. Whatever he sees in my face makes his expression soften. He puts his hands on my knees.

"Sorry," he says, shaking his head. "You didn't even get to finish your food."

"I don't care about that," I tell him.

"No, really," he says, "I apologize." He falls into this stilted, overly formal way of speaking sometimes. When he's nervous? Or uncomfortable. I'm not sure. "I hate that your brother did that. I can't stand violence."

I almost laugh. The idea that Rex, who's six foot four, built like a bodybuilder, held me up against a tree as he fingerfucked me, and could probably take apart any guy I've ever seen hates violence seems, well, laughable. But then I remember how he fixed Marilyn's leg the night we met. How he looked at my bruises and binder-clipped my pants. How he warned me about the weather and got upset with me because sometimes people die in the snow. How he made sure I was wearing my seat belt and cooked for me and stretched me so carefully in bed when I said it had been a while. How he held me in sleep, his arms heavy, but never crushed me. How he washed my hair in the shower and put a hand over my brow so shampoo didn't get in my eyes. How, at the diner the next morning, he winced when I burned the roof of my mouth on my coffee and silently pushed my water toward me even though I barely noticed because I do it all the time.

Rex stands abruptly and opens my refrigerator. He shakes his head and I know he's seeing my collection of takeout condiments and a stain from last week's leftovers that leaked.

"You don't have any food," he says resignedly, and waves me off before I can make any excuses. He opens the freezer and takes out... something. He rummages through my cabinets and pulls out a can of beans and box of instant rice and starts fiddling with my stove.

"You have to light it," I say. He picks up the fireplace matches that I've jammed into the oven door handle and gives me the same look Ginger gives me when she thinks I've said something particularly childish.

"Daniel," he says, bending down to look at the stove. "You really need to talk to Carl—this stove doesn't have a sensor on the pilot light."

I walk over, but it just looks like any other old stove to me.

"Uh. Is that bad?"

"It's not safe. If the pilot light goes out and the gas is still on... it's not safe."

"Okay," I say, trying not to snap at him for patronizing me, since it's obvious he's freaked out about something else.

He puts a hand on my shoulder.

"I'm serious. Are you going to call Carl?"

"Um, I don't really think he'll get me a new stove, Rex. Besides, I hardly ever use it."

His hand tightens on my shoulder like he wants to fight me on it, but he just turns back to the counter.

I don't know where he found it, but he's chopping a small onion and stirring it into the beans before I even see him find a knife that must have been here when I moved in. As happened before, after he's been cooking for a bit, his shoulders relax and he starts to talk.

"I don't want to get all heavy on you," Rex says.

"Hey, come on. I started it by talking about my brother. Just tell me why it flipped you out so much. Here, I'll put on some music," I say when he doesn't answer right away. I flip through my CD books for a few minutes trying to find the right thing. But what's good background music for an unexpected confessional from the guy you just started dating and whom you barely know? I figure you can't get more confessional than Tori Amos, and put on *Little Earthquakes*.

"You like Tori Amos?" Rex says, his back to me.

"Tori Amos is fucking amazing," I say, ready to go to the mat for Tori.

"I know," he says, "I guess I just thought you liked... I don't know, harder rock stuff?" He says this like he wouldn't know this "harder rock stuff" if he tripped over it. "Just, you're all edgy and stuff."

I'm about to prickle at this assessment when he sets a plate in front of me that looks like I'm in a Mexican restaurant. There's fluffy yellow rice and beans with onion that smell like spices I know I've never bought, and a miniburrito, which must have been what he found in my freezer.

"What the hell?" I laugh. "Wow, thanks. Have some," I say, but he waves it away.

He wanders around my apartment like he's hoping to distract himself, but he's shit out of luck because there isn't much to look at except one bookshelf and a bunch of CDs.

"I didn't have any friends," Rex says, looking out my window toward the woods. "In school. We moved so often I never had time to make any. And anyway, I was so shy I couldn't talk to anyone, even if I'd wanted to."

He wanders over to my bed, and then to the stereo. He flips through the CD book I left out and then turns the stereo off, Tori cutting out mid-"Winter."

"But people didn't really mess with me either. I was just invisible."

I can't imagine it. Rex invisible. Even now, it's like the whole room has arranged itself in relation to him.

"When I was fifteen, we moved back to Texas because one of my mom's boyfriends had some business there. Shitty little town called Anderson. The school was smaller, though, and after about a year, I made this friend. Well, he made me, really. Kept talking to me all the time at school even though I didn't say anything back. Real chatterbox." Rex smiles. "Funny-looking kid. This wiry red hair and a big old grin. Kinda scrawny. Anyway, he'd show up at my house and just take me with him wherever he went. He'd talk and I'd listen. And then one day he kissed me. I was so surprised I about fell over. He socked me on the shoulder and said, 'Just wondering,' and smiled at me. When I picked my jaw up off the floor, I kissed him back."

Rex wanders over to my bookshelf and he scans the titles. He goes right for *The Secret History*, running a finger over the mud-spattered spine. When he speaks again his voice is strained.

"We'd have sex in the woods, near this little park. No one really went there. One day these three guys found us. I didn't hear them. They started... you know, whaling on us. And Jamie. He was a little guy."

Rex walks back to the window and looks out, hands in his pockets. From the way he's talking, it's clear that Jamie wasn't just some fuck in the woods. I want to ask about what he was to Rex, but I don't want to interrupt. I can barely hear him when he starts talking again, his deep voice gone low and tight.

"One of the guys picked up a stick. Started hitting us with it. I kept trying to get up. To stop them from hurting Jamie. But I wasn't strong enough." When he says this, his muscles flex, arms tightening and shoulders bunching. "They ran away when some trucker wandered over to take a piss in the woods. He's the one who radioed for an ambulance, they told me later."

My stomach is in a knot. I stopped eating about two bites into Rex's story, but I wish I hadn't eaten those. I walk over to him, but his posture radiates "Stay away." I sit down on my bed facing him.

"What happened?" I choke out.

"I was out for days," he says, squinting at something out the window. "Busted eye socket and chin. Broken ribs. Took my appendix out." He rests his forehead against the window. "Jamie never woke up. Head trauma."

My swallow sounds loud in the quiet of the room.

"Fuck," I breathe. I don't know what else to say.

Rex taps the windowsill with the heel of his hand, and I can see him getting it together. "So, you can see why I don't take real kindly to your brother."

He sits down on the edge of the bed next to me and bumps my thigh lightly with his closed fist. "Listen," he says, "I think maybe that's not the kind of thing you talk about on a date. But I'm not real good with polite get-to-know-yous. So."

I like this about Rex. He goes for things and explains them if he thinks they need to be explained, but he doesn't seem to second-guess himself and he doesn't seem to regret anything he says.

I turn my nose into his shoulder and breathe him in.

"I'm so sorry," I say. "I know that's not—"

"Thanks," he says quickly, and I can tell he's done talking about this.

I scoot backward and lie down on my bed, holding my arm out to him.

He hesitates, but then sinks down beside me, turning into my body and throwing his arm over my stomach. I hold him as close as I can.

"After that," he says softly, leaning into my touch, "I knew I had to make it so I'd never be in that position again."

His voice is muffled in my neck and I feel the words before I hear them.

"I had to be strong enough. For whatever happened."

"Rex," I say, "it wasn't your fault." It sounds like a useless cliché before it's even out of my mouth.

He slides his hand under my shirt to stroke my back.

"Hey, Daniel?"

"Hmm?"

"Could I, maybe, stay here tonight?" He tenses, waiting for my answer. I'm embarrassed because my sheets are dirty, my bed's a saggy piece of shit, and I don't even have coffee to offer him in the morning. But his weight feels right.

"Yeah, please stay," I say.

I mentally run through all my clothes to see if I can offer him anything to sleep in and come up with nothing that would possibly fit him. I wonder if it's ungrateful to leave the food he made me congealing on the table. I should definitely brush my teeth.

Rex just strips and climbs under my covers. I jump up to make sure the door's locked and turn off the lights, and I duck into the bathroom to brush my teeth. I set my phone alarm and toss it onto the windowsill. Then I drop my clothes on the floor at the foot of the bed and crawl in next to Rex, shivering. His skin is giving off enough heat that I can feel it without even touching him. I press a small kiss to his shoulder and lie on my back beside him, barely touching. I'm not sure if he wants me to hold him or to be left alone. After a while, he grabs my hand and squeezes it, like we're a part of a string of paper dolls joined at the wrist.

We stay that way for a minute, and then he reaches over to my other hand and pulls me toward him. It's kind of awkward the way he hauls me onto him and I'm not sure what he wants. Then I realize that he's positioned me the way I woke up on Sunday morning, half on top of him with my leg thrown over his hip and my cheek on his chest. He's asleep before I can decide if I like it or not.

Chapter 7

October

IT'S BEEN a week and a half since my date with Rex and I've only seen him once, when we met for a quick coffee at the library on Saturday. I don't know why I thought I'd be *less* busy than I was in grad school once I got a job, but I was obviously wrong.

Peggy Lasher is officially my arch-nemesis. When I got to my office on Friday, I found an e-mail from her (with Bernard Ness, the chair of the department, cc'd) thanking me in advance for being willing to cover her classes in the coming week because her husband's mother had died and she would be leaving for New York immediately. I'm not proud of the fact that my first thought wasn't to feel sorry for her loss, or even pissed that she'd assumed I'd help her out; it was a gut-deep jealousy that she would be within two hours of Philly—unless by New York she actually meant Buffalo or something.

Of course, being pissed followed swiftly. When I mentioned it to Jay Santiago, who has become my go-to for reality checks about the department, he said that since it was such a small school the newest hire was often asked to cover classes. This was apparently school-specific, because as far as I know nothing of the sort was the culture at Penn.

Peggy's a Romanticist—not a specialty of mine—so I had to do some major cramming to feel comfortable teaching her classes. One was an intro to eighteenth- and nineteenth-century lit, which was okay because it was mostly stuff I'd read in grad school. But her second class was a 300-level class on Romantic poetry for English majors, which took every spare moment of my time to prepare for.

In a school the size of Sleeping Bear, reputation is everything. The students all talk to each other and if you have a reputation for being a bad or boring teacher, your classes won't fill, which is the first sign that a department won't keep you around. So, it was very much in my best interest to make Peggy's students think I was awesome so they'd take a chance on my classes next semester.

Friday morning, after Rex spent the night, we'd made plans to spend the weekend together at his house, so when I found the e-mail from Peggy I was doubly pissed because I knew it meant the end to our relaxing weekend. I explained about subbing for Peggy and he said he understood, but I've been a little worried that Rex feels like I abandoned him after the story he told me Thursday night. I can't stop thinking about it. Now that I know his mom and his first lover both died, his protectiveness makes a lot of sense. I still can't exactly picture Rex as the shy kid he described, but the idea of him going through something like that makes me feel sick.

And, somehow, more even than the beating and Jamie dying, it's Rex's decision to change his body that hits me the hardest. His need to believe that if he were only physically strong enough then he would be able to protect everyone he cared about. He didn't mention it, but he must feel like his size protects him too.

WHEN I get to Rex's, he's sitting at a small table in the living room grumbling while sketching something that looks like the plans for a dresser, Marilyn lying at his feet. There's a fire crackling, and the whole house smells like cedar and pine and maple, like maybe Rex ate pancakes for breakfast. He's wearing dark gray sweatpants and a white T-shirt worn thin, its sleeves pulling tight over his biceps every time he tenses his arm to erase.

"Hi," I say, and I dump my stuff next to the table, slinging my jacket over the chair opposite his. Because of all the time I spent covering Peggy's classes this week, I'm behind on my own grading. Rex told me to come on over and do it at his house and we could have dinner whenever I was done.

"Hey," he says, and reaches an arm out to me. He slides his chair back enough to pull me onto his lap, something I thought only happened to children and, like, cheerleaders or girls who were about to get proposed to. But he's warm, even in a T-shirt, and he smells so good.

"What are you grumbling about?"

"Hmm. Just work."

"What's up?"

"Oh, I want to do more woodworking and less odd jobs. Don't get me wrong," he says quickly, "I'm really glad the work's there. I just— well, I've been trying to figure out if I could, I dunno. People around here know that I make furniture, but it's not a big town. Obviously," he adds at my snort. "So, I was just thinking about how to make it more of a business. Transition more into custom jobs like that. Just a thought."

"That's awesome," I tell him. "Your work's beautiful. Of course you should get the word out. You need a website, for sure. And do you have pictures of the pieces you've sold? If not, I'm sure the people you sold them to would let you photograph them. Then people can reach you through the website to place orders. You know?" I trail off at the blank expression on Rex's face.

"Um," he says, "I'm not so good with computers."

"I can help you. It's so easy now. There're free sites you can use and tons of tutorials online."

He makes a noncommittal sound and kisses me, and I immediately lose track of everything except that I'm sitting on his lap and he's kissing me.

He tastes like Rex and coffee. Mmm, coffee….

Apparently, I said that out loud, because he chuckles and asks me if I want some. I nod eagerly and follow him into the kitchen, where he pushes me against the counter and kisses me, a long, deep kiss that bumps grading at least thirty slots farther down the things-I-want-to-do list than it already was.

"I missed you this week," he says, and pulls me into his shoulder.

"Me too," I say. "Sorry. It was a killer week. Freaking Peggy," I spit out.

Rex squeezes my shoulder with one big hand and I kind of melt against him involuntarily.

"Jesus," he says. "You're all knots. It doesn't seem fair that this Peggy woman can just make you do her work."

"She didn't *make* me. But, you know, I'm low man on the totem pole or whatever, so I've got to put the time in."

He takes my other shoulder in his hand and massages them for a minute. At first I tense up, but then every muscle relaxes, including the ones keeping my eyes open. I groan.

"Well, I don't think it's right," Rex says. "Are they at least paying you for it?"

"It doesn't really work that way in academia," I say.

Rex makes an irritated sound and his thumbs dig in harder.

"Ugh, you gotta stop; you're gonna put me to sleep," I tell Rex, but I'm kind of nuzzling him.

"After dinner I'll finish, okay?" His voice is husky. He tilts my chin up and kisses me. "Finish your work," he says, and the promise in his voice thrills me.

"Hey, which is your Wi-Fi network?" I ask Rex. "My piece-of-shit computer isn't picking anything up."

Rex looks surprised.

"Oh," he says, his shoulders going rigid. "I don't have one."

"You don't have the Internet?"

"Don't need it much. When I do, I go to the library. Oh, do you need it to get your work done? I should have told you, I guess. I just didn't think of it."

"No, it's okay, I just... man, I've just been in academic-world too long, I think; I didn't think to ask. I use it to double-check if I suspect a student's plagiarized. But, no, it doesn't matter. I can do that later."

I settle into the first paper, immediately irritated because the student doesn't seem to have a thesis. I let out a deep sigh. It's going to be a long afternoon. She also doesn't cite any of her quotes. The next paper's argument is so convoluted that I'm almost impressed with the fact that the student has managed to appear sane in class so far. Paper three has no argument whatsoever and not a single grammatically correct sentence. I sigh again and rub my eyes. Grading always requires waging a mental battle against my temper.

Rex looks up from his drawing and quirks a brow at me in question.

"Sorry," I tell him. "Grading always infuriates me. It's like my students don't listen to what I say at all. I mean, we go over thesis statements in class and I give them a handout about how to tell if a thesis is strong or not. Then they write these papers and they're just nonsense. I mean, actual nonsense. They aren't making an argument, they don't connect any of their ideas, and half the time I can't even tell if they've read the book they're writing about. It drives me fucking nuts. Listen to this. 'I will argue that the way Bartleby doesn't want to do anything proves that he's politically opposed to doing anything.' What!"

Rex clears his throat.

"You make it sound like they do badly just to piss you off."

I laugh, but he doesn't seem to be joking.

"You know, it's not really that easy for everyone," he continues. He's trying to sound casual, but I can tell he means it. "Sometimes people aren't good at things."

"I know that. But it's like they're not even trying—" I start to explain.

"You don't know that," he says. "Maybe they're trying their best and they're just not as smart as you. Or they're good at math but not your class."

Of course I know he's right. At every moment other than when I'm grading, I know that.

"You're right," I say. "I guess it just makes me feel like I'm wasting my time trying to teach them shit sometimes. Like they don't care about it anyway, so why do I spend all my time trying to make them?"

"Well," he says after a pause, "that sounds like a bigger question."

"Yeah, I guess it is. I don't really want to think about it right now. Sorry, I'm just so fucking glad it's the weekend. I'll just finish this."

Rex doesn't say anything. His shoulders are tense and his jaw clenched. He must think I'm such a pretentious ass right now. Really, it's never a good idea to grade while anyone else is watching.

"Hey, can we put on some music?" I ask. "It's so quiet in here I can't think."

Rex points to the cabinet next to the television.

"Put on whatever you want," he says.

"Yeah, sorry, I just, I'm so used to working in coffee shops or at the bar that I guess I've, like, trained myself to associate noise with concentration. I can just put my headphones on if you want."

"No, it's fine," Rex says. "Do you miss the city a lot, then?" He's looking at his drawing and fiddling with his pencil.

"Yeah," I say, standing before the cabinet and tracing the wood grain with my finger. "Did you make this?" He nods. "You're so talented." Rex smiles.

Wow, he has a lot of stuff I've never heard of. He has almost all records, but he definitely doesn't strike me as the sort of neo-vinyl fan who buys new records but never touched a turntable until college. Some of these are moldy.

"Who's Blossom Dearie?"

"She was a jazz singer. Mostly in the fifties and sixties. Recorded a lot of standards."

I put the record on. There's a scritch of static and then a light voice fills the room.

"Were these your mother's records?"

Rex's head jerks up.

"Yeah."

"I like it," I say, and go back to grading.

By the time I'm finished, I've gone through three more records, my comment-writing hand is cramping, my shoulders are tight, and I've decided that Rex is an incredibly distracting work buddy. Every time I look up from a paper, there he is, his sensual mouth tightened in

concentration and the tiny line between his eyebrows reminding me of
how he looked when he was inside me.

"Oh, thank god," I say finally, my forehead resting on the stack of
graded papers. "I need a drink."

AFTER WE take Marilyn for a walk, Rex makes omelets for dinner.

"Do you want to watch a movie or something?" I ask, putting my
plate in the sink.

Rex shakes his head.

"Do you want me to go so you can… do whatever?"

Rex shakes his head again, a dangerous smile playing on his lips. He
stands up and holds out a hand to me.

In his bedroom, Rex pulls me close, running his hands up and down
my back.

I put my arms around him, thrilling at his firm muscles and his
warmth. Every time I touch him it's like my whole body reacts. He slides
my T-shirt up and pulls it over my head, never losing contact. Then he
strips off his own.

"Lie down," Rex says, a warm hand splaying across my back. He
pulls my jeans and underwear off. "Just relax."

Rex massages my neck, strong thumbs digging into the muscles on
either side, then runs his fingers into my hair, massaging my scalp. I guess
he wasn't kidding about finishing that massage. He kisses the back of my
neck, then moves on to my shoulders. At first, I tense every time he moves
to a new part of my body, but he just keeps whispering, "It's okay, relax,"
and, little by little, I do. He spreads my arms, massaging my biceps, and
then down my ribs. My breath catches when his thumbs go to my spine. I
can hear little pops and cracks as his weight bears down on me.

With every breath and every touch, I feel like I'm melting into the
mattress. When Rex straddles me on the bed, I can feel his heat
everywhere. He kisses the back of my neck and the top of my spine as his
strong hands massage my lower back, pressing me into the sheets. His
palms skim my thighs and I tense up again.

"You're okay," Rex murmurs, and uses more pressure, massaging
the muscles of my thighs firmly. I bury my face in the pillow, hugging it
to me, tensing up again. No one has ever touched me like this. Cared for
me like this. It's like Rex thinks of my body as something he's responsible
for. Something precious. I shake my head in the pillow.

"Hey," he says, "look at me." He rolls me to my side so he can see my face. "What's wrong? Do you want me to stop?"

I shake my head violently but can't muster a single word.

"Do you want me to keep going?" I nod. Rex is looking at me carefully. I don't know how to explain it to him. I keep opening my mouth and nothing comes out. Rex gives me a sad smile. "Do you want me to take care of you? Make sure you're relaxed?" Is that a trick question? *Do* I want him to take care of me? What does that mean? I don't want Rex to think I'm weak, but I don't want him to stop. I want this to be like a dream, where things just happen and no one talks about them and everything is liquid and sleepy. I wish I were drunk so I could let him do whatever he wants to me and it wouldn't have to be my choice. I don't think I'm supposed to wish for that.

Rex presses a soft kiss to my cheekbone. "Just try and relax, all right? You don't have to think about anything. You don't have to do anything. Your only job is to relax, okay?" I nod.

Just relax. No big deal, right? Just relax. Years of experience have taught me that it *is* a big deal, though. If you relax, you're unprepared for what might happen next. If you relax, someone can sneak up on you. If you relax, you can't react quickly enough. Years of brotherly sneak attacks on the couch, being pulled into hallways and alleys, and slammed against lockers and walls have taught me so.

"Daniel, do you trust me?" Rex asks. I think I do. Intellectually, I know Rex isn't going to hurt me, but it's not as easy as I thought. Not as much of a choice as I thought. I take a deep breath and decide that it's just mind over matter. If I want to trust Rex, I just have to do it. I close my eyes and nod.

I'm rewarded with a kiss on the mouth and a smile. Rex looks genuinely pleased. I let out a deep breath, glad to have done the right thing, and spread my arms out again, letting go of my death grip on the pillow. If I open my eyes just a sliver, the green flannel of Rex's sheets is a nubbly landscape that I can pretend is moss. I've always wanted to take a nap on a bed of moss.

Rex's hands are back. I imagine that he's some kind of sinewy mountain cat padding across my back, pressing me deeper into the springy moss with his huge paws. I used to do this as a kid. I'd lie in bed with the covers over my face and pretend that my stuffed animals were bigger than me. I would pretend that my stuffed lion would gather me up in its paws like a cub and pull me on top of its stomach to sleep.

Even Rex's pine and cedar smell fits. Now he's a tree that has been standing for two hundred years, limber enough to bend with the wind, but sturdy enough to shelter me. His hands are on my thighs again, and this time it's like he's soothing muscles I didn't even know I had, stroking purely functional things to a sensual tingle.

"Okay?" Rex asks, and I want to ask him how a tree can talk. I just nod, though, my eyes closing a bit, casting the green hillside into the first shadows of evening.

It's working. I really am relaxing. Then Rex's hands touch my ass and I don't want to pretend anymore. He takes the globes of my ass in his hands and massages them and it feels like I'm drowning, sinking deep into something warm and viscous, like honey. I moan as his palms rest on the hills of my ass and his thumbs caress my lower back. Then he slides his hands to my hips and massages them, rotating them one at a time.

He kneels between my legs, spreading them to make room for him, and kneads my inner thighs and up to the crease of my bottom. He takes me by the hips and digs strong thumbs into my spine, pushing my knees up and apart. His hands slide back to my ass, fingers dipping into my crack, and I moan again. Every touch is electric. I never knew relaxing could feel so amazing. Every strong squeeze of his hands on my ass sends jolts of heat to the base of my spine and my cock, the only part of me that is not relaxed. I squirm a little, trying to maneuver myself into a position that isn't crushing my burgeoning erection.

Rex lifts my hips easily and settles me back on the bed tenderly, then urges me down again, his attention returning to my ass. I gasp when I feel his hand on my erection, and I let my breath out slowly as he gentles me again, caressing my ass softly to relax me.

I never thought about having tension in my hips or thighs, but as Rex spreads my legs farther apart, relaxing them, I feel loose and flexible, the tension draining from me, leaving me open to him. He scoots up, running a hand through my hair and I arch into his touch.

"Okay, baby?" he asks softly, like he doesn't want to break the spell.

"Feels so good," I murmur. When Rex slides down over my back and starts kissing my neck, I vaguely register that he's taken off his pants too, but I didn't notice. He kisses down my spine and, when he reaches the plump of my ass, he doesn't stop, kissing a line down my crack. I gasp and tense up again, but his hands stroke my hips.

"I want to taste you, Daniel," Rex says, his voice the tumble of a blood-warm wave breaking near my ear. "Can I taste you?" He follows this up with a lick to my ear and I groan, nodding manically. I can feel his hardness between my legs, a pulsing brand on my thigh.

"Tell me."

"Do it, please."

"Do what, Daniel?" Rex asks, his voice teasing and filthy.

"Ungh, I want—want you to taste me," I bite out, a rush of shame competing with arousal.

"Spread your legs for me," he commands.

He drops down again, grabbing the hills of my ass and squeezing them, then pulling them apart. His tongue touches my opening and a dark, hot pleasure opens me up as he licks into me.

"Oh god," I groan, burying my face in the pillow. Rex goes back to his massage, hands sliding down my thighs to my calves, relaxing every muscle he touches. Then his mouth is back, kissing and then licking my hole, his tongue relaxing this muscle too. He pushes me up farther, so he can bury his face between my cheeks, and then everything is liquid heat and a pleasure so much gentler than penetration. I feel the shift as my muscles relax and Rex's tongue breaches me. It's something caught so exactly between relaxing me and driving me to a fever pitch of arousal that my brain doesn't know how to process it and I slide back and forth between unclenching to his mouth and tensing with pleasure.

I'm crying out, now, desperate for Rex to push a little harder, slide a little deeper so this feeling can coalesce into something I know. But he keeps working me, sliding softly inside me and gentling my trembling muscles with his own.

"Rex, Rex, Rex," I call out, unable to control myself. I don't know what I'm begging for. Whether more or less—everything or nothing—I don't know.

Then Rex groans, the sound ripped from deep inside him. As he shifts, I feel his erection, impossibly hard, and he's trembling above me.

"Oh, Daniel," he says, and his voice is a tender animal that could consume me. "Fuck, Daniel, I need to be here right now." He slides three fingers into me as he says it, and my whole body clenches, shuddering when he breaches me.

"Unnhh," I say, pressing my hips into the bed and grabbing the sheets. Rex grabs my hips to keep me still. He reaches up to grab a condom from the dresser and puts his mouth to my ear.

"Was that a yes?" he growls, and I moan again. "Was that 'Yes, Rex, you can have my ass?'" I nod frantically, trying to turn and look back at him, but his weight makes it impossible. I'm out of my head with lust. The only thing I can feel is the empty throbbing in my channel where his tongue has left me wanting. I can almost feel him inside me, filling me up, and I clench at the thought.

"Fuck, baby," Rex says. Then he dives back down, his mouth sucking at my hole, tongue jabbing inside me.

"Rex, please."

"Please what?" he says, low and rumbling.

"Please, fuck me," I'm finally able to string together. I don't know how I can be this relaxed and this on edge at the same time, but when I feel Rex's heat against me I don't even tense up. He slides just past my muscle and my body welcomes him. He spreads my ass and slides the rest of the way in, filling me so perfectly that it takes me a moment to catch up with the sensation. By the time it does, he's all the way inside me, and my whole channel clenches with pleasure. We both cry out and Rex's hands tighten on my hips, pulling me up and onto his shaft.

He doesn't move, and it's like we're locked together in a perfect moment that we know will only get better. I swallow hard and Rex drops his forehead to my back. Then he begins to move—tiny pulses of his hips that stir friction between us. Gradually, his movements get bigger, until I can feel the drag of his cock against my inner walls. My own erection feels almost secondary, a sensation I never thought I would have. It's as if only where he's touching me matters. He slides slowly out of me, and I make a desperate sound, thinking he's leaving, but he strokes up my spine.

He rests the head of his cock against my hole, teasing me with it, pulsing himself shallowly in and out of my muscle, confusing the sensitive skin there with each penetration. Then he slides all the way back in with one firm stroke and it's like a fire stroking through my channel. He pulls my hips up farther and begins fucking me deeply, letting his weight bear him down.

He's supporting himself on his arms as he fucks down into me and I grab the corded muscle of his forearms, trying to gain some purchase. I can't stop the broken sounds that are coming out of my mouth and Rex is making a noise like a groan and a whimper. Then I arch into him and he slides against my prostate, flooding me with a wave of pleasure from my ass to my dick.

I cry out, and Rex pulls me up, locking his arms around my shoulders to maintain his angle. Every thrust bumps my prostate and I have no control over my body. I feel lightheaded, like every nerve is being strummed with Rex's strokes. He rotates his hips and drives into me, then freezes there for a long moment, letting me feel the pulse of his erection, letting me feel how completely he fills me.

"Please," I gasp out, and Rex moans. I can feel him shaking above me.

"Daniel," he says shakily.

Then he rears back and slams into me, grabbing my cock for the first time since he began his massage. The second he touches me, I'm done for. He pumps my shaft once, twice, three times, and then I'm coming in his hand, the pleasure washing through my whole body. My orgasm seems to go on even after he's wrung every jet of come from me, echoes of pleasure pulsing in my balls and through my ass. Then Rex is coming, his strokes growing short and hard. He thrusts himself deep inside me and moans brokenly, freezing in orgasm. Then his hips pulse a few more times as he presses the last of himself inside me.

I'm trembling from pleasure and can't catch my breath, but as Rex lowers himself on top of me, still softening inside me, I realize that I'm more relaxed than I've ever been.

"Jesus," Rex mutters as he slides out of me and drops the condom into the garbage can. I can't even open my eyes. I'm still on my stomach where I collapsed, Rex's sticky hand trapped between my belly and the bed. I roll onto my side a little and Rex wipes his hand on the flannel sheets. He snugs up behind me and kisses the back of my neck avidly, then slides his arm under my neck so he can wrap both arms around my chest. "Fuck," he says, as his spent cock brushes up against my ass and gives a little twitch. I moan absently and tuck my knees up. Rex nestles his groin against my ass and squeezes me tight.

I want to thank him for the massage, for relaxing me, and for what was definitely the best sex of my life, but I'm too relaxed to say a word.

I FEEL like my head is going to explode out my eyeballs and, when it does, I'm not even going to move; I'm just going to lie here with no head and no eyeballs. I've been in the library since I finished teaching at 2:00 p.m. I'm starving and there's no way I can do even one more hour of work on this conference paper. It's only Wednesday, and the week already feels endless, the relaxation of Rex's homey cabin and warm hands nothing but a memory.

I need to get some dinner, go home, and put myself the hell to bed if I want to finish this tomorrow. I gather my stuff and trudge downstairs.

"Daniel?"

I spin around and find myself face to face with Rex—well, face to throat; damn, he's tall.

"Hi," I say, smiling at him. "What're you doing here?"

"I'm just picking up some things, and I needed to look up some stuff." Well, that was specific. I nod, though, too tired to press him. "What are you working on?" He guides me over to the bench next to the wall and brings me down next to him. I lean into him a little.

"I have to give a paper at this conference in Detroit on Saturday. It's the biggest annual conference in my field and my panel got accepted over the summer, which is great, but I kind of forgot about it, what with moving and teaching and everything. Then this morning I looked at my calendar and realized it's, you know, really soon."

Even as I'm telling Rex this, my stomach is tightening. It's the first panel that I've proposed that has been accepted at a really prestigious conference, and I was jazzed about working on a new project when I wrote the abstract. Of course, sitting down this morning to start writing it, realizing I only have a few days, is a different story.

"I've got to finish it tomorrow so I can practice it and time it. Then I'm driving down Friday afternoon and coming back Sunday. I can't believe I left it this long. I just started it this afternoon. It's going to be crap because I'm throwing it together."

My stomach lets out an audible rumble even though I've moved past hunger to sheer anxiety. I'm blocking out hours in my head as I talk— three hours for teaching tomorrow, then I can work on the paper, then I need to do laundry so I have clean clothes for the conference; I should definitely check my car before I leave—and I miss something Rex says.

"Sorry," I say, "what?"

Rex narrows his eyes at me.

"I said when was the last time you ate?"

"Um. Breakfast?" I say. Which is technically true, even though breakfast was half a bagel I found in my bag from yesterday.

"Daniel, it's after seven." When Rex gets worried, that damned wrinkle in the middle of his forehead comes out—the one I can't help but associate with his face clenched in pleasure. I reach out absently and smooth it with my finger. His expression softens.

"Hi," I say, and I kiss him. I don't generally kiss in libraries, it's true, but no one can see us, and I can't resist touching him when he's this close.

He smiles and squeezes my hand. "Hi. So, can I take you to get some food?"

"Oh, that's okay," I say. "I was just going to grab something on my way home. I'm gonna crash out early, I think, since I have to try and finish this tomorrow."

"Okay," he says neutrally. "Do you want to have dinner tomorrow?"

"Yeah, that sounds great—oh shit!" I grab my calendar from my bag and flip through it. "Shit, shit. I can't. I'm having dinner with Jay tomorrow. I forgot."

"Who's Jay?" Rex lets go of my hand.

"He teaches in my department. He's helping me with this committee I'm accidentally chairing—don't ask. Anyway, we're having dinner tomorrow so he can explain everything. Sorry."

"Oh. So, I guess I'll just see you when you get back?"

Rex's eyes are slightly narrowed, and I can't tell if I'm supposed to offer to cancel dinner with Jay so I can see Rex before I leave for the conference? Am I supposed to invite Rex to come?

"You could come to dinner with us?" I say, and it doesn't sound at all sincere. "But it would be really boring for you because we're just going to talk about work stuff. Do you want to come over to my house after dinner?" I ask, hoping maybe this is a good compromise. "You could keep me company while I pack?" That is the lamest thing I've ever said. Only Ginger wants to hang out with me while I stuff things into a bag. But Rex smiles.

"I can do that," he says. He pushes my messy hair back and kisses my cheek, which stokes a small warmth in my stomach. I lean my head on his shoulder for a moment and breathe in his smell.

"Hey, are you falling asleep?" Rex says.

"Mmhmm."

"Are you sure you don't want to come home with me? I'll cook you dinner."

I groan. That sounds amazing, but all I really want is to go to bed.

"Thanks," I say, "but it's okay. I'll see you tomorrow night?" He nods. "Probably around nine? I can text you when we're done."

"Oh, I don't text," Rex says, straightening his spine and squaring his shoulders.

"Hunh. Okay, then, Mr. Technophobe. Well, we're just going to the pizza place around the corner from my apartment, so if I'm not at my place at nine, just come there."

"Okay," he says. "Can I at least drive you home?"

"Sure." He goes back to the computer he was using and puts what look like a few CDs and some printouts in his bag.

When Rex stops his truck in front of my apartment, he turns off the engine and turns to me.

"Listen," he says. "It's not going to be crap."

"What?"

"Your paper. You said it's going to be crap because you're writing it at the last minute. I know that isn't true. You're too hard on yourself. I'm sure it'll be great."

"You can't be sure," I tell him. I hate it when people say things like this almost as much as I hate it when they assume my writing's going to be bad. "You've never even read anything I've written."

Rex pulls his hand from mine and his jaw clenches. He looks out the window.

"Sorry," I say. I thought my tone was pretty matter-of-fact, but I've clearly hurt his feelings.

Rex shakes his head.

"No, you're right. I've never read anything you've written. I'm sure it's all real over my head."

He sounds disgusted and I feel like I should apologize, but all I did was state a fact.

"Good night, Daniel," he says.

He sounds far away. I lean over and give him a kiss and his hand comes up to cradle the back of my neck.

"Night."

I WASN'T looking forward to dinner with Jay, since I thought I'd need every last second to finish my paper. About an hour before we were set to meet up, though, it all just kind of came together. A rogue example turned out to be the perfect introduction, and it let me pull out a thread that had been lurking but that I hadn't known what to do with. I finished it in a flurry and I'll have time to check it over tomorrow night when I get to Detroit.

Dinner turned out to be good, though. Once I wasn't panicking about my paper anymore, it was nice to just chat with Jay about Sleeping Bear and what a weird place it was. He was in grad school in Phoenix, so the weather hit him even harder than it has me. He gave me the scoop on other folks in the department, affirming that Peggy was kind of the antichrist, and went over how he'd approached the student essays last year. He's a really nice guy, and very easy to talk to.

"So, I have to admit," Jay says after we've talked about the committee, "I was really excited when you took this job."

"Oh?" I say.

"Yes. Honestly, I was enthusiastic to get someone who came from a different background. You know, not the typical four-year college to grad school route. I imagine going to community college gave you a different perspective on teaching too."

He doesn't sound judgmental about it at all, which is pretty uncommon among professors. Most think going to community college is embarrassing. My advisor told me I shouldn't list it on my CV.

"It did, yeah," I say. "At CCP—the community college—people were there because they wanted to be. They were mostly older, or they were going part-time while working to pay for it. And some of the professors were really great. But a lot of the classes were easy. I mean, the English classes were good because the teachers would always talk about other books than were on the syllabus, so I could go find those and read them. But, yeah, they weren't very challenging.

"I could only afford to take a few classes a semester, but I went during the summers too, so when I transferred to Temple to finish out my degree, I only had a year's worth of credits left. That was all I could afford there. I mean, honestly, I wouldn't even have done it except I knew I could never get into grad school straight from a community college, so my degree needed to be from Temple. It's shitty, but that's how it is."

Jay nods, his attention intense.

"Anyway, I was really lucky because one of the professors I had for an English class was an adjunct at Temple. I would go to her office hours and we'd talk about books and stuff. She gave me a lot of good recommendations. She's the one who told me that if I was thinking of grad school, I'd need to transfer. I really didn't have a clue about how academia worked back then."

"I was on the hiring committee; I've seen your trajectory. It's very impressive, Daniel. Really."

I'm embarrassed, so I change the subject. We talk about the trip to New York that Jay's just returned from. He's trying to get an international Latino/Latina literature and theory conference started, which sounds great, and he was schmoozing with some folks he knows. We slip into the topic of other conferences and Jay realizes that he went to grad school with one of my professors, whom I'll see at the conference in Detroit. I swear to god, the academic world is frighteningly small.

I'm just describing my conference paper to Jay when Rex walks in and comes over to our table.

"Hi," I say. "Sorry, am I late?" I fumble for my phone to see the time, but it's only 8:40.

"No," Rex says. "I was early and I saw you guys, so I thought I'd come over. That okay?"

"Yeah, of course. Rex, this is Jay Santiago. Jay, Rex Vale."

"Nice to meet you," Jay says, standing to offer his hand, and he seems to wince the slightest bit at Rex's handshake. Rex nods at him.

"You too."

We're all standing when the check comes, so I shrug on my jacket and grab my wallet.

"I've got it," Jay says.

"No," I say. "You were doing me a favor. I've got it, please."

"No, no," Jay says. "You're the new hire; consider it a welcome to the department."

"Oh, you don't have to—"

"Nonsense," Jay says. "I've got it." And he hands the waiter his credit card without looking at the check.

"Wow, okay, well, thanks, Jay," I say, feeling a little awkward. "I appreciate it."

"My pleasure," he says, pulling on a black wool overcoat and leather driving gloves.

We start to walk out, Rex keeping pace with me.

"Enjoy the conference," Jay says. "Give Wendy my regards."

"Will do," I say.

"And the paper sounds wonderful, Daniel, really." He claps me on the shoulder.

"Thanks," I say.

"Nice to meet you," he says again to Rex, and Rex nods.

INSIDE MY apartment, Rex pushes me against the door and kisses me aggressively. My head bangs against the wood and Rex pulls back, breathing heavily.

"Sorry," he mutters.

"What's wrong?" I ask him.

Is he still pissed from last night? If it were Ginger I'd tease her. Say, "What, are you jealous?" But something tells me Rex wouldn't appreciate that.

"Nothing," he says. "Did you finish your paper?"

"I did, yeah. It all came together. You were right; it's going to be fine."

He smiles and looks a little sheepish.

"Listen," he says. "I didn't mean to be unfriendly. It was just harder than I thought to see you out with another guy."

"Well, you weren't so much unfriendly as you were totally menacing. And he's not 'another guy.' He's a colleague." I pat his chest and walk to my closet, grabbing my duffel bag and starting to toss things into it.

"But he likes you," Rex says, as if it's a fact.

"I mean, as a friend, maybe," I say. Wow, I guess he really is jealous. It's not a great look on him.

"No," Rex says. "More than a friend. I could tell by how he was looking at you."

"And how was he looking at me?" I ask.

"Like... like he was... appreciating you," Rex says, slowly, looking at the floor. I stop.

"I don't even know if Jay's gay," I say. "I hope he isn't, what with the easy rhyme and the cruelty of children."

"He is," Rex says.

"How do you know?"

"Um...."

"Oh my god, did you date him?" I ask. It would make sense. It's not like there are that many gay guys around here. At the thought, my stomach goes all funny.

"What? No," Rex says. "I just met him. But, when you first moved here, I overheard...."

"You overheard," I encourage.

"Just some idiots talking about the town being overrun by gay snobs."

I shake my head. I'm not that surprised.

"Anyway," Rex continues, the set of his shoulders stiff, "we haven't really talked about any of that. I mean, if you were to go out with him as more than friends, I... well, I guess that'd be your prerogative."

"Well, I better get to be Bobby Brown and not Britney Spears," I say, to cover the fact that my head is now spinning. He's talking about us dating other people. How it's okay if I date other people. Is that what he wants? Does that mean *he's* dating other people? My stomach feels sour. The idea of Rex with someone else… it makes me feel sick, and… sad.

I walk into the bathroom, grabbing the jacket I hung on the shower door in the hopes of steaming the wrinkles out while I showered this morning. It looks passable.

Then there's a crash from the kitchen.

Rex is kneeling next to what was—until, say, about ten seconds ago—my kitchen table.

"Are you okay?" I ask.

"I'm fine," he says, standing. "Shit, Daniel, I just leaned against the thing and it totally collapsed. Sorry," he says. But he doesn't sound sorry. He sounds embarrassed, and maybe a little pissed.

"Oh, it's not your fault," I assure him, walking over. "It kind of bit it the other day and I just, like, propped it back up. Haven't gotten around to fixing it yet. I should've warned you."

"Well, why didn't you ask me to fix it for you?" Rex asks, sounding irritated.

"Um. I didn't think about it," I say.

"But it's what I do for a living," Rex says, his hands out in confusion.

"Well, okay, I'm sure you'd do a better job than me, Rex, but I'm not some pathetic idiot who can't fix a goddamned table."

"I don't think you're pathetic," he says, sounding exasperated. "I just don't understand why you won't ever accept my help."

"What are you talking about? You fixed my wall and my light—"

"That actually was my job," he interrupts.

"You rescued me from a snowstorm. You've cooked me whole meals."

"Because I wanted to! I like to cook for you."

"You just think I can't do simple adult things," I mutter. I'm not sure where that came from, but I'm pretty sure I believe it. Rex's mouth drops open and at first he looks like he's going to shake it off. Then he looks around at my apartment and kicks at a leg of my kitchen table, splayed like a broken dancer on the floor.

"You live on coffee and bagels unless I cook for you," he says. "Your car is a deathtrap that you've held together with a wire hanger. You won't talk to your landlord about making your apartment safe to actually live in. You moved to Michigan and you don't have a winter coat! It's like you don't even care about what happens to you."

"No! You just think you need to rescue me. Even the night we met, you rescued me—me *and* Marilyn. That's all you've done is rescue me, like I'm some damsel in distress. Well, I don't need to be rescued! I can take care of myself."

"Can you?" Rex growls, advancing on me. "I'm not so sure."

"What the fuck!" My hands are fisted at my sides. "Are you fucking kidding me right now? Do you know how long I've taken care of myself? How many times I've been jumped or mugged or gotten my ass kicked? And I've *handled* it. I've handled *myself* just fine. You know how many times I've gone to lectures for the cheese cubes and stale crackers at the reception because I can't afford to buy food? Huh?"

I'm shouting now, so furious that Rex apparently thinks I'm just as weak and pathetic as my brothers do that my heart is pounding.

"I—I didn't mean—"

"Anyway, if you think I'm such a pathetic fucking mess then why are you even here?" I shove Rex's shoulder. Not hard, just in frustration, but it's like pushing up against a mountain.

Rex freezes. He opens his mouth like he's about to say something, and then just shakes his head, hands on his hips.

"Have a safe trip, Daniel," he says evenly. Then he walks out, closing the door gently behind him. His truck starts outside.

"Fuck!" I yell, punching the door. "Shit, ouch." I always forget how much that hurts.

I turn around and lean back against the door where Rex was kissing me a few minutes ago. My kitchen looks like a crime scene. The table is slumped onto the peeling linoleum, and the light over what used to be the kitchen table is swinging a little, casting eerie shadows. My duffel bag gapes open on the bed, my jacket on the floor. The whole place looks dingy and sad. It smells like ramen noodles and Band-Aids even though I haven't made ramen noodles lately and I couldn't tell you the last time I actually owned a Band-Aid.

Goddammit, this is why I don't date.

Chapter 8

October

I DIDN'T sleep well at all last night. Rex's face kept drifting into my head—that expression he got when I yelled at him. As if he were holding out something to share with me and I knocked it into the dirt like a bully with an ice cream cone.

I mean, is it, like, a requirement that just because he builds things professionally I'm not allowed to fix my own table? God, I can only imagine my brothers or my dad if they saw me calling my boyfriend for help because I couldn't even fix a simple table.

Wait. Did I just think of Rex as my boyfriend? How do you know if someone's your boyfriend? Oh Christ. *This* is why I don't date.

I just need to have a quick meeting with a student and then I can get the hell out of here. I can't wait to be gone. I definitely need a break. And a huge coffee.

"Hi," I say to Marjorie at the counter of Sludge. "Can I get—?"

"Don't you want to look at the board before you order?" she cuts me off, smiling a little too wide.

"Uh, no. I know what I want."

"Come on, just a peek?" She's twisting her hands together in a way that makes her look like a twelve-year-old girl, not a grown-ass woman.

I look at the board so she'll leave me the hell alone.

"What am I supposed to be—oh shit."

"Language, dear," Marjorie giggles.

On the Specials board, in bright green chalk, it says "The Daniel: 3 shots of expresso in a large coffee."

"Wow," I say. "That's…. Wow. I'm honored. It's *espresso*, though, just so you know; no *x*."

Oh Jesus, this is so embarrassing. Ginger is going to laugh her face off when she hears this. Marjorie looks a little pissed that I pointed out the spelling mistake, but she fixes it with the chalk. Then she looks back at me.

"Well," I say, trying to move things along. "Thanks again. So, I guess you know what I want, then."

Marjorie still says nothing, just looks at me expectantly.

"Uh…." I smile, like maybe that's the magic sign she's waiting for.

"Order it!" she says.

"I… did?"

"No, order it by name."

"You want me to order my own drink—the one you already know I want because you named it after me?"

"Well, no one *else* is ever going to order it," she says, clearly exasperated.

"Then why did you—Oh Jesus. Okay, I would like one 'Daniel' to go, please."

"Coming right up, Daniel," Marjorie says sweetly.

JAY SANTIAGO steps through my door just seconds after my student leaves.

"Hey, Daniel," Jay says with a smile.

"Morning," I say.

"You leaving soon?"

"Yep. On my way out."

"Listen," Jay says, sliding easily into the seat my student just vacated. "I really enjoyed our conversation last night. It was lovely getting to know you a bit better."

"Me too, Jay. I mean, you too."

Jay smiles warmly, then leans across the desk toward me.

"Look, Daniel, I don't know what your situation is, but would you be interested in doing it again?"

"Again, like, dinner again?" I say stupidly.

"Yes. I wonder if you'd like to have dinner with me again. If we enjoyed one another's company, that is, and it seems like we did."

Oh crap, crap, crap. I can't believe it. Rex was right.

"Like, as… friends?" I try, in a last ditch effort.

"No, as in on a date," Jay says.

"Oh wow," I say. "Um, well, thanks, Jay. I'm really flattered, I just—um, I'm seeing someone, though. Sorry."

"The man I met last night?" Jay asks, seeming unperturbed.

"Yeah. Rex." God, even saying Rex's name almost makes me smile, even though I'm still mad at him.

"Of course," he says. "I understand. Well." He stands and reaches his hand across the desk. "Enjoy the conference, then. The offer stands, if you'd ever like to take me up on it." He squeezes my hand once, lets it go, and, smiling, walks out the door.

Damn. That was the classiest ask-out I've ever seen.

My first thought is to call Rex and tell him he was right about Jay—both the gay thing and the into-me thing. But then what? I don't want to apologize. I doubt he thinks he did anything wrong. No, better to just take the weekend and cool off.

LEO'S BEHIND the counter when I walk into the music store I never knew existed. I think the reason I never knew it existed is because the sign out front says Mr. Zoo's Rumble. I don't even want to know. He looks up when the bell tinkles my arrival and breaks into a big, excited grin, which he quickly twists into a wry smirk, but not before I see how genuinely glad he is to see me.

"Daniel! Hey, man," he says. "You came!"

"This place is… something," I say, looking around. The whole front of the store is second-hand instruments of every sort that parents would kill to keep out of the hands of their kids: recorders, clarinets, dented brass things that might be cornets, cheap bongo drums, and one very sad-looking ukulele. Around these, in boxes, are old music magazines, sheet music, and stacks of broken jewel cases. On the other side of the counter where Leo sits are crates of CDs with signs written on the backs of cardboard flaps hung from the ceiling with fishing line, a few flapping in the breeze of the air duct above them. The crooked black Sharpie lettering spells out "World Music," "Rock 'N Roll," and "Country," but also "SoundTrax," "Mrs. Perelman's House," and "Busted/Take."

"Who's Mrs. Perelman?" I ask Leo.

"Oh, she was this old lady who lived above the store, and last year she, like, died, and so Mr. Zoo got all her music—I guess her kids didn't want it—and he didn't want to file it because it's old and didn't fit in his categories, so he just left it together."

"Mr. Zoo is a real person?"

"Oh yeah, Mr. Zuniga. He owns the place. So, what's up, Daniel? It's cool you came by!"

"Do you sell tapes?" I ask.

"Tapes."

"Yeah, you know, cassette tapes, the plastic rectangles with two circles in the middle."

"Um, right, yeah, we have some, but…." He runs a hand through his messy hair.

"What?"

"Just, there's nothing *good* on tape. Just crap people donate."

"That's okay. I just need a few. I'm driving to Detroit and I don't have a CD player in my car and I broke my tape adapter."

When I say I don't have a CD player in my car, Leo's face fills with intense pity, as if I've just confessed to him that I live on the streets and would like a warm meal and someplace to sleep.

"Yeah, man, of course, come on."

He's right, the tapes are mostly crap. They're shoved every which way into a bunch of shoeboxes under the counter. I sit down on the floor and pull a few out. Leo plops down across from me.

"Hey," I say to him suddenly, "shouldn't you be at school?"

"I already graduated," he says, looking down.

"Wait, how old are you?"

"Eighteen," he says. "And a half," he adds like a little kid. "But I did junior and senior year last year because I wanted to get out of there."

"Wow," I say, "that's awesome. You must be really smart to have been able to do that."

He smiles at me again, what I'm coming to think of as his real smile. He reminds me so much of myself in high school I can't believe it. And for the first time, I wonder if what Ginger said is true. If I seem totally different with her than I do when I'm with other people.

"So, how're you liking Holiday?" Leo asks.

"Um, it's nice," I say, setting aside a John Hiatt tape. "Really different from what I'm used to. I lived in Philly all my life, man, never thought about living anywhere else. It's just an adjustment, that's all."

He nods sagely.

"You're totally having a *Buffy*, early season four moment, that's all," he says.

"Sorry?"

"*Buffy the Vampire Slayer*. You know?"

"Never saw it."

Leo's eyes go wide. "What? Insanity! Aren't you an English professor? Who would ever listen to you talk about literary analysis if you haven't consumed, like, the greatest text of popular culture?"

"I'm not actually convinced that anyone *does* listen to me talk about literary analysis," I say.

"Okay, anyway, the point is, Buffy, right? In high school, she was at the top of the food chain. Pretty, popular, friends who worshipped her and had nothing better to do on a Friday night than follow her around on patrol. I mean, *sure* she had her problems, what with the whole Angel going dark thing—oh shit!" He stops, hand flying to his mouth. "Spoiler alert. *Major* spoiler alert. I am *so* sorry."

When I don't say anything he continues.

"So, yeah, she takes her hits and all, but basically she's queen bee. Then she starts college and it's like, all of a sudden she's not a big fish in a little pond anymore, you know? Like, Willow's super smart, so she meets people and is all into school and stuff—let's all just *pretend* she would ever actually go to UC Sunnydale, yeah, right—and Buffy kind of feels abandoned. Also, her roommate's a demon, no big deal. Plus, let's be honest, girlfriend is *not* really that smart, okay? Good under pressure? Totally. Wicked clever at outsmarting monsters? Sure. But college-smart? Um, not so much. And she feels out of sorts, you know, which is very un-Slayer-like.

"And that's you. Just out of sorts because you're in a new place and you don't quite know where you fit in." He pauses, nodding to himself. "But don't worry. No spoilers—because, obviously, the Slayer has to go back to being a badass—but Buffy totally finds her footing at college, and she starts dating Riley, and, okay, *that* actually doesn't work out that well, but the *point* is that you've just got to fall back on your own superpower and you'll be fine!"

"MY ONLY friend isn't even old enough to drink and Michigan named a coffee after me," I moan to Ginger when I'm five miles out of town, Meat Loaf's *Bat Out Of Hell II: Back Into Hell* in my tape deck. I'm feeling particularly in tune with "Life Is a Lemon and I Want My Money Back" at the moment. God, Jim Steinman, you are a genius.

Ginger does, indeed, laugh her face off when I tell her about The Daniel.

"Oh my *god*, pumpkin. I am going to go into every coffee shop in Philly and order The Daniel." She starts laughing again.

"Jesus fucking Christ, I am so glad to just get out of here for a little while."

"Won't you miss the lumberjack? How's it going? I need an update."

I sigh.

"I heard a sigh and I can hear Meat Loaf in the background, which I am considering an official cry for help." She pauses. "Is 'Paradise in the Dashboard Light' on this album?"

"Ha! You love the Loaf. No, that's on the first *Bat Out Of Hell*."

"Damn it. Okay, commence update."

"We got in a fight."

"Oh my god, *you* got in a fight? That would require actually talking with him about something that matters to you. That is *major*, sweetie!"

"Jeez, you sound like the imitation you do of your mother when you told her you got your period."

Ginger giggles. "You've entered the cult of womanhood! Congratulations!" she says in the weird mom-voice she always does.

"So, what happened?"

"It's just, I had dinner with a colleague. It was nice, you know, just talking about the department, about our research. He's from Phoenix, so Michigan's been culture shock for him too. Anyway, he was helping me with this committee I'm on because he was on it last year, so we met for pizza. Then Rex was telling me that he could see that Jay was interested in me, which pissed me off because, you know, it was for work. And then Rex got all mad at me because I didn't ask him to fix my table. I mean, I can fix a fucking table, you know? I don't need him to do it for me."

"Doesn't he fix things as his job, though?" Ginger asks.

"Yeah, but so what? Doesn't make me any less capable of taking care of it myself, does it? What, like I'm required to ask him just because he'd do a better job?"

"Whoa, babycakes, whoa. Slow down. Let me ask you a question. If you wanted a tattoo, who would you ask for one?"

"Is this a trick question?"

"Just hear me out, Daniel." Ooh, she's serious if she's using my name. I sigh.

"You."

"Right. Now, if I had to write some copy for the shop's site and I wanted someone to proofread it, who would I ask?"

"Me."

"Right. So, it's not like I *can't* proofread things. I mean, I'm not as good at it as you, but I can write a sentence. And you know ten other tattoo artists in the city. But you come to me because?"

"You're the best, obviously."

"*And?*"

"You're my best friend, idiot."

"Exactly. Look, sweetie, I know you're not actually a sociopath, but I'm also not the one trying to date you, okay? Sometimes you're totally dense about this shit. When you like someone and you respect their talent, you ask them to do things for you because you think of them first. Because the second you think of that thing, you think about them. Rex wants you to think of him first when something is broken. If he needed help writing something wouldn't you want to be the first person he thought of?"

"I guess," I mumble.

"And I've said it before, but it's obviously time you started listening. Sometimes people do want to help you and you get closer by letting them. That's what happened with you and me, remember?"

I smile.

"I remember."

"Good. Now what was the deal with Rex getting all caveman over this guy you had dinner with? That's so shitty. Though, good to know the lumberjack has at least one flaw. It was starting to disgust me, picturing him as some kind of buff Michigan Marlboro Man."

"Weeeell," I say.

"No!"

"Yeah. I thought it was totally professional and Rex was being crazy, but then this morning Jay asked me out. It was weird—he was so calm about it. Super suave."

"Wait, he and Rex met last night, or you just told Rex about him?"

"No, they met. Rex came to the restaurant after dinner to meet me."

"Did you introduce Rex as a friend or something?"

"No." I don't think I said he was anything, come to think of it.

"What a player!" Ginger says.

"What do you mean? Jay? He was really nice about it."

"He could totally tell you were with Rex and he asked you out anyway!"

"Well, you don't know that. And even if he did, it's not like he would know if we were monogamous or not."

"Come on, pumpkin, that is classic slimy moving-in-on-you-because-he-thought-your-boyfriend-wasn't-good-enough behavior."

"Don't say the b-word!"

"Be-havior?" Ginger laughs. "God, you're a fucking mess, kid."

I'm on the highway now, and "Out of the Frying Pan (And into the Fire)" is playing.

"The nightmares are back," I say softly.

"Shit. Bad?"

"Nah, not as bad as before. I had one the other night, though, and it was... weird."

"Weird how?"

"Well, I was really... happy? Rex gave me this amazing massage and we, you know, had sex, and I fell asleep with him and it was just, like, kind of perfect. But then I woke up in the middle of the night with the nightmare. And I've had it every night since."

"Did you tell Rex?"

"No. He didn't wake up, fortunately."

"You should tell him, Dandelion. Tell him about Richard *and* about the dreams."

"Yeah, maybe."

"Did you tell Rex about your colleague asking you out yet?"

"No, it just happened. Besides, he probably doesn't want to talk to me. He's mad at me."

"What are you, five? You hurt his feelings last night, and he was jealous. He might be upset, but you have to talk it through. Now, hang up the phone, blast Meat Loaf with the windows down, and relax. Call Rex when you get to Detroit. Okay?"

"Yes, mother," I say.

"God, you're so lucky I even speak to you."

"I know I am," I tell her.

I DID try Rex when I got to Detroit, but he didn't answer and I didn't leave a message. I called him this morning too—no answer. I texted Ginger. *Called twice, no answer. Told you he's mad.*

She wrote back. *Sometimes ppl have lives & its not all abt YOU. Xoxo.*

I know she's right, but I can't concentrate. My paper this morning went pretty well anyway, though, and I got some good questions that'll be useful if I want to try and turn the piece into an article down the line. It's been the usual sideshow of macho academic posturing, panels claiming to name the next turn in analysis, and badly concealed anxiety. Everyone's trying to make a good impression and pretend they don't care what anyone thinks. Everyone's trying to look like the smartest one in the room while acting like what they're saying is totally obvious. I hate conferences.

I've been looking forward to the last panel of the day, at least, because Maggie Shill, a nineteenth-century Americanist whose work I've always really admired, is going to be giving a paper about gilded age architecture and its influence on literary aesthetics of the time. Professor Shill teaches at Temple now, but she was hired after I left, so I've never worked with her. Her first book totally blew me away, though.

I slide into a seat just as the moderator is introducing the panel. I make a habit of never arriving to panels early and never sitting directly next to anyone so I can avoid any awkward small talk with other people in the audience who only ever want to know what you're working on and whether you're more successful than they are. The room's crowded, though, so I have to sit right next to a woman in an ill-fitting skirt suit who looks like she'd rather be anywhere but here.

"Sorry," I say as I accidentally brush up against her shoulder while I get myself situated.

"No problem," she says, and smiles at me.

When the first panelist gets up, she immediately begins to ramble on about how panels are designed to stifle thoughts and make ideas digestible and prepackaged; that's why they're called panels, like the containing squares in a comic book.

"Is that Maggie Shill?" I ask the woman next to me. I've never seen her speak, but the other panelists are a man and a woman who looks Latina.

"Oh yeah," the woman says, sounding embarrassed.

I'm shocked. This rambling mess is Maggie Shill.

"As I completed my paper," Professor Shill is saying, "I realized that it wouldn't do the world any good—no good at all."

"Oh Jesus," the woman next to me mutters.

"What's the deal?" I ask. "Her work is so good?"

The woman scrunches down in her seat like she's trying to avoid being seen.

"She's totally losing it," she says. She glances at me out of the corner of her eye. "She's my dissertation director, and—" She looks left and right to make sure no one's listening. "—she told me that she was too busy to write her paper so she was just going to wing it. I don't have any idea what she's doing, but I'm supposed to have drinks with her after this. Maybe I'll be struck by lightning instead."

Up at the podium, Professor Shill is still talking, her tone manic, her gestures wild. She's talking about interdisciplinarity and the role of the humanities, but saying nothing about the topic her paper was supposed to be about. Finally, she starts talking about how being a mentor is all she ever wanted and how her graduate students make it all worth it. The woman next to me slides down farther.

"Oh my god, this is not good," she says.

"So, she has no paper?" I confirm.

"Nope," the woman says. "It's so fucked-up. I was on the same flight as her coming here and when we got in last night she went to the hotel bar to meet some friends and got wasted. I saw her staggering around the lobby at, like, midnight, flirting with some business-looking guy. Then before the panel she grabbed me and told me to come to her talk and we'd have drinks to celebrate after. What was I supposed to say?"

Professor Shill is now denouncing the conference itself, claiming that she had the idea for the conference theme years ago and no one listened to her, but now no one will acknowledge her role. She sounds nuts.

"Dude, she's lost it," I say. Man, talk about disillusioned. I can't believe this is the same Maggie Shill whose work I've read all these years.

"Oh, she never had it," the woman says. "All she does is work and she, like, doesn't care if you have a life. She basically lives at school and does nothing but read and write. She's a machine. But she's off her goddamned rocker."

Maggie Shill reaches over to the panelist at the end of the table and picks up his paper. She tears it in half down the middle and drops it on the floor.

"In the end, it's just words on the page," she says, staring out at us, eyes blank. "Just words on the page that vanish into the air." Then she walks out of the conference room.

"Kill me," the woman next to me groans.

I DECIDE to get one drink at the hotel bar before I go back to my room and indulge in watching some shitty TV and zoning out.

"Daniel, hey."

I look up to see Andre, a cute grad student I've known for a few years. He started at Penn a year or two after I did and then transferred to University of Michigan when his dissertation advisor took a job there.

"Hey, Andre, good to see you." He gives me a hug and sits on the stool next to mine. "I should have known you'd be here—U of M's really close, right?"

"Yeah, Ann Arbor's only about a half hour from here. You're in Michigan too, now, right?"

"Yeah, up north of Traverse City. Crazy."

"Ooh, already saying Up North. Very Michigan of you."

"Sorry?"

"You know, Up North?" At my vacant expression, Andre says, "Up North is the northern lower peninsula, like where you live. Of course, everyone in Michigan will make a different argument about where exactly you can draw the line that indicates where Up North begins. It can get very heated."

I smile and shake my head.

"Fucking Michigan," I say.

"How's the conference treating you?" Andre asks.

"Dude, I just saw someone totally go off the deep end," I say, and tell him about Professor Shill.

"Oh wow," he says. "Well, that's what being a workaholic with no personal life will get you. You invest that much in paper and ink that can't give anything back to you and you end up losing your shit by forty."

Shit, when he puts it like that it sounds so depressing.

"Speaking of which," Andre says, his hand brushing my thigh, "are you here alone?"

"I am."

"You wanna…?"

Andre and I slept together at the last two conferences where we saw each other. He's sweet and really cute, with dark skin and long eyelashes and an adorable way of squeezing his eyes really tightly closed when he comes.

I shake my head. "I can't. I'm sorry."

Andre grins. "Whoa, did Dr. Mulligan actually meet someone?"

"Never mind that," I say. "Thanks, though. It was good to see you." I kiss him on the cheek and leave cash on the bar. He winks at me and finishes my drink.

BACK IN my room, I sink onto one of the beds without even taking my shoes off. I want to go to bed, but I had the nightmare again last night, so I turn the TV on and start flipping channels.

It's always the same. I'm walking to the subway from the bar after I get off work. It's dark and I can see the orange light of the subway entrance a block in front of me. Then, in that way dreams have of making fears concrete, the space doubles, then doubles again, until with every step I'm getting farther away from the subway, like I'm on one of those moving sidewalks at the airport and it's pulling me backward. Then the street narrows into an alleyway and every step I take is like walking through tar, every movement exaggerated.

I see their shadows before I see them, even though there's no light. They're cast long on the walls of the alley and the sound of their laughter echoes down to me. I turn around to go back the way I came, but it's a dead end—a crumbling brick wall that goes up and up until it disappears into the night sky.

When I turn around they're right there, two of them in front of me and one to my right. They're bigger than me, bigger than real people. I come up to their stomachs. They start saying things, silly dream things and scary dream things and things they really said.

The first punch splits my cheek to the bone, then a shove knocks the wind out of me when my back hits the brick wall, snapping my head back with a wet clunk. My vision goes double, but dream double, so now there are six of them, a sick tessellation of swinging fists and kicking legs and pain. I fall into one of them with a punch to the gut and he steps back in disgust, letting me fall to the alley floor. Only, now, instead of the filthy concrete, used condoms, needles, and fast food wrappers, the floor is made of Pennsylvania schist, the rock sparkling with flecks of mica. All I can think is that it's beautiful, like a spill of dark glitter. Then they're gone.

I breathe out, my ribs protesting sharply. My body, too weak with relief to move, slumps to the schist. A hot tear runs down my cheek, burning as salt slicks a bloody scrape, and I start to sob. Through tears, I see something moving on the wall. At first I'm grossed out, thinking it's a roach or a rat, but it's too big and blocky. Then it falls. It's a brick. Then another slides out of the wall and crashes to the ground next to me. I try to push myself up to run, but the alley shifts and what was the brick wall is now the ceiling, its bricks falling down on me as the wall crumbles apart. I get to my knees and more bricks rain down. One hits my shoulder and I hear bone crunch. I slump back down as more fall, the alley collapsing around me.

The bricks hit every part of my body except my head, busting my bones to dust, pinning my limbs to the ground like the frog I dissected in high school biology. Then brick hits brick, burying me, leaving only my head untouched. Then, finally, they cover my head, my face, and I'm in darkness, feeling each excruciating shock as more fall. I'm alone in the dark as my air runs out. Then I hear a voice, far away and echoey. I try to call out but can't, and the voice recedes. How long I'm stuck there depends. It's just darkness and pain as my breath runs out. Then I wake up gasping, my body tensed against the pain.

I know. It's just a dream and I'm a grown man. But it leaves me shaky every time because though the bricks collapsing didn't really happen, of course—Ginger jokes that I've listened to *The Wall* too many times—the rest of it did.

WHEN I started grad school I had no idea what to expect. I hadn't taken the college classes the rest of my cohort had, or read the books. I'd never heard of the literary theorists they mentioned and when one friendly girl with a shiny blonde braid asked if I was a deconstructionist, I told her I worked demolition in the summers if she needed something deconstructed. She laughed with me, bumping me companionably on the shoulder, except that I wasn't laughing because I had no idea what the joke was. Then she blushed. I thought I'd said something offensive and opened my mouth to apologize, but she looked offended and walked away, muttering something about anti-intellectual posturing.

I didn't speak in class because it quickly became clear that I had no idea what anyone was talking about. I read the books and the journal articles. Sometimes I read them twice. I knew I understood them because I noticed in class when someone misrepresented an idea or got a minor plot point wrong. The part I was missing, I realized little by little, wasn't the brains or the memory—or even the creativity. It was the language of academia with which my classmates seemed to come preloaded. They had gone to Ivy League schools and large research universities. They named the professors they'd taken classes with in college and the others nodded, as if they were talking about rock stars.

At first I didn't admit that I'd gone to community college for my first two years' worth of credits, working two jobs to pay for them over the course of four years. That it was only on the strength of one of my professors' recommendation that I was able to transfer to Temple for one final year. That I'm pretty sure the only reason I got into Penn for grad school to begin with is because I was a first generation college student who'd made good. Not that admitting anything was much of an issue because I didn't have any in-depth conversations with anyone. I could never go to their parties because I was always working. I often couldn't go to department lectures and guest panels for the same reason.

Finally, in May, I had a meeting with Marisol Jett, the chair of the department, to discuss how the year had gone, one of the requirements of my first-year scholarship. I'd had a class with Marisol that semester, but I didn't know her well. She intimidated me. At first I told her everything was wonderful, I appreciated the opportunity, I was thankful for the assistance—all the crap I'd learned to say to the people who bankrolled things I could never afford otherwise over the years.

But she snorted and smiled and called bullshit. She was straight with me—told me I had to start attending lectures and going to departmental functions, had to start speaking in class and getting involved. When I tried to explain how behind I felt—trying to find a way to express it that didn't make it seem like they shouldn't have taken a chance on me—she told me that she'd read my written work and that I had no reason not to be speaking in class. And she wouldn't hear any more about it. In fact, she seemed to have a pretty good idea what was going on with me in general. Without my needing to say anything, she told me that if a job was interfering with my attending functions, then I needed to reconsider my schedule or think about a loan. She told me that my fellow classmates would benefit from my perspectives just as I had learned from theirs. And she told me something that shaped everything that happened after.

She told that I might think of my background and my unfamiliarity with academic discourses as weaknesses, but that I should, instead, think of them as the greatest tools I had to do innovative, personal, and meaningful work. She told me to trust my perspective, and it was the greatest gift she could have given me. That summer, I worked sixty-hour weeks when I could get them, doing demo at construction sites and working every night at the bar, saving up against the coming academic year when my fellowship would mean that I had to teach classes at Penn to get tuition remission and a stipend, and wouldn't be able to work as much.

My second year was better. Much better. I started speaking more in class and made a few friends. I didn't see them much, since I was still working nights at the bar, but I felt more comfortable there. My third year, I finished course work and began studying for my Masters exams, which meant deciding what I would specialize in and what kind of project I wanted to undertake for my dissertation, which would get me my PhD. I was swamped all the time, trying to read everything that might help me with my work.

Then, that spring, I met Richard. He wasn't the kind of person I'd ever been around before, and, while I can see it for what it was now, at the time it felt like a compliment that he was interested in me. He asked me questions about my research and seemed interested in some of the theorists I was writing about. He always said, "Thank god you have the good sense to write about something real instead of all that fiction." It was a compliment to me but a dig at studying English in the first place. And, as Ginger later pointed out, it wasn't really a compliment to me.

The thing about Richard was that he didn't take any effort. He was never uncertain or insecure. He never asked me where I wanted to go or what I wanted to do. He'd say something like, "Italian okay?" And when I said sure, he'd say, "I know you're going to love this place," but never asked me later if he was right. He made it clear, after that first embarrassing date, that he'd pay when we went out. It made me really uncomfortable, but he also made it clear that if I didn't go where he wanted to go, he'd go without me. And he was never rude about it. On the contrary, he was always exceedingly gracious, explaining things logically and making it seem like it was strange that I cared, since money was no big deal. Of course it isn't, if you have it.

And he'd make light of it when he paid, joke around about how he liked that he could be the first one to take me for sushi or to a Korean steak house, even as he laughed at the faces I made as I tried raw eel for the first time. Then we'd go back to his apartment and he'd tell me exactly how he wanted me to fuck him. He liked it hard and fast and clean, and he'd come with me behind him, catching his own release in his hand so it wouldn't get on the sheets. Something about the fact that he wanted *me* to fuck *him* made it feel less like I was a charity case or a kept toy. Ginger said that was a fucked-up way to think about it, but it made a difference. I'm not exactly sure why.

I never spent the night; Richard was always at the lab by 8:30 a.m. because he said any later than that and the best equipment was taken. He never came to my apartment, which he referred to as "the crack house," even though he'd never been in my neighborhood, just heard things on the subway and read things in the online police blotter, which he checked religiously, as he did the weather. He was one of those people who truly believed that forewarned was forearmed—he taught me that proverb, along with "he who pays the piper calls the tune," which he trotted out in response to my embarrassment when he sent his food back twice at a restaurant on a busy Saturday evening.

I saw Richard maybe twice a week, and honestly, I didn't think about it that much. If I wasn't at the library, I was at the bar, and if I had any found time I was hanging out with Ginger at the shop, reading behind the counter with the comforting buzz of tattoo machines inking the words into my memory. Ginger hated Richard. She only met him twice. It's not that I was trying to keep them apart... exactly. More that I didn't even think of them as existing in the same universe, much less as able to interact.

I brought her with me to meet Richard and some college friends of his for a drink. I was only stopping in for one drink because Richard had asked me to, and then I was on my way to work. Ginger was going to the show at the bar that night, so I convinced her to tag along. It was a mistake. Richard was running late and wasn't there when we arrived and the bar—excuse me, cocktail lounge—had a ten-dollar cover. Ginger offended the bouncer and amused me by muttering about it being a pay-to-play, and when we walked in it was clear we were extremely underdressed. I was wearing black jeans and boots and a red T-shirt with the sleeves ripped off because I made more tips the more skin I flashed, and though Ginger was wearing a tight black tube dress, the tattoos that cover every inch of her arms, legs, chest, and back made her the center of attention.

We got drinks (twelve-dollar martinis flavored with herbs and served in tiny glasses) and stood at a table, waiting for Richard. The place was crowded, so I didn't think much when Ginger's shoulders tensed. She was constantly getting people coming up to her to touch her tattoos and ask her what they meant—or, less flatteringly, tell her that she'd be so pretty if she didn't have them—so I'd grown accustomed to running interference. I swung around to sit next to her, but she waved me back across the table and started talking about a tattoo she'd done that afternoon.

Later on she told me she'd sat down just in time to hear a man with an upper crust-y New York accent say, "I can't wait to clap eyes on Richie's rough-trade trailer trash. Richie says he's like a jackhammer." The table behind us had been, of course, Richard's college friends. Needless to say, we didn't have much to talk about and I was relieved when it was time for us to leave so I could get to work.

Richard walked us out and kissed me. "Thanks for putting up with those guys," he said. "You know how it is. They were probably nervous around you because you're so hot." He winked at Ginger and she just walked away.

After a year and a half or so of dinners and fucking that I thought of as dating, though I guess I never used the word to Richard, I stopped by Richard's apartment on my way to work because I'd left a book there the night before. I stepped out of the elevator—Richard lived in one of those posh buildings in Center City with a doorman and everything—and jogged down the hallway. I don't remember why I didn't call first. As I turned the corner to knock on Richard's door, I saw him standing in front of it. At first, I thought I was catching him just getting home and had a moment of being thankful for my good timing. Then I saw the arms wrapped around his neck.

Richard was making out with another guy right in his doorway. I must've made a sound—coughed, or gasped, or said his name—because Richard turned around. What I remember most about the moment his eyes met mine is that there wasn't any surprise in them. Not even a microsecond of shock, or guilt, or shame. His hair was mussed and the collar of his shirt askew, and he just smiled at me.

"Hey, Dan," he said. "Not a great time."

The man he was with was the opposite of me in every way: a gorgeous little twink, thin and blond, with big blue eyes and apple cheeks and an arm slung around Richard's waist with the casualness of long habit.

I had no idea what to say or do and, suddenly, what seemed like the absolute most important thing was that Richard not have the slightest inkling that I cared at all.

"I need my book," I said, and my voice came out scratchy and high. The twink shifted a few inches to the left, so I could squeeze through the doorway.

At work that night, as I mechanically poured drinks and stared at the lights strobing over the crowd, I played the conversation Richard and I had over and over in my mind, trying to make sense of the pieces.

Things Richard said:

"Well, it isn't as if we're exclusive," and, at my shocked expression, "I'm sorry if you thought that, Daniel, but we never had that conversation."

"Don't look at me like I've betrayed you. I would never cheat on a boyfriend, but when did we ever decide that's what we were?"

Socking me softly in the shoulder, "Come now, if you were my boyfriend you would've had to spring for a real birthday present." In fact, I'd spent more money on Richard's gift, a first American edition of John Dalton's *A New System of Chemical Philosophy*, than on any other gift I'd ever given.

Months later, I learned that I was about the only one at Penn who didn't know Richard and I hadn't been exclusive. Months later, I learned that Richard had been fucking his way through the entire city of Philadelphia and everyone had known. Months later, too, I realized that I hadn't ever even liked Richard that much, that the reason I'd never noticed that he saw other people or cared that we spent so little time together was because I was fairly indifferent to his company. Months later, I mostly felt incredibly stupid to have it pointed out so clearly that I had no idea what it was to be in a relationship, and quite ridiculous to realize how easy it was to be living a life completely different than the one of the person in bed beside you. But that night, I just felt shocked.

And it was probably because I felt shocked that I didn't pay better attention as I was leaving work and walking to the subway. The bar paid us in cash—one of many reasons I liked working there—and I had years of experience being careful walking around with it late at night. It usually helped that I didn't look like I had anything to steal: shitty old iPod, disposable pay-as-you-go phone, and my keys.

They might have seen me move the cash from my wallet to my front pocket outside the bar, they might have seen a bulge in my pocket and hoped it was a nice phone, or they might have just jumped me randomly. I don't know. But when I was a block away from the subway entrance, its awning awash in friendly light, two guys grabbed me and dragged me into an alley where a third man waited with a knife. They punched me in the face so I knew they were serious, and threw me against the wall where the guy with the knife leaned, looking on dispassionately. Gang initiation? Debt paid? I don't know. They found the money in seconds and broke a few ribs anyway. They shoved my face against the dirty wall and even took the time to rifle through my wallet, dropping it when they found nothing worth taking. Took one look at my ancient iPod and shitty phone and didn't even bother once they had the cash in hand.

I called Ginger and she came and picked me up, silent tears running down her face as she drove me back to her place and put me to bed under her covers.

And when I told Ginger about Richard the next morning, she said I should go to the police.

"Nah," I said. "I don't want to deal with it. What's the point anyway? They were probably just kids."

"No," she deadpanned. "Not about the mugging. About Richard. You should see if you can file an incident report for rampant douchebaggery," because she is the best friend in the history of the world. We both started laughing, which killed my ribs, so I tried to push Ginger, who, in trying to dodge me, fell off her chair. A regular Three Stooges routine.

I had nightmares about it for months afterward—no surprise there—but they went away for the most part, and I hadn't had one in two years.

So why the fuck am I having them again, especially starting on a night when I was really happy? My brain supplies a flash flood of answers, most of which are automatic analysis: you feel like Rex stole something from you, you feel like your world has been turned on its side, everything's collapsing, etc.

Before I can settle on any one of them, I turn the volume on the TV up and click over to the food channel that Rex mentioned liking, and I fall asleep to the sound of chiffonading, creaming, emulsifying, and zesting— or so the narration tells me.

THE NEXT morning, I wake up with the television still on and am greeted by a plump, motherly looking chef making some kind of breakfast feast of challah french toast and something called shirred eggs. My stomach gives a growl and I fumble around for the tiny coffeepot. I didn't eat much yesterday. My stomach was in knots every time I thought about my fight with Rex.

There are two sessions I should attend at the conference this morning, but I can't do it. I'm exhausted from all my socializing yesterday, from the fight with Rex, from all of it. And I can't help but think that I owe Rex an explanation. That, like Ginger said, I need to just tell him some shit about me and let him decide what to do with it.

And I think, maybe, I need to have the conversation with him that I never had with Richard. I'm not interested in Jay, but if Rex thinks I am then that must feel shitty. I never really thought of myself as jealous, but when I had that moment of thinking that maybe Rex used to date Jay and that's how he knew Jay was gay, my stomach definitely felt the way people always describe jealousy feeling in books. Besides, what if he thinks I don't care and he meets someone else? And, with that thought, I'm back on the jealousy wagon. The idea of Rex smiling his soft smile at another man makes me want to punch through the hotel wall. The idea of him cooking dinner in his kitchen with another man or finishing another man's food makes me want to throttle someone—anyone. And at the idea of Rex kissing someone else, black creeps into my periphery.

I fumble with my phone and call him again. Again, there's no answer. He's really mad. I know Ginger's right and he might just be busy, but I can't believe he could be so busy he missed every call and couldn't call me back. That's just not Rex. He has to be avoiding me on purpose. And I guess he has every right to be mad. I did yell at him when he was just trying to be nice.

So, that's that, then. I'm going to skip the morning sessions and just get the hell out of here. Go home.

Wow, I can't believe I just thought of *Holiday* as home. But, actually, the picture that flashed in my head as I made my decision wasn't of Holiday, or of my shitty apartment. It was of Rex's warm cabin, the windows glowing with sunlight or firelight, the full kitchen where Rex looks so hot cooking, the cozy living room with Marilyn snoozing on the hearth, and the bedroom where Rex makes me feel things I've never felt before.

Christ, I'm such a sap. Ginger would be grinning so hard right now if she could see this train of thought; my brothers would beat the shit out of me.

I throw my stuff into my duffel, not bothering about my wrinkled jacket, pull on some jeans, and splash the weak, hotel-room coffee into one of their to-go cups. And then I do exactly that. I need to talk to Rex as soon as possible.

Chapter 9

October

I'VE BEEN psyching myself up the whole drive home, singing along to
a tape that was in a John Hiatt case but turned out to be the Pet Shop
Boys—score!—and I've played the whole apology over and over in my
head like it's a conference paper: introduction, claims, supporting
evidence, conclusion, questions.

Driving through Detroit this morning made me homesick for
Philly. I almost called Ginger just to hear a familiar accent, but it seems
like every time I've talked to her lately she's ended up listening to me
whine, so I just turned up the volume and sang along, speeding as fast
as my poor little car would take me. I mean, the best thing about
Michigan so far is that the highway speed limit is seventy.

Around 2:00 p.m., ten miles from Rex's house, I think practical
thoughts like that I should go home and shower, or call again, or get
something to eat, but I know if I stop to do any of that stuff I'll lose
my nerve, so I just drive straight to his house, hoping he's home. My
stomach flips in relief when I see his truck in the driveway. I barely
register that his shades are down when they're usually open to let in
the sun.

When I get out of the car, I'm jittery from nerves and too much
caffeine. I knock on the door, but he doesn't answer. I'm pretty sure
he's home because I can hear Marilyn barking from inside and there's
nowhere he'd walk to on a Sunday without her. At least, I don't think.
But I guess I don't really know. I try the door and the knob turns in my
hand. I'm about to just push the door open and walk in, guns blazing,
yelling that I'm sorry, but pictures of Richard making out with another
man flash through my mind. What if I walk in on Rex with someone
else? I seriously could not stand that.

I'm not sure what to do. I knock again, noticing for the first time
that Rex doesn't have a doorbell. Then I hear Marilyn whining at the
door. What if Rex is hurt? What if someone broke in and shot him or he
passed out from carbon monoxide poisoning or something? That

happened to the mom of a guy I worked with at the bar. They just found her sitting in her armchair like she was watching TV, only she'd been dead for three days.

I push the door open even as my logical mind tells me there's not going to be carbon monoxide in a cabin in the woods, nor is there likely to have been an armed robbery. Still, the fear of Rex lying somewhere, hurt, is stronger than the fear of finding him with someone else. As the door swings open, Marilyn darts through it. I've never seen her do that before; she's so well trained. I swing around to run after her, not wanting to have to tell Rex I lost his dog on top of everything else, but she just pees on a bush by Rex's garage and trots right back to me.

I walk inside tentatively, feeling like I'm about to find blood-streaked bodies lying all over the house like in a slasher movie or *In Cold Blood*.

"Rex," I call. "It's Daniel. Are you here?"

Marilyn runs toward the bedroom, where the door is closed. Maybe he's sick?

"Rex?" I say at the door.

"Daniel?" a weak voice says from inside. I open the door and the bedroom is dark, the curtains pulled shut and taped together. There's a lump on the bed and I walk over to it.

"Rex," I say again, "are you okay?" I know it's Rex under there, but for some reason, all I can think of is how my brothers used to hide under the covers and jump out and scare me.

I reach for the bedside lamp, but Rex grabs my hand. He pulls the covers down slowly and I can see that he looks tense.

"Hi," he says. "I thought you were in Detroit." His voice sounds strained.

"Oh, yeah, well, I came back early. I wanted to talk to you. Are you sick? What's wrong?"

He smiles a little shakily.

"Sorry I didn't answer when you called. I just get these headaches." He makes a motion like he's waving it away and pats the bed next to him. I sink down and run my hand over his back.

"Well, I hear orgasms are good for headaches," I tease, leaning down to kiss him.

He winces.

"Mmm, I don't think so just now."

Now that I'm close to him I can see that the sexy wrinkle between his brows is deeper than I've ever seen it, and that his face is tight with pain. The bed smells warm, like he's been lying here a long time. Oh shit.

"Do you get migraines?" I ask him, keeping my voice very low and even.

"Yeah," he scrapes out.

God, that sucks. When Ginger gets them she's in so much pain she can barely even cry because it makes it hurt more.

"Shit," I say. "What can I do? Do you have medicine? Can I get you anything?"

"Can you take Marilyn for a walk?" he asks. "I let her out to pee this morning, but—"

"Yeah, of course. But what can I do for you? Do you have medicine?"

He mmhmms softly. "In the bathroom. But I can't keep it down."

I get up slowly and quietly walk to the bathroom, since light and sound are clearly not Rex's friends right now.

I find the medicine sitting on the sink in the bathroom, and the slight sour smell makes it clear that he's been sick in here. In the kitchen, I find a jar of applesauce and cut the pills into tiny pieces, hiding them in a spoonful of applesauce.

"Can you sit up a little?"

Rex drags himself up.

"Give me your wrist," I tell him, sitting next to him on the bed. With one hand, I squeeze the pressure point on his wrist that should help him feel less nauseated. "Try and swallow this," I say, holding up the spoon in the other. He makes a face, but swallows it. I put the spoon down and use my hand on the pressure point in his other wrist.

"Close your eyes," I say softly, and I keep the pressure on his wrists and start telling him about the conference. Just rambling on to distract him.

I tell him how Detroit reminded me a little of North Philly, with the big, crumbling stone churches and the streets arcing around them instead of laid out in a grid. I tell him how cool I thought it was when this badass old professor got asked a convoluted question by a young guy trying to prove how smart he was and she paused for a second and then told him that she wasn't really interested in that conversation because it didn't seem to have value to anyone but academics, and how I wish that someday I could be brave enough to call someone on their bullshit like that. I tell him that I watched the Food Network for the first time and want to watch it with him so he can tell me what everything is. I don't tell him how sorry I am for yelling the other night, though. I'll do that later.

Little by little, I feel him relax; his jaw unclenches and the rigid set of his shoulders loosens. I lean down and kiss him on the forehead.

"I'm going to take Marilyn out. I'll be back soon. You just rest." I tuck the blanket back up around him and close the bedroom door.

It's chilly, so I grab Rex's quilted flannel coat from the hook beside the door.

"Your dad's sick, huh?" I say to Marilyn when we get outside, and she barks in answer and bounds around me. I walk for a while, breathing in the clean-smelling air, and Marilyn runs off in front of me, scratches at something, then runs back, like she's scouting ahead. With every breath, I smell the combination of cedar, wood smoke, and musk on Rex's jacket and I pull it tighter around myself as if he were walking with me.

When we get back, a much happier Marilyn curls up in front of the fireplace. It feels a little cold in here, so I decide to light it. The only fires I've ever made have been by squirting gasoline in garbage cans in abandoned lots or in the alley behind my dad's shop if we had to burn garbage, but I've seen Rex do it a few times. How hard can it be?

Hunh. Kind of hard. Every time I get the kindling going, it burns up before it lights the rest of the fire. Finally, with some maneuvering that almost loses me the skin on the back of my right hand, I get a pretty respectable blaze going. Then I go back to check on Rex.

I sit down next to him on the bed. I don't want to wake him, but I want to see how bad he feels—if I should be getting him a prescription for something. I stroke his hair back and he whimpers. Poor Rex. He looks really awful.

"Rex," I whisper softly.

"Hey," he says.

"What can I do? Do you think you can keep any food down? I could get you something to eat?"

He laughs weakly. "I don't need food poisoning on top of a migraine," he says. "The pills are helping. Could you...." He trails off, like he wasn't going to say anything.

"What?"

"Maybe just stay with me a little while?"

"Okay," I say, "sure," and I kick off my shoes. Rex scoots over a little and looks up at me. His eyes are uncertain behind the pain, and I realize we haven't talked about anything yet. But it's not the time. I slip my jeans off and slide under the covers, careful not to jostle him. I lie on my back next to him, not quite touching, like the night we were at my house, only this time it's physical pain I want to protect him from. I hate that I don't know what else to do for him. That there *isn't* anything I can do. There wasn't that night at my house, either. I hate feeling helpless and for a second, I'm almost mad at Rex for making me feel that way. Then he reaches his arm out, encouraging me to rest my head on his shoulder, and my anger melts away. It isn't really at him anyway.

I lay my head on his shoulder and stroke his stomach lightly. He squeezes me a little, lets out a sigh and seems to relax. I listen to his slow breathing, my mind drifting.

When I wake up, it's dark and, for a second, I have no idea where I am. I tense, but my hand feels the warmth of Rex's body next to me and I relax. I tilt my chin up and kiss the underside of Rex's chin.

"Hi," he says.

"You're awake."

"Just for a minute."

"How do you feel?"

"A bit better. It's the tail end of it now, I think. It started on Friday night, and they don't usually last more than two days." He yawns. "I have to piss like you wouldn't believe."

Rex pushes himself up, his muscles trembling, and swings his legs over the side of the bed to heave himself upright. As Rex shakily makes his way to the bathroom, it gets me right in the gut: I want to take care of him. Not because I think he's weak, but because I care about him. It's so obvious. Ginger's been saying it to me for years, but I've never—not once—actually believed her because I've never felt it before. Every time I asked my brothers for help they gave me shit about it. Anytime I asked for help from someone at school, they made me feel stupid or like I wasn't trying hard enough. And the few times people offered help, it was obvious they expected something in return. Even my father's gruff attempts at taking care of my car just made me feel awkward, because he so clearly resented them.

And Ginger... well, Ginger always just felt like an exception. I wanted to take care of her, of course, but, deep down, it felt a lot like paying a debt. She saved me the day I wandered into her shop. Somehow, she saw me differently than my brothers or my teachers and the other kids at school did. Not as a fuckup or a loser or a pansy. She really saw me, and so of *course* I felt indebted to her. I felt like each small thing I could do for her might go a little way toward paying her back for giving me a chance to *be* something other than a fuckup and a loser.

It's not that way anymore. At least, I don't think it is. But it segued from that to true, deep friendship so slowly that I can't pinpoint when it happened exactly. And I've never felt it with anyone else. Definitely not with Richard, who would have viewed the idea of *me* taking care of *him* as absurd since, as he saw it, I didn't have anything I could offer him except a hard fuck, which, clearly, was a service others could provide. And other friends? I don't know. They never seemed to need taking care of—at least not from me.

But now, seeing Rex curled up in that big bed, struggling to get to the bathroom, all I feel is an itchiness in my palms to reach out and help him; a manic desire to somehow take his pain into my own body because I'd rather feel it than have to watch him suffer.

"You sticking around for a bit?"

Rex's voice startles me. I look up at him. He looks better. The tension is mostly gone from his face, though he still looks a little out of it.

"Yeah," I say, "if you want me to."

Rex smiles, but he looks a little sad. Was that the wrong answer?

"I mean, unless you just want some quiet, for your head," I amend. He pulls me gently toward him, hugging me to his broad chest.

"No, I want you here," he says, and I relax at the rumble of it through his chest. "The pills really helped. How'd you know what to do?"

"Ginger gets them—migraines. She always throws up and the only way she can keep a pill down is with the applesauce. She says it's like the migraine wants to take over, so it makes her brain reject the pill, but if she can't see the pill in the applesauce, it tricks the migraine and lets her swallow it. I think that's what her mom told her when she was younger, I mean. And the pressure points really help her. She's a die-hard acupuncture believer. Her hands get really cramped from holding the tattoo machine all day, and her back hurts from sitting bent over, so she goes to this guy in Chinatown who's done acupuncture for, like, sixty years. I swear to god, you look at this guy and you'd think he was forty, but he's seventy-five. Anyway, she says it really helps."

"Maybe I should try it," Rex says.

"Maybe. I read that for a while in the seventies, it got a lot of press because in China doctors were doing open-heart surgery using acupuncture instead of anesthesia. I asked the guy in Chinatown about it and he said that that was a hoax they did for attention when Nixon visited China, and that the patient was getting morphine, but that it's actually completely possible to render a part of the body pain-free using acupuncture if the person doing it is skilled enough."

"I really love that," Rex says.

"Yeah, it's pretty amazing," I say. "Especially since so many people end up dying after surgery from the anesthesia even when the surgery goes fine."

"No, I mean, I love how you tell me all this information about stuff. I love how you always have some fact about something."

"I don't mean to be a know-it-all," I say. My brothers hated when I'd bring up things I'd read, so after a while, I just shut up about it. But sometimes, I'd think it would be something they'd definitely be interested in, so I'd tell them. It never worked out how I thought it would, inevitably leading to them calling me a know-it-all or a smartass.

"Did I say that?" Rex asks, gently, tilting my chin up.

"No," I say softly. "Listen, Rex. I'm sorry about the other night. How I yelled at you. I *should* have thought to ask you fix the table. I'm just... not used to having anyone to.... I'm just used to looking out for myself, you know?"

He nods.

"I know. I think I get it. You've never had someone help you who didn't make you pay for it somehow. I shouldn't have walked out like that. I just felt stupid. I'd already made such an ass of myself acting like a jealous caveman about your colleague. I'm sorry about that."

He kisses me on the cheek, his lips a little shaky against my skin.

"So, you watched the Food Network, huh?" he says, taking my hand and walking into the living room.

"You heard that?"

He nods, grabbing the remote and flopping down on the couch, pulling me down next to him. He turns to the Food Network and I settle against his shoulder.

AFTER TWO episodes of a cooking competition show, I'm a total Food Network convert and my stomach is growling so loudly that I can hear it over the television.

"Can I make something?" I ask Rex, gesturing toward the kitchen.

"Sure." He stands up with me.

"You can just stay here and rest," I tell him. "I got it."

"No, I'll come."

"Man, you really do think I'm going to poison you, huh?"

"No. But I'll keep you company."

I don't believe him, but I shrug and walk into the kitchen, thinking I'll just throw a frozen pizza in the oven or open some soup. But when I look in the freezer and open Rex's cupboards, I don't find anything.

"You don't have any food," I say.

"I have a ton of food," Rex says, chuckling. "I just don't have anything encased in a block of ice or preserved to the point that it could be space food."

I glare at him.

"Here, let me do it," he says.

"No, no, I got this," I say, pushing him back down onto the stool by the shoulders. I totally do not got this.

Rex smiles and puts his arms around my waist, spreading his legs to draw me in to him. He kisses me and then leans his forehead against my chest. Then he stands up and opens the refrigerator, pulling things out.

"I'm going to show you how to make spaghetti," he says. "Okay?"

"Great."

Rex puts me to work cutting up a green pepper and some tomatoes.

"I'll teach you how to make the pasta yourself another time—fresh pasta is the best. But for now let's just use premade before you starve to death."

Rex bustles around the kitchen making a salad and putting water on to boil. I consider the pepper, trying to figure out how to explain why I got so mad before I left for Detroit.

"Listen, about what you said Thursday night," I say, concentrating on cutting up the pepper and not slicing my fingers off in the process. Rex looks up. "About how I won't accept your help?"

"Mmhmm."

"Well, a couple years after I met her, Ginger bought this motorcycle from a guy on Craigslist. She'd gone down to the guy's house and looked at it and everything and she said it seemed to run fine, so she bought it. Then, like, a week later, the thing totally died. Ginger asked me to look at it for her and I did—I'm not as good as my dad or my brothers, but I know enough to tell that the engine was total garbage and the gas tank was leaking. I mean, it's a miracle the thing didn't throw a spark and ignite the whole gas tank. Anyway, Ginger tried to message the guy through Craigslist, but, of course, he'd taken his profile down once the bike sold.

"So, Ginger asked me if I would go with her to talk to the guy. When we got there, the dude was like, 'Wow, I'm so sorry to hear that. It was running fine for me. You probably rode the clutch or something.' You know, because she's a woman, he thinks he can make it seem like it's her fault because she's not good with a bike or something, which is bullshit because Ginge's a great rider, she just doesn't know about mechanics. Anyway, the guy was a douchebag, but I made him give her her money back and everything."

"What did you do to him?" Rex asks suspiciously.

"Nothing!" I say, still addressing the cutting board. "I didn't hurt him, I just scared him. Told him what kind of loser I thought he was for ripping someone off like that. Anyway, that's not the point. The point is that I was really happy that Ginger asked me to help her, you know, because it meant that she trusted me and that we were really friends because you'd only ask a friend to do that. And, so, my point is that you were like me and I was like Ginger, only I didn't ask you, so it was like we weren't friends, and that's my fault because I didn't totally realize what was going on. But I do now. You know?"

Rex puts his hand over mine, taking my knife. I've cut the green pepper into such tiny pieces that it's almost pulp.

"That's wrong, isn't it?" I say, pointing to the green pepper.

Rex doesn't even look at the cutting board. He cups my face in his hands, forcing me to look at him.

"You're saying you understand that I want to help you because I care?"

"Um. Yeah," I say.

Rex looks at me seriously.

"You helped me today," he says. "You took care of me. Do you think less of me because I let you?"

"Of course not. I never said—"

"You never said it, but it's clear. Somewhere along the line you learned that it's a failure to accept help. That it makes you weak. Right?"

I try to look away, but he's still holding my face. I don't think anyone's ever looked at me so hard.

"Right?" he says again.

"Right," I say, and my voice cracks. I clear my throat. "But I know it's not true. That's what made me think of it: how much I wanted to take care of you today."

"You know it's not true here," Rex says, tapping my forehead. "But it'll take a while to believe it."

I shrug, but I keep looking at his beautiful eyes.

"Well, then I guess we'll just have to keep looking out for each other until we both believe it, huh?" Rex says.

"Okay," I tell him.

"Okay," he says, and he kisses me matter-of-factly, like we've just sealed a deal.

"Um, did I mess that up?" I ask again, pointing to the pepper.

"Nope," Rex says. "It's perfect for the sauce. It'll just cook faster now."

He shows me how to sauté the green pepper, onion, garlic, and tomatoes for the base of the sauce and mix oil and vinegar for salad dressing.

Rex nudges me with his shoulder, teasing me about being distractible. Apparently, I missed whatever he just said because I was watching him bend over to take the bread out of the oven. Rex's teasing is always gentle, which makes it feel like a whole different animal than my brothers' take-no-prisoners brand of humiliation.

"How are you feeling?" I ask him as we sit down to eat.

"I feel pretty damn good," he says, looking at me. I meant his head, but I don't think that's what he's talking about. I smile at him, but now that I'm not distracted by cooking, my mind is racing with questions. Should I tell him about Jay asking me out, or will that just give him more of a reason to be jealous? Should I tell him about Richard? Ginger said that's what you do when you... date someone. Is that what we're doing?

I shove spaghetti into my mouth until I can decide, but when I look up, Rex is looking at me, but isn't eating.

"'S good," I say with my mouth full.

"Something wrong?" Rex asks.

"No, I just. I was thinking, when I was in Detroit, that...." That what? That I should tell him what happened the last time I thought I was dating someone? That I should tell him how pathetic I am? Ugh.

"So, the main character in my favorite book is named Richard," I say.

"*The Secret History*?" Rex asks.

"Yeah! How'd you—oh." Right, the book had fallen out of my pants the night we fucked against the tree. "But how'd you know it was my favorite?"

"It was worn," he says. "And most of your other books looked like you bought them used, but not like they'd been read that many times. *The Secret History* had its corners all rounded, like it'd been handled a lot."

Jesus Christ, he's observant.

"Well, so, when I was in grad school, I met this guy and—this is so stupid—his name was Richard. And I had this idiotic thought that maybe he'd be like Richard in the book." I trail off, embarrassed that I admitted this.

"It's not stupid," he says, taking my hand. "It's actually incredibly sweet."

"It's nerdy," I say.

"Yeah, maybe a little. And… he wasn't?"

"Ah, no."

Rex nods and starts to eat slowly, as I talk. I tell him about meeting Richard and about how things were between us. Rex keeps eating, but his left hand is clenched into a fist where it rests on his knee, and he keeps squeezing it tighter and tighter every time I say something he doesn't like. When I get to the part about Ginger overhearing Rex's friends calling me trash, he makes a sound like a growl in the back of his throat, but stops himself from interrupting me. When I tell him about walking in on Richard kissing another man, Rex's face falls and he grits his teeth. He looks furious.

"I would never do that to you," Rex insists, his eyes on fire. He looks like he's about to say something else, but I just wanted to get it off my chest. I don't want to rehash my own pathetic history.

I push the serving bowl toward Rex.

"You should finish it. I bet you haven't eaten much lately."

He smiles gratefully and puts the last serving of pasta on his plate.

"Yeah, I can never eat when I have them. Poor Marilyn," he says. "She thought I was dying or something. She kept jumping up on the bed, trying to check on me, but I couldn't stand the movement, so I shut the door. She was whining all night, trying to get in."

I know the sound. It was the same sound she made the night I hit her. Remembering the way she lay on the ground, so helpless, makes me shiver.

"Hey," I say, "you never told me how you knew what to do for Marilyn."

"What, with her leg?"

He starts to clear the plates, but I wave him off, putting a hand on his shoulder to keep him sitting. I carry the plates to the sink and start to do the dishes.

"Animals used to follow my mom home all the time," Rex says. "There was always a dog sleeping outside our door, or some cats living under the porch. One day, I got home from school and found a turkey in our yard. Dogs were what she liked best, though, so whenever one followed her home or showed up at our door, she'd let it in and feed it. And then it'd just stay. The first one we had was Buster, like Buster Keaton. Sweet dog. Big hound. He used to sit next to my mom at the table and rest his chin on her lap. But usually, they'd live outside because we weren't home all day. They'd come home busted up from getting in fights with other dogs, or sometimes hit by cars."

I wince at that.

"So, my mom'd fix them up. She showed me how. It's just like people, really, only you have to make sure the dogs don't lick their cuts." He smiles absently.

"How many did you have at once, then?" I ask, imagining his mom as the Pied Piper of Hamlin, a trail of dogs trotting behind her.

"Only one or two at once," Rex said, and he gazes out the window sadly. "We could never take them with us when we moved. And we moved so often. Used to break my fucking heart, but my mom said that things come into your life when you need them. And there would always be another dog the next place we moved. She was right about that, anyway."

He still looks upset, though.

"Do you think that's true? That things come into your life when you need them?"

"Nah," he says, "not really. And, besides, even if it is true, she never said anything about leaving them. I would have dreams for weeks after we moved, where I was in the car with my mom and the dogs were all running behind us, baying, not understanding why we'd leave them behind. I mean, what about them? We came into their lives when they needed it, sure, but then we just left."

As if on cue, Marilyn comes into the kitchen, sniffing under the table for a snack. Rex bends down and puts his arms around her, squeezing her and then scratching her head. She plops down on the floor next to him and he leaves a hand on her head.

"Such a good girl," he says fondly.

"But, then," he says in an unfamiliar voice. It's deeper than usual, and a bit forced. "Then I think about you—how you came into my life that night. You and Marilyn. And, I don't know. Maybe there's some truth to it after all."

THE FIRE is dying as Rex and I lie together on the couch. We've been watching old movies I've never seen before, Rex providing color commentary.

"Did your mom know you were gay?" I ask when he tells me about some of the Hollywood actors who were gay. Whenever he talks about his mom he gets a wistful look on his face. I wish I had such fond memories.

"Yeah. I remember when I was thirteen or fourteen we were having a Tennessee Williams movie night and she asked who I liked better, Brick or Stanley—Paul Newman or Marlon Brando, that is."

"Oh, *Cat on a Hot Tin Roof* and *Streetcar Named Desire*?"

"Yeah. She was casual about it and I remember thinking that she talked about how beautiful the actresses were all the time. How sexy Marilyn Monroe was. How she loved Audrey Hepburn's voice and Elizabeth Taylor's eyes and Jayne Mansfield's mouth. How Gene Tierney was the most beautiful woman in the world. And she talked about the men too, of course. So, I didn't think much of it."

"Who did you like better?"

"Paul Newman. She never mentioned it again, but I think she was kind of glad I was gay."

"Why?"

"She wanted to *be* those actresses. She wanted to be the star, you know? And the women were always the stars. The men were just... catalysts. Is that the right word? So, I think she was glad that she wasn't competing with other women for my... I don't know, admiration? I'm not sure how to say it."

He shakes his head, looking flustered.

"After that, she talked about the men like she was teaching me about men in general. You know? A James Dean was someone to watch out for. Beautiful, but he'd steal your heart and drag you down with him. A Robert

Mitchum or a Gregory Peck were husband material, but James Dean was for having an affair. The guy she dated when we first got to California was a Humphrey Bogart, she said. Not handsome exactly, but attractive in some way you couldn't quite put your finger on."

"So did you want a James Dean or a Gregory Peck?"

"Hmm," Rex says. "I always had a thing for Montgomery Clift. He was the nice guy who got a bad rap. Handsome, but smart too. Maybe even a little bit... complicated?"

He runs his thumb over my cheekbone, and I can't help but wonder if that's what he sees when he looks at me: complicated. But *too* complicated?

"So, it was mostly you and your mom, huh?" I say, trying to concentrate on Rex again.

"Yeah," Rex says, that wistful look back again. "When it was just the two of us, I barely stuttered at all. We'd watch movies and act out all the parts. I don't think she even really got that I was shy since she never saw me interact with people. She thought I was smart. And I was a responsible kid, so she never asked if I had my homework done or anything. Just assumed I did. I cleaned the house; later I cooked. So, she just thought I was no trouble. A good kid."

I nod, imagining Rex as a little boy acting out scenes from movies with his mom. The picture that keeps asserting itself, though, is Rex as a firm-chinned Sam Spade type, even as a kid.

"She was always finding things at work to bring home for me," Rex continues. "That's how I started fixing stuff, actually. She would bring home junk that was broken and I'd mess around with it. She worked as a secretary for an office supply company for a while when we were in Houston. So she'd bring clocks and staplers and microwaves that got damaged and I'd take it all apart and put it back together again. I would spend hours on it. Once, for Mother's Day, I made her an alarm clock that hooked up to a miniature coffee machine and would start the coffee brewing like one of the expensive ones with a built-in timer. Turned out to be a bad idea, though, because she could never remember not to slam her hand down on the snooze button, which would make a big mess."

"Wow," I say. That's pretty impressive for a kid.

"And anyway, she always had boyfriends she spent a lot of time with. From work, usually. I don't know; later I figured out that most of them were probably married. Then, once we moved to California, they were always guys who wanted to pretend she didn't have a kid. I'd stay in my room when they came over, or just wander around."

Rex trails off, seeming embarrassed that he said so much. I smile and lean over until I'm kind of lying on top of him, my head on his shoulder. He starts running his hands up and down my back, then up into my hair and down over my ass. I can feel his cock start to fill beneath me, and I lean up for a kiss. It's an amazing feeling, having my whole body in contact with Rex's. We kiss lazily, just enjoying it. Rex pulls my shirt off and kisses my neck softly, his warm mouth moving over every inch of my skin. I lean down and lick a line up his throat to his stubbled chin, nipping at it. Rex moans and starts to sit up, his muscles tensed.

In her spot in front of the dying fire, Marilyn perks up. At first I think she's staring at us, which is slightly awkward. But then I hear the door open. Rex pushes himself up, swearing.

"Get your ass out here and fuck me hello, Rexroth!" a voice booms into the near-dark of the cabin.

Chapter 10

October

IN THE time it takes Rex to struggle to his feet and pull me up by my armpits when he displaces me, the following thoughts run through my mind in no discernible order.

1. Rex's boyfriend just got home. Rex has a boyfriend. Partner? Lover? Whatever. Some dude just told Rex to fuck him, ergo: bad news.

2. You are such a fucking idiot. How could you possibly trust him? All the sweet talk, gentle touches, and soft kisses were just to mess with you, or to get in your pants, or both. Oh god, you let him fuck you. You told him about Colin. About Richard. Seriously, could you possibly be more fucking gullible?

3. Rex is short for Rexroth? How did I not know that?

Then a fourth thought fights in, and it's in a voice that sounds a lot like Ginger's. It says, *Don't jump to conclusions. You don't know what's going on yet. Give Rex a chance to explain. Rex is not Richard.* But that thought doesn't have a chance because Rex walks over and flips on the lights and this guy is... beautiful.

His face is Scandinavian perfection and he's dressed like a model. He has high, sharp cheekbones, a perfectly straight nose, ashy eyebrows over blue-gray eyes, a square jaw and delicate chin, and a pouty mouth. He's about my height, but he seems taller. His blond hair is longish and tousled and he has a tiny beauty mark over his lip and another next to his eyebrow, as if he were the model for beauty mark piercings. He's stunning and I hate him on sight.

I can't fucking believe it. I confess to Rex how I found Richard with another man; Rex's... someone shows up right after. It really couldn't be clearer. If I were teaching the book of my life in class right now, I would use this moment as an example of irony. I've got to get the fuck out of here.

"Oops," he says, looking at me, his eyes sparkling. "Didn't know you had company."

"You didn't see the car out front?" Rex asks, tilting his head. The model gets a mischievous expression on his face and smirks at Rex, then looks back and forth between us.

"Maybe," he says. "But I figured it was yours. Not like you ever have any company except me."

His voice is deeper than what I'd expect from someone so pretty. He's not feminine exactly, just kind of androgynous in a rock star/model sort of way. He doesn't seem fazed in the least. I realize I've been staring at him with my shirt off, so I extract it from where Rex shoved it between the couch cushions and pull it on. It's inside out, but I refuse to acknowledge that. I can only hope that my expression right now is the unimpressed one I give the lead singers of bands who assume I know who they are, the rich guys who slum at the bars in my neighborhood, sure they can pick up anyone, and the students who think they're getting one over on me.

My brain has kicked into survival mode and all that matters right now is making it out of this house without either Rex or this guy realizing that they've had any effect on me whatsoever. Show nothing. Reveal nothing.

"Hi, Marilyn," the man says, looking right past me. Marilyn trots over to him and lets herself be pet. He bends down and rubs her belly. So, if he knows Marilyn, he's been around pretty recently—at least since this summer when Rex rescued us.

"Don't be a dick, Will," Rex says. "This is Daniel." Rex holds an arm out to me, but his eyes are anxious.

I intentionally pause before walking slowly over to them.

"Hey," I say, nodding and holding out a hand to Will. Will's grip is strong and his calloused hands don't quite match his pretty face.

"This is my friend, Will," Rex says, his emphasis on *friend* a little too deliberate. "Will," Rex says pointedly, "I didn't know you were coming to town."

Will seems to forget I'm there the second he lets go of my hand. He studies Rex's face and gives him a long once-over.

"Did you have a migraine?" he asks, and my heart starts beating in my ears. This guy *knows* Rex. There's no way they're just friends, or even fuck buddies.

"I'm fine," Rex says, waving him away. He puts his hand on the back of my neck. "Daniel took good care of me."

The warmth from Rex's hand and his words helps a little, but he's laying it on pretty thick. The last thing I want to do is leave Rex alone with Will, but my instincts are screaming at me to get out of here. I can't stick around, not even to see what's going on. I've got to get away before I do something I can't live down, like cry or give this Will guy the satisfaction of seeing that he's gotten to me. I awkwardly pat Rex on the hip and duck out from under his hand, pulling my shoes on.

"Daniel, don't go," Rex says.

"Oh, no, well, I have to teach in the morning, and it's getting late, so. I'm gonna head home."

"No, worries, Dan," Will says cheerily, "I can take it from here."

I stand quickly. This guy's stupid perfect face—I want to smash it with my fist. Rather than take a step back like most guys do when I'm in fighting mode, though, Will just smirks at me lazily and yawns. Rex puts a hand on my shoulder and turns me around, no doubt sensing bad energy between us.

But he's not looking at me like he's pissed that I want to punch his friend in the face. He's looking at me with satisfaction. Like I finally did something right. Like maybe he likes the idea that I'm jealous. Oh shit, I'm so fucking jealous.

"Later," I toss over my shoulder at perfect, stupid Will's face. Then I fist Rex's T-shirt in my hand and drag him down toward me, kissing him hard and deep. When I let him go, he sways, looking a little stunned. I smile at him and walk past Will out the front door.

AT LEAST I didn't have the nightmare last night. Because I didn't sleep at all.

My heart was pounding with adrenaline the whole drive home, but within about a minute my satisfaction at having laid claim to Rex in front of whoever the hell this Will guy is faded to stomach-clenching anxiety and I cursed myself for choosing a dramatic exit over sticking around and finding out what the story was. Those kinds of exits always seem so satisfying when I read them in books, but I guess with an omniscient narrator no one really needs to stick around for the down and dirty parts.

Finally, around six in the morning, I drag myself out of bed and stand in a hot shower, deciding to get some coffee and walk around for a bit in the hopes of shaking off the stressful weekend and everything to do with Rex and Will before having to act like a grown-up all day. I shake out my gray button-down and pull on gray corduroys and my wingtips. I really need to go shopping. I only have about ten articles of professional clothing and I've been swapping them around, but pretty soon someone's going to notice that I always wear the same thing. I pull on my only sweater, a thin red V-neck that Ginger gave me, in a Hail Mary play that the color might make me feel more awake, hoping it doesn't look ridiculous. Ginger said it looked great with my hair, but I think it might just make me look like I'm early for Christmas.

I grab my jacket and turn up the volume on New Order, deciding to wander a bit before heading over to Sludge. I'm immediately glad for my sweater, no matter how Christmassy, when the wind starts to blow. I definitely need to get a heavier coat. Maybe this weekend. My mind wanders to Ginger and how sometimes, on chilly days, I'd get us both hot chocolates and we'd climb the fire escape to the roof of her shop, looking down over South Street, the streets of beautiful old houses to the north, and the Italian Market to the south. I like my hot chocolate with vanilla and Ginge likes hers with cinnamon, and the smells of them would mix with those of the burger joint on the corner, the falafel cart down the street, the exhaust from cars inching down South Street, and the scent of rotting leaves and stale popcorn that always seems to drift through the streets as fall gives way to winter.

Up there on the roof is where I first told Ginger a secret: that after a spotty high school career of teachers who thought I was a loser punk with an attitude and skipping more classes than I went to because the teachers were idiots, I desperately wanted to go to college. Ginger smiled at me and said, "Of course you should go; you're the smartest guy I know." It's also where she told me about her older brother who'd killed himself when she was fifteen after their father walked in on him having sex with another boy. For a while after that, I worried that the only reason she wanted to be friends with me was because I reminded her of her brother or something.

Part of me wants to tell Ginger about the whole Will thing in the hopes that she'll tell me it's nothing, but it's way too early to call her. Will. There was something slightly off about that guy. Or, not off—just something that didn't quite add up. Guys that pretty are usually so used to getting whatever they want that they've never fought in their lives. But Will didn't seem the slightest bit intimidated by the threat of a fight. Maybe he was just so sure of his primacy with Rex that he didn't care? He did seem pretty concerned about Rex's headache. Still, not really possessive the way a lover might be—more... what? Annoyed, maybe, that Rex was in pain? I'm not sure.

Out of nowhere, someone grabs my shoulder and I wheel around and grab them around the neck.

It's Leo, and he looks terrified.

"Shit, Leo," I say, brushing him off and ripping out my earbuds. "Don't sneak up on me like that, man."

"Um, I was yelling your name, dude."

I've got to stop listening to my music so loud.

"Sorry," I mutter.

"No worries!" he says, looking cheerful again. "So, how was Detroit? Did you go to any shows? How was your conference? What was your talk about again?"

Jesus, it's too early in the morning to have that kind of energy.

"Detroit was fine. I didn't have time for anything but the conference. My paper went fine. It was about—"

"Oh, I remember. About turn of the century sensationalism in American newspaper illustration, right?"

I only remember briefly mentioning anything about my paper when I stopped in to Mr. Zoo's on Friday. I assumed Leo was just being polite when he asked, and I can't believe he understood what I was talking about, much less remembered it.

"That's right. How do you remember that?"

He shrugs. "Dunno. Not that hard. Sounded interesting." He's bouncing a little, whether with energy or to keep warm, I'm not sure.

"What're you doing out so early?" I ask.

"Oh, just wandering around," Leo says. "Couldn't sleep."

"Me either."

"Then I saw you and figured I'd come say hi. Hey, you wanna get a coffee? I know you always go to Sludge before class."

"How do you—? Never mind. Yeah, sure, let's go."

Marjorie greets me with a suspicious smile when I walk in the door with Leo. With no energy to resist her, I bite the bullet.

"I'll have a Daniel, please."

She looks disappointed for a moment, then smiles widely, as if she's beaten me. And maybe she has. I don't even have the energy to care.

"Ooh, yes, me too," Leo says.

"Dude," I say, sharing a look with Marjorie. "You're already bouncing off the walls; the thought of you ingesting that much caffeine actually makes me fear for the safety of this town and everyone in it."

"Nah, I'm good. Besides, coffee has a... whaddayacallit... paradoxical effect on me."

"Huh?" says Marjorie.

"It, like, chills me out," Leo says.

"Well, glory hallelujah, pour the kid some coffee," I mutter.

A stocky kid in trendy clothes comes in behind us. Leo's bouncing increases and his elegant nostrils flare.

"Two Daniels!" Marjorie announces gleefully, putting the drinks on the counter.

There's a snort behind us.

"Trying to be just like your boyfriend, Leo? Good luck with that," the guy in line behind us scoffs.

"Shut up, Todd!" Leo says, spinning around to look at him and almost knocking both coffees over with his backpack.

I put a hand on Leo's twitching shoulder and turn to the kid behind us. I stand, looking at him. It's the same vaguely threatening, totally unimpressed look that I gave Will last night, and this kid folds almost immediately, looking down at the expensive shoes I'm sure his parents bought him. Now *that's* what's supposed to happen.

"Excuse us," I say calmly, sliding money across the counter to Marjorie and taking the coffees. I walk out the door, certain Leo will follow me.

"Ha!" Leo says, grinning, elbowing me as we get outside. "That was awesome. You just *looked* at him and he practically shit his pants. How'd you *do* that? I mean, you're not even that big a guy and everyone's terrified of you. You've got to teach me that."

I decide to ignore the part about everyone being terrified of me, because I don't even want to know.

"Well, first of all, you have to believe, one hundred percent, that you could take them out if it came down to a fight," I tell him. "If you don't believe it, they won't either. That kind of confidence does 80 percent of the work for you. You look sure you could kick their ass, they're gonna be thinking they have something to worry about. Second, you have to not give a shit. And it's got to come from the inside out. If you're faking it, they'll know. Then the rest of it's just staring at them. If you know you could win a fight *and* you don't give a shit, the stare will do the rest of the work for you. Here, show me."

I square off with Leo, taking his coffee. He's only an inch or so shorter than me, but being that skinny, you've got to look all kinds of threatening to be taken seriously. I remember.

Leo laughs nervously, scuffing the toe of his Vans on the pavement.

"I've, um, never been in a fight."

"What about the day I met you?" I'd kind of assumed that getting picked on was a regular occurrence for him, but maybe not.

"Oh, yeah, well. I've gotten my ass kicked, sure. But I've never actually thrown a punch." He blushes and his eyelashes lower.

"Well, you've done the hardest part. It's a lot easier to hit someone than it is to take a punch. I can teach you, if you want." Wait, no. Is that irresponsible? But the kid's got to learn to take care of himself or who knows what might happen to him.

"Whoa, really? Hell yes. Teach me!" He does what is, perhaps, supposed to be some kind of martial arts punch-kick combination and nearly takes out both coffees again as he lurches toward me, light brown hair falling into his eyes.

"All right, Karate Kid. Some other time, though. If anyone sees us I'm going to look like I'm corrupting a minor."

"I'm not a minor; I'm eighteen. Hey! Wasn't his name Daniel?"

"Who?"

"The Karate Kid!"

"Call me Daniel-san and live to regret it," I tell him with a growl.

I hand him his coffee and we keep walking. My phone rings and my heart lurches when I see that it's Rex.

"Sorry," I say to Leo and wave the phone, turning my back to him.

"Hi," I say.

"Daniel." Rex's deep voice makes my heart pound. "I need to talk to you." I don't even realize my hand's in a fist until I hear my knuckles crack.

"Mmhmm."

"Listen, about Will. He showed up last night without telling me he was coming to town, okay. And you don't have to worry about him. Not at all."

"Look, Rex, it's not a good time to talk right now, okay? I'm with Leo and I'm about to go to my office. Can we talk about it later?"

Rex's voice is clipped when he answers. Annoyed? Anxious? I'm not sure, but I know I'm both.

"Yeah, of course," he says. "Can you come over tonight? After you're done with work? I'll make us some dinner." Damn it, the magic words.

"Yeah, I guess," I say. "Hey, how's your head?" I try to sound casual, like I'm just checking in on a friend.

"It's much better. Thank you." I can hear the smile in his voice and the knot in my stomach loosens a little. "Tonight," he says again, as if he's afraid I won't remember. "Whenever you're done, just come on over. You can work here, if you want. I'll be home by three."

"Okay," I say again.

"Oh, and Daniel, I, um, I have the Internet—you know, in case you weren't sure whether you could work here today because you need it. I have it now, so...." He sounds a little embarrassed.

"Oh, you do? Well, that's... okay, cool," I say. I guess he decided he needed it after all.

"I'll see you later," Rex says, his voice even deeper.

"Bye."

I turn around to find Leo practically in my face. I forgot he was there.

"Are you *dating* Rex Vale?" Leo asks, his eyes wide.

"Would you quit eavesdropping!"

"I ain't been droppin' no eaves, sir, honest," he says, in a dopey quasi-British accent.

"What are you—?"

"Hello! Sam, from *The Fellowship of the Ring*? Have you *seen* a movie released after 1985?"

I grumble something, feeling seriously old.

"So? Are you? Dating Rex Vale?"

"Kind of," I mutter, more to myself than to him.

"Oh shit, you totally are." He groans. "That is so incredibly hot." He looks me up and down and smiles that smile that's going to get him laid or laid out, depending. Me, I kind of want to punch him, but part of me can't help but be a little impressed. He's really elevated this whole small-town-gossip thing to an art form. It's like he watches television and movies and then goes out and slots people in his real life into the roles. Hell, it's probably what I would've done if I'd grown up somewhere like this where nothing happens.

"What do you know about it?" I ask him.

"Um, just that Rex is, like, the hot carpenter and you're the hot tattooed bad boy and I'm seeing tools and—"

"Stop, stop, stop! Jesus, Leo. Ground rule: don't ever talk about sex with my boyfriend again, got it?"

"Oh my god, he totally *is* your boyfriend," Leo says softly. "Okay, fine, sure, no problem. I will totally not talk about you and Rex having sex—whoa: poetry." The look on his face says, very clearly, "You can't stop me from thinking about it, though."

"Whatever," I mutter. "I think some old boyfriend of his is back, anyway, so it probably won't last long." I sit down on the bench at the edge of campus, picking at the sleeve on my to-go cup, and Leo sits beside me, knee jiggling up and down. I can't believe I'm talking about my romantic problems with an eighteen-year-old. Honestly, though, it's like I'm talking to a younger version of myself, anyway. Besides, when I was eighteen, Ginger definitely told me about hers. Of course, at eighteen I had a job and my own apartment, hovel though it was.

"I don't know," I say. "I'm going over there after class today. I guess I'll find out what the deal is then."

"No way does he like someone else more than you, Daniel," Leo says sincerely.

"Don't say shit like that, man; you don't know. No one knows why anyone likes anyone, and it's a total fucking mystery why Rex likes me." I shake my head, frustrated.

"Well, what'd he say on the phone just now?"

"That we had to talk."

"That all?"

"That I didn't have to worry about Will and that I should come over tonight. And that he has the Internet now."

"He didn't have the Internet? That is insane. Wait, is he, like, way older than he looks?"

"He's not *old*. He just said he doesn't need it that often so he goes to the library when he does. Watch it, kid."

"So, why'd he get it?"

"How the hell do I know? He started using it more, I guess. Or maybe now that it's winter he doesn't want to drag his ass to the library just to check his e-mail."

"Dude, he totally bought you the Internet!" Leo says, socking me in the shoulder. "That's so romantic."

I stare at him.

"Come on, it's obvious. You use it, right? So, he got it for you. Aw, man, I thought you were supposed to be smart."

I have to call Ginger right away and tell her that I have found the human being that we would create if we ever had a child.

ONCE I apprehensively gave Leo my phone number after he extracted a promise that I'd teach him to fight this weekend, I went to prepare for class. It's a miracle I didn't bungle both my classes given how distracted I was. I couldn't stop thinking about Will, and wondering what Rex was going to tell me when I got over there this evening. And, I can't lie: a tiny part of my brain kept running over and over Leo's idea that Rex got the Internet for me.

As I leave my office around four, I can't decide whether to take Rex up on his offer and go right over to his house or go home, change, and drive over later for dinner. I take two steps toward my apartment and then find myself reeling off in the other direction, toward Rex's. It's only a few miles, and a walk is just what I need to clear my head before I hear whatever he's about to tell me. The air's warmed up a bit and the sun is shining. The leaves are brilliant colors and everything smells clean. If there's one thing I'll say for Holiday, it always smells pretty good. There's no stink of fumes or garbage, and everything smells alive.

I'm just thinking how pretty the walk is when the skies open and it starts to rain. Then pour. Secure in the knowledge that my laptop won't get wet—my case is waterproof—I kind of enjoy it.

But when I knock on Rex's door, I know I must look like a drowned rat because he takes one look at me and pulls me inside, shaking his head.

"Daniel, don't you ever check the weather?" he chides, and I shake my head. I'm shivering now, and he drops my bag on the mat and pulls off my sodden jacket. I kick off my shoes.

"Jesus, you're freezing," he says, eyes flashing. He shakes his head at me in frustration. "Come here," he says and leads me to the bathroom, reaching over my shoulder to turn on the shower. I'm having major déjà vu of the first night I was here, in February, when Rex took me into that bathroom to look at my bruises. My cheeks heat a little, still embarrassed at how strong I came on that night. Doubly embarrassed if it turns out that, not long after, Rex was fucking Will, probably telling him about the pathetic loser who threw himself at him. I can see Will's perfect face smiling, enjoying the idea that his man is so irresistible. My hands fist and Rex jerks when I squeeze him.

"Sorry," I say.

He sticks his hand in to test the water, then reaches for my sweater to pull it off.

"I can do it," I say absently, pulling the sweater off from the bottom. He takes it from me and lays it out on the sink. Then he reaches for the buttons on my shirt. "I got it," I say.

"Daniel, stop," Rex says, his voice exhausted. I look up at him. "Please, let's not be back here. This is my fault. Because of Will. I know. But, come on."

I narrow my eyes at him expectantly. Rex looks at me exasperatedly, but there's warmth there too.

He steps closer to me and closes the door so Marilyn can't come in and drink the toilet water. He reaches for me and I step away from him.

"Well?" I finally say. Rex sighs.

"Will and I used to date. Years ago. But that was a long time ago. We're just friends now. But, every now and again when he comes to town, we'll—"

"Fuck," I finish for him.

"Yeah. But that's all it is."

I look up at him, trying to read whether it's true in his face. He meets my gaze intently, but he seems irritated or something.

"It didn't seem like that's all it was to him," I say.

Rex snorts.

"Yeah, well, Will is contrary that way. But believe me, that's all it is. He just likes to be alpha dog."

"Hmm," I say. "Interesting."

Rex blushes.

"Look," he says, running his hands up and down my ribs. "I know it was real bad timing last night. It must've seemed bad, what with everything you told me about Richard. But, Daniel, you have to know that I would never do that."

I let out a breath and nod.

"I love undressing you," he says. He kisses my neck, his mouth warm against my cold skin. "You always shiver just a little, and your nipples get hard." He strips my shirt off my arms and pulls my T-shirt off. Then he runs his thumbs over my nipples and my stomach clenches. "You're so beautiful." He kisses my mouth and I put my arms around him tentatively.

He undoes my pants and pulls them and my underwear down. He nudges me into the hot shower but doesn't close the door, and my eyes are glued to him as he strips and gets in with me.

He puts me under the water and rubs his hands up and down my arms to warm me up. Then he washes my hair, careful, as before, that no soap gets in my eyes. I lean back into him, my sleepless night catching up with me, and he wraps his arms around my waist. I turn in his arms to kiss him. As our mouths move together, Rex pulls me toward him, cupping my ass and squeezing with both hands. A bolt of arousal shoots through me. I press kisses up his throat, standing on my toes to reach his mouth again.

Rex kisses the same way he seems to do everything else: with a combination of confident power and gentle sweetness that completely gets to me. He pushes me against the wall with his body, tipping my head up so he can keep kissing me as we grind together. He cups my hip in one hand and runs the other between my cheeks to find my opening. His wet fingers slide inside me and I groan, the heat of his body and the heat of the water mixing with the heat of his fingers inside me to make me a little dizzy. Rex groans when I run my hands down his muscular back to pull him closer to me. His ass is tight as he rocks against me.

I look up into his eyes, the dark lashes clumped with water. I run my fingers across his hole and he shudders. I push gently and he winces. Is it in pain or arousal? His mouth is open and water is running down his jaw, glistening in his stubble. His thick hair is in dark swirls. He looks amazing, like he's standing under a waterfall in some exotic vacation spot I'll never visit. I rub a finger against his hole gently, just teasing, and he shudders and gasps.

"Good?" I say against his open mouth. "Or no."

"Good," he says, nodding, then he drops his head down onto my shoulder. A jolt of arousal rocks me. I reverse our positions, pushing him into the wall, and squeeze his ass in both hands. Like every other part of him, it's meaty and muscular and gorgeous.

When I feel him relax, I delve inside him again, my finger sliding in as he sucks in a breath. We thrust together as the water falls over our shoulders like the rain outside. Rex's hands are at the small of my back, as if to stop me from pulling away, and his head is lying back against the wall. I slide a second finger into him and he whimpers as I stroke over his prostate, his hole clenching down on my fingers.

"Oh fuck," he says. "It's been so long."

Good. A picture of Will fucking Rex in this shower flutters through my brain and I shake my head to clear it, latching onto Rex's nipples as I explore him with my fingers. His heat is addictive and I push closer to him, our erections sliding together and my fingers sliding deeper inside him. We both groan and Rex grabs our cocks in his big hand, bending his knees a little so we're the same height. I take the opportunity to slide a third finger inside him and he cries out, his hand tightening on our erections. Everything feels liquid as he works us together, and I massage his prostate with my fingertips, his jaw clenching in pleasure.

"Kiss me, please," Rex groans, and pumps us even harder. I can feel my orgasm creeping up the base of my spine. I grab Rex's face in my hand and slam our mouths together, my tongue sliding into his mouth as I push my fingers as deep as I can. He gasps into my mouth and begins to tremble. His thighs are shaking and his stomach vibrates against mine as his ass spasms around my fingers. I press into his prostate and he tears his mouth away from mine, his groans echoing in the small shower. His hand stutters and then heat thicker than water hits my chest and drips down my stomach. Rex's mouth is open and every one of his muscles is clenched, like some kind of glorious animal caught midjump. Then he lets out a shuddering breath and relaxes, his hole fluttering around my fingers.

"Daniel," he breathes, and he pulls me flush against him and kisses me so sweetly. He twists one hand in my hair and keeps stroking my erection slowly, watching my reactions. His eyes are molten gold, framed by dark lashes, and he's looking at me like he wants to eat me up. I lift my chin for another kiss, but he just keeps looking at me, his strokes getting harder and faster, and my breaths turn to gasps. Just as I'm about to come, he slows down a little and I squeeze my eyes shut in frustration, reaching for him as I shudder back from the brink. Instead of keeping me upright, Rex lets me melt into him and pulls me up so I can thrust against his belly. He holds me up with a hand under my ass and seals his other hand over my erection, encouraging me to thrust against him.

The warm flesh and firm muscle drags over my shaft as I hump against him, and he pulls me firmly to him. I cry out, the feeling both familiar and strange enough that I can't quite anticipate what's coming. The stretch in my legs and ass is making my balls tighten and tingle. I reach up and put my arms around Rex's neck so I can have more control and he holds me to him with one hand, the other finally palming my erection and stroking me hard and fast. I gasp and bite down on his shoulder as my orgasm blasts through me, jumping in Rex's hand as he strokes me through the aftershocks.

I can smell Rex's scent even with the water rushing down, and his skin smells like home. I squeeze him around the neck and his arms come around me, pulling me into a hug.

We both let out deep breaths at the same time and slump against each other, our hips still flexing a little, drawn together. When I look up, there's a soft look in Rex's eyes and he pushes my wet hair back and kisses me on the temple and then the mouth. There's just something about Rex that makes me feel so safe, so content. I've never felt anything like it. I know we have things to talk about, but in this moment, I'm so happy I can hardly breathe.

"Do you need to work?" Rex asks.

"Oh shit!" I run over to my bag. In my relief that there was no way my computer would be ruined by the rain, I didn't think about all the papers I have in there. I pull open my messenger bag, which is sitting in a pool of rainwater just inside the door, and sure enough, some rain got in.

"Shit, shit, shit." I pull out the stack of paper proposals from this morning, the papers clumped wetly together, and start to peel them apart, cursing myself for not springing for the bag with the roll-top. Fortunately, only the top third of the stack is wet and the ink isn't smeared, but if I let them dry stuck together they'll be unreadable when I pull them apart. I start laying out the wet sheets on the floor. Marilyn, curious, trots over and starts nosing at them.

"Here," Rex says. He spreads two towels over the coffee table and moves the papers there, holding Marilyn off with a word.

"Thanks," I say, grumbling at my bag and the papers and the rain.

Rex is laughing softly.

"What?" I say.

"You're just cute, that's all."

"What? No way. Why?"

I put the last paper on the table, their wet tops fanned out to dry. Rex is grinning at me. He shrugs a little.

"You're just…. Sometimes you're so professional, and you look real intense while you're working. Then, the next minute, you show up here drenched, with all your papers wet, and you're a mess." He steps closer to me, and the soft look is back. "Sometimes, you're sweet and nervous and you look at me like you have no idea what's going on. And the next minute you're all… prickly." He swats my ass.

"Hey!"

"And sometimes," he continues, tilting my face up, "you're so damn sexy I could just kiss you for hours." He kisses me, and I can feel myself relaxing into his arms, when he pulls away and looks at me again. "Then, I don't know. There are moments when I think you could kick my ass if you were mad enough." He looks at me assessingly, but I don't say anything. I wonder if I could.

Just to be sure it didn't get wet, I take out my laptop case and look inside. Nope, my piece of crap computer is totally dry, thank goodness.

"So, do you need to work? I have the Internet now, if you need it."

I look at him, curious.

"Why'd you decide to get it now?"

Rex looks a little embarrassed, but he says, "Well, you said you use it a lot, so I got it. I thought maybe you could do some work here instead of the library. And I know you don't love your place, so…."

Holy shit, Leo was right.

"You bought me the Internet."

"Well, in a manner of speaking." He fidgets. "Is that—I mean, is it useful to you?"

"You...." I don't even know what to say. I can hear Ginger in my head, yelling at me to just act normal, act like myself, don't overthink every little thing. What would I say to Ginger? What *would* I say to Ginger?

"You're so fucking nice," is what comes out. "Thank you. I really appreciate it."

Rex laughs and grins at me. Yes! I said the right thing. Note to self: just pretend Rex is Ginger. Wait. That's a terrible idea in several contexts.

"You're welcome," Rex says, and runs his hand through my drying hair, which probably looks like I got stuck in a thresher. "So, do you? Need to work, I mean?"

I do. When I regard the paper proposals drying on the table, though, my stomach growls.

"Well, they're wet just at the moment," I say.

"So, dinner?"

I nod and follow Rex into the kitchen. He starts pulling things out of the fridge and the cabinets. I never know what he's making until he puts it on the table, but I kind of like not knowing. It's like watching one of the cooking competitions he loves where you get the big reveal at the end.

"Can you cut things up and listen at the same time?" Rex teases. At least, I think he's teasing. He pushes four apples, a knife, and a cutting board in front of me.

"Oh god, this isn't one of those things where you're going to put fruit in all the food, is it? I keep seeing, like, cherries in all the salads here. It's disgusting."

"Well, Traverse City is the cherry capital of the world. They find their way into almost everything up here. But, no. I thought we'd make an apple crumble for dessert. Seems autumnal. That's the word, right? Autumnal?"

"Yeah. You bake too? Damn." Why is that kind of turning me on? Something about Rex's big hands and thick shoulders making delicate pastries in a white apron is crazy hot.

"Well, I don't do anything fancy. But this is easy. So, just take the cores out and the cut them into chunks, okay?"

I nod, and he starts doing... whatever else he's doing, cutting and sautéing and slicing a million things at once.

"So, how'd you end up here, anyway?"

"Huh?"

"In the cherry capital of the world," I say.

"Oh."

"Sorry," I say when he doesn't continue. "You don't have to tell me if you don't want."

"No, it's okay. I just—no one's ever asked before. It was because of Jamie, actually. He was from here, originally. Well, near here. I'd only ever lived in hot places when we met and I used to complain about how I hate the heat. When it was really hot and we'd be in the park or have to walk in the sun, he'd tell me stories about the winter in Michigan. The snow, and how he and his brother would build forts out of it and drink hot cocoa in there. It sounded magical to me. I'd never even seen snow in real life."

Rex smiles at the memory, his hands gone still and his eyes distant.

"Jamie told me he'd take me to Michigan with him one day for a real Christmas—he said Christmas without snow didn't even really count. So, I just kind of made my way here after my mom died. I was doing odd jobs. Fixing stuff for folks. I got here just before Christmas one year. I love Christmas," he says sheepishly.

He starts stirring again and continues.

"Anyway, I lived around here for a few years, really liked it. Then I was walking one day and I saw this place." He chuckles at the memory. "Man, it was a fall-down mess. Half the wood was rotten and the kitchen was a disaster. I asked around, found out the guy who lived here died and the county was going to tear it down. I convinced them to let me rebuild it instead. Took a while."

He's running his hand along the countertop as if he doesn't even realize he's doing it.

"Jesus. You *built* this cabin?"

He nods.

"Most of it. A bit was salvageable."

"That's... amazing." Rex smiles. "I guess now that I look at it, it does seem like a nicer kitchen than you'd expect to find in a cabin."

"You have much experience with cabins?"

"Um, no."

I turn back to the apples, unsure of what to say so I concentrate on cutting them into chunks while not chopping off any parts of myself. I can't imagine what it would feel like to build your own home. It must be amazing.

"So, about Will," Rex says, and my knife skids off the skin of the apple and thumps onto the cutting board, coming within a millimeter of my finger. Rex's head snaps up.

"Are you okay? Did you cut yourself?" I shake my head. "Here, give me that," Rex says, and takes my knife, tests it on his thumb, and hands me a smaller one. I open my mouth to say something, but he says, "I think I need to sharpen that one; this one's sharper."

I go back to cutting the apples up, but Rex is watching me now, probably worried I'm going to require his emergency services. When I look up, though, his gaze is fond. And he seems a little bemused.

"What?"

"It's not brain surgery, sweetheart," he says. "You can just cut them up." I look down at the cutting board. My chunks of apple are perfectly uniform. I cut the apple into rings and then strips and then chunks. Wasn't that what he asked for? I look back up at him, puzzled.

"Never mind," he says. "They're great—they're perfect. I just meant, you don't need to try so hard to make them perfect. It doesn't matter if they're all the same."

"Okay," I say, but I don't really know any other way to do it.

"Never mind," he says, and pats my shoulder.

"Okay, so about Will?" I prompt.

"Yeah. I just... he's my friend. A good friend. And I don't make friends real easy." He sounds sheepish. "I don't want my friendship with him to be a problem for you. That's all. And I didn't know he was coming to town. Sometimes he just shows up. If I'd known, I would never have let him just come over like that."

"How long did you date?"

"About a year."

"That's a long time."

"I think we both knew it was never going to be anything permanent," Rex says, and he sounds a little sad.

"Why?"

"We were just too different. And Will was never going to stick around here, you know? He couldn't wait to leave. I'm surprised he stayed that long. He got a job offer in New York and he took it. He stops in here when he goes to Chicago. His sister still lives nearby, so he comes to visit."

"And to see you."

"Yeah, sometimes."

"Do you still—I mean, if he hadn't left, would you still want to be with him?"

Rex pauses, like he's sincerely considering the question.

"Will and I had fun together," he says slowly. "I met him at a time when I needed someone who didn't take things too seriously. But, no. I don't think we'd be a good fit in the long run."

"What's he do in New York?"

"He does graphic design for a publishing company."

"Like book covers, or what?"

"Yeah, for… I don't remember what the company is."

"Hunh, that's cool," I admit reluctantly.

"He's a cool guy, Daniel. I actually think you'd like him." He shakes his head and chuckles. "You were something last night."

I raise my eyebrows at him, nervous he's about to call me on being a possessive psycho.

"I thought you were gonna drop him." He's smiling, so I guess that's not a terrible thing? "Will likes to mess with people. Find the things that get to them and then push those buttons."

"What a charming trait," I mutter.

"Well, you know a little bit about ways to push people away too, don't you?" Rex says gently. Is that what he thinks I do? *Is* that what I do? I never thought about it because I've never had anyone to push away.

"Here," Rex says, tossing me a lemon. "Put the apples in that bowl and squeeze half of that over them, okay?"

He gets out butter, brown sugar, and some other stuff that he puts in a mixer.

"So, I thought maybe we could all have a drink. You, me, and Will."

I cut the lemon in half and squeeze it on top of the apples. Rex reaches in and pulls out a bunch of seeds.

"Sorry," I say.

"No problem. I forgot to tell you about the seeds. So, what do you say?"

Do I want to meet Rex's ex-boyfriend slash sex partner? No. Because he seemed like a dick and I can't stand the idea of watching him touch Rex.

"When was the last time you slept with him?" I ask. "Am I allowed to ask that?"

"Of course, Daniel. The last time was, I guess, in the spring. April."

That's when he met Marilyn, I guess.

"Listen, if you don't want to, I understand. But he's my friend and I'd really like you not to hate each other."

"He hates me?" God knows what that asshole said after I left last night.

"No, of course not," Rex says. "It would just be nice if you got along. That's all I meant."

I narrow my eyes at him suspiciously, but Rex just opens his arms. "I kicked him out right after you left. He's staying with his sister."

"But he usually stays with you?"

"Sometimes."

I sigh. I know that my answer here is important. The question isn't actually do I want to have drinks with this douchebag, right? God, I need to go to dating elementary school. So, what's the question? Ginger, what's the question? *The question*, the Ginger in my head supplies, *is do you trust Rex? He's asking you to make his life easier and if you trust him, then you should do it.* Right.

"Okay, drinks," I say. "I trust you."

I get another of those warm smiles.

"Great," he says. "Should I call him and tell him to come over tonight, or is later in the week better?"

"No, he can't come over tonight," I say, swatting him in the stomach. "My clothes are wet and I look like a rag doll in yours."

"Mmm, I love the way you look in my clothes," he growls, leaning down to kiss my neck and collarbone where his shirt droops.

"Well, I feel ridiculous," I say, but I lean into his warm lips.

"Hmm, vanity," he teases. "A whole new side of Daniel."

"I'm not—mmhmm." He kisses me before I can protest.

"I know, baby. You just want an even playing field."

"Well, he looks like a fucking model, so I'd at least like to be wearing pants," I snap, irritated just thinking about Will's stupid face.

"He's got nothing on you," Rex says. Note to self: Rex is either a liar or blind. But very sweet. I kiss him again.

"Okay, how about tomorrow night?" Rex asks between kisses. "We could meet somewhere near campus and you could just walk over right after class."

"Fine," I say, distracted by his warm mouth.

"Thanks," he murmurs, and he pushes me against the counter and attacks my mouth.

I'M DISGUSTED with myself. I've been nervous about having drinks with Rex and Will all day. I mean, hell, I've poured drinks for major musical celebrities and attended lunches with academic ones, and I'm nervous to meet the guy Rex used to date? What the hell?

My stomach is tight with anxiety. I stayed at Rex's last night and made some toast—okay, burned some toast—there this morning, but aside from that, I haven't been able to eat all day. Even if I could've, I haven't had time. A journal article I submitted around the time I had my interview here got rejected this morning and I had to spend a whole chunk of unexpected time reformatting it so I can send it out again to another journal, which is depressing, but not unexpected. Between that and Will showing up, I really need that drink.

I'm a couple of minutes early when I get to the pub a few blocks from campus, so I grab us a table, praying that I don't run into any students, and pull out the readers' reports that the journal sent with my rejection letter. I'm having a furious internal dialogue with one of the idiot's comments when a hand falls on my shoulder and I jerk around to grab it.

"Oh, hey," I say to Rex. "Sorry." He puts his other hand on my shoulder and gives them a squeeze.

"No problem. Hi." He leans closer, but hesitates, and I can tell he's not sure if he can kiss me in public. Ordinarily, I'm fairly disgusted by couples who are all touchy-feely in public, and I've certainly never been one of them, but some equally disgusting primal neurotransmitter is screaming at me to lay claim to him in front of Will, so I tip my head back, inviting his kiss. His mouth is warm and he smells like Rex, which makes the tightness in my stomach unclench a little.

"What are you doing?" Will asks as they sit down, gesturing to the readers' reports, which, for some arcane reason, are printed on legal-size paper.

"An article I submitted for publication just got rejected and these are the notes from people telling me why," I say, when what I meant to say was, "None of your business." Oops.

"The strengths of this essay are that it is clearly written and that its author takes an imaginative approach to the—" Will reads from the top of the page before I notice what he's saying.

"Hey, fuck off," I say, pulling the paper away and stuffing it back in the envelope.

"Will," Rex says, disapprovingly, and pulls me into his side.

"Hey," Will says, hands up, "at least it's clearly written and imaginative. That's more than I can say for about 90 percent of the stuff I read."

Rex glances down at the envelope curiously. "Do these people have the final say?"

"For journals, yeah. They send your piece out to three people in your field and those are the readers. It's just so frustrating because I read the comments that they make and it's obvious that they didn't read the whole article, because they say that I didn't do things that I totally did. Just, in the second half. Anyway, whatever. It was a long shot to begin with."

"Let me get the first round," Will says, "as someone technically in the publishing industry, to express my sympathies that basically everything involved in it is crap."

I can't tell if he's fucking with me or not.

"Thanks, Will," Rex says. Then, to me, "I'm sorry, baby." He squeezes my hand and I shake my head. His clothes smell like pine and I take a deep breath of him.

"Were you in your workshop today?" I ask.

"Yeah."

"You smell so good," I say, as Will comes back to the table with a beer, a whiskey, and a martini. He puts them down in the center of the table and gestures to me. Is this some kind of test? Like, I'm supposed to guess what drink Will *thinks* I'd want? What the hell? Rex rolls his eyes, grabs the beer, and slides the whiskey to me. Will sips his martini and looks at me across the table. I stare back at him and down my whiskey like a shot.

"So, what do you think of Holiday?" Will asks. "You're from Philly, right?"

I nod. "It's okay. I like how clean everything is here. It smells kind of green. And the woods by Rex's are beautiful. There's not much going on, but I can't lie. It's nice to be able to walk around here and not worry about if it's safe or not. I feel like I could walk through the woods in the middle of the night and be fine."

Unease flickers in Will's expression, but he just nods.

"Yeah," Rex says, "unless you meet any serial killers, right?" He bumps my shoulder with his.

"I only said that once," I mutter. Out loud, anyway. "Did you grow up here?" I ask Will.

He nods.

"I left for college but came back for a few years after to stay with my sister. That's when I met Rex."

"Where did you go for college?" I ask. I mean where did he live, but it came out the way all academics say it: tell me your pedigree. Let's see if my school was better than yours.

"NYU," Will says.

"So, you like New York?"

"Yup." Will drums his fingers on the edge of the table in a fidgety gesture of boredom and I'm reminded of why I don't like small talk.

"Here, I'll get the next round," I say, though Rex still has half a beer left. "Gin?"

"Vodka," Will says. "Dirty." He waggles his perfect eyebrows.

Rex is looking back and forth between us like a betting man at a dog fight. I nudge his knee and he stands to let me out.

"Can I have a Corona?" he asks.

"Sure."

He starts to say something to Will as I walk away from the table.

"Can I have a Corona, a gin martini, dirty, and a Maker's Mark, neat, please?" I ask the guy behind the counter.

"Is the martini for the guy who was just up here?" the bartender asks.

"Uh. Yeah."

"He was drinking vodka before. Is he switching?"

"Oh no. Thanks. I meant vodka." God, am I drunk after one whiskey? I guess it was a double.

I put the drinks down and Rex slides over to make room for me in the booth, resting a hand on my thigh when I sit down.

"Thanks," he says. He's downed the rest of his first beer. I smile at him. God, he really is so nice.

"Cheers," Will says.

Will and Rex start talking about someone who lives in town, filling me in on the backstory, and I sip my drink a little slower. But it's official. I'm basically drunk. Damn, I've turned into a lightweight since I moved here. Not that that's a bad thing. Honestly, tending bar makes it pretty easy to be drunk whenever you want to. And I don't want to end up like my dad, working all day and then drunk on the couch watching sports all night.

I wonder how he is. And my idiot brothers. I haven't heard from them since I called the last time, no surprise. At least Colin hasn't sent me any more nasty texts. My mind drifts to my dad's house, the smell of Rex's beer making it easy. When I was in middle school, before Sam moved out, I'd do my homework at the kitchen table while my dad and my brothers watched sports in the living room. I wanted to be able to see them so it felt like I was part of the family, but if I sat too close someone would eventually step on my schoolbooks or spill a beer on my homework. I ended up not turning in a lot of worksheets because they reeked of beer.

I'm not sure how long I've been spacing out, but Rex is handing me my phone, which is ringing. It's Leo. Rex is looking at me with curiosity and a little concern.

"Hey," I say, and Leo's rapid-fire speech jolts me to awareness. He wants to take me up on my offer to teach him to fight on Friday, if I don't have plans. He says that part like since it's Friday night I must be going out or something, but where the hell does he think I'd go around here? We can't do it in my apartment because there's no room, and we certainly can't do it where anyone would see. "Hold on," I tell Leo.

"Hey, Rex," I say, looking up at him. "Um, would it be okay if I have Leo come to your house on Friday night and we use your yard?"

"Who is Leo?" Rex asks, his eyes narrowed slightly.

"I didn't tell you about Leo?" I push the phone against my chest to muffle it. Rex shakes his head, his expression studiedly neutral. "He's this kid I stopped from getting beat up the other week. He works at Mr. Zoo's."

"You've been to Mr. Zoo's?" Will says, like it's strange.

"What do you need the yard for?" Rex asks, puzzled.

"Um, I told him I'd teach him to fight."

Will buries his face in his martini glass to hide the fact that he's laughing.

"Why does he need—Yeah, of course," Rex says politely, though I can tell he's nonplussed. "Feel free."

"Thanks," I tell Rex, smiling.

"Hey, come to Rex's," I tell Leo, and give him the address. "Can you get there or do you need a ride?"

Will is laughing outright as I hang up the phone.

"You're teaching some kid to fight?" he says. "Who are you, Mr. Miyagi?"

"Would everyone stop it with the damn *Karate Kid* references!" I say. Rex and Will exchange a look.

"So, *who* is Leo?" Rex asks again.

I tell them about coming across Leo in the park and about the kids who were picking on him.

"But he's a kid," Rex says. "Like, a child?"

"He's eighteen, I think," I say.

"Oh my god," Will laughs, looking at Rex. Will points a finger at him. "You're jealous! Rexroth Vale, you are totally jealous of a teenager." Then he stops laughing and pouts. "Hey! You were never jealous over me."

Rex rolls his eyes and turns to me.

"It's fine," he says. "I never get any trick-or-treaters out that far anyway."

"Trick-or… oh, that's what Leo was talking about. Are you sure it's okay? If you have plans or—"

"No, no. It's fine. I don't."

"Thanks," I say, and rest my shoulder against Rex's. "So, do people go all out for Halloween here?"

"Not really," Will says. "Well, maybe some of your students will; I don't know. They do an early trick-or-treat thing for the kids so everyone's home before dark. No fun if you ask me. But, then, I prefer tricks to treats anyway." He winks at me.

"Did you go trick-or-treating as a kid?" I ask Rex.

"Naw, too shy," he says. "My mom would usually bring home one of those plastic pumpkins from whatever bar or diner she was working in, and some candy. You?" he asks me.

"Oh hell no. Ring a stranger's doorbell in my neighborhood and you would've gotten shot." I wait for Will to chime in about whether or not he went trick-or-treating as a kid, but he doesn't say anything. He gets up and gets another round, Rex waving no to a third beer.

"There are these ghost tours in Philly," I tell Rex. "You know, like haunted history stuff. And one year, Ginger and I followed the tour to see the route, then on Halloween, we dressed in all white and Ginger did this makeup so we looked dead—she's really good at makeup—and we hid in this one old graveyard in Old City that the tour went past. And when the tour guide started talking about the ghost of some elder statesman who supposedly haunted the graveyard, we jumped up and ran at the tour group. They all screamed and everything. It was perfect. But then, this old guy came running after us dressed in, like, a rotted potato sack with this long, bloody hair, and *we* screamed and ran. I guess he was *supposed* to be there to scare the tour group and we totally fucked it up."

Will has slid another drink into my hand while I'm talking and I sip it absently. I scoot a little closer to Rex, staring at Will. He's not so intimidating.

"Daniel," Rex is saying. "When's the last time you ate?"

"Um, at your house?"

He shakes his head. "That was a piece of toast. I think you need to eat something. Are you hungry?"

"I could eat," I say, as my stomach gives a loud growl. "Do you guys want?"

"Fries," Will says. Rex shakes his head. I order at the bar and stop at the bathroom. When I get back it's clear they've been talking about me— or, Will has been—because he stops midsentence.

I slide back into the booth and lean my head against Rex's shoulder just a little bit because I'm so tired all of a sudden. He puts his arm around me.

"So all it takes are a few shots of whiskey to turn the porcupine into a kitten, huh?" Will says. Is he talking to me? Rex's arm tightens around my shoulder.

"I don't like you at all," I say to Will, who grins at me. It seems to break the ice, though, because by the time the food comes we're all chatting about different places we've lived and Will asks me about teaching.

It's funny: Will is kind of a messy eater. He crams fries in his mouth like the kids I used to hang out with in diners, and it looks odd with his refined face and expensive clothes. I only notice it because I used to eat that way too. I grew up guarding my plate against my brothers and eating as fast as I could. It's one of the things I worked hard to fix when I noticed the other grad students at Penn didn't eat like me.

I eat about half my BLT and fries and push the plate over to Rex, who started eyeing it as soon as the smell of bacon hit his nose. He squeezes my thigh.

"You don't want any more?" he asks, like he always does, and I say "I'm done," just like I always do, and I have this weird picture in my head of that exchange happening a thousand more times. I shake my head, which is all fuzzy, though I feel better now that I've eaten.

Will is watching us, his greasy fingers leaving prints on his martini glass.

"You want to get out of here?" Rex asks me when he finishes the food. His eyes are warm and his stubble is a little longer than usual because he worked from home today. It looks soft, and in the light of the pub, I can see the red in it and a few strands of silver at his temples. I nod.

Outside, it smells bright and cold and Rex puts his arm around me again.

"I'll walk you home," Rex says, though you can almost see my apartment from here.

"Go to bed, old men," Will calls, waving behind him as he walks in the other direction without looking back.

Rex and I amble toward my house.

"Wait, how old is Will?" I ask, registering the old man comment.

"Twenty-six."

"Wow, so you dated when he was only, what, twenty-two?"

"Yeah, he'd just finished college."

I unlock the door and for once my apartment doesn't feel too oppressive. I left the window open a crack, so the ramen smell has dissipated, anyway. Kicking my shoes off and dropping my bag on the quasi-fixed kitchen table, I walk into the bathroom and brush my teeth twice. Nothing makes the day feel distant like the taste of toothpaste. I wander back outside and Rex has locked the front door.

"Do you want to stay?" I ask him. "I don't know if you can leave Marilyn alone, but…." I stand near the bed and pull my shirt off. I'm definitely a bit tipsy because all I can concentrate on are the lines of Rex's body and the way he's looking at me—like I'm some kind of treat he lets himself have sometimes. He walks closer and I can smell the spicy pine scent from his woodshop. He runs his hands down my arms and pulls me into a hug.

"Thank you for coming tonight," he says. "I know you weren't crazy about the idea. And I know Will acts like a child sometimes. But he's just defensive with new people, you know? Never wants to show his hand first."

I like how Rex explains things, like he sees the truth in why people do things. Even shitty things. He rubs my back softly.

"You're welcome."

"I can stay," he says, "if you want." I nod against his shoulder and pull his shirt off, breathing in the smell of his skin.

"You're so tired, baby," he says. "And maybe a little tipsy?"

"Maybe a little," I allow. "Sorry it's so cold."

"Isn't the heat on yet?"

"Um. No."

"Did you call Carl?"

I groan. I can't believe I gave him that opening.

"Daniel!" he says. "It's going to be really cold soon. You need to—"

I put my hand over his mouth.

"Do you need anything?" I ask, removing my hand.

"Can I use your toothpaste?"

I kiss him on the mouth.

"Mmm," he says. "Can I use it from the tube?"

I nod, and pull my pants and socks off before getting into bed. This bed is shitty; I feel a little bad making Rex sleep on it, though I've definitely slept on worse. His bed is so comfortable. My mind is drifting, picturing us on a bed the size of a room, when Rex slides in beside me, and pulls me to him, nestling my head in his neck.

"Sorry my bed's so uncomfortable," I murmur.

"It's worth it," he says.

I swallow a lump in my throat and turn my face farther into him.

"I just like you so much," I say. "How do you do that?"

And I think he answers, but I'm already sliding toward sleep.

Chapter 11

October

WHEN I get to Rex's, he's in his workshop, using a belt-sander on the surface of a tabletop, sawdust all over his chest and stomach and sticking to his sweaty arms.

"Damn," I mutter, and he looks up, lifting the sander from the wood and pushing up his safety goggles.

"Hi," he says, reaching for me, but pulling back when he realizes he's all sweaty. I pull him down for a kiss and brush the sawdust off my chest. He looks fucking sexy.

In some ways, he's the type of guy I've always been secretly attracted to: guys who could crush me as easily as the beer cans they swig from, wiping their hard mouths with the backs of dirty hands. But Rex is inclined less toward crushing and more toward putting back together. If only he could tinker me into shape as easily as one of his busted clocks.

"So, Leo should be here in a few minutes. We'll just hang out in the yard, okay? Just ignore us and keep doing what you're doing. It looks nice," I add, looking down at the satiny wood of the tabletop.

"Thanks," Rex says, running his hand over the grain. "Needs another pass."

"Do you like Halloween?" I ask.

Rex cocks his head and shrugs.

"I really like old monster movies." Of course he does. "Hey, I invited Will over for a beer while you guys are… training, okay?"

I nod. Will's irritating, with his power plays and innuendos, but he's not as bad as I thought. And he's Rex's friend. The only friend Rex seems to have. Of course, I didn't know about him until recently, so who knows who else could come out of the woodwork.

"Hello?" Leo calls from outside. "Oh, hey," he says. "Thought maybe I had the wrong house." He's wearing a battered army jacket and standing in the driveway with his skateboard propped on his foot.

"You can't skateboard on these roads," I say, confused. Leo blushes.

"Yeah, well, when you gave me the address I didn't realize it was in the middle of the woods. It's cool."

"Oh, sorry," I say. "Should we get started?"

Leo's face goes slack as he looks over my shoulder. Rex has come out of his workshop looking like exactly the kind of hot carpenter fantasy that Leo was spinning the other day. His muscles are bulging under the worn T-shirt and jeans, his hair is messy, and he's sweaty and covered in sawdust and curls of wood. Leo's mouth falls open.

"Hi, Leo, I'm Rex." He puts out his hand and it swallows Leo's up. "Can I get you something?" he offers, gesturing toward the house, and I feel like a bad host.

"No thanks," Leo says, having apparently managed to pick his jaw up off the floor. He's smiling and his big brown eyes shine as he looks at Rex with naked admiration. "I wish *you* would teach me a thing or two," he adds flirtatiously, sidling closer to Rex. Then he sneezes at the sawdust smell and I snort. Rex doesn't even seem to notice.

"I don't like fighting," is all he says. He squeezes the back of my neck, then goes inside.

I try to get a baseline on where Leo's at. He can't throw a punch, can't block without losing his balance, and can barely seem to distinguish left from right.

"It's hopeless," Leo moans after about half an hour, his face red with embarrassment and exertion.

I eye his skateboard.

"Can you actually skateboard?" I ask, realizing I've never seen Leo on it, only holding it.

"Yes!" he fires back.

I put the skateboard on the grass in front of me.

"Stand on it like you usually would."

He hops onto the skateboard and bends his knees a little to get his balance. I swing at him and he throws his hand up to block, but this time he stays upright. I do it a few more times and Leo stays balanced. He grins at me.

"Better," I say.

"Yeah, now all he has to do is ask the person who's about to punch him if it's okay if he sets his skateboard down and stands on it first," says Will through his car window as he parks. Leo's face burns and his smile is gone.

"Fuck off, Will," I say. "We're just building his basic skills first."

"Ooh, skill-building. Guess you really are a teacher, huh."

Leo is looking at the ground, his eyes darting up every few seconds to look at Will.

"Leo, this total asshole is Will; Will, Leo," I say.

Will walks up to Leo and looks him over. Leo falls off his skateboard. Jesus Christ.

"Hit me," Will says to Leo once he's picked himself up.

"Um," Leo says unsurely, looking to me.

"If you'd spent any more time around him you'd already have taken him up on that offer," I tell Leo.

"Are you su—?"

"Hit me!"

Leo arranges his hand into a fist the way I taught him and throws a weak punch from the shoulder, which would have landed somewhere around Will's nipple if it had connected. Will brushes him aside.

"No, no, no," Will says, "pick your heel up. No, your other heel. Bend your knees. Lean back. No."

"Will, we hadn't gotten there yet." I shoulder Will aside and stand next to Leo.

"Okay," I say. "You have to get the weight of your body behind the punch because you're skinny, okay? So, widen your stance a little and, yeah, get your back heel up. Now you can lean backward to get some momentum, right?" Leo does it and nods. "Good. Bend your knees like you do when you skateboard. Duck your chin a little. Not so much that you can't see. There you go. Okay, now lean back. This is like in baseball, how you start with the bat back to get more power, right? Good. Now relax your arm a little. Now try."

Leo throws the punch and almost falls forward.

"Better," I say.

"You've got to let him see how it feels to connect with something, Daniel," Will says. "Fucking hurts. Here, Leo, hit me."

"Yeah, end his modeling career, Leo," I say. "Please."

"You're a model?" Leo asks, his head jerking up. Will rolls his eyes and flips me off.

"No, I am not a model. Now fucking hit me."

Leo tries to replicate the stance, but somehow gets his feet all tangled up when he punches.

"Do it again," Will says.

Leo repeats the maneuver a few times, finally landing a punch near Will's chin. At the last moment, Will puts his fist up, so Leo hits that instead, and Leo drops to the ground holding his hand. Will shakes his hand out, not even flinching.

Will reaches a hand down to Leo, who blushes as he stands up. Will cups the back of his neck and Leo smiles tentatively, looking up at Will shyly through thick eyelashes.

"You," Will says, shaking him a little by the back of the neck, "are a terrible fighter." Leo drops his head.

"We just started," I mutter, but Will's right: Leo has no aptitude for this at all. Kid's just not a fighter, and I kind of like that he's made it to eighteen without needing to be.

Rex comes outside, hair still damp from the shower, and holds a beer out to Will.

"Why don't we leave them to it," Rex says. He must've been watching through the kitchen window.

"No way," Will says. "This guy's helpless. Can't let him wander around like that. God knows what kind of trouble he'll get into. Especially with that come-fuck-me smile."

"Right?" I say to Will. For once we're in total agreement. Leo looks mortified and Rex looks uncomfortable.

Will looks at me and back at Leo. He's not that small. Maybe five foot ten—only an inch or so shorter than Will and me. But he's skinny and he's got no instinct for fighting. Maybe I should just teach him what I taught Ginger, who had no interest in fighting, just in making sure she could get away if it came down to it.

"Let's just show him how to get *out* of a fight," I say. Will nods and comes to stand next to me.

"Okay, Leo. You're never going to be a fighter," Will says. "But you strike me as someone who pisses people off enough to need to defend himself. Believe me, I'd know. So, here's how to avoid getting your ass kicked when you find yourself in that situation."

"Rip off his ear, hit him in the nose, and crush his throat," Will and I say at the same time, and laugh. Huh, maybe he's not such an idiot after all. He's regarding me as if he's thinking the same thing. I can almost hear Ginger saying *jinx* in my ear.

"Jesus," Rex mutters under his breath, but he doesn't go back inside.

"Someone gets in your face this close," Will moves close to me, "they can't throw a punch. They're just messing with you. So, you grab their ear." He takes hold of mine and I give him a warning look. He winks at me. "Don't pull out, pull toward you, like ripping a piece of paper in half."

Leo laughs nervously, like he can't tell if we're serious.

"No joke," Will says. "That sucker'll come off no problem and it will fucking hurt."

"Also, it bleeds a lot and looks dramatic, so if there's more than one person, it'll help freak them out and discourage them from jumping into the fight," I add. "Okay, second, you smash the heel of your hand up into their nose. It doesn't take nearly the force or the precision of a punch to do damage, and you can do it in close quarters. Plus, it bleeds a hell of a lot and it'll make their eyes tear up so they can't see you as well." Will demonstrates on me.

"Third," Will says, "hit them in the throat, right here. It barely takes any force at all to totally incapacitate someone." He puts one hand on the back of Leo's neck and Leo's eyes briefly flutter shut. Will doesn't seem to notice, just presses the fingers of his other hand into the cartilage of Leo's neck. "Feel that? Now imagine I hit you there." Leo gags a little and Will lets him go. "If you hit a little harder, you'll crush their windpipe completely," he continues. He comes over to demonstrate, grabbing me by the shoulder so I can't pull away, and miming first a punch and then a chop to the throat. Leo looks a little freaked out.

Will still has me by the shoulder, so I drop my body weight down and twist away from his hand, coming around so that my fist is at his throat. I'm looking at Leo, about to show him the move, when Will swipes my feet out from under me and takes me down hard. I roll over and throw my elbow up so he can't grab me. Then I flip us over and pin Will with his hands behind his back. Will wriggles out of it somehow and pushes my face to the side. We're pretty evenly matched, I think, so I know I could probably take him if it came to it. This is just in fun, though.

"Stop it." Rex's voice cuts through the haze that has started to fill my ears, like always happens during a fight. He reaches down and hauls Will off me effortlessly, his biceps flexing, but his eyes never leaving mine. He pulls Will to his feet and then turns around and stalks into the house. I look quizzically at Will when he reaches a hand down to help me up. He looks guilty. Did he actually think he could have hurt me?

"I'm gonna—" I gesture toward the house, leaving Will and Leo outside.

Rex is in the kitchen, jerking things out of the cabinets and throwing them on the counter. The muscles in his shoulders and back are clenched and his neck is corded.

"Are you okay?" I ask, coming up behind him and putting a hand on his shoulder.

"I don't like fighting, Daniel," he says, his voice tight. It's the same thing he said to Leo outside.

"Don't worry. We weren't actually fighting, just messing around."

"I don't—" Rex clenches his fists and slams one down onto the counter before turning to face me. "I can't stand fighting." When I look at him more closely, he's trembling, his muscles clenched not in anger but in fear. His eyes look distant and he's swallowing convulsively. He drops his eyes from mine and I can see him trying to get himself back in control.

Oh fuck. I didn't even think about it. Rex already told me he hates violence. He told me about his lover who was beaten to death. When I asked him if I could teach Leo to fight, he hesitated. I thought he was confused about why Leo needed to learn, but of course he didn't want to watch it happen; he was just too generous to say so. He told me. He told me in so many different ways that violence upsets him and I didn't even think about it. God, all I had to do was mention the Internet once and Rex got it installed in his own house just so I could use it. He comes right out and tells me about how traumatized he was by violence and I just invite Leo over and start fighting with Will right in front of Rex. I am such an asshole. How could I be so oblivious?

"Rex, I'm so sorry. I didn't think—I should never have done this here. Fuck, I'm sorry."

I slide my palms up his chest and squeeze his shoulders, feeling them relax a little bit.

"I just...." Rex shakes his head and his fingers trace my throat and my nose and my ears, all the places Will touched me. I put my arms around him and pull him into a hug, stroking his back. His heart is pounding but he relaxes a bit more, burying his face in my neck.

"It's just," Rex starts again, his voice broken, "when I saw him on top of you, all I could think of was how I couldn't get to Jamie. How if I had just been stronger. Or if someone had taught me to fight like you're teaching Leo. Maybe I could have saved him. But they fucking killed him and I didn't—" His voice gives out until it's just breath against my neck.

"Rex," I say, hugging his trembling body closer to me. "There were three guys with a weapon. Even if you'd been stronger or known how to fight... man, there was nothing you could've done. And you probably would've gotten yourself killed trying."

I push Rex down onto one of the stools next to the counter.

"But maybe if I'd known how to fight better—"

"Have you been in a fight besides that day?" I ask gently, pulling up the other stool and sitting across from him.

He shakes his head. I'm not surprised. The only people who would take on someone as big and strong as Rex would be on drugs or wasted, and I doubt Rex is even around those kinds of people. After all, that was his goal in bulking up. It seems like it worked.

"It all happens so fast you barely even notice what's going on. I can't even really explain it, but adrenaline kicks in and everything is a blur. And you do whatever you need to do to make the other person hurt worse than he can hurt you. And you do it as fast as you can, because once that adrenaline wears off, it really, really hurts." I squeeze Rex's thighs between my knees. "Maybe, *maybe*, if you had been training for years, you could have taken on three guys, *if* they were crap fighters and waited to take turns going at you. But three on one? And all bigger than you? Out in the open?" I shake my head. "All one of them would've had to do is hit you in the head with that stick while you were fighting with one of the others and you would've been out." I take his hands in mine. "What happened to you and Jamie is horrible. But I'm so glad you didn't throw yourself into that and end up dead when it probably wouldn't have made any difference."

Tears are running down Rex's face even though his expression hasn't changed. He pulls me up so I'm standing between his knees and squeezes me tight, his face against my chest.

"I hate," he says venomously, "that you've been in enough fights to know that. But thank you." He rests his chin on my chest and looks up at me. It's strange to feel taller than him, but I take advantage of it and lean down to kiss him. I can taste salt on his lips, but his mouth is warm and he kisses me so sweetly. He pulls me down to straddle his lap and runs his thumbs over my cheekbones.

"I hate that you know all that stuff you were showing Leo, too," he says, "but I could tell you're a good teacher watching you show him."

"Yeah?"

"You explain things well. And you tied each new thing into something he already knew how to do. When he couldn't balance, you put him on his skateboard where you knew he could. So smart." His expression is heated and he kisses me again. "I love how smart you are." I laugh, putting my arms around his neck.

"Thanks. Hey, what were you going to make?" The ingredients are still strewn on the counter in front of me.

"Huh? Oh, um, I don't know; I just wanted to be doing something with my hands."

I kiss his neck and settle more firmly on his lap.

"I can think of something you can do with your hands," I tease him.

"Mmm." He pulls me down firmly onto him and kisses my mouth again. He's running one big hand up my back under my shirt when the door opens and bangs shut.

"Whoa," I hear Leo say, and I slide off Rex's lap. Rex clears his throat, but doesn't get up. Will has Leo by the back of the shirt, no doubt preventing him from walking into the kitchen.

"Uh, maybe we should just order a pizza instead?"

AFTER WE'VE eaten pizza, we're sitting around in Rex's living room and Leo is trying to teach Marilyn to roll over. She keeps sitting instead, as if Rex has taught her not to listen to people who tell her to do stupid things.

"Hey, don't you have any friends you should be hanging out with on Halloween?" Will asks, lazily running his finger around the mouth of his beer bottle. It's become clear to me that this is just how Will talks, but Leo turns red and looks down, embarrassed.

"Rex, how did you ever date such an asshole?" I say, without heat.

Leo's head snaps up.

"You two used to date?" he asks, and I can practically *see* the porn he's writing in his head right now.

"He doesn't mean anything by it," Rex says, leaning back into the couch and ruffling Will's hair. Will pulls away and shoots daggers at him as he fixes his hair. "He just doesn't always remember that other people *have feelings*." He shoots the last two words at Will.

"Jeez, sorry!" Will says, looking at Leo. "I'm sure you have hundreds of friends and it's so kind of you to grace us with your presence. Okay?" He makes a face.

"No, it's okay," Leo says with a sigh. "I guess I should go and leave you guys to your evening."

God, Leo's a nice kid. He gets up slowly, giving us all every opportunity to stop him. I shoot Will a look and see that Rex is doing the same. Will's eyes get big and then he rolls them at us.

"Wait, Leo," he says. "Don't go. Stay and we'll... uh—" He looks around wildly. "—we'll play a game?"

"Really?" Leo is back in a flash. "I love games! What are we gonna play?"

I look irritatedly at Will. Does Rex even own any games? He doesn't really seem like much of a game player. Besides, he's alone most of the time.

"Oh, wait, Rex doesn't have any games," Will says. Leo's face falls, like he thinks Will was just messing with him.

"We could do something else," I offer. "Watch a movie. It's Halloween; there've got to be some good horror movies on, right?"

Leo doesn't look thrilled with that idea either and twists his hands in his lap. Then he looks up, excited again.

"We could play Celebrity! You just write the names of different celebrities on pieces of paper and then you draw the names out of a hat and try to get us to guess them as fast as you can."

Will looks at Rex, his eyes shifting quickly back.

"Um, no, that's no good," he says. "Old man Rex over there won't know any celebrities unless they're circa Hedy Lamarr."

"Who?" Leo and I say.

Rex opens his mouth like he's about to tell us, but Will interrupts.

"How about Pictionary?" Will says. "Two teams of two, and each team can just tell the drawer what they're drawing. No work involved."

I shrug.

"If you guys want. I can't draw for shit."

"Yeah," says Leo, "I can't really—"

"Here, kid, you can be on my team and the lovebirds over there can be together." Will pulls Leo over to him and Leo goes easily, shutting up the second Will touches him. I flip Will off, but move over to Rex.

"Sorry in advance," I tell Rex. Rex brings out pads of paper and pens and we start to play. I am an embarrassingly bad artist, trying to communicate things with stick figures and totally not-to-scale objects. Rex gamely guesses, following my trains of thought pretty well. He's a good artist, though. Everything he draws is neat and precise, with simple, clear lines like a blueprint. Leo, like me, isn't good. He draws fast and large, taking up the whole page only to scribble it out and start over, which drives Will crazy. He guesses at rapid-fire pace, going in a different direction practically every time Leo draws a new line, to the point where the kid gets flustered and starts narrating what things are, which loses them the round.

But Will is an amazing artist. He begins to draw and, with only a few pen strokes, pulls a whole story out of the page. His drawings have style and personality even when they're things like milk or flyover states.

We're playing to ten and we're tied at nine, our team having lost the last round, so if Will and Leo get the next point, they win. It's Leo's turn to draw and I gave him The Talking Heads.

"A corpse! A mummy! A mannequin?" Will guesses. "A guy blowing a bubble! A guy blowing a bubble through a straw! A guy fishing with his mouth! Two guys mouth fishing? Two guys blowing bubbles? Come *on*, Leo, what the hell *is* that? Wait, fellatio! Come on, Daniel, you gave the kid 'fellatio'?"

"I can assure you I did not."

"People with dentures! People with dentures blowing a bubble! People with wax lips and clown noses sucking each other off! Robots! Dick-sucking robots!"

"There are no dicks, you asshole!" Leo finally yells. "That is not a penis!" He points to his paper.

"Draw, draw, draw!" Will yells. "Oh, they're talking. Talking heads?" he says suddenly, with a grin that suggests he's known it all along.

"Yes! Fuck!" Leo yells furiously just as the timer on his phone goes off.

Will lets out a whoop and launches himself sideways into Leo, knocking them both onto their sides on the rug, Marilyn pawing at them curiously.

AN HOUR later, after Will and Leo have bonded over a Halloween episode of *Buffy* that they swear is ingenious, Will has shuttled Leo home and the three of us sack out on the couch, drinking beer, and I rib Will about having a crush on Leo. To my surprise, Will looks guilty, and I can't help but wonder if it might actually be true. Before I have a chance to examine it too closely, though, my phone rings and I know it's Ginger, since no one else ever calls me.

"Happy Halloween!" Ginger crows when I answer.

"Happy Halloween, Ginge," I say, as Rex and Will start laughing at something.

"Ooh, are you with Rex?" she asks. "Put me on speaker!"

I put the phone on speaker and gesture to Rex.

"Hi, Ginger," he drawls. "Nice to meet you."

"Hi, Rex. You have a hot voice. Don't ever stop talking to me."

"I already like her more than you," Will says.

"Everybody does," I tell him.

"Not me," Rex says, smiling at me.

"Who is that?" Ginger says. God, I hate speakerphone.

"He's Rex's ex-boyfriend, Will, who showed up out of the blue to try and sleep with Rex." Oops, didn't mean to say that last part. Will is staring at me, wide-eyed.

"Uh, well, okay, then," Ginger says uncomfortably, clearly wanting information from me but unwilling to ask for it in front of Rex and Will. "Have a good night, Dandelion."

"Ha! Dandelion?" Will whoops.

"Don't make me kick your ass, pretty boy," I say, glaring at Will.

"Pretty boy?" Will says, getting in my face. "Pot, meet kettle."

Rex picks up my phone and takes it off speakerphone, talking to Ginger as Will and I glare.

"Ginger, I have two beautiful drunk men who are about to fight in my house. If I didn't *hate* fighting, it would almost be.... Yeah, I should. Huh. Okay, thanks. Nice to talk to you. I hope so too. Thanks."

Will is staring at me. I'm staring at Will. I won't hit the idiot because Rex wouldn't like it, but dammit, I want to. Rex shakes his head.

"Hey, tough guy," he whispers in my ear. His voice is low and his breath raises the hairs on the back of my neck. I lean into him a little, but keep my narrowed eyes on Will in case he makes a move. Then Rex digs his thumb into the incredibly ticklish spot on my ribs that only my brothers and Ginger know about and I'm done for.

"Goddammit, Ginger!" I yell, squirming. Rex and Will laugh, the tension gone.

"Now would you two idiots stop it," Rex says, dropping onto the couch. "I can't even be flattered that you're fighting over me because you're not. Not really. You're just fighting because it's what you're used to and I don't like it."

"Sorry," I say, sitting down on the arm of the couch.

Will's face is unreadable.

"You are kind of scrappy," he says to me with a touch of admiration, and I can tell he's thinking about our tag-team effort to teach Leo this afternoon.

"Yeah, well, you're not as much of a pansy as you look either," I grudgingly admit.

Rex shakes his head, looking between us. He points Will into the armchair and pulls me down onto the couch next to him. Marilyn wanders over, looking up at us on the couch, and I fold myself into Rex to make room for her. I'm helpless against the look of hope she gets when she wants to snuggle. Rex usually makes her sit on the floor, but I like the feeling of her lying on my feet. She puts her paws up on the couch and I pat the space next to me.

Rex sighs, but just strokes my hair as I put my head on his shoulder and pat Marilyn's head. Rex puts his arm around me and flicks on the TV, flipping channels until he gets to the classic movie channel he likes so much.

"Hey, it's your monster movie," I say when I see it's *Frankenstein*. Rex squeezes my shoulder and I relax against him.

"Poor Frankenstein," Will says. "Bastard couldn't catch a break, could he?"

"The doctor is Frankenstein," I say absently, my eyes fixed on the screen. "That's his creature."

"Call him whatever you want," Will says. "He's miserable and alone and he's about to be mobbed by a whole fucking village. Sucks."

"—SISTER OKAY?" Rex is saying quietly when I wake up. I dozed off during *Frankenstein* and it looks like now it's a movie about rats or something. Marilyn is a warm weight on my feet and Rex smells delicious. I'm kind of lying on him now; I must have been out for a while. I decide I'm not in the mood to talk to Will anymore and I close my eyes and relax into Rex again.

"She's all right," Will says, and then starts talking about some boyfriend or her boss and I'm not really listening, just thinking about how comfortable I am and how I wish Will would disappear in a puff of magic Halloween smoke and leave me alone with Rex so we could go to bed.

I must have fallen asleep again for a minute. When I drift back awake, Will's voice sounds different.

"He really likes you a lot."

My first thought is to sit up and ask Will who the hell likes Rex, but then my sleepy brain catches up and I realize he must mean me. I know I should tell them I'm awake, but I can't make myself do it. I want to hear what Rex says in response. Also, part of me is curious to hear how he and Will interact when it's just the two of them. Sure, Will isn't turning out to be quite the asshole I thought he was, but I haven't seen much that makes me understand why he and Rex are friends either.

"Yeah, you think so?" Rex asks, his voice vulnerable. He's stroking my hair, which feels amazing. "Sometimes he's just so... I dunno. Like he doesn't want me close."

"He's lying on top of you," Will jokes.

"Ha, smartass. You know what I mean."

"I do," Will says, sounding serious. "And I think for a guy like Daniel, what he's like when he's drunk or tired says more about how he feels than he'll say out loud."

"Yeah?" Rex asks.

"Well, you saw how he went right for me today and the other night. I can tell he's been fighting his whole life. That shit's ingrained."

"Well, you weren't exactly discouraging it," Rex says.

"Hey, man, I reacted to him. You know I don't start fights. I'll fight back, but I don't throw the first punch unless I have to. You know that. Daniel… he doesn't like it, but he's used to it—you know, like, he throws the first punch to stop whoever from throwing the second and third and the fourth. I get it."

"He didn't hurt you, did he?" Rex asks.

"Nah. Stronger than I thought, though. When you said he was an English teacher I thought he'd be a pansy."

"Funny, he said the same thing about you."

"Anyway, I saw how he jumped when we startled him at the bar yesterday. He's either been jumped a bunch of times or he's been abused. Maybe both. Am I right?"

"It's not your business, Will," Rex says gently.

"That's fine, babe," Will says, and I resist the urge to jump up and throttle Will for the term of endearment. "All I meant to say is that for someone who's used to fighting, the fact that he defaults to relaxing around you means something. That's all. Besides, the way he looks at you…."

"Yeah," Rex says fondly.

Wait, how do I look at him?

Will changes the subject even though now I'm desperate to hear more. I don't like that he could tell so much about me, having only known me for a few hours. More than that, though, I'm curious. Because he's right.

I never relax around people the way I do around Rex. I hadn't really thought about it because I've been anxious about other shit, but I've never fallen asleep on anyone except Ginger. I've never put my head on someone's shoulder while we were sitting next to each other. It's never even crossed my mind. And yet, with Rex, I have. I've done those things and not even really thought about them. Maybe Will is right. Not only do I like Rex, but I let my guard down around him in a way I can't even verbalize. Maybe Will's not such an idiot after all.

I wake up the next time to Rex shifting beneath me. I sit up and look around the darkened room.

"Will gone?"

"Yeah, he just left," Rex says, smoothing my messy hair back from my face. He stands up and reaches out a hand, pulling me up. I rest my forehead on Rex's chest to stop my head from spinning. I guess I was a little drunk after all. Rex strokes my back gently.

"He's not so bad, I guess," I say into Rex's chest.

"He said the same about you," Rex says, and I can hear the smile in his voice.

Chapter 12

November

ON WEDNESDAY afternoon I'm in my office, trying to get some work done on one of my book chapters, and am more than happy for the interruption of my phone ringing.

"What's the good news?" Ginger asks. She's been texting me for days, trying to convince me to come home for Thanksgiving.

"I can't come for Thanksgiving, Ginge. I'm sorry. There isn't time to drive and I definitely can't afford to fly. I'll come for Christmas, though—sorry, Chanukah."

"Bummer, babycakes," she says. "Who will I eat Thanksgiving burritos with?" We usually get these amazing burritos with turkey, sweet potato, stuffing, and cranberry sauce from a weird hole-in-the-wall place near Ginger's and listen to Elvis (at Ginger's insistence) on Thanksgiving.

"Maybe I'll keep the shop open and only give Thanksgiving-themed tattoos. But, like, literal ones. Like, I'll tattoo turkeys, Thanksgiving foods, the genocide of indigenous peoples, et cetera. Whattaya think?"

"I like it. Maybe you could also tattoo Wednesday Addams as Pocahontas from that Addams Family movie where they go to camp and are tortured by Disney movies."

"Good one!"

"Sorry, Ginge, really."

"No worries, pumpkin. I know money's tight. If I could afford to fly you out, I would. But if you abandon me for Chanukah, I'll Jewish-guilt you until you're dead. I need your ass on my couch, eating Chinese food and listening to Christmas music, or our friendship is basically over. And, lucky you, Chanukah goes all the way up until Christmas this year, so your schedule should be fine."

"I'll be there," I tell her. Chanukah at Ginger's is one of my favorite traditions, even though I hate Christmas music. Ginger thinks it's cruel and unusual that there is no Chanukah music and she's not one for klezmer or Adam Sandler, so she's reclaimed Christmas music. She even rewrote some of the lyrics.

"So, are you having Thanksgiving at Rex's?"

"I don't know. It hasn't come up."

"Well, is he going to be in town or does he go visit family?"

"He doesn't have any."

"Family? What happened?"

"He didn't know his dad, he's an only child, and his mom died when he was a teenager. Actually, except for Will, I haven't even met any of his friends. I'm not sure he has many."

"That's sad." Ginger and I both have fraught relationships with our families, but at least we have them.

"Do you think I should ask him? I mean, I don't know if I should bring it up. Maybe holidays make him sad, or maybe it would seem like I'm trying to invite myself over, or what if—"

"Um, Daniel. Those are kind of the things you're *supposed* to talk about in a relationship."

"Oh, right. Sure."

Maybe I'd rather go back to my book after all.

"DANIEL!" LEO exclaims as I walk through the door of Mr. Zoo's.

"Hey, man," I say.

"Need more tapes?" Leo asks with a cheeky smile.

"No, but you might want to check your cases. Some Pet Shop Boys fan is going to be surprised by a John Hiatt album. I'm looking for a record."

"But I thought you didn't have a record player?"

Jesus, does this kid remember every goddamned thing I say?

"It's, uh, for Rex."

"Aw, Rex," Leo coos.

"Careful there, kiddo. At least I can remain upright in his presence, which is more than I can say for you when Will is around."

Leo turns a satisfying shade of red.

"Um, the records are over there," he mutters, pointing.

I flip through them, looking for something special. Something that Rex would love. I can't quite figure his taste yet. Everything he listens to is old, passed down from his mom, but he likes Tori Amos and he's seemed to know several other bands I've mentioned. I consider getting him a few things I really like, but I'm not sure he'll like them. I linger over an Etta James album and a Lou Reed, then consider some of the bands I first saw play live, but that seems sappy. I finally decide on an Emmylou Harris record and take it up to Leo.

"So, what's the occasion?" Leo asks.

"No occasion. He just did something nice and I want to say thank you." Jesus, it sounds like I'm describing National Secretaries Day or something.

"That's nice of you. What did he do?"

Leo seems to have no clue that certain things are none of his business, but the kid is growing on me, and it's not like it's particularly personal.

Last night, Rex came over carrying something that looked like the beautiful piece of wood I'd seen him working on in his woodshop a few days before.

"What's this?" I asked him.

"You needed a new kitchen table," he said. His posture was comfortable and commanding like usual, but I could see uncertainty in his face, no doubt because of my totally ungrateful response to his previous efforts regarding my table.

I took a deep breath. No one had ever *made* anything for me before, and I couldn't even imagine how many hours it must have taken Rex to craft this piece. Rex doing that—showing up like that—was a test. Not that Rex engineered it as one; he's not manipulative like that. But it was a test of whether or not this could be okay between us and I knew it. This was Rex showing me that he cared.

I smiled and stepped aside. Rex fitted in the legs and skimmed the wood with a tender hand. The table reminded me of him: sturdy and comfortable and welcoming.

"It's amazing," I said, and Rex's smile told me I'd passed the test for sure.

So, now, here I am at Mr. Zoo's because I wanted to get Rex a record or something to say thank you.

"He made me a new kitchen table," I say. "Mine broke."

"Whoa! That's amazing."

Yeah, it really is. Leo looks at me and then down at Emmylou and gets a weird look on his face.

"What?"

"Um, no offense or anything," he says, "and I'm sure it's a good album and all, but that's kind of a lame present for someone who, like, *carved* you something out of a tree with his bare hands."

Shit. Shit, he's totally right.

"Sorry!" he says.

"No, you're fucking right," I say, letting out a breath.

"You swear a lot."

"Yeah, I guess I do. Sorry." He just smiles. "So, you got any better ideas?" I ask. "And if you insinuate anything to do with sexual favors, so help me...."

"Well, what have you already done for him?"

"Done?"

"Yeah, like, what nice things, so I don't repeat them."

Nice things. What nice things have I done for Rex? Fuck all, that's what. Better question: what nice things has Rex done for me? Rescued me after a car accident and given me a place to stay for the night even though I was a total stranger. Saved the dog I hit with my car. Fixed the desk in my office when he barely even knew me. Warned me about the weather. Come to pick me up in the middle of a snowstorm when my car died. Cooked for me. Taken me to dinner. Given me a massage. Gotten the Internet at his house for me even though he doesn't use it himself. Made me a kitchen table even after I yelled at him the last time he brought it up.

And me? I took his fucking dog for a walk when he had a debilitating fucking migraine. I fucking disgust myself.

I drop my head down onto my arms on the counter and groan.

"Shit, Leo!" I say.

"What? What's wrong?" Now I've scared the kid.

"What's wrong is that I'm a shit boyfriend. Absolute shit. I don't know what I'm doing. I have no fucking clue."

Leo is wide-eyed, staring at me with his mouth half open. God knows why he liked me in the first place, but whatever hero worship he had is, I'm sure, dying a writhing death on the counter between us as we speak. I'm a grown man and I have no idea how to date someone. No idea at all.

"Um," Leo starts, with a mommy-and-daddy-are-fighting expression. "Well, my sister always says she'll forgive a guy anything if he buys her flowers."

"Uh-huh, and how old is your sister?"

"Sixteen."

"Yeah. Well, you should tell your sister that's a crap policy."

"Okay, well, why don't you take him on a really nice date? My sister says—"

"No offense, Leo, but I'm going to go ahead and say I don't care what your little sister thinks about dating."

"No, no, this is a good one. She says a well-conceived date shows that you pay attention to the person. That you know what they like to do and you want to show them a good time."

That makes sense. I was probably supposed to ask Rex out on a date after he took me to dinner, so things were equal. I've never asked someone on a date before. Never planned one. But I know what Rex likes. Old movies and good food. This will be fine.

"Right, okay." I tell Leo. "A date. I can do that."

But he doesn't look totally convinced.

ON FRIDAY, I pick Rex up at his house because it seems a date-like thing to do. He looks amazing in tight black jeans that mold to his muscular thighs and round ass and one of those thick oatmeal-colored sweaters that I associate with ski lodges and Irish whiskey ads. The thick sweater makes him look even larger than usual, like if he held me I'd be warm and safe forever.

"Wow," I say. "You look amazing."

Rex's smile is brilliant. Against the light sweater, his skin looks tan and luminous, his reddish brown stubble darker than usual. His hair falls in his face as he leans down to kiss me and I can't help but push one hand into the soft strands and pull him closer with the other, feeling the incredible warmth he always gives off. Now there's a light scent of wool and cedar added to his usual pine and wood smoke smell.

"You wouldn't say where we were going," he says, "so I went with something versatile."

"Oh, well, it's nothing too exciting, so—"

"I don't care what we do," Rex says, elbowing me gently like I should know better.

"No, I know. I just wanted to take you out on a real date. I've never really done that before. Anyway, should we go?"

I'm actually really pleased with myself for finding anything to do in this town that Rex might like. I'm taking Rex to dinner and then to see *The Phantom of Liberty*, which, according to the chair of my department, is a classic of Surrealist French cinema from the 1970s, and he can't believe I didn't know that there's a film series on campus. I figure with his love for classic movies, Rex will be totally into it, and since it's French, he's less likely to have already seen it.

Rex is in a great mood. At dinner, in a cozy round booth, Rex tells me about custom furniture pieces he's seen that he'd like to try making and teases me about things he's heard people saying about me around town. Apparently, Carrie and Naomi, the high-school-age waiters at the diner, talk about my clothes, my hair, and—Rex elbows me—how cute I am. I get the feeling that, since Rex barely talks to anyone when he's out, he overhears a lot. Probably even a lot that he isn't telling me.

When I tell him about Marjorie and The Daniel, he lets out a low, rolling laugh I haven't heard before.

As we're eating our entrées, Rex says, "How much of you asking me on a date is because of Will?" He doesn't sound mad or disappointed or anything, just curious.

"What? None of it."

He raises an eyebrow.

"I'm not judging. God knows I got jealous enough of that guy Jay, even if he wasn't actually after you."

I squirm.

"Oh, um, well, you were right, it turns out. About Jay. I forgot to tell you before because of Will showing up, but he sort of asked me out on Friday, before I left for Detroit. Last Friday, I mean."

"What did you say?" Rex asks evenly.

"I said no," I say, studying his face for a reaction. But he looks as calm as ever.

"How come?"

His voice is casual but his expression is intense. Like he's trying very hard not to lead me in answering.

"I—because I… we—I guess I thought we—I mean, I don't know… maybe we're not.…"

"You said no because we're dating?"

I wouldn't have necessarily put it like that. *Rex is not Richard*, I repeat over and over in my head, as if Ginger were yelling it at me. I nod miserably, but a warm smile spreads across his face.

Rex speaks slowly, like he's considering his words very carefully.

"Because you don't want to date anyone else? Or you do, but you're just not interested in Jay?"

I grab my wine and swallow a few gulps.

"Both. I mean, no. The first one. And I'm not interested in Jay. But, I mean, you can—date other people. Like, because we haven't had that conversation, I know."

"I think we're having it right now," Rex says. He scoots closer to me in the booth, so our knees are touching. I look down at his thighs, let them take over my whole field of vision. There is no conversation. There is nothing but Rex's powerful thighs.

"I don't want to date anyone else, Daniel," Rex says. His voice is low and possessive, his hand covering my thigh. My head jerks up. He's looking at me tenderly and my heart starts to pound. I swallow again, my throat dry.

"Neither do I." It comes out like a whisper.

"Lucky me," Rex drawls, smiling.

I grin at him and start to laugh, totally relieved.

After that, we don't have time for dessert if I want to get us to the movie in time, so Rex says we'll go back to his house later and he'll show me how to bake something. Just the idea of watching his big hands and powerful body as he bakes sends a flush of arousal through me. I picture him peeling off that heavy sweater and doing it shirtless in those tight jeans.

Rex throws an easy arm over my shoulder as we walk to the movie, pulling me into his warmth. Suddenly, I can't believe that this is my life. I have a... there's no other word for it: boyfriend. I have a boyfriend and we're out on a date, and he has his arm around my shoulder. I don't even have a frame of reference for this feeling.

The theater is in the basement of a building on campus that I've never been in before.

"It's an old movie from the seventies. A film series," I tell Rex as we walk downstairs. As soon as the words are out of my mouth all the stupid self-satisfaction I felt at picking something Rex would like fades away. It's just a movie. And we went to dinner. I took Rex to dinner and a movie. It's literally the most clichéd date of all time. "I just thought you might like it," I finish lamely.

Rex just smiles at me. A soft, intimate smile. He cups the back of my neck and pulls me in.

"Thank you," he says softly, and kisses my ear.

Oh. Well, that's okay, then.

Once we're seated, Rex takes my hand. There are only about ten people here and I'm relieved to see that none of them are my students.

"Am I allowed to know what movie it is?" Rex asks.

"*The Phantom of Liberty*," I say. "Have you seen it?"

He shakes his head and runs his hand through his hair.

"Thank you for tonight."

"It's kind of the least I can do," I say. "I mean, you carved me something out of a tree with your bare hands."

"Not really," Rex says with a warm smile.

"Seriously, Rex. I don't know why I didn't think to ask you before. I just, you know, I've *never* asked someone out on a date before. I mean, obviously, I know that's what you're supposed to do, but it's never been part of my life at all, so."

"I know that," he says, stroking the back of my hand with his thumb. "There are no rules for relationships, Daniel. There's no one way things are supposed to go. You know that, right?"

I nod. But... aren't there? I mean, not like Leo's sister's dumb kind of rules, but aren't there things you're supposed to do, like take your boyfriend out to dinner? There's that word again.

"None?" I ask.

Rex looks at me intently and I can see him really thinking about it. He shrugs.

"If you care about someone then you look out for them, right? You're careful with them. But it's the same as with friends or family. Those are just people rules, though. There are no rules for me, no. I mean, no rules like: you have to buy me flowers or cook me breakfast in bed. No greeting card rules."

"Fuck!" I say exaggeratedly. "Was I supposed to bring you flowers?"

Rex smirks and puts his hand on my thigh. He touches me all the time. It's almost like he doesn't notice it. Like I'm just an extension of his body and so of course he would touch me. But, no, that makes it sound thoughtless. It's like when I'm near him he decides that it's his right to touch me. It makes me feel so connected to him. At first, every time we touched I wondered if it might be the last time. I felt greedy about those touches because I wasn't sure when the next one was coming. Now, it's like whenever he's touching me he's telling me that I'm his. That he's taking me on as something within his purview.

"We can make our own rules, cowboy," he drawls as the lights dim.

I laugh at the French translation of the title, *Le Fantôme de la liberté*, realizing it's a play on the line, "a spectre is haunting Europe—the spectre of communism," from *The Communist Manifesto*, *fantôme* being the French for spectre. That makes me start thinking about the chapter I've been working on and I make an effort to clear my mind so I can pay attention. There may not be greeting card rules to dating Rex, but I'm pretty sure you're not supposed to be writing your book in your head while you're on a date.

The movie begins and Rex's hand tightens on my thigh. I glance at him and see that his jaw's clenched.

"You okay?"

"Yeah, fine," he says, and pats my leg.

The movie is definitely weird, but it's interesting. I have no background in film. Like I told Rex, I never even watched many popular movies as a kid. Superheroes and some horror movies and that's about it. But I'm glad Rex likes them because I'll be happy to get an unofficial education.

After a half hour or so, I notice Rex glancing over at me more and more often. At first it was sweet; he seemed like he couldn't keep his eyes off me. Now, though, it seems like he may just hate the movie.

"Are you bored?" I whisper.

"No, no," he says quickly, and looks back at the screen. About twenty minutes later, though, his hand is back on my knee and he's tracing complicated patterns closer and closer to my crotch, which is making it hard to pay attention. Not that I need to pay particular attention because the movie's kind of disjointed. A boy and his aunt are making out and Rex is stroking my leg. Some people are sitting on toilets at a dinner table and Rex leans down to softly kiss my neck. I pull away a with a shiver and shoot him a dirty look because I don't want to get all riled up in a theater at the school where I teach.

He kisses my cheek chastely and looks back at the screen, but he seems off. Fidgety and tense. Did I offend him?

I'm still wondering when the movie ends. The end is actually really beautiful, with the sounds of a riot at a zoo and the only thing on the screen a puzzled ostrich's head bobbing back and forth seeking out the sound.

As we walk out, I cast a look at Rex. He doesn't look mad, I don't think, but he's got his fists jammed in his pockets and he's staring at his shoes.

"Weird movie, huh?" I say stupidly as I start the car.

"Yeah. So," Rex says as if to change the subject, "ready to learn how to bake?"

"Sure. What are we making?"

"Do you like gingerbread?"

"Yeah, I love it."

"Great."

He sounds cheerful, but his knee is bouncing and he's holding on to the seat with both hands. I'm not that bad a driver, I don't think. Although,

I've never driven with him before, only ridden in his car, so maybe this is how he always is as a passenger.

"I googled the director before the movie," I say. "I didn't realize he was the one who made this famous short movie with Salvador Dalí in 1929. The one where they cut open a woman's eyeball?"

Rex doesn't say anything and I find myself rambling on in the silence of the car.

"I loved the end. And the thing about the inversion of consumption and evacuation at the dinner scene was really interesting. I mean, that's culture, right? Just a set of customs that tell us it's polite to shove food into our faces in front of each other but not polite to take a shit. And it could just as easily go the other way, like in the movie. It makes total sense, you know? Like, what's so special about the things we hide away anyway? Would they become unimportant if we just did them out in the open? And vice versa the things we think are fine. It doesn't actually take that much for something to become taboo. Or, at least for us to stigmatize things and give people total complexes about them."

I trail off as we pull into Rex's driveway. Rex unlocks the door and as we walk inside, he sighs.

"You hated it, right?" I ask.

He shakes his head.

"Well, then what did you think."

"It was interesting," he says vaguely.

"Okay...."

He crouches down and pets Marilyn, who trotted over when we walked in.

"Okay," I try again. "Well, I'm sorry if you didn't like it."

"I liked it fine," Rex says, standing. He definitely sounds mad now. "I just don't have a *thesis* about it to tell you, okay? I don't have a clever theory to share or anything. All right?"

Where the *fuck* did that come from? Jesus, I must have sounded like a total pretentious asshole in the car to have pissed him off that much. That's the problem with nervous rambling. People think you're attached to the things you say rather than talking out of your ass.

"Jesus," I say, putting my hands up. "I just meant that you didn't have to pretend to like it if you didn't. I was just trying to do something you'd like. Isn't that what I'm supposed to do?"

Rex doesn't say anything.

"Oh, right," I continue. "There are no rules. Well, that's fine for you. It's really easy to throw the rules out if you already know them. But I don't. Anyway, if you hated it, it's fine, but you don't have to be such an asshole about it."

"All I meant—"

"Oh, I know what you meant! You think I'm being the pretentious professor who thinks he's so fucking smart. Well, screw you. That's not what I think."

"You don't actually know everything that I'm thinking, Daniel," Rex says, his voice scary. "You can't read minds! I know you think that you can just look at everyone in this town and know what they think about you or about politics. But you can't."

"I don't think that!" I say, furious and frustrated. "I've never said that. Is that what you fucking think of me? That I think I'm smarter than everyone else? That I think I know everything? Because if that's what you think you had better say so right now."

Rex says nothing, the look on his face unreadable.

I storm into the kitchen and pour myself a glass of wine from the bottle on the counter. Am I supposed to leave now? Is that what you do when you have a fight with someone who you can't hit? Fuck! There's another rule that doesn't exist, I guess. So, then, how am I supposed to know what to do?

Rex comes into the kitchen.

"I don't think that," I say to him again, leaning on my elbows on the counter. How can I make him understand? This is what people always think. My brothers, my father. That I think I'm better than everyone just because I went to grad school. But it *isn't* what I think. I just like talking about books and movies. And I notice when people look askance at me for it. That's all.

I drop my head down between my shoulders, but I can feel Rex's heat at my side. I'm so furious with myself for this lame date that I want to punch myself in the face. Or punch a wall hard enough that my knuckles will be swollen tomorrow in reminder. And I'm fucking embarrassed. I guess Leo was right not to look convinced.

"Fuck, Rex, I suck at this! I'm shit at romance, or whatever the hell a date's supposed to be. I don't know how I'm supposed to act. I don't know what I'm supposed to say or do! I don't know how it's supposed to go, and don't tell me there is no supposed to because I know there is. I know there is because if I were doing it right you wouldn't be looking at me like that right now. I wouldn't have pissed you off and…. Dammit!" I yell.

I hit the counter with my fist, since I'm relatively sure I won't break it. The counter, I mean.

"I can't even take you out on a date without fucking the whole thing up. I should never have taken you to that stupid movie. You're right, it was fucking pretentious of me and of *course* you hated it!"

"I didn't hate it!" Rex yells. "Would you stop? I didn't hate the movie, Daniel. I didn't… I didn't fucking understand it, okay?"

He puts his hands over his mouth, like he's just said something he can't take back.

"Oh, well, I mean, Surrealism's pretty disjointed, so—"

"No. I mean—shit," he breaks off shaking his head. "I couldn't read the subtitles. I can't… I don't read very well." He shakes his head again, like he's frustrated with what he said. He looks up at me as if it takes a lot of effort. "I'm dyslexic," he says. "Severely."

It takes me a minute to process this, since Rex seems so completely competent at everything, but once it sinks in, the pieces fall into place like the reveal at the end of a mystery novel.

Rex taking my phone number rather than writing his own, Rex not texting, Rex having no use for the Internet, Rex cooking without recipes. Jesus, of *course*. And that night with Will and Leo, when Leo wanted to place that game where you had to read things off scraps of paper, Will made excuses because he knew Rex wouldn't be able to do it. Because he knows. And Rex never told me. Fuck, that can't be good.

I realize that I haven't said anything and Rex is now looking back down at his hands. I'm not sure what to say. I can tell this is a big deal to Rex, and I don't want to say the wrong thing.

Absent anything helpful to say, I decide to take a page out of Rex's book and I put a hand on his shoulder. He's shaking. He looks so tired all of a sudden; his forehead is wrinkled and his mouth is tight.

"I'm not—" He shakes his head in frustration. "I'm not stupid." He spits out the word. "It's just that things get all jumbled up. Especially if I'm nervous. I mean, I *can* read. Subtitles go too fast, though." Every word is tight, bitten off. It's clearly killing him to tell me this.

He walks into the living room and starts to build a fire. I follow, sitting on the couch and just watching the strong line of his back, his clever hands kindling the fire quickly. Marilyn trots over and licks my hand, then settles into her favorite spot in front of the fire. God, it must be amazing to be Marilyn. Warm, taken care of, pet all the time, nothing to do except eat and shit and cuddle and sleep by the fire. Never having to worry about whether you're acting right or if someone's going to misinterpret what you said. Never trying to figure out what you want.

Rex sinks down onto the couch next to me, looking at me intently.

"Sometimes I can hardly think when I look at you," he says, almost like he's talking to himself.

"Wha?" I garble out stupidly. He traces my eyebrows with his thumbs and then lets his hands fall away as he leans his head back onto the couch and sighs. He looks lost for the first time since I've known him.

I straddle Rex's lap and put my hands on his shoulders, so I'm looking into his eyes.

"I know you're not stupid," I tell him calmly. "I think you're incredibly smart. You have an insane memory. Amazing spatial skills. You can fix everything and you know how things work just by looking at them. You are anything but stupid."

Rex lets out a breath. He seems… relieved, maybe? That he told me. His hands come up to settle on my hips. He nods, though barely.

"When did you realize it?" I ask, rubbing his shoulders. "Were you diagnosed?"

He shakes his head.

"I was bad at school, always. I understood what the teachers said, but books and worksheets were all muddled. But I didn't know any different, so I didn't realize it wasn't the same for other kids. I didn't talk to anyone. Never said, 'hey, why are the letters all jumbled on the worksheet' so someone could tell me they weren't."

The thought of Rex as a little boy, so painfully shy that he doesn't even know he's different, gives me a funny emptiness in my stomach.

"Didn't your teachers ever talk to your mom or something?"

"We moved so much I was never in the same school for long. My teachers thought I was dumb, or lazy. No one asked about it, though. Why I didn't do the work. After a while, my mom stopped keeping my records because we moved every six months sometimes. She never asked to see my homework or my grade on a test. She didn't care about stuff like that. Didn't know about it, really. By the time report cards got mailed home, we were long gone, so she never knew I did badly and I never told her. I don't think she would've noticed if I just never went back. So…." Rex glances up at me nervously. "I didn't. I never finished high school. After Jamie—I never went back."

Rex looks embarrassed. I run my fingers through his thick hair, the few silver strands glinting among the brown.

"Ginger never finished high school either," I say carefully. "She dropped out in her junior year to do her apprenticeship at the tattoo shop. Her parents were furious."

He nods and I can feel him relaxing, his tense thighs softening slightly, shoulders unclenching.

"I just don't want you to think I'm ignorant," he confesses. "At school, people thought I was… like, learning disabled because I never talked and I…." His voice is thick with shame and he won't meet my eyes. "Before I learned… ways to deal with it, people would—" He shakes his head. "I just… part of why I like it here is that people don't think it's weird that I didn't finish school. Yeah, I just don't want you to think I'm—"

"I don't think that," I reassure him. "I'm just…. Rex, I'm sorry. I didn't notice. I feel terrible about tonight. I just feel like I should've—"

"I didn't want you to," he says heatedly. "Don't you see? I mean, look at you. You're a professor, for god's sake. You read and write for a living. I didn't want you to think I was like one of those students who do everything wrong."

I feel a rush of hot shame. I sat in this house, reading student papers out loud, pissed because they didn't write proper thesis statements, and all the while Rex sat and listened to me being a judgmental dickhead, assuming the students didn't care, never considering that maybe it was just hard for them. What a stingy, prissy thing for me to do.

"Fuck," I mutter. "I shouldn't have talked about my students that way. It's not even really what I think when I'm not grading."

Rex nods.

"It's just, people are good at different things, you know?" he says. "And just because you tell someone how to do something doesn't mean they can just understand."

"I know. You're right."

"I can tell you that it doesn't make you weak to let me in, but it doesn't mean you can just do it, right?"

Touché. I hang my head. Of course he's right. I feel like shit. Like exactly the kind of privileged, life's-a-breeze, pastel-wearing rich kids I met in school. Is that what I've become? So isolated in my little academic bubble that I think what's true for me is true for everyone? Fuck me.

Paging Daniel, as Ginger would say: this isn't actually about you.

"Every day there are things I have to figure a way around or pretend or fake," Rex is saying. "Things I never do because I can't stand how flustered I get when I get nervous. How everything goes to mush. I don't want to feel like I did as a kid: smart enough to know everyone thought I was an idiot and too fucked in the head to do anything about it."

"Hey, don't say that," I tell him.

"It's pathetic, Daniel. I ordered the special when we went to dinner the first time without hearing what it was because I could barely keep my dick in my pants, much less concentrate on reading with you sitting right next to me. With your hair and those goddamned eyes. I couldn't even think."

His eyes are boring into me. God, he seemed so in control that night until that whole thing with Colin, but now I remember that his pasta had artichokes, which he didn't like.

"What was I going to do, ask you to read the menu to me like a child?" There's bile in his voice I've never heard before. "I fucking hate it." His hands tighten on my hips until they're almost painful.

Rex drops his head forward onto my chest.

"Fuck," he says. "I'm sorry. I didn't mean to get all self-pitying on you." He lets out a deep breath, slides his hands under my thighs, and stands up, lifting me too. "Gingerbread?" he asks. And just like that, it seems, the topic is closed. I nod, dazedly, and follow him into the kitchen.

He pulls things from cupboards and the refrigerator.

"Rex?"

He freezes and when he looks at me I can see the uncertainty he's trying to cover up with his motions.

"I think you're perfect. I mean, shit, that sounded sappy, but, I mean perfect in my opinion." Ugh, how do I explain what I mean? That all those things that he is came together like the perfect recipe.

"For you?" he says.

"Hmm?"

"Perfect for you, maybe?" He looks shy and pleased. All I can do is nod.

He hoists me up onto the counter and kisses me silly.

"Daniel," he says, "the things you say sometimes. You kill me." He kisses me and it's hot and sweet, flushing heat from my stomach to my throat. I start to harden, arousal tingling through me. I chase his mouth, but he pulls back to look at me. His whiskey brown eyes are warm and there's a bit of color across his cheekbones. His lips look swollen from mine and that line between his eyebrows is a perfect crease.

"Einstein was dyslexic," I say, a little out of breath.

Rex cocks his head. "Yeah?"

"Mmhmm, and Lewis Carroll, who wrote *Alice in Wonderland*. Oh! And Ozzy Osbourne. Forgot about him. And, mf—"

Rex kisses me hard and pats my cheek firmly. Then he pulls me down off the counter.

"All right, so I'll tell you what to do and you do it, okay?"

"You wish," I snort, pushing my hips against his.

Rex explains things clearly and gropes me often enough that the time flies. Before I can believe I made something that didn't come from a can, there's gingerbread on the counter.

"Holy shit," I moan, tasting it, "that's delicious. So, with cooking and baking, how do you learn the recipes?"

"Um, well, I get a lot of them from watching cooking shows. If I can see someone do it then I can do it myself. But for baking I usually have to look at a recipe the first time." He looks at me intently. "I *can* read. You get that, right?"

"Yeah."

"It just takes a while. And it gives me a headache."

"Wait, like the migraine you got?"

He nods.

"Reading gives you migraines?"

"Just if I look at something too long. Or on a computer screen."

"So, what were you reading too long when you got the migraine last month?"

Rex looks embarrassed.

"Just—well, just some stuff about starting your own business."

"For your furniture?"

He nods, but his eyes track sideways like there's something else.

"I can help you," I say, hoping it sounds casual rather than pitying. "I mean, you could still read the stuff, but if you wanted help looking through it all to find what's useful. I'm good at research. And then you wouldn't have to read on the computer. I could just print it out at school— it's free for me—and I could—"

Rex pulls me to him and wraps his arms around me, tight. His sweater now smells of gingerbread in addition to wool and smoke and cedar and it's about the best thing I've ever smelled. He feels like what I always imagined Christmas would be like in the perfect families I read about in books.

"Fuck, you smell so good," I say into Rex's shoulder, where my nose is wedged. He chuckles. "How do you always smell so good?" I'm a little annoyed by it, to be honest. It seems unfair that Rex, looking like he does, and feeling like he does, should also smell this fucking delicious. It's like he was designed specifically to conquer every one of my senses. Don't even get me started on how good he tastes.

He laughs again. Apparently I said that out loud.

He strokes my hair away from my face and keeps a hand at the small of my back.

"You smell great," he says. "Like pencil shavings and coffee shops and peppermint."

"My shampoo might be peppermint," I say, trying to picture the bottle.

Rex smells my hair, running his fingertips over my scalp in a rough massage. It's such a particular feeling, and it makes me shiver. Then he puts his nose to the crook of my shoulder, where it meets my neck, and breathes in. He drops to his knees, puts his arms around my waist, and breathes me in again. He drops lower, and my breath catches when he buries his face in my crotch, hands on the backs of my thighs.

"You smell amazing everywhere," he says.

I laugh, but then Rex unbuttons my jeans and nuzzles my crotch and my laugh turns breathless. He kisses my belly and then lower, taking me in his mouth. His mouth is hot and slick and his tongue wraps around my shaft, cradling me. His hands rub up and down my thighs as he takes me deeper in his mouth. It feels amazing, but something's off. Rex has his eyes squeezed shut and his hands are opening and closing on my legs convulsively.

"Rex," I say. "You okay?" I run a hand over his brow.

He pulls back and nods.

"Sure," he says. "Let's go to bed."

He grabs my hand and walks toward the bedroom. When he has me down on the bed he starts stripping my clothes off single-mindedly, the crease in his forehead deepening. He kisses me deeply and I moan into his mouth. I pull off his sweater and T-shirt to find his chest flushed and hot. He's all heat and vibration and movement. If I didn't know better, I'd think he was afraid I was going to leave any second. The intensity in his eyes is half passion and half concentration. His mouth is everywhere. Hot on my neck and shivery over my nipples. He licks into my belly button and nibbles my hip bone. Then he's back, kissing me as I kick off my pants and unzip his.

He palms my ass, kneading the flesh and sliding down to lick at the head of my erection. He's like a tornado, trying to engulf every part of me in sensation.

I can't reach his pants to get them off and he turns around and pulls at them in frustration, swearing when they get caught around his knees. Every muscle in his back is tense and his hands are shaking when he turns back to me. I sit up and then go up on my knees so I can look him in the eye. He's breathing heavily and his eyes are darting all over the room.

I put a hand on his jaw and kiss him softly. Something is definitely wrong. It's like Rex was trying to distract me with his body so I'd forget about what he'd told me. I look at him. His muscles, his strength. Maybe they aren't just to feel safe physically. Maybe his body is something he feels like he can offer even with his dyslexia.

"Thank you," he says shakily. He sounds so nervous.

I cock my head to ask for what.

"Just… for not saying I'm pathetic or stupid."

"Fuck, Rex, no way. You're not! I could never think that."

He's nodding, but not in agreement. More to say, *okay, whatever.* I should know. I've done it often enough when I don't really believe someone but want the conversation to go away.

I cup his cheeks and kiss him again.

"Shh," I say. "It's okay."

I kiss one corner of his mouth and then the other, then I kiss him again. I kiss him over and over, each time a little longer and a little deeper until finally he opens his mouth. His tongue comes out to touch mine tentatively, like we've never done this before. I push Rex onto his back on the bed and his hair splays out on top of his sweater, the dark strands beautiful against the light wool. If this were a scene in a book, it would look like a halo.

I kiss Rex deeply, trying to put everything I feel into it—how much I want him to trust that I don't think he's stupid. How wonderful he is. How grateful I am that he likes me, for whatever reason. How strong he is. I kiss him until his arms come around me, heavy weights against my back, and he starts rocking his hips up into mine. His eyes are glazed and he looks tired.

I reach between us and cup his erection in my hand, stroking softly. A full-body shiver runs through him and he bites his lip.

"What do you want, baby?" I ask him. "Please, I'll do anything you want."

Rex opens his mouth and closes it again, hesitating. He closes his eyes and spreads his knees so that our erections rub together.

"I… I want." His voice is scratchy and I can hear him swallow.

I brush his hair back and look into his eyes.

"You want me to fuck you?" I ask, and his hardness jumps in my hand. His eyelids drift shut for a moment, then flutter open. He nods, shakily.

Arousal shoots through me at the thought of burying myself inside Rex's tight body. The idea of opening him with my cock, turning all that muscle to a quivering puddle of pleasure makes me dizzy with lust.

"Oh fuck yes," I say, and I kiss him, letting him feel how much I want him. "I've thought about you like this so many times," I say.

"Yeah?" His lips quirk into an almost-smile. "Usually people just want me to top," he says, biting his lip, "but I—oh!" he moans as I palm his ass, enjoying the firm roundness and the incredible heat between. I can imagine that people don't look at Rex and see someone who wants to get fucked. But it was right there in his eyes. In how he trembled against me, so eager to give me pleasure like he thought it might be the only thing he could offer, but so heavy with the responsibility it required. He wants this, wants me to take care of him. And I need it too.

The dynamic between us has been the opposite ever since Rex found me in the woods all those months ago, and I've barely noticed because I've felt so messed up about everything else in my life, so off-kilter because of my feelings for Rex. I've let him take care of me or resisted it, but I haven't been taking good care of him. And maybe before, I could tell myself it was because I didn't know how. But right here, right now, in this bed, I *know* how to take care of Rex. I know how to take him out of his head and how to force him not to think about anything but the feeling of our bodies moving together.

I jerk open the drawer and grab the lube, determined to make this as good for Rex as he always does for me.

Richard liked it hard and fast, liked me to slam into him over and over, like I was the star of some rough-trade fantasy come to life. He'd jerk himself off, and if he came before I did, he'd pull off me, leaving me to finish myself off, uninterested in sex lasting for one minute after he was done. Something tells me Rex won't be anything like him.

I roll Rex over onto his stomach with his knees spread and kiss the back of his neck, paying attention to how warm his skin is, how every tiny movement he makes ripples through the muscles of his back like a finely tuned machine.

"Daniel, I—" Rex starts uncertainly, but I don't let him finish.

"Shh," I say. "You just don't worry about anything, okay?"

He moans, which I take as assent.

I run my hands along his rib cage and watch goose bumps rise on his arms. I kiss down his spine toward his gorgeous ass and watch the shivers ripple over his skin. I kiss the dimples just above the swell of his ass and then lick them. Rex groans, fisting the sheets, his face now buried in the sweater.

"Your body is so fucking gorgeous," I tell him, squeezing handfuls of his ass and watching the flesh bounce perfectly. I kiss the insides of his thighs and he jerks, his breath coming faster. I reach under his hips and pull his erection so it's pointing down between his legs, then I run my tongue along the sensitive skin between his hole and his balls, then down over the tip of his erection, which is leaking his arousal.

With one hand, he reaches back and pats my cheek clumsily, trying to look over his shoulder and failing. He's muttering something into the pillow but I can't make it out.

I spread his ass apart and tentatively run my tongue over his hole, never having done it before. Within seconds I can tell that it's about to become my new favorite thing to do, though, as Rex's whole body comes off the bed.

"Oh god!" he practically yells.

I chuckle and put a soothing hand on his hip as I lean back down. I lick over his hole, feeling it spasm, and then, as he slowly relaxes, push the tip of my tongue inside. Rex is moaning like crazy and the feeling of this big, powerful man coming undone with the motion of my tongue intoxicates me. I rub at his slick hole with my thumb, encouraging him to open to me, and then I slide my tongue inside.

Rex whimpers, then goes slack on the bed.

"Oh god, oh god, oh god," he says as I flex my tongue inside him. "Oh god, Daniel." All I can feel is the slick heat of Rex's hole and the way it's seemed to short-circuit the rest of his body.

"Please," Rex says so softly I barely hear him. I slide up his body and bury my face in his neck. I can hear his breath coming fast, feel the incredible heat coming off his skin. "Daniel, please," he scrapes out.

"You need me inside you?" I say low in his ear, and he shudders. He nods immediately, reaching for a condom and passing it back to me.

"I want you just like this," I tell him, running my hand down his spine. He nods again and I can see the relief in his face.

I slick up my fingers and slide one inside Rex's heat, watching his shoulders for any tension, but he just moans softly. I push his knees farther apart and add a second finger, feeling him clench a little around me. He's all slick heat and strong muscle and I crook my fingers, searching for his prostate.

He cries out when I find it, his knees falling even farther apart as he tries to hump against the mattress.

"Uh-uh," I say, and lift his hips away from the bed. I slide a third finger inside him and stroke his erection lightly. He writhes against me.

"Ready?"

"Yes," he moans, "please."

"So polite," I murmur, pressing against his prostate once more before removing my fingers. He shudders and hangs his head, now up on his knees and elbows.

With one hand steadying his hip, I slide against the crack of his ass. I'm hard as a rock and just the feel of him sends bolts of pleasure to the base of my cock. I give his erection a few hard strokes as I start to slide inside him.

We both groan as I breach his muscle. It's like I'm being swallowed up by the most perfect pressure, his body hugging my erection so tightly I can barely slide in.

"Oh fuck, Rex," I say.

"Don't stop," he says quickly.

"Not on your fucking life," I say, pulling back a bit and adding more lube before sliding forward again. This time I slide all the way inside him, and it's not like anything I've ever felt before. Usually I feel a sense of relief when I slide inside a guy's ass, the sense that soon I'll get to come and it'll feel great. Now, I feel something like desperation. Desperation to be inside Rex for as long as possible. Desperation to make him feel as good as I do. And, yeah, okay, desperation to come.

"Jesus, you feel amazing," I say.

Rex just grunts in response, but I can see him nodding against the bed. He pushes back against me, fitting us even closer together. I hadn't realized I wasn't moving. I drop a quick kiss on Rex's spine and then I pull back and start thrusting into him. I feel like every single nerve is concentrated in my groin—like all feeling has left my extremities and migrated there, turning me into one desperate, heat-seeking missile of pleasure. As I push into Rex, he pushes back against me, driving me even deeper. I press his shoulders down, changing the angle, and he cries out.

I'm hitting his prostate now as I thrust into him, and I feel like with each snap of my hips, I'm trying to push the pleasure out of my own body and into his. The muscles of his back are tensed and his hair is spread out against that fucking sweater and his arms are thrown out to the sides like he's pinioned on the bed.

All of a sudden, it's imperative that I see his face.

I pull out and Rex makes a sound of complaint.

"C'mere," I say, and pull him over by the shoulder.

Rex's face is flushed and his hair is a mess and I can see the impression of cable-knit on his cheek, and he's the most beautiful thing

I've ever seen. I tilt his hips up and push his knees apart and then I'm right back there, sliding us back together, connecting us as we should be. I drag his chin to mine and kiss him with everything that I have, feeling his erection pulse between us.

"Daniel," Rex says brokenly as I start thrusting again. His voice is choked and he squeezes his eyes shut as he moans. With every thrust, he rolls his hips to meet mine, causing us to meet powerfully and sending tiny explosions of ecstasy through me. I can feel the tingling in my lower back and belly and I push my orgasm back, determined to make this last as long as I can.

I pull all the way out of Rex and slide back into him as slowly as I can, the initial feeling of breaching his body almost as intoxicating as the glorious slide deep inside him. I pinch his nipples, just watching his face, trying to read what he needs from me there. Seeing Rex like this, all his strength at the mercy of my body—and him loving it—is about the hottest thing I've ever seen.

Rex arches his back against my assault on his nipples and throws his head back. I kiss his neck and take his weeping erection in my hand. I pump him firmly and his hips pulse, driving me even deeper inside him. I can barely think. Every beat of my heart is thumping in my ears, pulsing in my stomach, and pushing blood into my cock until I feel like one big heartbeat, pulsing inside Rex's body.

I kiss his mouth and his arms come around me, holding me against him.

"I'm so close," he says against my lips, and, curling his hands around my hips, he pulls me even closer against him.

I kiss him once more, then pull all the way out and slam back into him, feeling the tendrils of my orgasm begin to unfurl, starting in my balls and the base of my spine and pulsing outward. I slam into Rex's heat again and again, and then it's as if time stops because Rex freezes, his whole body clenching up. He convulses, his channel squeezing me with impossible pressure, and then he's coming, shooting against my chest in pulse after pulse of heat. With a roar, I milk one last convulsion from him and he falls back against the bed, moaning.

"Oh my god," I mutter. That was the hottest fucking thing I've ever seen.

I'm right on the edge, staring at Rex's beautiful face. I touch the tip of his spent cock, mesmerized by one last bead of come quivering there, and Rex clenches violently. It's like his whole channel is a fist, squeezing me. I cry out, and Rex does it again, clenches around me. And it's over;

I'm spiraling into an orgasm that wrings every drop of pleasure from my body. I'm thrusting deep inside his body and my ass is clenching and I can hear myself groaning, but all I can concentrate on are the bolts of electricity tearing through me, pushing everything out of me.

I collapse on top of Rex and his arms immediately enfold me.

"Oh, Danny," he murmurs, "Oh."

The nickname shoots straight through me, bringing the warmth of a very different kind of pleasure.

But even though every nerve is singing, I'm asleep in seconds.

I awaken sometime in the night to feel Rex moving against me. I'm half-asleep, but I wrap my arms around his neck and our mouths find each other again. I can't see anything, but I can feel Rex's hard body and his heat, and I can feel his erection pushing against my thigh. I roll so our chests are touching and throw my leg over his hip, opening myself up to him. All the time, we never stop kissing. For a moment I even think I'm dreaming, but Rex wraps his huge hand around my half-asleep cock and brings me to full hardness. In the dark, he's everywhere, arms and legs and chest and hands and sweet, hot mouth. As we grind together, slowly working ourselves back up, Rex hums into my mouth with pleasure.

He drops an arm over my hip and dips his fingers into my crack.

"Can I...?" he asks and I kiss him yes. Then he has the lube and his fingers are moving inside me, slicking me up and transforming my liquid, dreamy arousal to hard need.

"Come here to me," he says, and pulls me on top of him as he lies on his back. We grind together while he fingers me and my eyes have adjusted to the dark just enough to see that his eyes are closed and he has a little smile on his face. I close my eyes too, and pretend we're in one shared dream.

He lifts my hips and fits me on top of him, sliding me down so his erection breaches me slowly.

I cry out in ecstasy, and I have the strangest sensation that I'm still fucking Rex. That my cock is inside him at the same time as his is inside me. I know my oversensitized body is just playing tricks on me, but every pulse of Rex's cock inside my body feels like an answering movement to my own, earlier motions. In the dark, it's like all that's holding me up is Rex's erection inside me and his hands clutching my hips.

"Oh, baby," he says and he starts to move, pulsing his hips as I roll mine, our bodies coming together in a liquid rush. I lose track of time, drifting in and out of my own pleasure and Rex's, my fingers ghosting down his face, his neck, his chest, to the place where we're joined.

Rex moans and laughs shallowly, and he starts bouncing his hips up off the bed, burying himself so deep inside me that my stomach clenches as the weight of my body bears me down on him. Rex lifts me by the hips and then thrusts up into me over and over until I'm just a puddle of heat and pleasure, my cock bouncing against my stomach. I want to grab it, jerk myself off, but in this strange, dreamy world of sensation, all I want is for my body to be taken over by Rex; I'm completely in thrall to him.

Finally, after what feels like hours or maybe only seconds, Rex runs his thumb over the head of my cock, spreading the slick fluid down my length. I cry out and steady myself on his shoulders, sure I'll fall if I don't stop the spinning in my head and the buzzing in my groin. Rex strokes me hard and the orgasm pours out of me, until I'm jerking on his cock, spewing come down on his belly, the milky whiteness quickly disappearing in the dark.

My breath stutters and I feel like a rag doll as Rex moans and keeps thrusting inside me. The sensation is almost overwhelming and, just as I know I can't take any more, I feel him come, his groan vibrating his chest beneath my palms, scalding heat flooding my ass as Rex becomes a part of me.

Absently, I realize that means that we just had sex without a condom and, from Rex's sudden stillness and intake of breath, he must suddenly realize it as well.

"I'm sorry," he says. "I wasn't thinking—I didn't."

I should feel a cold rush of fear, but for some reason it doesn't come.

"Are you... I mean, are you clean?" I ask him.

"Yeah," he says, "but I didn't mean to—"

"Shh," I say. "You felt amazing."

He relaxes beneath me.

"I'm clean too," I assure him, and he picks up my hand and kisses my palm.

"I still didn't mean to—without asking you."

All I feel is relieved and shaky with pleasure.

I lean down and kiss Rex softly, hoping to show him that I'm okay with it—more than okay. He kisses my mouth, then my eyelids, and then he maneuvers me so that I'm lying on my side, back to his chest as he slowly slides out of me.

I feel his hesitation, so I take his hand and bring it to my opening. He slides his fingers inside me, feeling his come leaking out of me. I'm sure it won't feel so nice in the morning, but right now, the thought that Rex will stay inside me all night feels like a warm blanket.

"Oh Jesus," Rex murmurs. He snugs his hips up tight against my ass, gathering me close to him with his arm, and buries his face in my neck.

I have the brief, absent thought that I'll never be able to fall asleep with him holding me so tight, and then the darkness swallows me.

Chapter 13

November

"FUCK, FUCK, fuck!" I say as a thin tendril of smoke snakes toward me. By the time I turn back to the stove from jerking the charred toast out the toaster oven, the eggs have congealed in the pan. They don't smell burned, though, so I scrape them onto the plate. I put more bread in the toaster, tipping the burned pieces in the trash. I hate wasting food, but no way am I serving Rex charcoal. Aside from the fact that it's pretty embarrassing to have an advanced degree and not be able to apply heat to bread evenly, it's not really the message of comfort I want to send.

Granted, maybe cooking isn't the best medium for the message, but I wanted to do something for Rex to make up for our disastrous date last night. The toaster oven dings and I grab the toast, miraculously unburned, and scrape some butter onto it.

"What're you doing?"

Rex appears in the doorway just as I'm about to carry the plate to him, wearing a pair of sweatpants and nothing else. He looks warm and sleepy.

"I was going for breakfast in bed, but…."

"Sorry," Rex smiles. "Want me to go get back in bed?"

What a question. He looks positively edible himself, with his powerful shoulders braced in the doorway and the muscular expanse of his chest and stomach taking up the whole space between. His hair is messy and his stubble makes his full mouth look amazing.

"Hell yes," I say, but in the time I've been gawking at him, he's already started to move toward me. He sits on one of the stools at the counter and pulls me to stand between his legs. He looks serious, like he's trying really hard not to bring up last night's confession about his dyslexia but badly wants to. Then he pulls the plate toward him and his expression softens.

"I can't believe you cooked," he says, picking up his fork while keeping one arm twined around my waist. "Here, share with me." Oh, right. I only made one plate.

He forks some egg into his mouth, still looking at me fondly. Then his expression becomes studiedly neutral. He chews slowly. Swallows. Tries to smile. He puts down the fork and picks up the toast, looking relieved as he takes a bite. He puts the toast down and pats my back.

"It okay?" I say.

Rex nods, but doesn't open his mouth. He's patting my back like you would an elderly relation.

"Rex," I say. "Is it bad?"

He coughs a little and clears his throat.

"It was a real sweet thought, Daniel," he says. He kisses my cheek and pulls the plate closer to him with a deep breath, squaring his shoulders. He takes another bite of egg, but before he gets it to his mouth he sighs and looks at me out of the corner of his eye.

"Um," he says.

"What the hell?" I say, and I grab the fork from his hand and eat the eggs.

Holy. Fucking. Shit.

"Fuck!" I say. "That tastes like death. Why the hell did you eat it?"

Rex starts chuckling.

I take a bite of the toast—that, at least, can't be bad. It's not even burned.

Wrong.

The toast tastes like I pulled it out of a burning building, the congealed butter only adding to the gross consistency. I look at Rex desperately. How can eggs and toast possibly taste that bad?

"That's the worst thing I've ever tasted," Rex says, laughing, but he pulls me to him and kisses me, so it barely even stings.

"Ew, get away," I say. "You taste like death eggs and fire toast!"

Rex laughs deeply and buries his face in my hair.

THE NEXT week, Rex and I hang out at his house a lot. It's this weird feeling I haven't had since I was a kid: this sense that I want to spend all my time with someone. The last time I felt it was with Corey Appleton in seventh grade. I was captivated by him, just wanted to watch him do… whatever. The way he sharpened his pencil seemed to suggest something deeply contemplative about his character and his choice of apple juice over soda at lunch indicated a sweetness that pulled me in. Of course, when I groped him after school, sure that his companionable arm around my shoulder was a message, my heart pounding so hard with hope that I thought I might pass out, I found that nothing about his pencil-sharpening gestures or his choice of beverages had indicated shit. There was nothing sweet about the way he shoved me against the brick and definitely nothing contemplative about the way he told everyone at school what I did.

I've learned a lot about Rex this week too. He really is shy. I can see how hard he works to be polite to strangers, but years of saying as little as possible to avoid stuttering has made him terse. It's clearly made people intimidated by him.

He's also incredibly healthy. He exercises and eats well and stays hydrated, but he's not obnoxious about it. It's like his body is the only thing he can depend on, so he tries to make it run as well as possible, like customizing a luxury car.

There's something about Rex that makes me feel calm. As if I'm scattered until the moment I see him and when he touches me I fly back together in a configuration that makes sense.

And ever since he told me about his dyslexia, things feel more settled between us or something. It makes sense, in that it must have been weighing on him, trying to keep it a secret. At first, I was surprised it didn't come out sooner. I mean, how many times might I have asked him to read something to me or look something up? Then, when I thought about it, it became clear how hard he's worked to make sure those situations didn't arise. How much thought he must've put into avoiding them. How on edge he must have been, wondering if he'd be forced to out himself every time we were together. I hate that he felt like he had to do that, but I'm glad he can just relax now.

He's worked incredibly hard to educate himself. Partly as a reaction to people thinking he was stupid due to his dyslexia, and partly because he's just interested. He's taught himself vocabulary and listened to books on CD.

He keeps trying to teach me to cook, but I'm hopeless, mostly because when he starts moving around the kitchen all I can do is watch him. He'll be explaining how to mince something or how long it takes to make a hardboiled egg, and I'll be watching the way his muscles bunch as he wields the knife or the way he blows his hair off his forehead. When he's trying to show me how to roll out pasta dough or knead bread, I'm looking at his huge hands and strong forearms (which I'm basically obsessed with).

Once, I was so distracted by the thought of him kneading my ass the way he was kneading the bread that I was shocked to find cheese in the bread when I bit into it. Rex thought that was quite amusing, but I think he knows how hot I find watching him in the kitchen and milks it on purpose. Jesus, no wonder I can never re-create anything I see him do.

I'm cutting up pears for some delicious-sounding dessert when Rex comes up behind me, slow so he won't startle me into cutting my finger off. He learned the hard way that I zone out sometimes when he came up behind me while I was making a fire and I almost clobbered him with a large piece of kindling.

"Sweetheart," he says against my neck, "you don't need to make everything so exact. You can just chop it up. It doesn't need to be so much work."

"I am just cutting it up," I say. He's said this to me before, but I'm not sure why he wouldn't want it done perfectly since it's about the only thing I can do when it comes to cooking.

"Here, look," Rex says, easing the knife from my hand but keeping his arms around me. Hmm, it really shouldn't be so hot to have Rex around me with a knife….

In a few easy, practiced movements he takes the pear apart. He knows exactly how deep to cut to miss the core, just how much force it takes to rend the flesh. It's effortless.

Everything seems this effortless for him. He just has this way with objects, like, at his touch, the world becomes manageable, falling into place to be taken apart or put back together at his will.

"Got it," I say, my throat suddenly thick with something like jealousy at Rex's ease. Except I know it's not that simple. Hell, I know just how uncomfortable he often is because of his shyness, his dyslexia. I still can't help but feel like a major failure for not noticing his dyslexia earlier.

He puts the knife down and picks up a bit of pear, holding it up for me. I eat it from his hand, then kiss him, knowing he can taste it on my tongue.

"I know you think you have to be perfect at work. Out there," he says, gesturing with his shoulder while keeping both hands on the counter, trapping me against his body. "But you don't have to try so hard here. Not with me."

I open my mouth to protest. But… *is* that what I'm doing? I never thought about it like that. I suppose I have been… on my best behavior around Rex. But that's just because I don't want to scare him off. I look down at Rex's big feet, unsure of what to say.

"I just meant, you don't have to think so much about everything you do."

Yeah, I've heard that before. I challenge you to find someone who went to grad school who hasn't.

"You know, it's not actually that easy to just change the way you *think*." It comes out a little more bitter than I meant it to.

"Daniel." He cups my chin and forces me to look at him. "I get it. The self-consciousness? Believe me." He huffs out a breath. "But I've seen you try so hard to figure out what someone was thinking about you that your eyes about crossed. You're thinking about things all the time. How people react to you. If they misinterpreted what you said, understood your joke. You're so used to feeling like you don't fit in that you're always trying to be one step ahead. Figure out which Daniel's called for in the situation. But...."

He trails off, stroking my hair like he doesn't want to hurt my feelings.

"But?" I prompt.

"But you can't read people's minds, baby. You can't always figure out what's gonna happen just by being smart. And even if you could—" He shakes his head. "—you shouldn't. You shouldn't have to try so hard to fit in because you're scared."

I tense, but Rex's hand is still gentle in my hair.

"I know, I know, you're never scared, right?" He gives me an unreadable smirk. Amused? Doubtful? Indulgent? "Just, people are gonna like you or they aren't. There's no sense in trying to change how you act to suit them. It'll just drive you crazy."

I open my mouth to say something, to insist that I don't do that. But then Rex is kissing me, holding me in place with his soft hands and his hard body, until all I can think about is how damn good he smells and how amazing he feels.

"I like you, Daniel. Just you. I like you so much." Rex's voice is low and sincere and I can feel in his kiss how much he means it. It makes me feel... treasured. Appreciated in a way I don't recognize. "And I want to keep getting to know you. The real you. Okay?"

"I... like you too. A lot." Jeez, and the award for Understatement of the Century goes to.... But he's right. I love getting to learn all the strange little things that make Rex Rex. I may have been on my best behavior with him, but I've also been more relaxed when I'm around him than I can ever remember being with anyone but Ginger.

"Like, you know that feeling," I try to explain, "where it's Sunday night and you have school or work the next morning but then it's a snow day and you don't have to go in? You feel like that."

"I feel like a natural disaster?" he teases, but his gaze is intent.

"No," I say, forcing myself to say what I mean. "A relief. You feel like a huge relief."

Rex's eyes go very soft.

"You feel like a relief too, Daniel," he says.

I decide to take Ginger's advice, pushing down the roiling fear of rejection in my gut. "Hey, Rex?" I ask. "What are you doing for Thanksgiving?"

"Nothing," he says, his eyes narrowing.

"Would you want to maybe have it with me?" I try my best to keep my tone casual so he doesn't feel any pressure to say yes.

"Yes," Rex says instantly. "Yes, please." He kisses me hard and pulls me into his arms.

"I like this whole not overthinking thing," I tell him.

So, YEAH, this week has been pretty great until I run into Will at Mr. Zoo's when I go to invite Leo to Thanksgiving. And I remember that he knew about Rex's dyslexia and purposely hid it from me. Until I remember that he's touched Rex and therefore I hate him. Okay, so, apparently I've also turned jealous and irrational this week. At least where Rex is concerned.

Will and Leo don't notice me at first. Leo's behind the counter and Will is leaning on it, his chin in his hand as Leo talks quietly. When I wave, Leo turns bright red, as if I've caught him doing something he shouldn't be. Will just straightens up and levels me with a look that dares me to tease them about their obvious flirting.

"Hey, Daniel, how's it going?" Leo asks, fiddling with the tape dispenser.

"Can I have a word?" I say to Will, and walk back outside before he can answer.

"Let me guess," Will says, as he leans against the shop window. "This is about Rex."

Now that he's standing in front of me I don't know what the fuck I'm thinking. What I want to say is, "Why didn't you fucking tell me about Rex's dyslexia!" But, why would he? He barely knows me. Rex was his lover. It's not his place to say a goddamned thing. But I'm so angry with him for knowing and so angry with myself for not noticing that I say it anyway.

"Excuse me?" Will says.

"Fuck!" I say. "I know, I know. Never mind. Goddammit!"

"Look, Daniel, everyone Rex has ever cared about either died on him or left town, okay? Then, here's you. The hot professor from Philly who's slumming it in our little town until something better comes along. I mean, I get it; I do. You're so Rex's type it isn't even funny. The perfect lost cause. I'm not surprised he's all over you like a dog on a bone. But, before you come in here with your accusations and your self-fucking-righteous demands about Rex, I want to ask you one question. Are you here to stay? Or the second the ivory tower says jump are you going to say *From what window?*

"Because, in case you can't tell, Rex thinks you might just be passing through. I can tell just by looking at you together: he's hung up on you something good, but a part of him won't let himself open up to you because he thinks you'll be fucking out of here on the next train. Frankly, I'm shocked he told you about his dyslexia. And if I were a betting man, I'd say he didn't. I'd say it came up some other way and he was too much of a mensch to outright lie to you about it. So you just watch yourself, Daniel, is what I'm saying. You're crazy about him; I can see that too. But I don't trust you. I think you're scared and I think, when it comes down to it, that you'll hurt him."

Will delivers this whole monologue without pausing or looking away once.

Fuck. When he puts it like that, I guess Rex really did only tell me about his dyslexia because of our shitty date. Was it *not* actually a sign that he trusted me, but just a sign that he felt sorry for me? *Would* he have told me otherwise? I don't know.

And even though I should be furious at Will for what is clearly his low opinion of me, the way he told me off reminds me so much of Ginger that I'm filled with a rush of warmth and longing. Longing for Ginger, but also the briefest thought that maybe Will and I could be friends.

"Do you want to come to Rex's for Thanksgiving?" I ask him. And I allow myself a brief moment of satisfaction as his self-possessed mask falls away and he looks genuinely surprised and, I think, a bit pleased.

"DANG, I like this Will guy—sorry, pumpkin. He's so got your number."

"Yeah, yeah."

"So…" Ginger pauses. "*Are* you going to stay? I know you didn't want to at first. You said you were going to go on the job market again."

"I dunno, Ginge." I'm sure she can hear the conflict in my voice. "I mean, I'll definitely at least look at the job list when it comes out. See if there's anything too good to pass up. But… fuck, I really don't know. I just never thought I'd be in this position. God, I used to pity the people who had partners they had to take into account when they were on the job market. It just makes everything harder."

"Partners, huh?"

"What? No, I just meant—"

"I know what you meant; don't hurt yourself."

"So, we're having Thanksgiving. Me and Rex."

"That's great, sweet cheeks. I'll be eating The Burrito with my window open, so if I choke while I'm alone then the smell of my rotting corpse will waft out the window and I'll be found more quickly," she says dramatically.

"I think having the window open in November would make it so your corpse didn't really smell that much, actually. Seriously, though, you're not going to your parents' at all?"

"Psh. I might stop by," she says. "Of course, it's not much use trying to go to dinner at the house of someone who sucks up all the oxygen in the room. Makes it kinda hard to eat, ya know?"

Ginger's mother is the kind of nervous, hovering woman who counts how many glasses of wine Ginger's had and tells her about all the neighbors' children's accomplishments but never acknowledges Ginger's. It doesn't help that Ginger's older sister is certifiably off her nut and always needs to be the center of attention, or that her parents refuse to say her older brother's name and pretend that they never had a son.

"Christ," I say. "Do we *know* anyone with a normal fucking family?" There's a charged silence on the line. "Ginge?"

"Well, actually…."

"Actually…?"

"I kind of… met someone. And his family seems about as normal as they come."

"Holy shit, you already met his family? Tell me."

"Well…. You know him, actually. You remember that sandwich place that opened down the street from the shop at the beginning of the summer?"

"The one you said had real bagels?"

"Yeah. Anyway, you remember the cute guy who worked there?"

"Uh, dude, not to judge, seriously, but that guy's like eighteen."

"No, not the kid with the glasses! The redhead."

"Oh shit, right. He's hot, in a Josh Homme kind of way."

"I *know*, right? That's exactly what I thought. I went in there for a bagel and cream cheese a few weeks ago before I opened the shop. I was half-asleep—you know how I am before I've had my coffee—and I dropped the bagel on the floor as I was putting cream in my coffee."

"Uh-oh. Thou hast not seen rage like the rage of a Ginger sans bagel and coffee."

"Seriously. So, I drop the bagel and I'm just like swearing a blue streak, right? And that's when he comes in the door. And he looks at glasses guy behind the counter in horror—like, what the hell did you do to make this lady lose her shit. Glasses guy's kind of terrified, so I say, 'Oh, no, it was my fault; I just dropped my bagel,' thinking he'd nod and smile. But he walked behind the counter and made me another bagel and cream cheese, then put it in a bag with three other bagels and filled up a to-go container of cream cheese—that awesome chive stuff. And he hands it to me and says—get this: 'Just in case the vagaries of your day find you needing another one.' I mean, who the fuck says that? At first I thought, ruh roh: potential overly sincere Renaissance festival douchebag? But then he winked at me. A really filthy, flirtatious wink. And, of course, I went back for another bagel the next day."

"That's hot, Ginge. So, you've met his family?"

"Oh, not intentionally. Turns out glasses guy is his cousin and his dad comes by to fix stuff in the shop all the time. His mom sometimes brings him lunch. It's hilarious. Every time he's all, 'Mom, I make food here,' and she's like, 'give your mother a kiss and shut your mouth.' Priceless, babycakes! Anyway, they're so nice."

"So, why don't you have Thanksgiving with him? What's his name, by the way, so I don't just think of him as Josh Homme—or as The Ginger, which would be confusing."

"His name's Christopher. And I don't know. I think it's too soon. Like, he'll be having dinner at his parents' and we only started dating a couple of weeks ago, so."

"You could always invite him over for a postdinner Thanksgiving burrito at your place," I offer.

"Huh. Not a bad idea, sweetie. Not a bad idea at all."

"CAN YOU grab some butter?" Rex asks me.

We're at the grocery store buying some last-minute additions for Thanksgiving dinner. Or, security items, really, since Rex has planned about three alternate dinner menus. Really, I have no idea what we'll be eating, except that there's a turkey, which I got back to his house yesterday to find in the sink.

We've already been to an indoor farmer's market about twenty miles from here that Rex apparently frequents, where I embarrassed myself in front of several vendors and Rex by buying fennel because I thought it was the celery Rex sent me to get, so god knows why he's asking me to pick up anything. Still, I can hardly fuck up butter, can I?

"Oh, I'm sorry," Rex says, "I need unsalted. I should've told you to get the red package."

The box I'm holding is blue.

"Never mind. We'll just grab it when we get over there," Rex says, obviously writing me off as a shopping buddy entirely. Doesn't matter. I'm pretty content to trail along behind him while he looks at food. He dragged me out of bed at six this morning to get to the farmer's market before they could sell out of… whatever he bought there. He made three pies last night as well as some kind of sauce for something. And I've never seen him so excited as when we were wandering through the market. It feels strangely domestic. I've never cared about cooking, obviously. But I haven't really cared that much about eating either. I mean, it's a necessary thing that sometimes tastes good, but especially when I'm by myself, it's just a chore. An interruption, like laundry or cleaning.

But Rex makes cooking and eating feel like part of my life—our lives. He expresses something of himself through cooking. Not just his personality, but his care. It's like he cares about what I eat—if it's healthy, if I like it. And so everything to do with it feels important. Even grocery shopping. Because I can feel him looking at the food the way you'd look at a shelter dog or something: as a thing that might come home with you, if it's the right fit. Something that will be incorporated into our lives. Life. Our life.

It's all there in the way he chooses an onion or a bagful of apples, his attention totally focused on it. I can see the path from apples in the store to apple pie. Can see his hands kneading the pie crust. And I realize that the more I pay attention to Rex as he moves through the store, the less I think about myself. The less I notice if people are staring at me and the less I wonder what they're thinking. The less I pay attention to who sees when I knock over a pyramid of limes.

I noticed that this week, when we were talking. When I paid close attention to Rex, it was like I escaped the present. Kind of like I do when I'm reading. It's so fucked. I started reading and making up stories to escape how shitty things were. Then, that habit made it hard for me to be back in the real world—hard to connect with anyone. Which made me super self-conscious and want to escape. Jesus. Anyway, I've decided that if I'm going to escape, it's better to escape into Rex than into a fantasy world where no one will ever find me.

THE SECOND we've unloaded the groceries, Rex remembers something he forgot and runs back out to get it. Will and Leo are coming over to help us cook, and Rex promised them breakfast, so I'm going to give it a go. Rex didn't look impressed by this idea when I yelled it to him as he was walking out the door, but he gave me a resigned smile of what I can only assume is the thank-god-I-bought-extra-eggs variety and nodded, so I guess that's that.

I've seen him make pancakes and I know I can look up a recipe online, so I think it'll be fine. I'm not even going to try eggs again because I still can't figure out how they tasted so disgusting the last time, and I'm not risking it again. Pancakes and bacon and then Rex will put us all to work on dinner.

The bacon is in and I'm pouring the first pancake into the pan when Leo and Will show up, bickering.

"It's set in the eighties," Will is saying. "That does *not* qualify as historical fiction, even if you didn't happen to live through the decade. Wait." He freezes, looking shocked. "Oh my Christ, you really *didn't* live through any of the eighties, did you?"

Leo rolls his eyes and walks over to me.

"Happy Thanksgiving, Daniel! Thanks for inviting me!" He's practically bouncing in place. Well, the kid definitely has manners.

"Ask the professor," Will continues. "Daniel, a book set in the eighties is *not* historical fiction, right? Tell him, please."

"When was it written?"

"2009," Leo says.

"Actually, I probably would call that historical fiction, because—" I start to say.

"Oh, shut up; no one asked you," Will grumbles.

"Um," Leo says, "I think your pancake's—"

"Shit!" I yell. My pancake is black and smoking in the pan.

"Let me guess," Will says. "You're used to letting people cook for you?"

Before I can throttle Will, I scrape the remains of my poor pancake into the trash and put the pan in the sink.

"What's this?" Leo asks, peeking into the pot on the stove.

"Hemlock," Will mutters.

"Oh my holy god," Leo says, sounding genuinely upset.

"What?" I ask, thinking he burned himself or something.

"Are you *boiling* bacon?

"Um. Is that wrong?" I say.

"Argh! I want to *punch* you!" Leo says.

"Sadly, we all know you can't," Will says, elbowing him out of the way and using tongs to pull a piece of bacon out of the water. It definitely doesn't look the way it does at the diner.

"Bacon, bacon," Leo chants, like some demented, carnivorous monk.

"Why the fuck would you boil bacon?" Will asks.

"Um. I thought it would be like hot dogs?"

"Jesus Christ, you boil hot dogs. You poor thing. I take it all back. Thank god Rex found you."

"Thank god Rex found him, why?" Rex asks, walking in the door.

"Rex," Leo says plaintively. "I—he—and—he *boiled* the bacon."

Rex looks in the pot and then looks at me and bursts out laughing.

"I didn't know!" I say.

Rex puts his hands on my cheeks and kisses me, shaking his head.

"Why don't you, um, pick some music for us," he offers, running his hands through my hair fondly. To Leo, he says, "I have more bacon."

"Oh, thank you," Leo says worshipfully.

"Shouldn't you be at your parents' house," I mutter, and walk into the living room to pick some records.

"HEY, DAD," I say, my phone on speaker while I arrange cheese and crackers on a plate in the living room, the only food-related job Rex will give me. "Happy Thanksgiving."

"Hiya, Dan," my dad says, and I can hear the roar of football on the television in the background and my brothers yelling at the screen.

"How are you?" I ask.

"Oh, fine, fine. You know. Same as always. How's the car?"

"It's fine," I say. Which isn't entirely true. It keeps stalling out if I don't drive it every day. Though I don't really need a car to get from my apartment to campus and around town, it's nice to be able to drive to Rex's now that it's cold.

"Hey, shithead, throw another empty beer can at that TV and I'll throw a full one at your head!" my dad yells. Has to be at Brian, who has a habit of throwing things at the TV when sports don't go his way. "So, you're okay?" my dad asks me.

"Yeah, I'm good, Dad. I just wanted to wish you and the guys happy Thanksgiving."

"Boys," my dad calls, "your brother's on the phone."

There's a long pause.

"Hey, Daniel." It's Sam. "Happy Thanksgiving."

"Thanks, Sam. How's everything going?"

"Fine, thanks," he says. "Liza's bringing a turkey over in a bit since these idiots were drunk by 10:00 a.m. and didn't even order chicken."

We always used to get fried chicken from this cheap place about ten blocks from my dad's house on Thanksgiving.

"That's nice. How's Liza?"

"She's fine. Good. Work's busy."

There's a long pause.

"All right, kid, well, I'll see you later," Sam says, and hangs up.

My phone beeps with the disconnection.

"You okay?" Rex asks, sliding an arm around my chest.

"Um, yeah. I'm done," I say, gesturing to the cheese plate.

"Okay," Rex says, but he holds me against him for another minute and I breathe in his comforting smell.

Dinner is delicious—of course. Leo turned out to be quite the little helper and I can tell he liked feeling like he had something to do. He never says why he's here with us instead of at his parents' house, but I'm glad he is. At one point, he started asking everyone to tell about their best Thanksgiving ever. Rex was silent and I caught Will's eye and all three of us started cracking up at the same time.

"What?" Leo asked, and I didn't have the heart to tell him that he was probably the only one of us who had a single happy Thanksgiving memory.

Will took Leo home around ten, and Rex and I exhaustedly abandoned the dishes until tomorrow, choosing to take Marilyn for a walk instead.

It's beautiful out. Cold and sharp, but with no wind, so you can smell everything. By the light of the moon I can just see Marilyn as she trots ahead and circles back to us, joyfully peeing on trees and nipping at low-hanging branches.

Rex has his arm around my shoulders and I feel so fucking peaceful. It doesn't hurt that I'm also full and wearing Rex's heaviest sweater and coat.

Marilyn stops to contemplate a bush and I find myself pushed up against the strong trunk of a tree, with Rex in front of me.

"We have got to stop meeting like this," I say.

He huffs out a laugh and kisses me, one hand pulling off my hat to tangle in my hair. Rex really likes to touch my hair. He kisses my neck and then both cheeks. Then he kind of sags against me, hugging me and the tree. He says something, but it's so muffled by my shoulder that I can't hear him.

"What's that?"

"I said, I'm really glad you're here. That we did this." I think he means Thanksgiving dinner, but I'm not totally sure.

"Me too," I say. "It's actually the only time I've ever eaten turkey. That wasn't in a sandwich, I mean."

As I'm about to say something incredibly sappy, my phone makes a loud and unfamiliar sound.

"What the?"

It's a text, but I always keep my phone on vibrate.

Rex chuckles.

"Will."

"Huh?"

"I bet Will changed your ringtone. He does that. It's a gesture of goodwill, I promise."

"Some fucking gesture," I grumble as I open the text. And immediately grin, tilting the phone to show Rex.

There, lying against Ginger's purple velvet couch, is a naked (and red-haired) chest. And on it, a huge, half-eaten Thanksgiving burrito.

Chapter 14

December

THE LAST week of classes, my students are in the usual frenzy, flooding my office hours for help with their final papers, writing me desperate e-mails at 3:00 a.m. (probably from the library) to beg for extensions, and falling asleep in strange contortions in the middle of classes. Usually, I kind of like this final week. It feels buzzy with the promise of winter break and the end of another semester. Unfortunately, this semester, in addition to grading all my final papers, I also have to read all the essays for that damned committee I accidentally volunteered for.

As a result, I've been locking myself in my office every day since classes ended. I can't bear trying to work in my shithole of an apartment. It's dark, depressing, and, now, freezing. I do have to smile every time I see the table Rex built, though, which looks amusingly out of place among my otherwise disposable furniture.

Rex. I can't stop thinking about him. It's like once we started spending more and more time together I got addicted to him or something. Everything reminds me of him or of something I want to tell him. I keep starting to text him things and then deleting them because I don't want to inundate him. I asked him about texting tentatively last week. I wasn't sure if, given plenty of time to read them, texts would be fine for him, or if he wouldn't like them. He said he'd never texted with anyone so he didn't know, but he was happy to try. I promised him that I wouldn't care about his spelling, which he's very self-conscious about. So, finally, this morning, after accidentally falling asleep and spending the night in my office, I sent him a simple, if sappy, text: *Hi. I miss you.*

About five minutes later, he texted back: *Come here when yore done?* It made my heart beat with anticipation. I didn't exactly mean to sequester myself, but I know from long experience that the only way I can make grading bearable is to tackle it all at once, so I've been motoring through it all for the last few days. I've been grabbing to-go food from the diner or eating out of the vending machine in the basement and I really need a shower, but I'll be goddamned if I'm not done by tonight. I'll submit my grades to the registrar, drop my essay selections in the main office, and then I'm done for a blissful month. Just thinking about it makes me giddy with desperation to finish.

I text Rex back—*Absolutely. See you tonight*—and then dive back in. Now that I'm so close to seeing Rex, though, I'm back to what's been distracting me for weeks. Will's comments before Thanksgiving about whether or not I was in Michigan for the long haul. Whether I was with Rex for the long haul. I'm fucking crazy about Rex. That much I know. But I don't even really know what a long-term relationship would look like. I've just never thought about it before. Does it mean, like, holidays and vacations? Barbecues and choosing paint colors?

There's a hollow feeling in my stomach thinking about it. But it isn't precisely anxiety. It's something more tentatively... hopeful? What would it even look like to do those things with Rex? To be responsible for someone else—*to* someone else?

I shake my head to clear the fog and squint at the stack of essays in front of me. It's page after page of potential and futurity and possibility and, for the first time in a long time, those seem like good things to me.

"HI," REX calls as I drag myself through the door, my vision practically blurry from staring at papers for four days straight.

I drop my stuff by the door, scratch Marilyn's soft ears, and slouch into the kitchen with her trailing behind me. I didn't even go home to change before coming here, I was so desperate to feel the sense of calm that only Rex can provide.

The whole house smells wonderful: a combination of wood smoke, trees, snow, and cooking that smells like, well, home. Rex is wearing a tight navy blue henley worn almost transparent in places. It's pushed up over his powerful forearms and he's doing something at the stove when I walk into the kitchen. His smile warms me immediately, and before he can turn toward me, I plaster myself across his back and hug him from behind.

"Hi," I say, and it comes out as a tired moan.

Rex turns in my arms and leans back to contemplate my face. He strokes my cheekbones and rests his thumbs under my eyes.

"You look beat," he says. I drop my head forward to rest on his breastbone and he holds me close. Every few seconds, I wonder if he wants me to let go—I know most guys don't love to hug—but it's as if he can read my mind, because each time the thought occurs to me, he gathers me tighter against him. I must fall asleep for a microsecond because the next thing I know, Rex is guiding me down onto one of the stools and I feel that lurch in my chest that happens when I'm awakened suddenly.

"You're all done?"

"Yeah, thank god," I say.

We talk a little bit about a new commission Rex has for a sleigh bed and he makes magic happen on the stove and the next thing I know, my forehead cracks against the counter. I have such a clear memory of this kid, Martin, in tenth grade who was always falling asleep during class. We'd all watch his head start to slump and usually he'd jerk himself awake. But once a week or so, he'd fall out of his chair, waking up halfway down and scrambling to catch his balance. At the time, I thought it was hilarious. Now I wonder what shit job he was working until late to make him that tired at fifteen.

"Jesus, are you okay?" Rex asks, rounding the counter toward me.

"Shit," I say, rubbing my head. "Sorry, what were you saying?"

"You're asleep on your feet, sweetheart," Rex says. "Why don't you go take a hot shower? When you're done, dinner will be ready and then you can crash."

"Do I smell that bad?" I tease as he hoists me up by the elbow.

"Only a little," he says, brushing my hair out of my eyes. "Go on."

I manage to stay awake in the shower. Under the hot water, my mind wanders to my apartment and I realize that I should make sure to start running the taps every day so they don't freeze. At my old apartment in Philly, the kitchen taps would sometimes freeze because I never used them.

I feel a little better after my shower—more floaty than lightheaded—and wander back into the kitchen to find Rex putting what looks like roast chicken, mashed potatoes, and peas on the table.

"Oh my god," I groan. "That's, like, the dinner I've been waiting for my whole life." It smells amazing and looks perfect, like one of those fake dinners on a 1950s TV show.

Rex crosses to me in three steps and practically knocks me over when he kisses me, hard.

"You look so fucking hot in my clothes," he growls, and kisses my neck. His smallest T-shirts are baggy on me and I'm wearing the sweatpants he left out for me the night we met.

"Got a binder clip?" I tease and Rex smirks.

"Nope," he says wolfishly, looking torn between pulling my sweatpants down himself and waiting for them to inevitably succumb to gravity.

The chicken is as amazing as it smells and I basically stuff my face while I tell him about finishing my grading. He gets a pained look on his face when I mention accidentally falling asleep in my office last night, but doesn't say anything. I have all sorts of elaborate plans for how I'll let go of my borrowed sweatpants, letting them fall tantalizingly to the floor in the hopes that Rex will follow through on the promises of seduction that his eyes have made throughout dinner, but when the moment comes, all I can really do is stagger to the bedroom and let Rex guide me down to the bed.

My eyes close the second the soft mattress and warm smell of Rex cradle me, and I reach out a hand to where I thought Rex would be but he isn't there.

"Hmm?" he says, and I must've made a sound.

"Are you sleeping too?" I ask.

"Yeah, I'll be right in," he says, even though I catch sight of his alarm clock and it's only 9:36. I wake up a few minutes later when he settles into bed beside me and roll toward him. He puts on headphones and settles in on his back, propped up on a few pillows. I put my head on his chest and sling an arm and a leg over him.

"What're you listening to?" I ask, but if he answers I'm already asleep.

I WAKE feeling the kind of rested that only ever happens after being totally exhausted. A glance at the clock tells me I slept for twelve hours. I hear the shower running and slide out of bed, suddenly desperate to feel Rex's skin against mine. I knock on the door because I still can't imagine barging in on someone while they're in the bathroom, even if it is Rex. He opens the door, not even in the shower yet, and pulls me in.

"You're up," he says. "Perfect timing."

I watch him strip in the mirror as I brush my teeth, a glob of minty spit falling into the sink when he drops his boxers, revealing his thick erection.

"Can I be of some service?" he asks, smiling at my open mouth and stepping into the shower.

I rinse my mouth and practically trip over my clothes to join him. I'm barely even under the water before I reach for his gorgeous cock, the skin like velvet over steel, and he murmurs his approval, caressing my nipples with his thumbs. He drags me under the water with him and takes my mouth, hard, groaning as I squeeze the base of his erection. He pulls me into him, clutching my ass roughly as he grinds our hips together. We kiss, straining together, hands roaming one another like it's been months rather than days since we were last together like this.

I nip at Rex's neck and he practically lifts me off the ground, crushing me to his chest.

"Please, baby, I need you," he grits out, voice rough with lust. His pupils are huge in his whiskey-colored eyes, wet eyelashes shadowing them, making him look intense and desperate. His cock is so hard he's pulsing against me and I can tell it took some effort to even form the words. I nod at him, tacit permission for him to take whatever he needs from me. I love when he gets like this.

Rex spins me around and squeezes conditioner from the bottle to slick me up. He kneads my asscheeks as he spreads the slickness at my opening and slides two fingers in. Christ, his fingers are big. It takes my body a moment to adjust, but when my muscles rearrange themselves, a bolt of desire shoots from my ass right up my spine and leaves me shivering.

"All right?" Rex asks, more growl than query, and I nod frantically.

"Now you, please."

He swears, and squeezes more conditioner out to slick himself up. He takes my hands and puts them on the bar inside the shower door, bending me over and lifting my ass to him.

"Stay," he says.

He swipes his fingers over my hole one more time, making me clench in anticipation and moan when that's all there is. Then I feel his heat hovering over my back, and he slides against me, filling me slowly. I can feel the trembling in his thighs as he seats himself fully inside me. He's so tall he has to crouch to fuck me like this, and that tremble makes everything more intense, like he's willing to do anything to get inside.

"Oh god," he moans, resting his forehead at the nape of my neck. I clench around him and he swears, curling his hands around my shoulders from the front, and dragging me down even farther onto his cock. As he penetrates me this last little bit, it sends shock waves of pleasure through my ass, and I can't help but clench up again.

"Move," I beg, so of course he stays still, kissing and sucking the back of my neck. I can feel him, pulsing inside me with the beat of his heart. Now that we're not using condoms, it's like I can feel his blood close to the surface, his heat always just about to merge with mine. Then he starts to move, tiny little pulses of his hips that seem to stir my pleasure so slowly that I'm moaning and panting before I even realize I'm doing it.

He reaches down and spreads me open wider, and I can see our blurry reflections in the mirror through the shower door. Rex is looking down at where we're joined and I wish I could see us through his eyes. Our hazy shapes in the mirror look like smears, shaking against each other with desire, straining to become one.

Rex ghosts his finger over my hole, around his erection, then pushes at my rim experimentally. My breath catches and I go still, my body tensed, every bit of my attention focused on the spot. He just keeps running his finger around my hole, sending shivers through me, until he flexes his finger slightly, sliding it in alongside his cock. I shudder, the sensation of being too full making me writhe away for a moment. But when he eases his finger out, I immediately want it back.

"Do that again," I breathe, dropping my head down and trying to relax.

Rex pulls out and slams into me, that first stroke catching me so off-guard that I cry out. He fucks me deeply for a few more strokes, then surges in to the hilt and pauses again. He squeezes more conditioner and then his finger is back, sliding gently into me alongside his erection. Rex moans and I shiver, my breath coming fast. Rex slowly pulls out, leaving just his finger inside me, and he curls it to nail my prostate. I cry out, the sudden bright pleasure so intense and so different than the diffuse pressure of his cock that it's shocking. He leaves his finger inside me and slowly slides back in, filling me.

"Oh, fuck, fuck," I mutter, trying to squirm away, but he won't let me. He's trembling again, clutching at my hip with his other hand. As his erection slides in, it presses his finger against my prostate, turning my insides to liquid heat. I tentatively clench my internal muscles around him and pleasure shoots through my channel. Rex convulses against my back, groaning. I can't take much more of this. I feel wracked on Rex's cock and finger, my whole body straining simultaneously to get away and to move closer. I can hear myself moaning brokenly but it sounds like it's coming from miles away. The water sounds close, though, like we're fucking under a waterfall.

Rex gives one more flex of his finger against my prostate, then slides his finger out. I'm panting, my legs barely able to hold me up. I've left my hands where Rex put them: on the door rail. As Rex starts to fuck me in earnest, long, deep strokes that fill me so perfectly, I let go to grab my own rock-hard erection. Rex, his hand now free, catches my wrist before I can, and guides it back to the door rail, squeezing his own over it.

"No," he says roughly, and I groan in frustration, but can't seem to form actual words of protest.

Rex pulls my hips up farther, so I'm almost on my tiptoes, and keeps fucking me. The heat prickles in my lower back and I can see my erection jump each time Rex's hard cock slides past my prostate. I squeeze my eyes shut, trying to concentrate on not stroking myself off. There's something about the way Rex tells me what to do when we're fucking that makes me want to do whatever he says. It's like he owns my body and controls it. And I let him.

Rex puts a hand to my belly, just above my groin, holding me tight to him. Then he starts thrusting up into me, changing his angle so he penetrates me even deeper. I can feel my whole channel throbbing with pleasure and a little bit of soreness from his powerful thrusts. Then Rex slides his hand down and starts jerking me off. The second his rough hand closes around my erection, I'm done for. My balls are pulled up so tight I can't believe I haven't come yet, and every nerve ending in my body feels electric. Rex thrusts into me a few more times, and my orgasm shoots through me, the fingers of pleasure stroking me inside and out, pushed out of me by Rex's cock and pulled from me by his hand.

My whole body clenches in white-hot pleasure and I can hear Rex cry out, distantly, as I clench around him. His hand is shaky on my cock as he gives a few last thrusts, and then he's coming too, legs trembling, chest heaving, and cock branding me inside with heat. My own cock gives a final, sympathetic pulse, a few last beads of pleasure welling from me as Rex collapses on my back, his breath loud in my ear.

"Fuck, baby," he moans against my neck, and he slides out of me in a rush of heat, leaving me feeling empty in his wake.

I feel wrung out, my opening still spasming a little as Rex's come slides out of me. I have the absent thought that I should find that disgusting, but actually it's really hot to feel evidence of his pleasure still inside me.

Rex spins me around and pulls me to him, kissing my mouth. I put my arms around his neck and kiss him passionately, trying to communicate how good he made me feel.

Our kisses turn lazy and we get out of the shower shakily, our eyes meeting in the mirror as we pull our clothes back on. It's only as we leave the bathroom that I realize we didn't even wash our hair or anything. Not that I could possibly care about that now. I'm so warm and satisfied, as if Rex fucked the stress right out of me.

In fact, I'm in such a postorgasmic haze that I barely notice Rex asking if I want breakfast, just mindlessly trailing after him into the kitchen.

"I need to do laundry and go to the store," I say, half to myself. "I haven't done anything but grade all week and I have no clean clothes, nothing to eat at my house."

"You can do it here, if you want," Rex offers, pushing a mug of coffee I didn't see him make toward me across the counter. I sink onto one of the stools to drink it and immediately change my mind as my tender ass meets the hard wood.

Rex must see my wince because he kisses me in a way that would be creepy and possessive if he were someone else but, because he's Rex, is possessive and hot.

"Okay," I say. "If you don't mind. I'll go to the store and drop my stuff off, then grab my laundry and bring it back?"

"Sounds good," Rex says. He's looking at me closely and his eyes are soft.

"What?" I ask, suddenly self-conscious.

"Nothing." He shakes his head and kisses me on the cheek. "You want some breakfast before you go?"

I shake my head and go change back into my gross, dirty clothes from yesterday.

"Okay," I tell Rex. "I'll be back in a few hours."

He smiles and kisses me, his hand falling to rest on Marilyn's head, where he strokes her absently.

My phone rings as I close the door behind me, and I grab for it, assuming it's Ginger, since no one else really calls me except Rex. But it isn't Ginger; it's Sam.

"Listen, Dan," Sam says when I pick up. His voice sounds thick and weird. Nasal. "Pop's gone."

"What?" I ask stupidly.

"Pop's dead," Sam says, and it sounds like he might be crying. I'm not sure. I've never heard him cry.

"What do you mean?" I ask. I've read about this in books but never experienced it: the feeling of being unable to process a simple sentence even when you know what all the words mean. Vaguely, I wonder if this is what Rex feels like when he tries to read—grasping after meaning and finding only nonsense.

"Damn it, Dan, Pop's dead," Sam says, as if I'm being intentionally obtuse. "He had a heart attack and died."

"When?" I hear myself ask, as if at the other end of a tunnel.

"Yesterday."

Momentarily, fury pushes aside some of the fog in my head. Yesterday. I look at my watch. It's almost noon.

"Why the fuck didn't you call me?"

Sam's talking, but I barely hear him. There's a roaring in my ears so loud that I look around, wondering if someone's riding a motorcycle down the street outside Rex's house.

"Dan! Dan?"

"What," I say.

"Did you fucking hear me?"

"No," I say.

"I said you don't have to come if you're busy or something, but—"

"Are you fucking crazy? Of course I'm coming. I'm leaving now."

I close my phone and slide it into my pocket, staring at the snow-heavy branches of the fir tree next to the driveway. Little lumps of snow drop off it onto the hood of my car as the wind sways its boughs. It's beautiful. When it snows in Philly the trees are all bare.

I jump when I feel a hand on my arm.

"Hey," Rex says, "I thought you were going to—baby, what's wrong?"

"What?" I ask.

"You were just standing out here. What's wrong?" Rex cups my face and I try to blink away the weird black spots at the edges of my vision.

"Um," I say. "Um. My dad died. I have to go home now."

"Oh no," Rex breathes, and he looks so sad.

"I have to go home," I say again, fumbling for my keys.

"Let me just grab my keys and I'll drive you," Rex says.

"No, I mean I need to go *home*. To Philly."

But of course my damn car won't turn over. I pop the hood and start automatically going through the list of things that are usually wrong with it. Honestly, there's no way the thing is going to last the winter. It started okay for me yesterday, but now it's just dead.

"Fuck," I say, kicking at the tire.

"Baby," Rex says, coming back outside with his keys. I shrug him off and slam the hood. Rex reaches out a hand to me. "Let me drive you," he says.

"No, Rex, I need to go home, now."

"I know," he says. "You need to go to Philadelphia. But your car's dead and you're in no condition to drive anyway. A last-minute flight will be very expensive. I don't have any jobs lined up this week. Let me drive you home. Let me help you take care of everything."

Let me help you. Let me help you. This is it. This is the moment that everything we've talked about has been leading to. Either I trust Rex enough to let him help me or I don't.

"I can't ask you to—" I start to say.

"You didn't ask. Daniel, look at me."

Rex pulls my chin up. I can't quite breathe.

"Baby," he says again. "I'm so sorry. Please, let me help."

I nod, and Rex is in action immediately. He puts me in his truck, starts the ignition to get some heat, and runs inside. He's back five minutes later, carrying a duffel bag and thanking someone on the phone. He hangs up and gets in the car.

"Okay," he says.

We pull up in front of my apartment and Rex leads me to the door. I look up at him, confused.

"You need to grab some clothes," Rex says. Right. Of course.

Fortunately, I think I have some clean underwear and a pair of jeans that aren't too dirty. I start to put things in a backpack robotically. Rex runs his hand over the wood of the kitchen table he built, which is currently home to stacks of library books.

"Daniel?"

Has he been calling my name?

"Huh?" I say.

"It's freezing in here."

"Sorry," I say. "I can try and turn it up."

"No, baby, we're not staying. I just meant.... Never mind," he says, and crosses to me. He brushes my hair out of my eyes. "Do you have a suit?" he asks gently.

I stare at him, unsure why I would need a suit. Rex clears his throat.

"For the, um, the funeral?"

Right. The funeral. What a strange word. Fyooneruhl. Not very many words with an f and then a long U-sound. Future. Fuchsia. Fumarole. Fugue.

"Daniel?"

I take my only suit out of the closet and roll it up into my backpack. I add my toothbrush and toothpaste to the bag.

"Do I have to do something with the pipes?" I ask Rex. "So they don't freeze or something?"

"We can call your landlord and let him deal with it."

"What about Marilyn?" I ask, suddenly remembering the dog.

"I called Will. He's going to take care of her. Is there anything you need to see to at school?"

I shake my head. I submitted grades before I went to Rex's the night before and I'd dropped the essays off in the main office.

"Okay," Rex says, and as we walk back out into the Michigan snow, I have the strangest feeling that it's the last time I'll ever see my apartment. But of course that's ridiculous.

IT TURNS out that Rex is one of those people who know how to get places. He has an atlas in the truck, and I ask him if he wants me to look up directions, but he says he doesn't need me to. For the first few hours, I keep expecting him to ask me to check something, but he never does. Rex doesn't talk to me, for which I'm grateful. I have no words right now and to demand any of me would be cruel. I can't even answer no when he asks if I'm hungry. I know I should offer to take a turn driving, but when I gesture vaguely at the steering wheel, Rex just shakes his head and squeezes my knee.

I'm not sure if I sleep or not, but it's been dark for hours before I notice. Rex gets off the highway in Youngstown and the Springsteen song starts playing in my head. Good song. We pull into the parking lot of a motel.

"Are we stopping?" I croak.

Rex nods. I bite my tongue. I want to keep going, but Rex has been driving all day and he must be tired.

In the room, Rex tells me he's going to go get some food and starts the shower for me. It feels like it's been months since we showered together this morning. I get into the shower like he says. I have the strongest memory of the week my mother died. I didn't quite understand at first, but when I realized she was never coming back I started to make a wish when the clock turned to 11:11. A kid at school had told me that if you wished on 11:11 it would definitely come true. I would stay up late so that I could make the wish twice a day, that whole week. I wished for my mom to come back and my dad to be gone instead.

Rex opens the door and the water has gone cold. Again, I haven't even washed my hair.

"Come here, love," Rex says.

"Sorry," I mutter. "I think the hot water's gone."

"It's okay. Don't worry about it."

Rex has laid out Subway sandwiches on the small table by the window.

"I got you turkey," he says, but I'm not hungry. I shake my head and lie down on the big bed.

"Daniel, you haven't eaten anything all day. I know you're not hungry, but you need to eat. Just a little." I close my eyes. "Please," Rex says, and when I open my eyes I see how tired he looks. How worried. About me, I guess.

I nod and haul myself up again. Rex is clearly starving because he finishes his sandwich in about two minutes. I take a bite and it tastes like glue. When I try to swallow, it's like I've never eaten before. The sensation is so strange. Like a brick has lodged itself in my stomach. I take another bite and chew until it's paste, hoping it'll just slide down. I swallow it, but on the third bite my mouth refuses to open. I know I'll throw up if I try.

"Sorry," I say, and push the sandwich across the table to Rex.

"We can save it for later," he says, but I shake my head quickly. Just the idea of eating it later, slick turkey clinging to moist bread, makes my stomach heave.

"You eat it," I say. Rex hesitates, but he's obviously still hungry and acquiesces. It's gone in minutes.

I'm aware of Rex's eyes on me and I dread the moment when he asks how I'm doing, when I have to find some words—pull them up from where they're roiling in my stomach along with those two bites of sandwich.

But he doesn't say anything, just cleans up the trash and lies down on one side of the bed, flicking the TV on and flipping channels until he gets to the Food Network. I wander into the bathroom and brush my teeth, hoping to get rid of the taste of the sandwich. I wish I hadn't slept so much last night because all I want to do now is fall into bed and sleep forever.

Rex has one arm behind his head, his biceps bulging under his head. I crawl onto the bed and kiss the smooth muscle. He stretches his arm out, making a space for me to lie against him. On screen, a group of little kids are chopping, frying, slicing, and mixing like professionals. I relax a little bit, and Rex cradles me in his arm.

"Daniel," he says, and I tense, expecting the inevitable questions. "I'll do anything you need, okay? Anything." His voice is low, intense, and I can tell he means it.

"Thanks," I say. "I'm okay. This is good."

Rex must have tucked me under the covers because when I wake up screaming they're tangled around me and at first I think they're the bricks falling on me, crushing me. Then something really is crushing me. Rex gathers me in his arms, stroking my back and whispering nonsense, trying to soothe me back to sleep.

WHEN I see the first signs for Philadelphia, I feel a rush of joy. And, even if it's under terrible circumstances, my first glimpse of the skyline makes me smile. Rex squeezes my knee.

"Can you tell me where to go from here?"

"Yeah. Oh shit, I never called Ginger." Oh well. She won't mind if we just show up.

I give Rex directions to my dad's place. It's surreal to be driving down these streets with Rex. I have him park in the alley outside the shop to make sure no one smashes his windows, but when we get out of the truck, I can't make my feet move. Rex comes around to the passenger side and hovers next to me. I've begun to get used to this, his constant presence, strong and warm and calm, lending support but asking nothing of me.

I look up at him, trying to drink in as much of him as I can before going inside. His hair has gotten long, I realize all of a sudden, and it waves around his face, intensifying the shadows under his cheekbones and highlighting his strong jaw. He's fucking perfect and I have no idea how I got so lucky. All I want is to cling to the way he's looking at me for a few seconds longer before the illusion that I'm someone worth spending time with is shattered.

"Look," I say, running my hand along his side. "Whatever stupid shit my brothers say, don't listen to them, okay? They're assholes, I know. I just don't... don't want you to think that I'm like them."

"Don't you think I know that?" he says gently.

"Probably."

"Come here."

Rex kisses me, so softly, so sweetly that it makes me want to cry. Because what has he done these last few days if not proved that he knows me?

"Okay," I say. "Thanks."

We walk in through the shop entrance and the smell of oil and hot metal and rust is so familiar it makes my head spin. The shop's not open, of course, but it's a smell that never goes away. It's what my dad and my brothers always smell like, no matter how often they shower.

The shop door connects to the kitchen and I walk in, Rex at my heels. The kitchen's a mess, as usual, with stacks of pizza boxes on every counter, sauce-crusted pots in the sink, and beer cans stacked in precarious pyramids against the wall. The TV is on and I can hear my brothers' voices and smell the sweet malt of what is probably a *lot* of beer.

I reach back and catch Rex's hand, squeezing it hard.

"Here goes nothing," I say, immediately embarrassed that such a dumb cliché is the first thing that came to my mind.

Squaring my shoulders, I walk through to the living room. Sam is sitting in the recliner, staring at the hockey game on TV. Liza's next to him, perched on the arm of his chair. Brian is sitting where he always sits, on the floor in front of the TV, leaning against the couch. Colin is on the couch, knees splayed open to take up twice the space he really needs and ensure no one will sit next to him. It's almost like I never left, the scene is so familiar, except all three of them look terrible. Sam's eyes are swollen to slits, Brian looks like a child, with his shirt inside out and his hair hanging in his face, and Colin—it may be the first time in years that I've seen Colin look almost vulnerable. He isn't wearing his usual look of scorn; his mouth is slack and his brow furrowed like he might actually be thinking about something other than his next barb.

"Hey, guys," I say, when they don't seem to notice us. I can feel Rex's warmth at my back. Three dazed heads swivel to look at me.

"Hey," Sam and Brian say. Colin's expression immediately turns sour and he looks familiar again.

Only Liza gets up.

"Hey," I say to her. She hugs me briefly.

"Sorry, Daniel," she says. I nod at her.

"Um, this is Rex," I say. "That's Sam, Colin, and Brian, and this is Liza," I tell Rex, pointing. Sam nods at him, Brian gapes, and Colin's eyes narrow. Liza holds out her hand and Rex shakes it, smiling at her.

"Nice to meet you all," Rex says politely, but I notice that his voice is deeper than it usually is. He looks so out of place here, like a figure in a painting razored from its background and pasted in another. He's so clean and fresh and honest. In our shabby living room, he also looks huge. I look around, trying to see it through Rex's eyes. The floorboards are dark with oil that's been tracked in from the shop year after year, the shellac peeling in places near the front door. The plaster is uneven, so the yellow light from the overhead fixture highlights every dip and bulge. The reclining chair is broken, forever over-reclined, so it has pillows shoved in the back so you can still see the TV. The couch is threadbare, with a grimy red blanket thrown over the back that my mother crocheted when she was pregnant with Brian and wanted something to do with her hands.

And suddenly I want to be back in Rex's clean, cozy cabin more than anything. Want to be watching a movie in front of the fire or sitting on a stool in the kitchen watching Rex cook. Want to be walking Marilyn in the woods around Rex's house or lying in Rex's big bed while Rex reminds me how good it's possible to feel.

When it's obvious that the guys aren't going to say anything to Rex, I walk farther into the room and, seeing no safe place to sit down, stand against the wall next to the TV.

"Um, so what the fuck happened?" I ask. "Was Dad sick?"

"If he was he didn't say so," Sam says. Liza has walked back to his chair and is resting her hands tentatively on the back of it, as if she thinks Sam might tell her to leave any moment.

"I don't think he went to a doctor or anything," Brian adds.

"So, he just dropped dead all of a sudden?" I say. "Can you please tell me what happened?"

"We were in the shop," Sam says. "Everything was fine. Then I heard a crash in the office and Pop was on the floor, grabbing at his heart. Luther called 911." Sam's getting choked up. "He died at the hospital."

"Shit," I say. "So, the doctors said it was a heart attack?"

Sam nods.

"What else did they say?"

"Are you a fucking medical doctor now too?" Colin's voice is poisonous.

"No, I just want to know what happened."

"We're having the funeral tomorrow," Liza says, taking pity on me.

"Jesus, that's fast," I say. Of course, at this point it's already been three days since they didn't call me right away.

"Well, we can't keep the shop closed and Vic got us an in at his cousin's funeral parlor," Sam says.

"Seriously, Sam? Vic's a fucking slimeball."

"Just because you don't like him…," Brian says.

"Dude, he's a criminal; come on." I look at Liza, hoping for some backup, but she's looking at the floor.

"Well, you weren't here to make other arrangements," Colin says, his voice shaking with anger. "So we took care of it. If you're too good to go to the funeral because you don't approve of Vic, then that's your fucking business."

I grit my teeth, at this point just trying to get all the information before I get the hell out of here.

"Of course I'm going to the funeral. What can I do to help?"

"Nothing," Sam says. "It's taken care of."

He gives me the details.

"Okay, well," I say. I feel like I should say something but I have no idea what.

"I'm sorry I wasn't here, but I'll see you tomorrow," I say.

"Not like you ever gave a shit about him anyway," Colin mutters.

Fury lances through my chest, propelled by the old familiar cocktail of frustration, pain, and injustice.

"You know that's not fucking true, Colin," I say, furious to hear my voice shaking. "I just didn't have that much in common with him." Rex takes a step closer and puts his hand on the small of my back.

"I'm sorry," Brian says, "but who the fuck are you?"

"Well, yeah," Colin says, standing up. He sways on his feet. Shit, he's trashed. "What would Pop have in common with a stuck-up little faggot?" He puts his finger in my face. "He looked out for you and you didn't even care enough to stick around."

"Colin," Sam warns.

Colin's staggering drunk, but his speech is horrifyingly clear. He actually believes that they're the loyal sons who loved our dad and I'm the selfish piece of shit who took him for granted and then bailed. I can feel it: the tickling in my ears and tightness in my throat that means I'm going to cry if I don't do something quick. So I do the only thing that always works. I get mad instead.

"What the *fuck*, Colin!"

I shove him, thinking that this unsteady on his feet he'll go down like a sack of cement. But, even wasted, Colin's a fighter, and he sways back to center like a punching bag, grabs me by the shirt, and slams me against the wall so hard the light flickers. I hear Liza's intake of breath. Colin's face is a mask of fury. He's the only one of us who looks like our mom, with light brown hair and light blue eyes.

He's my height, but he's built like a tank. I've never won a fight with Colin. Not ever.

Then there's a large presence at my shoulder and Rex peels Colin off me. His expression is neutral, but when he speaks his voice is murderously calm.

"Don't. Fucking. Touch him," Rex says, and you would have to be out of your goddamned mind to start anything with that voice. Colin, though I've wondered over the years, is not out of his mind.

The tension in the room is thick. Sam has half risen from the recliner and Brian is standing in front of the TV as if he might be able to change the channel and end up in some other living room in some other house, with some other family. He looks anxious. Brian is always anxious when Colin isn't in control.

"Um, so, *who* are you?" he asks Rex again.

"Rex," Rex says, glancing at me as if to check what he should say.

"He's my boyfriend," I say. I feel a flash of elation at saying it for the first time, followed by a deep pang of shame, the only emotion I've ever associated with desire for men inside these walls.

Sam looks at the floor and Colin sinks back onto the couch.

"Well, I guess it's obvious who the girl is, Danielle," Colin says, using his old nickname for me.

It doesn't matter that years of studying gender theory have given me the ability to reject the gender binary outright. It doesn't matter that I understand my negative reaction to being called the girl is due to a whole lot of entrenched cultural misogyny and not my own feelings about women. It doesn't matter that I love when Rex fucks me, which is, of course, basically what Colin's accusing me of.

All that matters in this moment is launching myself across the pathetic pressboard coffee table cluttered with beer cans and junk mail, and beating the shit out of Colin, which is what I'm attempting to do when Rex grabs me. At least he let me get in a couple of good punches, but I'm still vibrating with fury.

"Fuck!" I yell, and I'm actually glad when Rex grabs me this time, because I was about to punch the television, and god knows if I'd broken that, all three of my brothers would have jumped on me and murdered me before Rex could do a thing about it.

I slam out the front door and turn into the alley where Rex's truck is. I'm leaning against it when Rex joins me.

"Well," I say. But I have nothing to add.

Rex fixes me with a look that manages to be incredibly sympathetic without pissing me off.

"I don't care for your brothers," he says, jaw clenched.

I laugh.

"Fuck, me neither. Let's get out of here."

I FEEL better after the fight with Colin, actually. My anger for him is familiar; I know it'll fade. It feels better than the creeping numbness I've felt the last few days.

It's about nine when we get to Ginger's shop, and I have a huge grin on my face as the door chimes tinkle their customary welcome. Ginger is in the back of the shop, doing inventory. She's wearing these hideous purple overalls that she loves and a black bandeau top that shows off the tattoos on her arms, chest, back, and neck. Her curly black hair is shaved on one side and she's wearing her usual tangle of thin silver chains around her neck.

She's pretty but not beautiful, with a pale, heart-shaped face and intelligent brown eyes. But when she looks up and sees me, she cracks a grin that turns her into the most beautiful girl in the world. Her eyes flash and her nose crinkles and she squeals and rushes toward me, jumping on me in joy.

"You came back early!"

She smells like Ginger. Like baby powder deodorant, eucalyptus shampoo, jasmine perfume, and, over it all, the metallic tang of ink.

"My fucking father died," I say, as she untangles herself from me and her boots hit the floor.

"Oh shit, babycakes," she says. Then she looks behind me. "Is this Rex?" she asks.

Rex steps forward and holds out his hand.

"Ginger?" he says. "Nice to meet you."

She scoffs at his hand and hugs him too, though it's considerably harder, since he has about a foot on her.

"Come upstairs," she says. "You're staying with me, right?"

"If it's okay," I say.

"Obviously," she says, rolling her eyes at me. Fuck, I've missed her. "Hey, guys," she calls into the private tattooing rooms, "close up for me?"

"Yeah, I got it," a voice calls back.

"Hey, Marcus," I call.

"Hi, Daniel," he calls back.

I SINK down on Ginger's purple velvet couch, which, despite all the shit I give her about how ugly it is, is actually quite comfortable. I love Ginger's apartment. It's a perfect reflection of her. The wood back of the couch is painted gold and it and a leather armchair flank the wagon wheel coffee table. Hung above the doors and windows are animal skulls encrusted in black glitter. She painted the ceiling so it looks like it's cracking, and the cracks run from a spot near the window where she's painted it to look like a realistic skeleton hand has broken through the ceiling and is reaching down. The walls are hung with friends' art and her own. There are paintings by her friend, Jonah, which are Day of the Dead animals; collages of outer space by some woman who traded them for a tattoo years ago; a gorgeous nude of a man covered in tattoos that she traded two of her own paintings for.

I love Ginger's work. Many of them are based on tattoo designs, realistic black and gray skulls morphing into candle flames and melting wax, panthers morphing into sleek, black-haired women, and a very creepy one of a snake swallowing a grouse. My favorite hangs over the bed. It's a self-portrait Ginger did from a photograph of herself from behind, so it's really just her hair and shoulders. The detail in her long curls and short stubble are amazing. It's stark and mesmerizing but framed in a heavy old baroque-looking gold frame. I've spent hours tracing the lines of the curls with my eyes when I woke up hungover in Ginger's bed.

Rex is doing what everyone does the first time they come over to Ginge's, which is walking around her apartment checking out all her stuff. He lingers over a puzzle box on a stand near the bed. Ginger did a tattoo of a really complicated Escher piece on this guy a few years ago. He was a puzzle maker—that's how he described it. His signature work was these puzzle boxes carved out of chunks of wood from his family home, which partially burned down. He was a weird guy. Anyway, he came back when the tattoo had healed because Ginger wanted to take a picture of it for her portfolio and he brought her the puzzle box as a gift. It's gorgeous, the wood stained this really dark chocolate brown. I've fiddled with it a million times.

Rex is turning it over in his hands, poking and prodding it. I should have known he'd go right to it, with his love of taking things apart. After a minute, though, which is how long it usually takes people to give up and assume it doesn't open, Rex pulls something and pushes something else, and the first pieces come out.

"Holy…." Ginger mutters and we both walk over to Rex.

"Is it okay? Sorry, I should've asked," Rex says, looking like a kid whose favorite toy might get taken away.

"No, no, it's fine. Please," Ginger says, raising her eyebrows at me as Rex gleefully sets his attention back on the box.

After five minutes he has it open and casually starts to put it back together again.

"Wait!" Ginger yells. She reaches into the center of the box and pulls out a piece of paper. In cramped handwriting, it just says, *I'm impressed.*

"Oh my god," I say.

"What?" Rex asks, sounding nervous. He looks between me and Ginger. She's gaping at him.

"No one's ever opened that thing before," I tell Rex. "Not even Ginger. We had no idea there was something inside either."

"Holy mother love bone," Ginger says, a grunge oath she reserves only for things that truly delight her. "Dandelion, you hooked a genius."

"I know, right?" I link my arm with Rex's. He's actually blushing and he looks quite pleased. "Except, now, all I can think of is what happens to the idiots who open the puzzle box in the *Hellraiser* movies."

Ginger laughs—she loves *Hellraiser*—but stops abruptly.

"Um, so your dad?"

It comes rushing back so suddenly that I can't believe I ever forgot. I sink down onto the couch and Rex sits next to me, looking ridiculously beefy reclining against purple velvet. I tell Ginger about my dad. About getting the call and how the guys waited a whole day to bother telling me. When I get to Colin's accusation that I didn't care that Dad was dead, Rex is vibrating with anger.

"Rex might have had to pull me off Colin," I say.

"Had he called you that before?" Rex asks hesitantly, and it takes me a minute to remember which of Colin's vile comments he might be referring to.

"What, Danielle?" Ginger asks.

"Or the girl? Not," I add quickly, "that being called a girl is an insult. Just, you know Colin."

"Oh, I know," Ginger says. "That little asshole. *Not*," she adds, looking at me and drawling suggestively, "that there's anything wrong with assholes."

"Oh fuck, I've missed you," I say. "Got a drink?"

Ginger nods and grabs a bottle of whiskey from the kitchen. I take a sip and feel the heat feather down my throat and spread through my breastbone.

"How is it, then?" Ginger asks seriously, finally raising the question I've been dreading.

"Oh, fine; a little harsh for my taste," I say, raising the bottle at her.

"Ha-ha," she says. Then she just waits. I close my eyes and lean back against Rex's shoulder. His arm automatically comes around me and all I want to do is turn my face into his neck and never come out.

"I'm not sure," I say finally. "I'm… I feel all messed up, but… not precisely sad. More like—fuck, I don't know."

"Finish your sentence," Ginger says. Jesus, she's pushy. I can practically feel Rex taking notes.

"I don't know if I'll miss him. But, I guess a part of me always thought maybe the way things were was temporary. That, eventually, we'd be closer? Understand each other better. So now I feel like the… like that potential future has been… interrupted. Stolen from me."

"More please," Ginger says. I close my eyes again. I hate when she does this. I love when she does this. It's like I don't know what I'm thinking or feeling until I say it out loud.

"I was thinking, over Thanksgiving, that I don't really know him. I don't know what makes him tick—made him tick. Like, if he were the main character in the book I was reading, it'd only be chapter two. I'd know his name and who was in his daily life, but I'd be waiting to find out that thing that would make me care about his story. At least, that's how I felt before. There was a whole book left. The promise that maybe if I kept reading I'd learn enough to make me like him—care about him. Only now, it's like he was just a secondary character—a tertiary character. And the author hadn't even thought about any more of a story for him. There just *isn't* any more of him. And, I don't know. That makes me fucking sad because I think probably he felt the same way about me. I know he cared about me, at least a little. I mean, I think so. And Colin and the guys, they knew him. And they're fucking devastated he's dead. And I'm jealous because…."

"Because?" Ginger prods.

"Because they were a family and I wasn't part of it," I say, and though I've never had the thought before, I know it's what I really mean the second it comes out of my mouth. I swallow hard and my mouth tastes like blood. I take another gulp of whiskey and let my head fall back on

Rex's shoulder. I look up at him and see moisture gathering in the corners of his eyes. When he looks at me his eyes are so soft.

"I guess now we're both orphans," he says, and even though his voice is a masculine growl, it's such a little kid thing to say that it breaks my heart.

"I guess so."

I clear my throat.

"So, how was the family for Thanksgiving," I ask Ginger, desperate to change the subject before Rex and I end up bawling all over each other.

"It's been worse," she says slowly.

"Just because we're both orphans now doesn't mean you can't feel free to rain shit down on your family," I say. Ginger smirks.

"The mother was a passive-aggressive ice queen from hell who told me I needed to lose ten pounds and then maybe my tattoos would look like an avant garde fashion statement instead of a desperate attempt to thumb my nose at society's standards of beauty before men could reject me for being unconventional-looking."

Rex's mouth drops open.

"No, that's seriously how she talks," I say.

"I think you're beautiful," Rex says. Then a look of panic crosses his face. "I mean, I know that's the opposite of your point. Shit, I'm sorry." He looks at me, as if I can smooth it over.

"I love you," Ginger says to Rex. "I love him," she says to me.

Me too, I think, before I can even process the thought. Fuck me.

"The father was a black hole of spinelessness except when he was kissing the mother's ass in the hopes of some small crumb of encouragement, approval, or affection. It was nearly vomit-inducing, except that I couldn't possibly give the mother the grim satisfaction of thinking she'd turned me bulimic."

Rex's hand has found its way onto my thigh and its warm weight is comforting. I hand him the whiskey and he takes a few swallows.

"The sister attempted to break down all known laws of physics by simultaneously being completely self-centered and totally obsessed with what everyone else thought about her. It boggles the mind how one human being can possibly speak so many sentences about herself in a row and still have it seem like she's saying mean things about you. Truly, she has apprenticed at the feet of the master. In related news, she and the mother got matching haircuts, so the sister now also looks like the fifty-year-old president of a Chabad house. The end."

I pass Ginger the bottle silently.

"I know what we need," she says. She walks over to the record player.

"Tom Waits," I whisper to Rex so Ginger can't hear.

After that perfect static smear, Tom Waits counts off, "1, 2, 3, 4," and the opening strains of "Ol' '55" start.

"Called it," I say, and Ginger raises the bottle to me in a mocking toast.

Then Rex's stomach growls so loudly that I can hear it over the music.

"Sorry," he says. "Are you guys hungry?"

It's after ten and poor Rex hasn't eaten anything since we stopped at a rest stop outside Pittsburgh. I shrug.

"I could eat," Ginger says. "Here, I'll order something. Or, do you want the tots?" she asks me.

"Ugh, no, not tonight, sorry," I say. There's this bar a few blocks away that makes these diabolical tater tots that they kind of treat like nachos, with Cheez Whiz, some meat that I probably don't want to know about, and horseradish ketchup.

"I can make us something," Rex offers.

"Good luck," I say. Ginger waves him into the kitchen, winking at me.

"Jesus," Rex says from the kitchen. "You're as bad as Daniel."

"I'll get the menus." Ginger has a folder of menus from every restaurant within a thirty-block radius, organized by current level of favor.

AFTER WE eat, I'm sleepy and a bit drunk. I feel a little raw from all the talking about feelings and shit, and also a little shy with Rex, like maybe he's mad I didn't tell him what I told them in response to Ginger's prodding.

"Tell me something happy," I tell Ginger. Whenever we talk about heavy shit, we always end with something happy, like conversational dessert. "Tell me about Christopher. The burrito holder," I say to Rex.

"He smells really good, but like a grown-up," Ginger says.

"That's important," I say, nodding.

"He holds eye contact for the exact right amount of time, so you can tell he's focused on you but it doesn't feel creepy."

"Mmm."

"He called me Gingerbread once and I only hated it, like, 65 percent."

"Whoa."

"Yeah. You can meet him, maybe. Tomorrow?"

"Maybe. Tomorrow's the funeral. Tomorrow night?" She nods. Rex's arm tightens around me when I say the word "funeral," like it's an emotional bomb against which I need to be supported.

"Tell me how you guys met, Rex."

"You didn't tell her?" Rex asks, and he sounds a little hurt.

"No, I did," I say. "She wants to hear how you tell it."

"Well," Rex says, "I was out walking in the woods around my house. I'd heard wolf howls the night before, so I wanted to check it out."

"You said you were hunting!" I accuse.

"No, you asked what the gun was for. I've only been hunting once. You just thought everyone in the country goes out to shoot their dinner every night. Besides, sweetheart, it was dark."

Oh yeah. It was dark. I grumble and gesture at him to get on with it.

"Point is, I was worried about running into a wolf or something, when I heard this awful sound. Couldn't tell what it was, but a while later I heard this guy talking to himself. I shined my light toward the sound and there's this man holding an animal. When the light hit his face, I froze because I'd never seen someone so beautiful."

My heart beats faster and I look up at Rex. He looks a little embarrassed.

"Clearly a city guy, wearing a suit and all, but he looked so out of place or something. Not just in the woods, but in the suit. And he looked terrified. At first I thought he was just really worried about the dog, but then he was looking at me like I was something out of a horror movie."

"You had a gun," I say weakly.

"When I got close to him to take the dog, he started babbling about whether the dog was a boy or a girl. It was adorable. I liked how he talked. Like I was smart and could understand whatever he was on about. He was just... different. I thought, if I can help that dog, maybe this guy will give me the time of day. So I brought them back to my house even though I never bring people there. I was trying so hard not to check him out that I took about twice as long to fix the dog's leg as I needed to.

"When I ran a shower for him, I felt like a total pervert because here was this beautiful kid who'd gotten in a car accident and all I could think about was how to get him out of that ugly suit. When he took his shirt off and I saw those tattoos, I was done for."

Now I can tell Rex is really talking to me.

"You took my shirt off."

"Whatever," Rex says, smiling at me. "He got drunk on a couple shots of whiskey, and then paraded into the kitchen with my pants so close to falling off that I almost swallowed my tongue."

"They were too big," I say, elbowing him.

"I made him a sandwich and he told me a bunch of stuff about the job he was interviewing for. I thought, shit, this guy is smart and gorgeous. And, from what I saw with the dog, a sweetheart. But he clearly thought we were in the middle of nowhere, so I knew there was no way he'd ever be back.

"He let it slip that he was gay and I thought he was going to pass out. I could see how scared he was, but he just stared me down like he was daring me to have a problem with him being gay. It was… hot. So when he started freaking out, I couldn't help myself. I kissed him. I knew I'd only get one chance, so I figured I may as well go for it when he was incapacitated with fear."

He winks at me and I roll my eyes, but my memory of that kiss is still vivid.

"Then we were on the couch and he was all drunk and warm and adorable."

Rex shakes his head.

"When he kissed me it was all I could do not to rip those damned sweatpants off and—um, you know. But he was drunk and he'd been in an accident and it wouldn't've been right. It killed me to do it, since I knew I'd never see him again, but I went to bed and left him on the couch.

"The next morning, he was dead to the world, sacked out on the couch with my sweatpants practically falling off. Like he'd been put on that couch specifically to show me what I could never have. I banged around in the kitchen for a while, hoping he might wake up, but he was out.

"I had to take the dog to the vet before I went to work, so I left him there. I wanted to program my number into his phone. Get his number and put it into mine. Leave him a note saying if he ever came back through Michigan he should look me up. But it felt pathetic. In a day or two, the guy would be gone, back to Philadelphia or New York City or wherever, and he'd never be back."

I can't help but notice that Rex mentions New York, where Will moved, as well as Philly.

"And anyway, I didn't want to leave a note—even one to say *Take care*, because I didn't want him to think I was stupid and spelled everything wrong. Which I do."

Rex trails off.

"Got home that night and he was gone. Spent the next few months cursing myself for not leaving my phone number. Or something. But then, just when I'd convinced myself I'd never see him again, there he was."

"There you were," I murmur, my eyes closing.

"Come on, you narcoleptic," Ginger says, shaking me. "He always does this," she says to Rex. "We'll be listening to a record or something and he just conks out like a baby in a fucking car seat."

"I know," Rex says. "At first I thought he was constantly sleep deprived."

"Nah, he's just always keyed up. Then, when he finally relaxes, he just falls asleep before he even notices."

Rex seems to contemplate this while Ginger takes the whiskey away from me and clears the trash from dinner.

"You guys take the bed," Ginger says, and Rex immediately protests.

"Oh, stop," she says. "I've slept on this couch a hundred times. It's fine. No way are the two of you going to fit on it. Unless"—she waggles her eyebrows at Rex—"you want to ditch this sad sack and cuddle up with me."

"Back off, bitch," I say, smiling at her. "Thanks, Ginge." I hug her and she squeezes me just like she always does.

"I'm sorry, babycakes," she says.

I strip down to my boxers without thinking about it. Nothing Ginger hasn't seen before. Rex seems uncharacteristically shy, and crawls under the covers before he takes his shirt off, like we're in high school or a nineteenth-century novel or something.

Ginger's bed is a safe place, and almost immediately after crawling under the covers, a warm lethargy creeps over me, relaxing me.

"Thank you for bringing me here. For being here with me, I mean," I say to Rex softly. I can hear Ginger brushing her teeth in the bathroom.

Rex kisses me lingeringly.

"Anything for you," he says. Then he gathers me against his heat and I drift off to sleep, held in Rex's arms and Ginger's familiar bed.

Chapter 15

December

REX DRIVES us to the funeral with one hand on the wheel and the other heavy on my thigh. He's been so calm this whole time, so steady. I could see it in him the night we met—how solid he was.

THIS MORNING I woke up to Ginger crawling into bed next to me while Rex was still asleep, one arm thrown above his head.

"He's gorgeous and awesome," Ginger said matter-of-factly.

"I know, right?" I whispered back. "What the hell is he doing with me?"

She smacked me lightly and rolled her eyes.

"Listen, Ginge, will you come with us to the funeral? I'm afraid I might murder one of the guys and then the two remaining ones will turn on me, which will make Rex kill them and really I don't want to be responsible for Rex going to prison on top of all this…."

"Obviously, I'm going to the funeral with you, you idiot," she said, but she smiled.

Rex ran down to the bodega on the corner and got eggs and bread. After a late breakfast, Ginger called my brothers at my dad's house to get the specifics of the funeral while Rex and I changed. She figured they wouldn't be rude to her at least. I don't know why she'd think that after all these years. She started with the phone on speaker, but after Brian made some disgusting comment and Ginger told him he should go eat a dick and he replied, "Why don't you get Danielle to do that since it's his favorite thing to do," she took it off speaker and went into the kitchen.

Rex let out a controlled breath, shaking his head, and clenched his fists.

"Honestly, Daniel, I'm impressed you can even be in the same room as them," he said.

"I…. Brian's not usually so bad. When I was younger, we were— well, not friends, but friendlier? We'd play catch or poker sometimes when he didn't have anyone else to hang out with. And Sam. He calmed down a lot after he and Liza got married. He never really gave me too much shit because he was so much older."

I knotted my tie and shrugged into my jacket, which Ginger had taken one look at when I pulled it out of my backpack and immediately hung in the bathroom to steam while we all had our showers. Rex ran his hand down my lapel.

"This is the suit you were wearing the night we met," he said softly. I couldn't believe he remembered. I was only wearing it for an hour.

"It's the only one I have," I said. "How do you...?"

Rex's eyes never left mine.

"I remember everything about that night, Daniel."

He looked like he wanted to say something else, but then he took a deep breath and his eyes skittered away from mine and back to knotting his own tie.

"SO, WHAT'S the deal with this funeral?" Ginger says from the backseat. "I mean, are you all secretly Jewish or something? I thought you guys waited, like, weeks before you buried people so you could do whatever voodoo you do to make bodies that can rise from the grave."

Rex snorts.

"Fucking Vic," I say. "He and Sam worked out some kind of deal with his cousin or something. I don't know. They wouldn't hear a word against him. Jesus Christ," I say, running a hand through my hair, "I just hope this doesn't turn into that scene in that movie you made me watch after you broke up with Stephen."

"Oh yeah, *Death at the Funeral*," Ginger says. "Ha, good movie." Then to Rex she says, "The body falls out of the coffin."

"Yeah, I saw it," he says, his hand tightening on my thigh.

"Knowing Vic, he might bury Dad even if he's not actually dead just to make a buck," I say, going for levity, but it just comes out a little shaky.

"In case you hadn't noticed, Dandelion turns morbid when he's uncomfortable," Ginger says to Rex, leaning forward to stick her head between our seats. Rex smiles at her in the rearview mirror.

"Yeah, I'm getting that," he says, rubbing my leg with his warm hand.

"Dude," I say, "you're kind of turning me on. Do you *want* me to show up to my father's funeral with a hard-on?"

Rex shoots me a dark and filthy look that says if he had his way he'd have me showing up everywhere with a hard-on, but he just pats me on the knee and puts both hands on the wheel.

"Brian said there's going to be some kind of party in the shop?" Ginger continues.

"Yeah. For everyone who can't make it to the cemetery today. You know my family: it'll just be a shit-ton of beer and fried chicken and they'll drink and cry and undoubtedly those creepy twins will smoke in the shop and set a garbage can on fire. There are these friends of my dad's," I tell Rex, "who no one can tell apart. Like, sincerely, I don't even think my dad could tell them apart. He just always calls them The Twins, and no one's ever seen them when they weren't together. They're super skinny so it kind of looks like they're just one person that got sliced in half."

Rex's hand is back on my knee, gently. It's as if he can hear how fucked-up I feel in everything I say. I feel better than I did on the drive to Philly—seeing Ginger's helped a lot—but now I feel kind of... sick. Just vaguely nauseated, like I've forgotten something important or am about to get in trouble. I shouldn't have eaten those eggs.

BESIDES ME, Rex, and Ginger, my brothers, Liza, Luther, and a few of the other guys who work at the shop are the only ones there. It's a graveside service, and, credit to Vic and his cousin, my father's body does not fall out of the coffin. Sam shook my hand when we walked up, and nodded to Rex and Ginger. He looks sharp, in an overcoat I've never seen before, and I'd lay money that Liza went out and bought it for him. He holds Liza's hand the whole time. Brian looked okay when we started, but now he's crying. He's trying to stay quiet, but tears and snot are dripping down his face and his sleeve is shiny from wiping them away. He doesn't have a dress coat and Colin made him take off his Eagles down jacket at the graveside. It's fucking freezing out here, so now Brian is shaking too.

Colin. It's the strangest feeling, but Colin looks how I feel. He looks sick. He has circles under his eyes, and his hair, which is usually buzzed, has grown out some and looks crumpled from sleep. His lips are chapped and cracked from the cold and his eyes are puffy. When they lower the coffin into the ground, Colin squeezes his arms around his stomach and I realize I'm doing the same thing. Trying to hold it together from the outside in. Only he's failing.

I've never seen Colin cry. His eyes are scrunched up and his neck is corded and I can tell that he's nearly puking with the attempt to stay quiet. Sam is crying, Liza holding his arm. Tears are running down Luther's weathered face and he's making no attempt to hide them.

I am not crying. I am not sad. I am sick and numb and guilty with not crying.

I haven't been to a funeral since my mom's. At that one, everyone put roses on top of her coffin. One of my mom's friends gave me a rose. White. She told me, "Put it on top of Mommy so she can take a part of you with her." This—of course—terrified me, and I put the rose next to the grave, hoping no one would notice. One of our neighbors walked up last, and when he turned back after putting his rose on her coffin, he kicked my rose into the grave. For months, I had nightmares where I was just sitting in class or taking a shower and I would feel a tugging in my stomach. I'd look down and see the stem of a rose sticking out of my belly button. Then a hand would reach for it. My mother's hand. She'd take hold of the stem, thorns cutting her palm, and she'd pull. The stem would slid out of my stomach, ripping its way through, until finally the white bloom, now stained red with my blood, slid out. She would drag me into the darkness, tethered by the stem.

I tighten my arms around my stomach and Rex pulls me into him.

"You okay?" he asks softly, his mouth next to my ear. I shiver and nod.

It's just so ridiculous. That something like grief could course through each of these people, desperately contained, as the ritual unfolds, for the sake of… what? And the idea that my father is now a dead body inside a wooden box—absurd.

For a second, my mind wanders to the cholera epidemics, when fear of accidentally burying a family member alive resulted in coffins fitted with strings tied around the toes of their loved ones that led to bells, so that if they awoke, interred, they could signal for help. I've taught Poe's "The Cask of Amontillado" and "The Premature Burial" in classes before and always pictured these suitably dark, crumbling, atmospheric tombs. But it's 2:00 p.m. and the sun is shining and it's muddy. There's a man talking about my father who never met him and never will. My brothers are pillars of grief, mourning a man they adored. And I'm standing here thinking about nineteenth-century American horror stories. It's too fucking absurd. I make a noise that sounds disturbingly like a giggle.

Colin's head snaps up and his eyes meet mine. His face is red with pain, his lips bitten to blood. His look is disgusted. Murderous.

My brothers hate me.

Or, at least, don't care about me.

And I don't like them.

I'm standing between the only two people in the entire world who give a shit about me, and who the fuck knows how long at least one of them will stick around.

The service ends and Luther and the others walk off after hugging my brothers—manly, aggressive hugs, with back slaps and shoulder squeezes—and nodding uncomfortably at me. Luther shakes my hand.

Liza's still holding Sam's arm, but now she takes Brian's hand too, and he leans into her like a little kid. They stand there gazing at the grave. Colin is nearly vibrating. He's wearing a suit that's too short in the arms and a raincoat that I recognize as my dad's, which is tight in the shoulders. His shoes are worn and polished, now spattered with mud. Colin's losing his shit. Crying audibly and shaking his head like it's happening to someone else and he can't understand it. He takes off toward a copse of trees. I shake off Rex's arm and walk in the other direction, toward the bathroom, thinking that if I'm going to throw up I may as well do it in a toilet.

I can see Ginger take hold of Rex's arm to stop him coming after me. Bless her.

My face and ears feel hot and flushed. Once, when I was five, just before my mom died, we went to the Jersey Shore and I played in the water all day. Brian would bury me in the sand and I'd have to break free before a big wave came. I built a sand castle and waded into the waves to pee in the water so I wouldn't have to leave the beach. It was, I thought at the time, the best day I'd ever had. I got a terrible sunburn and my skin peeled for a week. That's how I feel now: so full up with heat that my head is throbbing.

I make it to the bathroom and puke into the toilet. I feel like something that's been lodged in my guts for years has come loose. Everything I said to Ginger and Rex last night was the truth. I do feel a kind of regret that I'll never be close with my father, a kind of mourning for what could have been. But I'm also so angry that it feels like poison is coursing through my veins.

My head is throbbing and my mouth tastes like puke and I'm making a sound I don't even recognize. In my head is only screaming. Screaming because you loved my brothers more than me even though, at first, I tried to do everything you wanted—anything to make you smile after Mom died. I tried to put on a play to distract you and you told me that only girls put on plays. I made it onto the track team and you tried to act pleased, but we both knew if it wasn't football or basketball or hockey then you didn't care. Screaming because you let my brothers tease me and beat the shit out of me and made me believe that was normal. Screaming because when I told you I was going to college you told me that it was a lot of money to let someone else tell me what to think. Because when I got into grad school you said, "That's nice, son," and never mentioned it again. Screaming because when I got my PhD, you didn't care. Screaming because when I moved away, you couldn't talk to me about anything except a damn car.

Screaming, screaming, screaming because when I told you I was gay—even if you never said it—you looked like you wished I were dead.

I throw up again, until there's nothing left to come up. Acid is burning my throat and the back of my nose. I drink a bunch of water from the tap and stuff gum into my mouth that Ginger gave me earlier. She said, "Chew instead of punching." Smart girl.

I leave the bathroom, just wanting some fresh air, and start walking in a random direction. I'm sweating, the kind of cold, oily sweat that comes with puking, and the cold air blowing through my clothes is making me shiver. Goddammit, I should go back to the grave and find Rex. I either want to fuck him so hard I can't think of anything else or drink until I pass out.

The smell of cold dirt clears my head a little and the breeze freezes the snap of mint in my mouth. I feel a little better and veer toward what looks like a storage shed, thinking I'll duck inside to sit down for a second and text Rex that I'll meet him at the truck in ten minutes. The door's open and I walk inside.

At first, all I see is Colin's back, shoulders shaking, and my only thought is that I should turn around and walk out, because the way Colin looked back at the grave site, if he gets me alone it won't be good.

I don't even notice the other figure at first because it's so dim in the shed. Then it registers that Colin is crying *on* someone, someone whose arms are wrapped around my brother's shaking form.

A man.

A man is… holding my brother. There's no other way to describe it. A man is holding my brother gently, and Colin is clinging to him, crying his heart out.

The man is broad and taller than me and Colin—much taller. His dark eyes meet mine over Colin's head. I can see him tense and Colin must feel the change in his body because he turns around, though the man keeps hold of his shoulder. Colin looks destroyed from crying, but when he sees me his expression changes to something I've never seen before. Absolute panic. And it's so clear that I almost laugh.

"Holy fucking…," I start to mutter, but I can't even get any words out. I drop into a crouch, my elbows on my knees, just looking up at Colin. With a man. My brother, who has treated me with nothing but revulsion since he found me giving Buddy McKenzie head in an alley, is gay. I can see it all in his panicked face.

Colin looks back at the man, as if he's going to help, and then he holds out a hand to me, as if to placate. I stand up.

"Look, Dan," he says, "don't—"

But I throw myself at him before he can finish the thought.

"You fucking *liar*," I yell, grabbing him by the lapels of our father's coat and dragging him close.

My vision blacks out with fury. I thought I was angry at my father before, but this is murderous rage. I ram into Colin, every single nasty, homophobic word, every disgusted look, every punch and slap and shove slamming into me with the force of a brick wall. My weight bears him down to the dirt floor and I get in two punches to the face before he shakes off his surprise and fights back. He boxes my ears and gets me once in the stomach, but I am filled with a heavy rage so strong it feels like I could rip his head off and barely even break a sweat.

I push his shoulders to the ground and put my forearm to his throat. His fist slams into my lower back, just missing my kidney, and I rear back. A punch to my mouth, one to his stomach, and then we're just wrestling on the floor, grappling, grabbing whatever parts of each other we can, both trying to inflict the maximum amount of pain. It's only when a strong arm rips me away that I realize I'm still screaming at Colin.

It's Rex.

The man who was with Colin is still standing exactly where he was when I walked in, watching.

Rex pulls my back tight to his front and I break off, my voice gone. Colin scrambles to his feet, bleeding from his nose and mouth, and spits out blood on the dirt floor. I can't catch my breath.

Colin hangs his head.

"I—" he starts to say. "I—please, Danny—"

"Don't fucking call me that, you fucking *liar*," I yell at him, lurching forward, but Rex holds me back. My voice is broken.

"But, can I—?"

"How *could* you?" I yell, and my voice gives out completely. I'm vaguely aware of tears running down my cheeks, but I never look away from Colin. His expression is pure self-loathing and I realize that I've seen echoes of this expression my whole life. It's just that I always thought they were directed at me, not reflected back on himself.

Rex is holding me up, now. I can't believe it. I cannot wrap my mind around it.

And I can't even imagine how destroyed Colin must be over our dad if he let a man hold him at the cemetery where we all were.

Rex is making desperate eye contact with the other man, clearly trying to figure out what's going on, but the guy is stone.

I shake my head when Colin doesn't say anything, and turn to leave.

"Dan," Colin says from behind me, his voice strained. "Don't tell Brian and Sam. Please. Please?"

I spin around to look at him. He's crying, tears running through the blood from his nose and leaving pink tracks down his face. His scraped up hands are out to his sides, beseeching. For a moment, all I want is to do exactly that: tell Brian and Sam and watch Colin's world come tumbling down. But I take a deep breath and give Colin a single nod. Then I close my eyes and leave, because I don't have a voice for any of my questions, and I'm pretty sure Colin doesn't have any answers for me.

REX CATCHES up to me a few yards from the truck, where Ginger is standing, waiting for us. When I see her chomping on a huge wad of gum, I realize I must have lost mine sometime during the fight with Colin, but I don't know if I swallowed it, it fell out, or what. I lift a nervous hand to my hair, hoping I won't find it there.

"What in the fuck happened to you?" Ginger says, blowing the gum out of her mouth like a spitball from a Bic pen. I shake my head in disbelief.

Ginger looks at Rex, who's by my side again.

"Seriously, babycakes, what the fuck is going on?"

"Colin's gay," I say, and it's a screech, like how my voice is after a particularly late night of bar tending when I've had to shout at people all night.

Ginger laughs uncomfortably and cocks her head.

"I don't get it," she says.

"Colin is fucking gay, Ginger," I say. "I just saw him."

She searches my face and when she sees I'm not joking or messing around, her mouth drops open.

"Holy...," she breathes out.

Rex tries to put his arm around me, but I feel like fire ants are crawling all over me. I'm covered in dust from the floor of the shed; I can feel that there's blood on my face in addition to tears, and traces of the puke taste are creeping back into my mouth. For all that, I can't stand still. The idea of getting in the truck makes me nearly come out of my skin.

"I'm going to walk," I say, though it sounds like every word scrapes my throat. "I'll meet you guys at Ginger's."

"Are you kidding? It's like six miles," Ginger says.

"I'll be fine," I say, shoving some more gum into my mouth. "I just need to get some air."

Ginger and Rex are looking sideways at each other in an extremely irritating way.

"I'll walk with you," Rex says.

"No," I say. "Thanks, but you don't have to. I'll see you later."

"It wasn't a question," Rex says, and tosses Ginger the keys to his truck.

I WALK in the general direction of Ginger's, looking at the city I've lived in my whole life as if I've never seen it before. Rex trails along gamely beside me, not saying anything, but never letting me more than a few paces out of his reach. At first it's fucking irritating and I want to turn and yell at him that I'm not a child. That I've gotten along just fine without him for this long and he can fuck off back home. But the truth is that I haven't.

I haven't gotten along just fine. In fact, I've barely gotten along at all. And always, always, some of it has been because of Colin.

I've been mad at him and—if I'm being honest—scared of him for so long that I've forced myself to forget that I used to worship him. When Mom died, he was the one I ran to after the nightmares woke me up. When I was eight and he was fourteen, I'd watch him get ready for high school, wishing that I looked just like him. He was the one who first got me into music, blaring rock stations whenever he was in the shop instead of sports radio. He had a great voice too, and he would wail along with Steve Perry, Axl Rose, and Freddie Mercury while he changed oil and rotated tires. I'd sit in the doorway to the kitchen and listen, thinking maybe we'd start a band someday. When I was ten and he was sixteen, even though by then he was too cool to bother with me, he crashed our dad's car and broke his arm and I ran back and forth from the kitchen to the living room to bring him sodas and chips, desperate to make him feel better.

He was never exactly nice to me back then—he'd always pat me on the back a little too hard and take the last cookie out of my hand—but it felt fraternal, just regular brotherly shit, the same as he gave to Brian and Sam gave to him.

It changed before he ever found me with Buddy McKenzie, though. Around the time I was twelve or thirteen, I gave up on trying to be like the rest of them. I stopped pretending I was watching the football games or that I cared when they discussed the fall lineups. I didn't hang out in the shop anymore, letting my dad tell me which tool was which. I stopped laughing at their unfunny jokes and pretending that I didn't care when they "accidentally" ripped my library books. I stopped talking and asking questions. I pulled back every overture that I'd learned from experience would be met with disapproval and rejection because that's when I knew.

Knew I was gay. Knew that I wanted to get the fuck out of that house. Knew that I wanted a different kind of life than beer and ball and cars. And they knew it too.

Colin was the worst, but it was all of them. They took it as disapproval. They became convinced that I thought I was better than them when the truth was that I just knew they would never like me if they knew who I really was and what I really wanted. Love me. They would never love me.

And they didn't. Not really. They stopped. But only Colin turned truly poisonous, as if he saw my retreat as an attack.

Now, though. What? Did he see me doing what he wanted to do? I don't think so. Colin may be gay—Christ, the sentence even sounds insane in my head—but he loves working at the shop, loves the cars, loves sports. And he fucking loved our dad. Would do anything he said. So, when he saw how badly my dad reacted when I told him that I was gay, it would have made it a thousand times harder for him to do the same. If he even knew then.

And instead of confiding in me, he turned it inside out and terrorized me instead.

I can't imagine how it must have felt, calling me a faggot all these years and seeing my dad and my brothers go along with it. Fuck. How could he do it?

We've been walking for three or four miles when Rex breaks the silence.

"Can we stop for a coffee or something?" he asks, startling me.

"Yeah, of course," I say.

We duck into a café and I order coffees to go while Rex uses the bathroom. I realize, as he comes back, that he probably meant he wanted to stop and sit down to drink a coffee and get warm.

"Did you want to sit?" I ask, hoping he'll say no.

"Um, no, it's okay," he says, uncertainly.

I really think he wants to stay, but I jump on it and walk out the door. I just can't be around any of these people right now, sipping their fucking chai lattes and triple skinny caramel whateverthefucks.

Rex slides his hat back on and takes the coffee.

"Thanks," he says. I can tell he wants to say something, but he just keeps walking with me.

After another few blocks, he drains his coffee and tosses the cup.

"I never went to my mom's funeral," he says.

"What? Why?" I ask, realizing that while I've been busy wrapping myself in a blanket of my own shit, Rex is probably dealing with some pretty heavy memories of his own.

"When I took up with Jamie," he says, his voice low and his chin tucked into his jacket, "I started spending all my time with him. Just, he was the only one who talked to me, and that felt… good. I didn't see much of my mom in the evenings because she had this boyfriend, John, who didn't like me, and she was working all the time during the day. So, I didn't think anything of staying out with Jamie. Maybe six months after I met Jamie, John got a job in Colorado and my mom told me we were moving out there. But I didn't want to leave Jamie, didn't want to start all over again."

He pauses, looking around for something to do with his hands. I hold up my half-drunk coffee to him. He takes it, smiling gratefully and wraps his hand around it.

"I told her I was staying. We had a real go-round about it. The only time we ever really fought." He shakes his head. "I told her I was tired of following her all over. Told her I was staying. And I did. Jamie said I could stay at his place, said his parents wouldn't mind, but of course they did. So I'd sneak into his room after they went to bed and sneak out again before they got up in the morning. I'd eat breakfast and lunch at school and scrounge something up for dinner. Then—" He stops short to avoid a dog-walker's tangle of leashes and looks longingly after the dogs.

"Then, you know, That thing happened with Jamie about three months after. In the hospital, I kept wanting to call her, but I didn't want her to worry. Gave a fake name at the hospital and skipped out before they could discharge me. Didn't know what to do, so I hitched to Colorado. I'd missed Jamie's funeral while I was in the hospital. By the time I got to Colorado...."

"Oh god," I murmured.

"She was already gone."

We walk in silence another block or two.

"How did she die?" I ask, hooking my arm through Rex's.

"Pancreatic cancer. She must've been sick for a while and never knew it. She hated doctors. Wouldn't ever go. She'd been losing weight for a year or so, but she was always trying to lose weight. Always on some diet or another. She was happy about it. Bought a new dress and all."

"John didn't let you know?"

"I guess he tried, but he only had Jamie's parents' number, and I wasn't there. She died two weeks before I got there. If it had taken me even a few days less to get there.... So, I've never been to a funeral before today."

I pull him close to me with the arm hooked through his, bumping our hips together.

"Fuck," I mutter. Because what else is there to say?

WHEN WE get back to Ginger's, she's in the shop and waves us upstairs to her apartment. I feel like I should say something more to Rex, but how do you soothe a pain someone's lived with for so long as opposed to just irritating it again?

I sit on the couch and I'm vaguely aware when Rex sits next to me and slides his hand into mine.

Is Colin *dating* that guy? Maybe I read things wrong. Maybe they're just friends. Or.... I shake my head.

"So, do you know the man who was with your brother?" Rex asks, like he plucked the thought right out of my head.

"No." After a while, I continue. "I just—I can't understand how he... could be with a man. He thinks I'm disgusting. Or, even if he just hates being gay even though he is, who would want to be with him if he hates them? And that man—I mean, not to stereotype, but he looked pretty, um, powerful? Like, it's not as if Colin could just close his eyes and pretend he was with a girl, you know?"

"Well, you never know what people are into," Rex says.

I know he's right. Christ, I've never known it better than today because never in a million years would I have imagined seeing Colin being held by another man.

I feel the kind of confusion that's seeped into my bones. The kind of confusion that makes me question everything. That makes me wonder if maybe Colin never hated me at all? Or maybe he hated me even more than I ever imagined, just for different reasons. I can't think about it right now because if I do I'll go crazy. I can't think about any of it.

"Rex, I...."

"What, baby?" he asks, immediately turning to me.

"I know this sounds trashy or pathetic or whatever, but I just really want to get wasted. I can't—" I shake my head. "I can't deal with any of this right now and maybe if we were home I... but we're here and I just... I just can't."

"I understand," Rex says, though he looks apprehensive. "Well, I'll look out for you, of course. What do you want...."

"Just whiskey," I reassure him.

He nods, clearly relieved.

"Jesus, what did you think I wanted?"

He looks embarrassed and ducks his head.

"I don't know. Just... you've said things before that made me think maybe you used to—" He searches for the words. "Escape in more extreme ways."

"Yeah, I used to dabble, I guess, but I don't do that shit anymore."

"Good," he says, and his hand tightens on mine.

"I just—I don't want you to think I'm a loser who drinks all the time. I don't, really. I just... sometimes it helps."

"I can help too, you know."

"Yeah?"

"Yeah," he says, cupping my face and running rough thumbs over my mouth. "Maybe this isn't the time or the place, but I'm here."

I look into his beautiful face. His expressive mouth that always tastes like home. His whiskey-colored eyes, which, if we were alone together, would be the only drink I'd need. I throw a leg over his lap and straddle him the way I did the night we first met. Only this time, he doesn't pull away. He holds me tight, even though I'm sweaty and dusty and bloody and disgusting. Even though I'm a mess. He holds me tight and looks into my eyes as I kiss him. I twine my fingers into his thick hair and kiss him with everything I have. Not trying to turn him on, just wanting to crawl inside his warmth, his comfort, and hibernate until it's safe to come out.

Unfortunately, Ginger didn't get the memo because that's when the door opens.

"Whoopsie," she says as we pull apart. Then her face turns stormy. "Daniel Mulligan, are you getting blood on my couch? Take a shower, you dirtball!" Then she turns to Rex and smiles sweetly. "Why don't you help him out? I'll take care of dinner."

"Whiskey, Ginge," I ask her nicely.

"I know," she says.

In the bathroom, Rex strips me out of my dirty clothes, murmuring disapprovingly at the bruises he uncovers. He pushes me under the hot water before taking off his suit. There's a knock at the door as Rex steps into the shower with me.

"PS," Ginger says, "You've got exactly eleven minutes before that water turns ice cold." Shit, I forgot that.

"Better be quick, then," I say, and drop to my knees in front of Rex, nuzzling into his crotch, just wanting to feel close to him. He starts to harden immediately and his hand strokes my hair, but he pulls backward.

"Daniel, no, you don't have to—"

I pull his hips back toward me and lick down his length, from root to tip.

"I want to," I say. I just want to do something for him. Something right, for a change.

"Baby, please, maybe it's not such a—mmmf!" He breaks off in a moan as I run my teeth gently over the tip of his erection. He tastes like Rex, salty and a little sweet, like a hot martini. I take him all the way into my mouth, hands running up the backs of his thighs, and as he starts to rock his hips toward me, I don't have to think about anything except the feel of his fingers in my hair, his muscles under my hands, and his pleasure. I suck him hard, palming his ass.

"Shit, Danny," Rex says as I swallow around the tip of his cock. I'm trying to make him come hard and fast and still have enough hot water to wash my hair. All it takes is applying everything I've learned Rex likes over the last few months at once. A lick here, a nibble there, a finger here, and he's gone, coming down my throat with a torn-off moan. But when he reaches for me to return the favor, I just reach for Ginger's shampoo. I can't feel that vulnerable right now. I won't be able to hold it together.

Rex is looking at me strangely. I lean in to kiss him, but he pulls away, catching my chin in his hand. What more does he want from me?

"Hey," he says, his voice deceptively gentle. "I know you're not okay. Next time, let's both be here, all right?"

I drop my eyes to the tile and get shampoo in them for my trouble.

"Sorry," I murmur.

"No," he says, "please, no. You felt amazing, I just... I don't like when you're so far away. I feel like I'm taking advantage."

"Okay," I nod, knuckling water out of my eyes.

"Daniel, god. I—" He looks at me searchingly, so intent on my face that I nearly look away. But he doesn't finish his sentence. Just pulls me close to him and puts my forehead against his shoulder as he washes the shampoo out of my hair. The hot water is about to go, so I pull him out the door just as it turns freezing. It's not a shock anyone should experience if they can help it.

I brush my teeth. The taste of all that gum is starting to make me feel sick again.

I throw on jeans and a T-shirt and walk into the living room to pour myself a drink as someone knocks on the door. Ginger comes bustling out of the kitchen to answer it.

"Hey, folks," the guy who must be Christopher says. He holds up a bag from his sandwich shop in one hand and a bottle of Bulleit in the other.

"Well, I like you already," I say lightly, taking the whiskey from him. With his free hand, he high-fives Ginger, then pulls her into a kiss.

"He likes me," Christopher says, winking at me. "That means I'm approved, right?"

"Maybe," Ginger says. "What'd you bring me?"

"Half a Reuben made with pastrami and half a grilled cheese BLT, two potato knishes, and a cream soda."

"You're approved," I tell him, as Ginger rips into the bag like a velociraptor.

"Are there pickles?" Ginger asks.

"As I value my life," Christopher says.

"Hey," I say, holding out a hand to him. "I'm Daniel."

"Yes, I know," he sighs. "The man I have to impress in order for Ginger to even consider taking me seriously. Nice to meet you." His smile is gone as instantly and naturally as if it were never there. "I was really sorry to hear about your father. Family—no matter what, it's intense."

"Yeah," I say. "Thanks."

"Hi," Rex says, coming out of the bathroom. "I'm Rex."

"Daniel's boyfriend—" Christopher nods. "—Christopher. Nice to meet you."

"I like him," I say to Ginger. "He says good, nonstupid sentences."

"Yeah," Ginger says, "and he never says idiotic sexist shit that's disguised as a compliment."

"Rare," I say.

"Virtually nonexistent when coupled with good looks and good deli."

"Statistically."

Christopher and Rex look at us like we're crazy.

"Aaaanywaaay," Christopher says, eyebrows raised, "I'm just making the delivery. I know it's not a great time for socializing. I hope I get to meet you under better circumstances soon, Daniel."

Ginger raises an eyebrow at me. I raise one back at her.

"No, stay," I say. "At least for dinner. You brought it, after all."

"Yeah, stay," Ginger says, her smile sweet and private. Then her expression changes. "As long as you're not sharing mine." She clutches her mismatched sandwich close and takes a step backward. Rex laughs.

"Okay, sure, thanks," Christopher says.

WE EAT, drink the bourbon Christopher brought, and talk. It's nice and strangely normal despite it being the first time that Ginger and I have each had a date with us. And, of course, despite it being the first time that Ginger and I have each had a date and my father has just died and my homophobic prick of a brother has turned out to be gay. But who's counting.

Christopher lives up to his good entrance. He's nice and interesting and not at all a douchebag. And he's clearly out of his head crazy about Ginger, which is a big plus. Rex has turned a little shy and isn't saying much. Ginger and Christopher are doing most of the talking, and Patty Griffin is playing in the background.

I had a drink before I ate half of my sandwich and another afterward. I'm finishing my third now and I can feel the tingling in my fingers and the looseness in my joints that says the Bulleit has hit its mark. I hand Rex the other half of my sandwich and head off what I'm sure would have been his protests that I need to eat with a head shake.

"I can't," I say, and settle in with my drink. Ginger and Christopher are on the couch and Rex is sitting in the armchair. I'm sitting on the floor, elbows on the coffee table (read: hand near the bottle), but if I lean back a little, I can rest against Rex's shins.

Patty sings "When It Don't Come Easy," and I pour another drink and lean back against Rex's legs, closing my eyes. This song kills me. Rex spreads his knees, so I'm leaning against the chair, and I rest my head against his knee. I have one arm around his calf before I even realize it, like his leg is a stuffed animal or something that I'm trying to cuddle with. Patty sings "Florida," and all I can hear is her voice, like sand tied up in honey and light.

Against my closed eyes, the funeral plays over and over, the coffin lowering into the grave somehow morphing into Colin hitting the dirt when I bore him to the ground.

Suddenly, my stomach lurches as a memory hits me, shaken loose by who knows what combination of grief and booze. I'm ten and Colin is sixteen, a junior in high school. It's the winter after Sam moved out and Colin is in a perpetually bad mood. He lifts weights in the back of the shop every spare minute and if you interrupt him, god help you.

One afternoon, there's a snowstorm and the elementary schools close early, though the rest stay open. My dad's garage isn't open full-time yet, so he's at a shift at one a few miles from our house, so I can't call and have him get me. I trudge home around noon, the snow turning to ice, and go in through the garage so I can leave my iced-over snow things there to dry. When I go into the kitchen, I hear the radio on in what was Sam and Colin's room, which Colin now has to himself, so I go push open the door, thinking Colin left the radio on, since he should be in school.

Colin's lying on the bed, his pillow over his face. He's still wearing his shoes and one is untied. Thinking he'd fallen asleep, I walk over and pull the pillow off so he doesn't get too hot. When I do, his eyes open to slits and I can smell the stink of my father's rum. I force myself to look at the memory closer, because the part I remember clearly—Colin slapping me, telling me never to come into his room, and then going back to sleep—isn't, I don't think, the point. The point is the bottle of pain pills my dad was prescribed after he slipped a disc in his back. The point is that it's half empty and Colin is drooling drunk and buried in his bed.

My eyes fly open. The record is over and Ginger is putting on another.

Did Colin try and kill himself? I want to talk to him. I want to ask him a hundred questions, but I can't imagine reaching across the chasm and trying to actually communicate with him. How can I hate someone this much and suddenly feel so sorry for them? How can the person who made me so miserable suddenly be the only person who might understand what it was like to grow up in my family?

I gulp down the rest of the bourbon.

It feels like everything is moving very slowly. The room seems fragmented: squares with pictures in them and corners and the soft square that's the bed. Then it all blurs.

"Daniel," Rex says softly. I realize I've got a death grip on his leg.

"Daniel," Rex says again, his voice near my ear.

"Huh?" I tilt my head up to look toward him. It's like I don't even recognize him, it's so shocking to see him in the context of Ginger's chair.

"Come here, love," he says, and he lifts me into his lap effortlessly.

But why? Then I realize Ginger didn't put the record on and Christopher is looking at me with a sad expression. Why are they all staring at me? Aside from the fact that I'm a grown-ass man who just got hauled into someone's lap. Rex looks strange. Smeary.

He brushes his hand over my cheeks and I realize that I must be crying. They're looking at me because tears are streaming down my cheeks even though I hadn't noticed. But when Rex touches me, it's like the clock starts again and I'm suddenly aware that my back hurts where Colin punched me, and my face hurts where Colin punched me, and my chest feels tight, and these are definitely tears.

"Rex," I say, but I don't have anything to say to him. It's more like I'm asking for something, but I don't know what it is. "Rex," I begin again, thinking maybe the sentence will finish itself.

"I'm here, baby," he says, and he pulls me into a hug, rubbing my back. I'm so embarrassed. I feel like a little kid, doing this in front of everyone. Jesus, I don't even know Christopher. I pick my head back up. Ginger is walking Christopher to the door.

"I'm sorry," I say to him, but he shakes his head and waves me off like it's nothing.

"Feel better," he says, and he pecks Ginger on the cheek and leaves.

Ginger walks over to me.

"I'm going to check on the shop," she says. "You're okay here?" I nod.

The door closes behind her and I look at Rex.

"Sorry," I say, confused. The tears are still running down my cheeks, but I don't feel like I'm crying. I feel like I'm leaking.

Rex shakes his head, then pulls my face to his and kisses my lips softly.

"Do you think I should call Colin?" I ask.

"What do you think?" Rex says.

"I don't think he would talk to me. He never has. But... I don't know. What if he... what if... you don't think he'd hurt himself, do you?"

Rex is immediately alert.

"What makes you say that?"

"I… don't know. I just had this feeling like maybe he's tried it before. But I don't quite remember."

"It can't hurt to call," Rex says, proving he's never tried to call Colin before.

I fish my phone out and find Colin's number. It rings and rings, but I hang up before his voice mail comes on.

"You don't want to leave a message?"

"I don't know what to say." But my finger is hitting redial anyway. This time, I leave a message. "Colin, it's Daniel." I pause, not knowing what to say beyond this point. "I, um, I kind of wanted to talk to you about some stuff. But, I don't know. Maybe not. About today, I mean. And maybe always? Um. Anyway, call me if you want. Or not. Okay, bye." I hang up the phone, roll my eyes at myself, and drop the phone on the coffee table in disgust. Rex pats me on the back awkwardly; not even he is able to pretend that wasn't the dumbest message ever.

I retrieve my glass from the floor and pour a finger of bourbon into it. Ginger knocks tentatively at her own door.

"Come in," I say, and swallow the bourbon, sinking down onto the couch.

"You okay?" she asks. I nod, suddenly irritated to be here instead of in my own bed. Well, really Rex's bed. My bed sucks.

"So Colin's gay, huh," Ginger says. "What in the fuck is the world coming to?"

I just shake my head. I feel woozy.

"Will you put Patty Griffin on again?"

"Sure," Ginger says.

When she sits back down, I reach for the bourbon and pour us each another.

"You guys are my favorite people," I say. "Thanks for being with me at the funeral today." I miss my mouth when I take a sip, my lips weirdly numb, and spill.

"Shit," I mutter, and pull my T-shirt off with one hand, swiping at my chest with it.

Ginger eases the cup from my hand and puts it on the coffee table.

"Hey!" I protest weakly.

"Daniel," she says, leaning forward to look me in the face. "I love you more than anyone in the world. You're my favorite person too. I just wish you didn't have to be wasted to say it." She gives a meaningful head toss in Rex's direction.

"I don't," I insist, trying to figure out whether it's true or not.

"I know it's a terrible day," she goes on. "I'm not judging. I just… you get that your brothers are drunk all the time, right? You get that your dad was drunk all the time? I just don't want you to go back to a place you can't crawl out of. You know?"

My head is pounding. I know she's right. But I've actually been doing really well since I moved to Michigan. I guess not working at a bar helps.

"I'm gonna crash," I say, and head to the bathroom to brush my teeth. She and Rex are talking quietly when I come out.

"Daniel," Ginger says quietly. "Are—"

"We're fine," I say. I scrub my hands over my eyes. "I know," I say, answering her earlier question. "I know and I don't want to be like that. I've been doing good lately, I promise." Then I drag myself over to the bed and fall in, my head spinning. It feels like I sink all the way down. I try to kick my pants off, but only get one leg out before the room starts spinning.

After a few minutes of breathing deeply, the room stills and Rex gets into bed. When he lifts the covers, he sees the state of me and huffs out a breath. He untangles me from my pants and drops them over the side of the bed, then gathers me to his chest and strokes a warm hand up and down my spine.

"Sorry, Rex," I say. "Didn't mean to be so terrible today."

"You weren't, sweetheart. Don't worry."

"I threw up and got in a fight at a funeral 'n made you walk in the cold 'n got drunk," I slur into his neck. His hand feels so good it's melting my spine. I can practically feel myself slumping into liquid on top of him, dripping down to fill in any empty spots.

"I'm sorry you threw up," he says, and that makes me start to laugh, only it comes out wrong and Rex pulls me tighter to him.

"Feel so much better when you're around," I tell him. "'S not fair you get to be with you all the time."

I can feel Rex smile. I hope he doesn't think I'm a drunk. Like my brothers. Like my whole fucking family. I burrow my head into his neck, thinking that maybe if I can get close enough I'll just be absorbed into him.

"It's okay, baby," he murmurs into my hair. "I've got you. It's okay."

"I want to leave tomorrow," I say, my voice so rough it's barely even there.

"What about the wake? Party thing?"

I shake my head and pull the blanket up so it's almost covering my head.

"Don't want to go. They won't care anyway."

"All right," Rex says. "Sleep now, love. Just sleep."

I DON'T even notice when Rex drives us straight to his house when we get back to Michigan.

"Oh, sorry," he says in the driveway. "I didn't ask if you wanted me to drop you off?"

Do I want that? I have no clean clothes and I desperately need to do laundry. There's no food in my house. I could go get my laundry and do it here, I guess. No, I can't, because my car is dead. And if—

"Hey." Rex squeezes my shoulder. "Let's go get your laundry and bring it back here. We can stop and get some groceries and I'll make dinner while you do laundry. We can just go from there, okay?"

I nod, relief flooding me.

While I'm doing laundry, my phone rings, practically scaring me to death, and I walk into the living room to answer. It's Virginia Beckwith, my dissertation advisor and all-around mentor from grad school.

"Hey, Virginia," I say. "How are you?"

"Well, Daniel, I'm well. You?"

"I'm okay," I say, not wanting to get into any of the shit about my dad, not to mention field questions about why I didn't come see her when I was in town.

"Listen, you remember the junior faculty position that you applied for last year at Temple?"

"Yeah, sure. I thought the interview went well, but then the line got canceled because they didn't have the funding to hire anyone. At least, that's what they told me."

"Yes, that's my understanding as well. You were at the ASA meeting in Detroit, no?"

"Yeah."

"So, you probably heard about the, er, incident regarding Maggie Shill?"

"Oh, I saw it."

"Yes, very bad form, of course. Well, Maggie Shill was up for tenure at Temple this year and because of the… incident, she didn't get it."

"Oh wow."

"Point being: I got a call from the chair of last year's search committee. He asked me about you—where you had ended up, whether you were happy there. Since Maggie Shill was denied tenure, she's leaving Temple, which means a nineteenth-century Americanist position has opened up. They don't have the funds for a senior hire, so they're opening it to junior faculty. The chair of the committee indicated to me that they would very much like you to apply for the position."

"Wow, Virginia, thank you. I mean, yes, that's great."

"Yes, it is. I don't like you up there in Michigan, away from even a decent library."

"Yeah."

"Well, listen, I'll e-mail you the details. Of course, it's early still, so the official call won't be out until next month, but I wanted to make sure you could get a head start on putting your materials together. Yes?"

"Yes," I say, because that's what you say to Virginia.

"All right, then. You're well?"

"Um, yeah, I'm fine. How are you?"

"Fine, fine. All right, Daniel. I'll send you that information. Bye-bye."

"Bye."

"What's up?" Rex asks, clearly having heard from the kitchen.

"The, um, the job I really wanted last year—well, almost the same job—might be open again this year and they want me to apply."

"That's great," he says. "Right?"

I nod. But there's a weight settling in my stomach that feels like a cannonball.

"What's the job?"

"It's a nineteenth-century Americanist job."

"Isn't that perfect?"

I nod again.

"It's at Temple," I say.

"Where's that?" Rex asks.

"Philadelphia."

"Right," Rex says. "Well, of course they want you."

"Just to submit an application."

"Still," he says. He kisses me on the cheek. "Listen, Will's going to come over in a few minutes to drop Marilyn off, okay?"

I nod.

"I think your laundry buzzed," he says, and heads back to the kitchen.

Marilyn comes bounding into the laundry alcove as I'm switching the loads, nuzzling my hand and trying to jump up on me, which I let her do because I think it's cute and because Rex can't see.

"Hey, girl," I say, dropping to my knees to hug her around the neck. "Did you know that my timing is epically off?" She licks my face as if to say *I know better than anyone, since you were driving down the road at the exact moment I was trying to cross it.*

"Daniel?" Will sticks his head around the corner. "Rex says you're good with cars?"

"I'm okay," I say.

"Mind taking a peek at mine?"

"Yeah, sure." I grab my coat and follow him outside. "What's wrong with it?"

"Nothing, I don't think, but I'm heading back to New York and I just want to make sure she'll make the trip."

"You're leaving?" I say, gesturing for him to pop the hood.

"Yeah. I took some time off work to see my sister, but now I have to get back."

I look up at him. His jaw is set and he looks stressed.

"You'll break poor Leo's heart," I tease as I scan his car's guts. "Does he know yet?"

"I'm going to tell him now."

"Well, be nice to him; he's a good kid."

Will stares at the ground.

"I know."

"Your car is fine. You obviously just had it serviced. So what is this really about?"

Will looks slightly sheepish at having been caught.

"I guess you really do know about cars."

"I know enough."

"Listen," he says, his tone sincere, "I'm sorry about your father. Really sorry."

"Thanks."

"Turns out you're not so bad. Maybe if we were both back east, we might even be friends."

I nod when he pauses since he seems to expect it.

"So, okay, look. I want to tell you something. About me and Rex."

My blood goes cold and I snap my head up to look at him.

"No! No, shit, sorry, nothing like that." He clears his throat. "I want to tell you something about before we broke up because I think maybe you're actually pretty good for Rex. I know he cares about you a lot and I think you care about him too."

"I do," I say quickly. "What?"

"As I'm sure you already know, Rex and I broke up because I left town. Well"—he makes an expansive gesture—"mostly. Anyway, when I told Rex I was leaving he said, 'I guess part of me knew it was coming. I hope you'll take care of yourself.' That was all. And after that—he was never the same. He was still sweet, supportive Rex and he asked me about my plans and everything. But he was gone, even though we didn't break up until I left, three months later. He was there, but he'd dropped the gate down, right? He wasn't going to be vulnerable with me after that. If anything, he was more invested in lending a hand, being a help. But that was it."

As Will talks, the cannonball that's felt like it was lodged in my stomach since Virginia's call turns into a block of ice. I'm shivering and something like panic is creeping up the back of my neck.

"So," I start to say. "So, um."

"So," Will says. "I'm trying to help you. I don't mean that your relationship with Rex is the same as mine—far from it. But I think maybe you and I are more alike than I wanted to admit. Which means that maybe I know a thing or two about how you operate. Like, maybe you didn't grow up with a whole hell of a lot of positive fucking reinforcement. So, maybe you get that from people in your profession. And maybe you think you need that because you can't get it anywhere else. And if that's your choice, that's fine. I just think...."

"What?"

"I think Rex is good for you too. So, if you think that you can leave and he'll be here waiting for you if you change your mind and come back... he won't. He might mean to be. He might swear up and down that you should follow your dreams—in fact, I'm sure he would because that's the kind of guy he is. But he shuts down if he thinks someone is leaving him. He shuts down and then it's too late. And maybe I just don't want that to happen to you the way it happened to me. And I really don't want to see Rex hurt. That's all."

He sighs and kicks at a rock on the driveway.

"I probably shouldn't have told you that," he says. "But I'm glad I did. Don't fuck it up. I want you to be here the next time I come into town."

I nod. Though I'm loath to admit it, what Will said about Rex makes a lot of sense. Rex offers help to protect himself. It's something to fall back on when he's uncertain. Something he can offer to show he cares without making himself too vulnerable. But how can I tell the difference between that and what he says is how we trust each other: by letting each other help? I really don't know.

"Daniel?" Will says, snapping my attention back to him. "Take care of him, okay?"

"Okay," I say. Will shakes my hand and gets in his car. "Will," I say, and gesture for him to roll down his window. "You're not so bad either. Have a safe trip." His smile is pure victory as he backs out of the driveway.

I sit down on the front step. I don't quite understand how my life got so out of control. How did things turn so fucked-up just when I thought I was getting everything together? And why do I feel so... so fucking vulnerable?

No, not just vulnerable. I feel panicked.

It started with the phone call about my dad, sure. But, everything with Colin—I still can't wrap my mind around it. It's like I have to re-see my whole life—every interaction with him—through a new lens. He hasn't called me back either, no surprise there. Then Virginia's call....

The Temple job is everything I thought I wanted all throughout grad school. Secure, prestigious, teaching smart students, working with brilliant faculty, having the budget to bring speakers to campus, having access to great libraries and archives. It was perfect.

Last year.

And now? Now, just the idea of leaving Rex fills me with the strongest panic of all. And the look on his face when I said Temple was in Philly... he looked resigned. Like he knew it would happen. Just like Will said.

Fuck! Everything is spiraling out of control again, the way it used to when I was a fucked-up kid with no self-control who would act before thinking anything through. Only back then the sensation was thrilling, like a kite string unspooling into who knows where.

Now I just feel like I want to puke.

I go back inside to finish changing my laundry loads, but find that Rex has already done it.

"Did you?" I gesture toward the laundry when I find Rex in the kitchen.

"Yeah," he says. "Will gone?"

I nod.

"You didn't have to," I say.

"It's okay," Rex says. "You were helping him with his car. I can help you, right?"

I look around the kitchen. Rex has bread dough rising and something that smells heavenly is in the oven.

"Dinner will be ready in about an hour," he says. "Why don't you relax? Take a bath or something. I'm going to go to my workshop for a bit."

My breath starts to come faster as I notice the salad dressing he's made from scratch in the mustard jar on the counter. All I can hear is what Will just told me and Rex saying he can help me. It's like there's a screaming in my head that is Rex pulling the gate down, just like Will said. My heart is pounding so loud and so forcefully that I can feel it throbbing in my ears. I blink to try and wet my dry eyes, but they're all prickly.

"Please don't be all helpful!" I blurt out. "Don't slam the fucking gate down and pull away!" I'm babbling. I can hear myself, but I can't stop. I need, need, need to break through Rex's unflappable calm.

"What?" Rex asks, puzzled, approaching me with arms out like you would a wild animal.

"Rex, Rex, please don't!" I'm full-on panicking. My voice sounds incredibly loud even though I can feel that I'm almost whispering. I am begging Rex not to shut me out, not to give me help instead of himself, not to leave me, and he is staring at me like I'm out of my mind.

"Baby," he says, "please. I don't know what you're talking about. Please, just calm down and talk to me. Tell me what's wrong."

"Will said—" But I'm breathing too fast to explain. I squeeze my eyes shut, trying to calm down, but all I see is that coffin, heaped with dirt, my white rose sliding over the edge of another grave, my brother clutching a bottle of pills, his fist connecting with my face. And all of it shrinks backward at only one thing: Rex. And I'm convinced I'm going to lose him.

"Daniel, Jesus," Rex says.

He scoops me up and carries me into his bedroom. He puts me in bed and crawls in after me.

"Lie down and just breathe," he says.

I try to breathe, but now the tears are coming too fast for me to hold them in. And this time, I know getting mad won't do anything.

"Please don't be helpful," I gasp, kneeling on the bed.

"Tell me, baby. Tell me what Will said," Rex insists, holding my face in his hands.

"He said when you think someone's leaving you slam the gate down," I manage to get out through my tears, "and then you're nice, and polite, and helpful, but you're—" I sob. "You're not there."

"Oh, sweetheart," Rex says. He pulls me into his lap. I am a fucking mess of tears and snot and shame.

"Please, I can't lose you," I tell him.

It all comes out in a rush of pain and fear and sadness, and I cling to Rex, sobbing into his chest.

"Please," I'm saying to him over and over until I hardly know what I'm begging for anymore, only that it's the most important word I've ever said.

Rex holds me, cradles me in his arms, and rocks us back and forth, stroking up and down my back and running his fingers through my hair. When I'm finally calm enough that I can breathe without hiccupping, Rex pulls away just enough to look at me.

"This is about Temple?" he asks. "You think that I expect you to leave, so now I'll pull away like I did with Will?"

I nod frantically. Rex smooths back my hair and nods too.

"Look, we don't have to talk about that right now, okay? We have time to figure everything out."

His thumbs smooth my tears away and everything about him is so gentle, from his fingers on my face to the way his strong arms are holding me. And his expression is soft and open in a way I've never exactly seen it before.

"Daniel," he says, stroking my face. "I'm not going anywhere. Don't you know? Don't you know how crazy I am about you?"

My hands fist in his shirt and I stare into his eyes, blinking slowly. I guess I did know, but I never imagined he might say it.

He cradles my neck in his hand, thumb stroking my nape.

"I—I love you so much."

He says it quietly, but it's like a bomb going off.

I freeze. And yet, a warmth starts to bloom in my chest, melting the block of ice in my stomach. And apparently it melts it into tears, because I'm leaking again.

"You do?" I say, stupidly, which I *know* is not how this is supposed to go.

He shakes his head, like he can't believe I don't already know this.

"Yeah. Of course I do. How could I not?"

I throw my arms around his neck and cry into his hair. I have never cried like this in my life. Huge, surging gasps of tears that leave me feeling lighter instead of heavy, hopeful instead of desperate.

"I—I—" I start to say.

"Shh," Rex says. "You don't have to say it back. I know it's hard for you and—"

What I was trying to say is that I know I'm messing this all up. But I don't need to. Because Rex is holding me close and making the kind of promises that I could never have known how to believe before now.

He leans back, lying down slowly and taking me with him. He pulls the covers over us, enveloping us.

I feel like a washcloth that's been wrung out, so drained I can hardly do anything except attempt to move every part of my body as close to Rex's as possible.

"Oh god, I fucking love you," I choke out into Rex's neck, and I can feel his whole body electrify. "I do," I mutter. Saying the words makes my world tilt to the side. Saying the words is the greatest jolt I've ever had. Rex's arms come around me and pull me down so I'm lying on top of him and he holds me like he's never going to let me go.

Chapter 16

December

THE NEXT morning, I wake up in Rex's arms feeling like days have passed. I feel floaty and spacey from crying, a sensation I'd forgotten since I last had it after my mom died. My eyes feel swollen, lashes stuck together with salt and gunk, and my head is muddled. I feel like a soft, cringing snail whose shell has been pried off. But instead of getting out of bed to shower it all away, I force myself to close my eyes and not freak out.

I name the sounds I can hear. Birds. Are the birds in the winter different? I wish I knew something about birds. The wind blowing through the pine trees just beyond the house. A sound that might be snow, but I can't tell. The hum of the generator. Rex's breathing. Then I move on to smells. My nose is a little stuffed up from crying and sleeping, but everything smells like Rex's house. Homey.

Before I make it to breaking down the individual smells, though, Rex stirs next to me and I have to open my eyes to look at him. He's so beautiful I still can't believe that I could just reach over and touch him if I wanted to.

I don't understand the way I feel. It's no different than yesterday, but everything's changed. I don't know what kind of tether love is between us. The man lying next to me... all of his... stuff. Not belongings, but thoughts, feelings, history. I don't know what I'm supposed to do with it. Am I responsible for it and he for mine? Does love imply a promise of some kind? These are things I feel like I should know, but I just... don't.

"Hey," Rex says, and I feel like a bit of a creep for staring at him while he sleeps.

"Hey." There's so much I want to say to him, but I'm not sure how to start. "Um," I say. "Do you think it's snowing?"

"Yeah," Rex says after listening for a moment. "I think we're supposed to get a few inches today." I stare absently at the window for a minute even though the shade is closed.

"Daniel." Rex's warm hand lands on my shoulder. I realize I'm still wearing my clothes from yesterday, though Rex must have stripped sometime in the night because he's in his underwear. "Last night," he continues. "I meant what I said." He seems a little anxious, as if I'm going to claim not to remember anything, but he looks right at me.

"Me too," I say, but I have to look away. I don't know why I feel so embarrassed, but I do. I fiddle with the edge of the blanket, telling myself that if you love someone, you should probably be able to sustain eye contact with them, but I feel so shy.

"Can you look at me, please?" Rex says, tenderly but with the hint of an order.

I look at him, my heart racing.

"I love you," he says, and somehow it doesn't sound like a grenade of found language the way it always does when I hear other people lob it at each other casually. *Loveyou*, as they hang up the phone; *Loveyou*, when they're running out the door. *Loveyou*, as they race to class, already texting someone else.

No, it sounds like something Rex has made up just now to try and tell me something real.

"I love you too," I tell him, trying to make the words real also. "I really do," I add, feeling like my delivery was lacking. I sounded terrified, tentative.

"I believe you," Rex says, smiling at me. "Come here." He scooches up to lean on his pillow and pulls me down on top of him. His kiss is sweet and slow and doesn't demand anything in return.

"I just... I...." I mumble against his mouth.

"What?" Rex asks, stroking my cheekbones. His eyes are so warm, and I remember him telling me he'd do anything for me. I remember him telling me there is no right way to act in a relationship. I remember thinking that those things were easy for him to say, but I couldn't comprehend them. But maybe, just maybe, he was telling the truth all along.

"I don't know how to do this," I confess softly, running my fingers over his straight nose and down the dip of his upper lip. "I don't know what... it means to... I mean, I *do* love you," I insist, fingers scritching over his stubble. "But what if we don't mean the same thing when we say that? We can't mean the same thing, can we? No one ever really knows what anyone else means when they say those things, you know? So, maybe you say it and you mean this one thing that means you expect something and I say it and I don't know you expect that so I don't do it and then you think I don't really mean it, only I do, but maybe it just means something different and—"

Rex puts two fingers over my mouth. I'm breathing shallowly, but he's smiling, serene.

"Do you want to know one of the things I love about you?" he asks.

"I, uh, yes?"

"You're so brave."

"Huh?"

"All this stuff about meaning and never really understanding each other—that's big words stuff."

"Big words?"

"You know, philosophers and theories and all the smart stuff you read. Big words stuff. But you really believe it. Hell, you're probably right. We might not mean the same thing when we say love. But you're brave because you said it anyway."

"I...." I don't know what to say to that.

"But you started to say 'I don't know what it means to.' What were you going to say?"

Oh Jesus, he really *did* learn from Ginger.

"Just what I said: like, I don't know what you mean when you say love, and you don't know what I mean, and—"

"That's not what you were going to say."

I drop my eyes to the blanket and shake my head, tracing the plaid with a trembling finger.

"Say it, baby."

I squeeze my eyes shut.

"I don't know... what it means... to have someone love me. And I know how I feel about you, but... I don't know how to act about it."

Rex kisses my closed eyes.

"I know," he says softly.

"Sorry," I murmur. He deserves so much better.

"No," he says. "We'll just figure it out. Together. Can't say I'm such an expert either."

I open my eyes and look at him. I know he loved his mom. I know he must have loved Jamie. And Will? I'm not sure.

"No?" I say.

"No."

He kisses me and I stare at him. Can it really be this easy? Can you really just love someone and go about your daily business? How do you hold it all inside?

"What are you thinking about so hard?" Rex asks.

And maybe that's the point. Maybe the point of *I love you* is that it *is* a tether. A connection so you can find your way back to someone even when shit seems huge and unmanageable on your own. A promise to help just because you care about someone, a promise to help that doesn't mean pulling away.

There's a little warm flame above my stomach but below my throat. It's been there for a while, I think, but I didn't notice. Everything with my dad and Philly and Colin and the Temple job got in the way, so I forgot about it. But last night, it roared back to life. Okay, so maybe I don't know how to do this. But I can learn. I didn't know how to be a student once, either, but I learned. I didn't know how to teach, but I learned. I dug in and watched other people and I learned. Not just how to do it, but how to do it well. And I can learn this too.

I smile at Rex.

"I was just a little scared," I admit. "But I'm okay, I think."

He cocks his head a little, but he seems to get that I'm just working shit out.

"See?" he says. "Brave."

I push him back into the pillows and kiss him. There's a type of joy bubbling under my skin that I've never felt before. It's light and hopeful and a little cautious, but it's there.

We kiss for what feels like hours, mouths meeting and parting exquisitely, tongues tangling together passionately, then turning sweet. We just kiss and, after a while, every touch of Rex's mouth is like a touch to my whole body. I feel electrified, so shaky with warm pleasure that I can't imagine what I would do if Rex stopped kissing me.

He manages to get my clothes and his underwear off while barely breaking the kiss. My hands move over his face, his neck, and down to his broad shoulders and strong arms. I'm on top of him, but I feel weightless, like his touch is the only thing anchoring me to the bed, the room, the earth.

I'm dizzy and my mouth feels swollen when Rex finally pulls away. His eyes are sleepy with pleasure and his mouth is puffy. When he backs off, I can feel how raw my mouth and chin are from his stubble. Not distracted by his kisses anymore, I can also feel that we're both rock hard, our erections caught between us.

I wrap my arms around Rex's shoulders and kiss his throat and I can feel his cock jerk against my stomach. I push Rex's thighs open on the bed and grind my hips into his. He groans, brokenly, and his arms come around me.

Flipping us like my hold on him was nothing, he pushes me into the bed, breathing hard. He shakes his head, as if to clear it, and leans down, hovering over me, and kisses me once more, just a press of swollen mouths.

"I love you, Daniel," he says. "I love you and I want you so bad."

His words send a wash of heat through my chest and a pulse of arousal through my groin. My hips strain upward to meet his, but he slides down the bed and rolls my hips up off the blanket, slinging my legs over his shoulders in one effortless motion.

"Fuck, I want you," he says, and then his mouth is on me. He licks my straining hardness from base to tip and I can feel his moan against my skin. When his mouth closes around me it's like I'm suspended in a bubble of pleasure so exquisite I can't move for fear it will pop. He holds me in his mouth and swallows around the tip of my erection and I cry out, writhing on the bed.

Rex rolls my hips farther back, exposing my ass to his mouth, and he licks into me.

"Oh fuck," I cry, the sensation so sudden that at first I try to get away.

But Rex's grip on my hips, his big hands spreading me open, are undeniable.

He relaxes my clenching opening with his soft tongue, and it's a sensation I'll never get used to. How can something so soft feel this powerfully good? I'm totally helpless under his touch, my breath coming in gasps as he opens me and slides his tongue inside.

"Oh god. Rex," I moan. I fumble in the drawer for the lube and pass it down to him, but he ignores it. He just keeps licking and sucking at my sensitive opening until my cock is leaking a constant stream of precome and I'm breathing so fast I'm dizzy.

When he finally draws back with one final, slow lick over my hole, I whimper and let out a breath, my hands fisting in the blanket because I don't even have the strength to lift them to Rex's hair.

"Unngh," I say, which means *No one has ever made me feel like you do.* Rex kisses up my stomach, licking the precome that's pooled there, and then he bites gently at my nipples. He kisses my throat and my jaw under my ear and I *mean* to return the favor, but my body is so lost in confused pleasure that I actually can't move.

"What are you doing to me?" I manage to whisper, and when Rex kisses my mouth softly, I can taste myself on his lips, dusky and warm.

"Just loving you," he says softly. He kisses the corners of my mouth and my eyebrows and then his slick fingers are at my opening.

He slides two fingers inside me and my eyes roll back at the jolt of pleasure his fingers send through my ass. Rex groans low in his throat and watches my face. He strokes me from the inside, curling his fingers over my prostate lightly so the pleasure flushes through me but doesn't overwhelm. He leaves his fingers there, moving gently inside me, just exploring with no urgency. As if he has all the time in the world. This building pleasure has ratcheted up so slowly that when it catches up to me I feel torn apart by sensation. Rex's fingers inside me, his muscular bulk hovering over me, the heaviness of his thick cock against my hip, and his mouth a breath away from mine.

His attention is so complete that I feel like, for just a moment, I'm seeing myself through his eyes, my body shaking with pleasure laid out before him, my lips trembling for his next kiss, my eyes wide and desperate. I'm pinned by his gaze, his body, his fingers inside me, and the love I can feel in his every touch.

Rex slides a third finger inside me, still just resting there, filling me up, stretching me with nothing but slow, gentle strokes, like seaweed inside me, undulating with an errant wave.

My eyes fill with tears. I'm not sad, just overwhelmed, full to the brim with his body and his attention and his love.

"You feel so good," I say softly as he kisses away my tears. He slides even closer to me, the fingers inside me reaching deeper. His voice is a low, resonant growl.

"From the first moment I saw you, this is all I've been able to think about," he says, eyes never leaving my face. "Being inside you in every way possible."

I cry out at his words, my eyes squeezing shut as he pulses his finger against my prostate and my whole channel throbs with pleasure.

"Ohgod, ohgod, ohgod," I'm muttering, barely aware I'm making a sound at all. "Please!"

"You want me inside of you, baby?" Rex growls, voice hot and possessive and just for me.

"Yes!" I'm shaking, my ass quivering and clenching around Rex's thick fingers.

He teases my rim with his thumb and my opening spasms.

"Are you sure?" he asks, teasing edging into his voice. "I could bring you off this way, put my hand inside you and just stay here, like this." He kisses me gently, almost a tease of lips. My whole body clenches at his words and my eyes go wide.

"You like that idea," he says. "Being so full of me you can't move. Just lie there and feel my fingers moving inside you."

"Oh god." I can't even think. But I want Rex's pleasure too. Want to see him come, smell it, feel it inside me. I shake my head a little.

"Later," he says, and I nod frantically. "Right now I need to be inside you." I can feel his erection, huge against my hip.

I hear the click of the lube, but I'm floating, my eyes on Rex's. When he eases his fingers out of me, I cry out at the loss, and Rex kisses me, his mouth consuming mine as he pushes inside me.

I gasp into Rex's mouth and he groans, burying his face in my neck. I can feel him trembling against me, and his hardness spreads me open so completely that my legs fall apart and I throw my head back.

"Oh, baby," Rex says. He takes my ass in his hands and eases my hips back farther, then he readjusts his angle and thrusts the last bit into me. He feels deeper than he's ever been, like he's touching something inside of me that has never been touched before.

Eyes on mine, he pulls out and thrusts back in again, slowly, and the skin and muscle he so sensitized earlier tingles with delight. I'm caught, already on the edge, as if any movement of Rex's might send me spiraling over. Rex is moving so slowly that I almost can't tell when he's pushing into me and when he's sliding out. With my hips held off the bed, I'm totally at his mercy, my cock pulsing against my stomach with pleasure.

"Please," I gasp into Rex's mouth.

He pulls out and slams back inside me, nailing my prostate and causing my whole body to clench up in pleasure. He fucks me deep and hard, pulling my shoulders down to amplify his thrusts. I know I'm whimpering and babbling and I don't care because he feels so good. He's watching my every reaction and on his next thrust, he holds himself inside of me and pulls my hips down, penetrating me even deeper. I can feel the thickness of him pulsing inside my channel and pressing into my prostate, and as he holds me locked to him, he starts to move his hips, pushing impossibly deeper with tiny thrusts.

I can't move away from this deeper penetration and I can't control it. My mouth falls open and Rex licks my lips. He pulls my shoulders up, lifting me even closer into him, so my weight pushes him even deeper inside me.

"I can't—" I say. "I need—" Rex kisses me hard and thrusts up into me. My insides are liquid, but his erection feels huge, so deep inside me I feel like we're one. Rex cups my face in his hands as he kisses me and I wrap my arms around his neck.

"I love you," Rex murmurs, "I love you." He kisses me and lays me back down on the bed. I can't think anymore. The whole world has narrowed to Rex. I try to say that I love him, but it comes out garbled, a mash of *I* and *love* and *you* that makes Rex smile.

"Keep your eyes on me," he says, and he pulls out of me slowly, my muscles clenching and spasming around the emptiness he's left behind. I feel bereft and I cry out, hating the sudden loss of him. He slides four fingers inside me, the fullness huge, but different, and presses on my prostate.

"Oh fuck, Rex, oh god!"

He fingers me, rubbing at my gland until I think I'm going to explode. Then he slams his cock back inside me and I erupt without him even touching my cock, spewing come between us, starbursts exploding through my ass and tingling up my spine as I clench around him. It's a pleasure that isn't just orgasm but the culmination of every touch he's bestowed on me since we started kissing, like my whole body is answering Rex's. I can tell he's watching me and when I can open my eyes, finally, he's breathing heavily.

"You're so beautiful," he says, his voice raw.

"Now you," I say, my whole body sensitized. "I want to feel you come inside me."

Rex groans and rolls his eyes like I'm killing him. He kisses my throat and then starts thrusting inside me again, the sensation so amplified after my orgasm that I know I won't be able to take it for long. I scrape my fingertips down Rex's spine, the muscles bunching as he pushes inside me. He's groaning, hips pistoning, and then he freezes, muscles taut.

"Oh, Danny," he says, and then he releases deep inside me, with pulse after pulse of branding heat. His hips keep moving, like he can't control himself, sending little tingling aftershocks through my rectum. Finally, he collapses on top of me, lips soft and breath warm against my shoulder.

As he slides out of me, groaning, he slips his fingers back in to feel his release work its way out of me. He can never help himself. As he goes to move his hand, I catch his wrist, holding his fingers inside me.

"I like it," I say. "I don't feel so empty." Rex's face tells me how much he likes that. He kisses me deeply and is asleep within seconds. I lie awake a few more minutes, thinking that maybe I can do this whole love thing after all. That seemed like a pretty good start.

THE WEEK since Rex and I got back from Philly has been relaxing and feels intimate in a way that still catches me up short when I notice it in the moment.

It's been years since I had this much time off with no school, no job, and nothing expected of me, so, of course, now I'm starting to feel guilty for not taking this time to work on my book. This morning, I dragged myself out of Rex's bed early and borrowed Rex's truck to slog to the library through the snow. I've fiddled with my car, but despite trying every trick I know, it's like the car died with my father and refuses to be resurrected. I should just sell it for parts and buy another, but I can't afford even that right now.

My dad's death feels like a bruise, tender when I bump it unwittingly but otherwise dormant. I'm not sure if that's how I should feel or not, but I'm trying to take a page out of Rex's book and decide that I'm supposed to feel however I feel.

It's Colin I'm worried about. Colin I can't *stop* worrying about. He never returned my call, but I'm not really surprised. I mean, he's been gay all this time and never called me before. It's not like I think he's psyched to bond over it or anything.

I work in the library until I realize Rex has left a message to ask if I want pasta or chicken for dinner and it hits me in a rush that, for the first time, I have things structuring my time other than the time the library closes or the amount of juice left in my laptop battery. It's still a little strange to remember that if I worked all night, Rex would miss me. It's even stranger to realize that I would miss him. I've only stayed at my apartment one night since we got back to Michigan, and it felt... depressing. Lonely. I don't want to look around for another place, though, because what if I get the Temple job? It's a long shot, I know, but Virginia seemed to think I have a real chance.

I haven't been letting myself think about that, though, because thinking about it means thinking about leaving Rex, and thinking about leaving Rex makes me feel like I'm going to puke. I know he said we'd have time to talk about it, but I haven't brought it up.

I text back *Chicken* as my stomach growls, in the vague hopes that maybe he means the roasted chicken that he's made before.

I make a quick stop at Mr. Zoo's because I've had Republica stuck in my head all day and am hoping I can pick up a used copy.

"Are you *always* here?" I ask Leo as I approach the counter. He looks up from a book that he tries to hide under the counter before I can see it. "Whatcha reading?" I say casually.

"Oh, noooothing," he sighs. He looks tormented.

"Leeeooo," I whine back at him, "what are you reeeeading?"

Miserably, he holds up a thick book printed on the kind of newsprint that can only mean…. Yup, it's *Conquering the College Application in Ten Easy Steps*.

"That's great, man," I say. "I know you said you wanted to get out of here, but I didn't know you wanted to go to college."

"You don't think I should go?"

"Uh, that's really not what I just said, is it?"

"No." Leo slumps on the counter.

"Okay, I'll bite. What's wrong?" I ask, pretty sure the answer is spelled W-I-L-L.

"Nothing," Leo sighs, clearly delighted I've asked.

"Oh. Okay, then," I say. "Do you have—"

"Ugh!" Leo exclaims, looking up at me. "Will's gone." He's pouting and he looks genuinely miserable.

"I know, man, I'm really sorry. I know you liked him. God knows why," I add under my breath.

"Thanks," Leo sighs. "Oh my god, shit! Shit! I'm so sorry. I'm complaining about—and—I'm so, so sorry about your dad."

Leo looks horrified, his eyes huge, the lovesick sulk immediately replaced by sympathy.

I nod. "Thanks. Listen," I say, not wanting to talk about it, "have any Republica?"

"Um, I dunno, I never heard of them," Leo says. "Go ahead and look, though."

I do and they don't. I look at a few other things, keeping track of Leo out of the corner of my eye. He's back to reading his book, cheek in hand, but he's sighing pitifully again.

"Leo," I say, and he drags puppy dog eyes up to meet mine. "You want some help with those applications? Or with your essay or something?"

"Really? Oh, man, that'd be so great. I don't even know where I want to apply, or what I need to do."

"Okay. Are you working on Saturday?" He shakes his head. "Why don't you come over to Rex's around noon? Or, wait, my apartment?" I probably shouldn't just be inviting people over to Rex's, should I? "Shit, no," I say, picturing the state of my apartment and the approximately 200 library books that seem to have taken up permanent residence on the table Rex built. "Rex's house. Okay?"

"Uh, okay. Just text me if you change your mind," he says, looking at me like I'm nuts. "Again."

I give him the finger and a wave and head to Rex's.

"OH, FUCK me, it *is* the roast chicken," I mutter, the smell hitting me as soon as I walk in the door.

"Well, you're easy," Rex says, coming out of the kitchen. He pats me on the ass as I sling my bag onto the floor and pulls me in for a kiss when I stand up.

"Mmm, smells so good," I say, kissing his neck. "The chicken smells good too," I say against his ear.

As we eat, I tell him about Leo.

"He's really broken up over Will leaving. Do you think it's just a crush, or did something actually happen between them?"

"Will wouldn't mess with a kid," Rex says.

"You sound pretty sure, but Leo's not exactly a kid. And he did proposition me the first time we met."

"He would be to Will, though. Will goes for... um, the opposite."

"What, like... daddies?" I make a face, thinking of Will in that way.

"No," Rex says, blushing, since I guess my comment kind of implicated him. Whoops. "Just, older, bigger guys."

"Nothing wrong with that," I mutter, running my hand over Rex's beefy chest.

He smiles at me, the happy, private smile that I've been getting used to. It makes me feel warm through and through.

"Um, so, I invited Leo over on Saturday to help him out with his college applications."

"That's nice of you."

"But, um, I invited him... here. Is that okay?"

Rex smiles again.

"Yeah. It's great." He eats a few more bites. "Listen, about that." My head shoots up, sure he's about to say that actually I shouldn't have invited Leo over. "I know you and Ginger have plans for Chanukah, but will you be here for Christmas?"

"Oh, um, I guess so. I hadn't thought about it. Why?"

Rex slings an arm over the back of my chair.

"I thought maybe we could have Christmas together. You know, like, decorate and make dinner and…." He looks down. "You think it's lame."

"No! No, I don't. I just… honestly, the closest to Christmas decorations I've come in the last twenty-five years is shitty seasonal ale. No, that's not true. Brian did stack all the beer cans into a pyramid that looked like a Christmas tree one year."

Rex strokes my cheek.

"What would you like for Christmas dinner?"

I immediately look at the remains of the chicken on the counter and Rex laughs.

"You really like roast chicken, huh? Okay, we can do that. I think I might have some decorations in my workshop somewhere."

He starts to clean up, but I wave at him to sit down and gather the plates. Doing the dishes is the least I can do since Rex always cooks.

"Actually, Ginger made these awesome ornaments out of beer cans a few years ago. She used Bud Light cans because they're blue—you know, for Chanukah. She cut them into these little angels. They were pretty awesome. She had a tree in the shop that she put them on. She gets very pissed off that Chanukah doesn't have a tree so she just does one anyway. Don't even try and call it a Chanukah bush, though, or you'll get an earful about fucking Adam Sandler."

Rex raises an eyebrow.

"Adam fucking Sandler, I mean. She hates him."

"My mom used to collect ornaments," Rex says, staring out the window behind me where snow has started to fall again. "They were all these Marilyn Monroes. Lots of different poses. The one where her dress blows up from *The Seven Year Itch*, one from *Diamonds Are a Girl's Best Friend*, some of just her face."

He looks back at me and smiles self-consciously.

"What happened to the ornaments?" I ask him, but he just shakes his head.

"I don't know."

"HOLY SHIT," I say, as I look through the pile of Leo's transcripts and SAT scores that is scattered over Rex's kitchen table. "I mean, I know test scores aren't everything, but, shit, Leo, these scores are amazing." I frown at his transcripts. "I don't understand. You aced calculus your freshman year; why did you take geometry and algebra after that? You should have been taking college-level math."

"My parents wouldn't pay for it," he said. "And the school district wouldn't pay to bus me to Traverse City for Advanced Placement classes, so. Besides, you don't know what I looked like as a sophomore."

"What do you mean?"

"I couldn't have gone to college classes; I looked about ten."

"Aw, a little *Doogie Howser!*"

"Seriously, Daniel, update your references."

"Okay, well, I see why you graduated early. You took every class your podunk little high school offered."

"Dude, I think 'podunk' is, like, totally ethnically offensive."

Rex walks in from his workshop before I can google "podunk" to see if Leo's right. He smells of fresh wood shavings and sweat and it's only the fact that there's a teenager in the room that keeps me from jumping his bones.

"Hey, Leo," Rex says.

"Hel*lo*, Rex," Leo says, his flirtation-o-meter apparently tuned back to Rex's frequency now that Will's out of town.

"Um," Rex says, "I'm gonna make lunch; you guys want something?"

"Oh, thank god," Leo says. "Yes, please. I'm starving, but I didn't want to say anything in case Daniel offered to cook."

"Hey!"

"No offense," Leo tosses over his shoulder at me, then he's back to watching Rex's muscles flex as he pulls food out of the fridge. I understand the impulse.

"You know, Leo," I say, shuffling through the stack of applications he's printed off, "I can't help but notice that most of these schools are near New York City." Rex gives me a look over Leo's head that says *Be nice.*

"Ermghm," Leo says, blushing.

"And I can't help but remember that Will lives in New York City." Leo's hands twist into a complicated formation behind his back. Rex is shaking his head at me, amused. "I just meant that if you go to New York to look at schools, maybe Will could show you around," I say innocently.

Leo shakes his head and drops back into his chair.

"Will doesn't give a shit about me," he says with more bitterness than I'd realized he was capable of, and I feel instantly bad for teasing him.

"I'm sure that's not true," Rex says, but I can tell he won't outright lie to the kid so he can't say anything more than that.

"Oh yeah, then why did he leave town right after he kissed me?" Leo blurts out, looking furious and hurt. "Oops," he says, clapping a hand to his mouth. "I wasn't supposed to tell you that."

"Will kissed you?" Rex asks, sounding curious but confused.

"Will kissed you?" I say. "Jesus, rob the cradle much?"

I'm joking—mostly—but Leo's lip starts to tremble and his chin starts to wobble. I look desperately at Rex.

"Shit, Leo, I'm sorry," I say. "I was just kidding."

"No, you're right," he says. "Will just thinks I'm a kid. He doesn't care that I—" Leo breaks off, shaking his head as tears course down his cheeks.

Rex comes around the counter and pulls a chair up next to Leo's, putting a hand on his shoulder.

"Leo, Will went back to New York because he couldn't take any more time off from work. He was here to help his sister out for a bit, but he was always going back."

"But, um," I say, wanting to do my part in making Leo feel better, "if you do end up going to school in New York, then maybe...." I trail off when I notice Rex shaking his head at me very subtly.

Rex rubs Leo's back and then gives him a hearty, definitive pat.

"Will's a good guy," he tells Leo, "but you don't want to get involved with him."

"You did," Leo says, managing to sound jealous, scornful, and flirtatious all at the same time. Ah, youth.

"Different," Rex says, and he goes back to making lunch.

"Look, man," I tell Leo, "it's Will's loss, okay?"

The smell of bacon fills the kitchen and Leo perks up.

"Bacon?" he says, and Rex just smiles.

WHEN REX wakes me up on Sunday morning, six inches of snow have fallen and more is predicted for later this afternoon. It's early—only six or so—and I bury my face in his neck with an indistinct sound of protest.

At Rex's urging, I've started working at his house when I don't need to use the library. He cleared off a large table he kept in his workshop and set it up for me in the living room, replacing the small one he only used occasionally. Writing felt effortless last night, and I know better than to waste a flow like that, so I didn't stumble in to bed until about 3:00 a.m.

Rex was warm and sleepy and immediately pulled me into his heat. But I definitely do not appreciate having to wake up three hours later.

"'S too early," I complain into his neck. "Go back to sleep."

Rex rubs my back softly and I relax against him.

"Wake up, baby," he says. "I'll make breakfast. Go get in the shower and you'll feel better."

"Ungh, why?" I'm whining. It's probably not attractive and I make an effort to stop.

"'Cause we gotta go soon."

"Where?" Rex's hand is back, running up my spine and into the hair at the nape of my neck.

"Surprise," he says. Then he kisses my cheek and slaps me on the ass. "Up," he says.

"Tyrant," I growl, but I roll out of bed and head toward the bathroom. It turns out that a slap on the ass is a very effective alarm.

After I shower and we eat breakfast, we get on the road. The only concession he makes to my questions is to tell me to wear his extra pair of snow boots, which are way too big on me.

"So help me god, Rex, if you woke me up at 6:00 a.m. on a Sunday morning to take me on some kind of winter hiking trip, I will end you," I say as we walk to the truck and I trip over my too-big boots almost immediately.

Rex just chuckles and kisses me as he grabs me by the shoulder. He puts me in the truck and reaches over me to buckle my seat belt. When he's level with my face, he kisses me breathless. He nods, as if satisfied I won't complain any more, and then gets in the driver's side, putting one hand on my thigh.

We drive for over an hour but I fall asleep almost immediately despite the coffee I downed right before we left. When I open my eyes, the truck's parked in a snow-cloaked field. In front of us and out my window, the snow is undisturbed. It looks like we're in the middle of nowhere. The sun is shining and it's nearly blinding, like the truck is our boat on an ocean of snow. It's beautiful.

"Come on," Rex says. I tug on my hat so it covers my ears and wrap one of Rex's scarves—plaid flannel, of course—around my neck, already shivering. We walk around the truck and it looks like we're in the woods, but the trees look too regular, too perfectly aligned.

"Where the hell are we?" I ask. No one is around and the quiet is overwhelming. Rex takes my hand and we trudge through the snow, Rex's powerful legs cutting through it easily and me walking in the trail he

makes. After a few minutes, a little hut comes into view and I can see a
tractor—or something like that—parked outside. On the hut is a row of
cheery green wreaths twined with red ribbon.

"Holy shit, are those Christmas trees?" I ask. All around us, rows of
trees stretch as far as I can see.

Rex nods. As if on cue, a cheery-looking couple steps out of the hut,
door bells tinkling their exit.

"Hello, gentlemen," the man says. He's got to be eighty years old,
but his eyes are sharp and he's smiling.

"Here for a tree, I presume?" the woman chimes in. She's got pink
cheeks and her white hair is in a bun. I actually have to hold my hand in
front of my mouth to keep from laughing. This is the most ridiculously
stereotypically Christmas couple I've ever seen. All the guy needs is a
beard and a team of reindeer pawing at the roof. Rex, of course, is the
picture of manners.

"Hello," he says, his voice soft like it always is when he's speaking
to strangers. "We'd like to cut down a tree, please."

"Of course, of course," the man says. I zone out as he and Rex
discuss type of tree—who knew there were different kinds of pine
trees?—height of ceiling, spread of branches, etc. The woman looks at me
kindly and I try to smile in a way that doesn't reveal my actual thoughts,
which are, at this moment, running toward gore-splattered horror movie
posters of the *American Gothic* aesthetic featuring a background of
beautiful trees and this pleasant little hut.

"All right?" Rex is saying—to me, it would seem.

"Huh? What? Yeah, great," I stammer, looking around.

Rex is holding a saw. I do not like Rex holding a saw. Wait, *cut*
down a tree? As in, cut *down* a *tree*? Rex waves at the couple and takes
my arm—fortunately for me, not with the hand holding the *saw*.

"Um, Rex," I say, as we set off down one of the rows of trees. "Are
you about to use that saw to… to *fell* a tree?"

"Is that what you say?" he asks.

"I don't *know*," I reply, "because where I come from saws are
something out of horror movies and trees live in parks so if you cut them
down you go to prison."

Rex laughs. He sounds truly delighted. I look up at him and his face
is radiant. He's striding through the cold air and shin-high snow like he's
never been happier to be anywhere in his life.

"When we find the one we want, we cut it down. Then Wallace will
come with the tractor and take it to the car for us."

"Wallace?"

Rex shakes his head.

"Where do you go sometimes?" he asks. "Back at the hut, what were you thinking about?"

"I was thinking that those two looked like Mr. and Mrs. Claus on a diet and that it was, like, the Platonic ideal of Christmassy coupledom and so of course it was too good to be true, so they would probably turn out to be creepy serial murderers who cut our heads off with saws"—I gesture to the one in his hand—"and turned us into mulch for next year's trees."

Rex is staring at me.

"Oh, and then I started thinking about *American Gothic*. You know, the painting of the couple with the pitchfork?" He nods. "Only, they weren't actually a couple; they were the painter's dentist and his daughter, but the point is that there's this horror movie called *American Gothic*, and the cover of it is like the painting only the couple are these murderers who trap people in the house and kill them. And on the poster you can see people, like, clawing at the windows and stuff, trying to get out, and the pitchfork is all bloody and the woman is holding a knife dripping with blood." I laugh.

"That's what you were thinking about while I was talking to Wallace about Christmas trees?"

Rex looks serious.

"I mean, I don't really think that they're serial killers, Rex."

"I get it now, I think," he says.

"Come on, I was just kidding."

He nods. He drops the saw and where it falls there is a perfect impression of a saw in the snow.

"You look at things that you think are nice or happy or cheerful and you think they're too good to be true. You think they're too good to be real, so they must actually be bad."

"I...." Well, actually, yeah, that is exactly what I think, but he said it like it's a bad thing.

"You're suspicious," Rex says, like he's seeing me for the first time. "Suspicious that something you might like or want is a trap. That if you trust it, it'll all go wrong. No?"

"Well, I mean—"

I drop my head and stare at the saw-shaped hole in the snow. Rex tilts my head up. I don't know what to say, but it seems somehow crucial that I say the right thing. Rex looks like he's in actual, physical pain.

"I… I used to," I say. His face softens. He takes the ends of my scarf that have come untied and tuck them back in. I look back down at the snow.

"I… do you… you don't like that, I guess?" I ask, unable to meet his eyes. Rex bends his knees to look me in the eyes.

"I don't like that you've had to think that way," he says. "But I get it."

"I thought that about you," I admit. "For a while."

"Yeah," he says.

"I just—you *were* too good to be true. So handsome and strong and kind. Understanding. And I felt like, if you *were* true, then why the hell would you want me? You know? And so I guess it was just easier to think that you didn't."

"What I think you still don't get, Daniel," Rex says, "is that, for me, *you* were too good to be true."

I snort and Rex grabs me by the shoulders, his expression fierce.

"When I first met you, all I knew is that you were this real educated, real smart professor and I'm the guy who never graduated high school. Who can barely read." His face flushes. "You're gorgeous and sexy and ambitious. You're from the city, used to hanging out with famous bands every night, and you showed up in this little town in the middle of nowhere where I barely leave my house."

"Rex, I—"

"But my point, Daniel," he says, his face close to mine, "is that all those things are true. We are good for each other. But not too good to be true. Complementary. That's the word, right?"

I nod.

"The other night, you said that we mean different things when we say I love you. That you don't know what it means to have someone love you. This is what it means. It means doing things together and learning what each other needs. I give you what you need. You give me what I need. And they're not the same. And that's fine. It's not too good to be true. It's just good."

I'm nodding spasmodically as Rex talks. My hands fist automatically, which looks ridiculous with the gloves I'm wearing.

"But I have to tell you that… I just—still, every time you start to say something serious like this, a part of me thinks you're about to end it. I don't mean to go there, but I just—I'm sorry."

I search his face for any clue that I haven't just set us back months. Rex lets out a breath.

"I know," he says. "I can see it in your face."

"It's just where my mind goes, automatically," I say, wanting to explain.

"Well, I think we've established that where your mind goes and the truth aren't exactly the same place," he says. "Seriously? Is all you think about serial killers? I think you watch too many horror movies."

I laugh, incredibly grateful that Rex is willing to joke about it.

"Hey," he says, "I love the places your mind goes. I didn't mean to make you self-conscious about it. Just... you know, you don't have to think that way about me. You'll see."

"Okay," I nod, trying not to sound suspicious. Rex kisses me, his hot mouth a shocking contrast to the cold air around us. I gasp into his mouth and try to put my arms around him, but I lose my balance in these damned boots and start to stumble. Rex tries to grab me, but he overbalances and we both fall into the snow, Rex landing on top of me.

Rex uses his position to kiss me again, and I try desperately to roll us over so he can be the one getting snow jammed into his collar.

"Ha, get off me!" I say. Rex is laughing, trying to find a way to stand up without squashing me. When he finally manages it, and pulls me up with him, he kisses me again, our faces both cold with snow. He reaches down and plucks the saw from its pocket of snow, putting his other arm around me.

"What does that look like to you?" he asks, indicating the spot where we rolled around.

"A murder scene," I say, but I'm smiling at him.

"Hmph," he says.

"Well, what does it look like to you, then, Mr. Sweetness and Light?"

"A snow angel," he says, with an expression that clearly says that this is *not* what he thinks. "See? Complementary."

"Fucked-up angel," I say and grab the saw from him. "Come on. Are we doing this or what?"

It's cold and I've got snow places snow should never be, but I feel warm from the inside out. Rex is gleeful, explaining to me the different types of trees and how long they last. He points out what makes them different, but I'm content just to walk next to him and practice thinking happy thoughts: this is *our* tree. We're going to decorate it together. We're having Christmas together. There will be a fire, and food, and the dog. There will be Rex.

"Hey, you okay?" Rex says, stopping when he realizes I'm a few paces behind him.

"Yeah," I say. "Just happy."

Rex's smile is pure joy. He looks like a little boy who was told he did a good job.

By the time we find our tree, there are families wandering the lanes alongside us, kids plowing through snow that's up to their thighs, pointing at which trees they want—always the biggest ones.

"That one," Rex says, pointing to a medium-sized tree at the end of the row. It doesn't look any different than any of the others to me, but what the hell do I know? The last Christmas tree I had was made of beer cans.

Rex kneels in the snow and starts to saw through the trunk of the tree. I've never seen anyone cut down a tree before. It's strange.

"You want to try?" Rex asks.

I don't, really, but it seems like one of those things that we're supposed to do together. I take the saw and slot it into the notch Rex has started. After sawing for a few minutes, I'm exhausted. Rex touches my back and takes over again. When he's sawn through, we stick the saw into the snow so we can find it again, and walk back to get Wallace. Rex gets on the tractor or baler or whatever it is with Wallace, but there's only room for two, so I wait for them by the hut.

I'm watching an adorable little girl trying to braid tree branches when my phone rings. I expect it to be Rex, stuck in the snow with Wallace, or Ginger, calling to confirm when I'll be in Philly for Chanukah. But it's Brian.

"Dan," he says.

"What's wrong?" I ask, before he can say anything, because damn trying to be less suspicious, Brian has never called me in my life.

"Um," he says, "have you heard from Colin?" His tone of voice says he assumes this is ridiculous but needs to ask.

"No," I say. "Not since the funeral. Why?"

"We haven't seen him since the funeral either," Brian says.

"What? But what about the party at the shop?"

"He didn't show."

"Is he at home?"

"No, man, we didn't think of that!" Brian says, like a jackass. "He isn't at home and he hasn't been at the shop. We haven't seen him since the funeral. I keep calling his phone and he never picks up."

"I haven't talked to him, Brian," I say, "but if I hear from him I'll let you know."

It's a testament to how anxious Brian must be that he doesn't say a single nasty thing as he hangs up the phone. I dial Colin's number and his phone rings to voice mail.

"Colin," I say, "um, it's Daniel again. Look, Brian just called me and he says no one's heard from you since the funeral. I just… want to make sure everything's okay. Okay? So, even if you don't want to talk to me, maybe call Brian or Sam? Okay, bye. Oh, and I didn't say anything. Okay, bye."

"All right, son, you're all set," Wallace says, pulling the trailer thing with the tree in it up in front of me. Rex hops off and hands Wallace some money. I reach for my wallet, but Rex waves me off.

"Thank you," he says, shaking Wallace's hand. He looks so happy.

"Merry Christmas, boys," Wallace says, waving.

Rex smiles at me and then grabs the bundled-up tree like it's nothing more than a baseball bat he's casually resting on his shoulder and sets off for the truck. He straps the tree to the roof and we set off. Rex is unusually talkative, explaining some of the things Wallace told him about tree farming. I love seeing him so happy, but the call from Brian is nagging at me.

"Hey, what's up?" Rex asks a few minutes later. I glance up at him.

"You don't think…." I begin. "I mean…." I shake my head. "It's just, Brian called while you were getting the tree. And he said no one's heard from Colin since the funeral. He's not at home, won't answer his phone. I just… I don't know, I just wonder if he's okay. I've called him. A few times. And he hasn't called back."

A few nights ago, when I took Marilyn out for her evening walk, I called Colin again. At first I was just going to leave a generic, "Seriously, dude, are you ever going to call me back," message. But as I was walking, I started to think about how it might have been if Colin and I had been allies instead of enemies. How different things would have been. How different *I* might have been. So, when his voice mail picked up, I said, "Hi, Colin. I'm so angry with you because you cheated me out of a brother. I don't understand why you never told me. I mean, I can think of lots of reasons, but I don't know what yours was. No matter what it was, though, I think it sucks. I think it sucks that you let me think I was alone in this, when I wasn't. I wasn't, was I, Colin?"

My hands were shaking when I hung up the phone, and Marilyn was sitting at my feet, looking up at me like she was worried about me.

The next night, I snuck into the bathroom after Rex was asleep and left another message.

"Colin, it's Daniel. Look, I'm mad at you, but I still want to talk to you, okay? I want to know what the fuck's going on with you. Why were you so horrified when you found out I was gay? Because I know you weren't faking that. You almost killed Buddy when you found us together. I just want to know why. Please call me back, okay?"

"Do you know any of his friends he might go stay with?" Rex asks. "Any of them you could call?"

"No. I don't know any of his friends. I don't even know if he has any. If he hasn't talked to Brian and Sam then he hasn't talked to anyone."

I stare out the window, the snow suddenly seeming oppressive instead of magical. I try to shake it off, though, because today is supposed to be about the Christmas tree—about making Rex happy.

"He's probably with that man, don't you think?" I ask. "The one from the funeral?"

"That makes sense," Rex says. But I'm not so sure.

WE SPEND a lazy day decorating the tree with some tinsel and lights that Rex says he found in his workshop but that I suspect he may have bought especially for us. Marilyn is confused to see a tree inside and we have to keep taking her outside to stop her from peeing on it.

"I'll take her," I say when she circles the tree again as Rex is about to start dinner.

Outside, a few more inches of snow have fallen since this morning and the scene of snow-draped pine trees outside Rex's cabin, with its warmly glowing windows, looks like a postcard that I can't believe I can walk into it. I fiddle with my phone, flipping it open and shut uncertainly until it almost breaks in half. Jesus, I really need to get a new phone. I mentally add it to the ever-increasing list of shit I need to buy in a couple of paychecks.

I flip the phone open and call Colin before I can change my mind. But, of course, it goes right to voice mail.

"Colin," I say, my teeth chattering. "I have this memory. At least, I think it is. I'm not totally sure it really happened, but... if it did.... It's—it was a snow day at school and I came home early. You were in bed, drunk, and I remember Dad's pills, for his back. Anyway, I remember a lot of them, Colin, and I just. I wanted to make sure—I wanted to see if.... Look, just don't do anything fucking stupid, all right, you asshole? Because I.... Just, please be okay. Okay?"

I'M LYING in front of the fire, groaning, stuffed so full of Christmas brunch that I can barely move. I don't even know how I'm going to be able to eat the roast chicken Rex is making for dinner. If I tip my head back a little, I can see the lights on the Christmas tree reflecting in the window, making it look like I'm surrounded by trees. Last night, Christmas Eve, Rex and I watched *Little Women*, which is one of Rex's favorite Christmas movies—the 1933, Katherine Hepburn version, not, Rex explained, the 1949 one with Elizabeth Taylor. It was pretty good, actually, though I never cared for the novel. If one of my brothers burned the only existing manuscript of my book, he would be in a world of pain.

We watched because Rex told me how he and his mother used to have a set of Christmas movies they watched every year and how he hadn't done it since she died. Their lineup was *Little Women*, *Holiday Affair*, *It Happened on Fifth Avenue*, and *The Bishop's Wife*. He was shocked to hear that I'd never even heard of any of them except *Little Women* and hadn't actually seen a single one. I made it about twenty minutes into *Holiday Affair* before falling asleep and drooling all over Rex, so we went to bed instead.

Now, Rex is in his workshop doing something mysterious that he wandered off to after brunch when I collapsed on the rug to try and digest. Presumably, it's something to do with a Christmas present, since we're about to exchange them.

I have Rex's present hidden in the closet. I really wasn't sure what to get him. Everything either seemed too generic—music, clothes—or so expensive I didn't have a prayer of affording it. Like, probably there are some tools or something that he'd like for his workshop, but hell if I know what they would be even if I could afford them. I thought about something for the kitchen, but it's pretty well stocked, and I wouldn't know where to start there, either. I hope he likes what I finally landed on. I felt pretty good about it last week, but now I'm nervous it's not a good idea.

I'm flying to Philly tomorrow to have Chanukah with Ginger and stay for a few days and I've been thinking about whether I should try and track down Colin. I've left a few more messages for him, but he hasn't called back. I know it sounds sick, but, I mean, I would have heard about it if he killed himself, right? Someone would have found him and—

"Ready!" Rex saunters in with a wrapped box in his hands.

I groan, reaching out an arm toward him so he can help me up. He drops the box on the couch and smirks at me, then lies down beside me on the floor, leaning on one elbow so he can look at me.

"Do you think it's possible to actually die from eating too much?" I ask.

"Yeah, probably," he says, dropping a light kiss on my stomach and then lying back. I groan and flop over so I can bury my head in Rex's neck. His arm comes around me and he lets out a warm rumble of contentment. Marilyn barks once, then comes over, turns in a circle, and lies down with us in front of the fire. I start to laugh, then clutch my stomach.

"What?"

"It's just so goddamned picturesque," I say, waving a hand at the Christmas tree, the snow falling outside the windows, and the dog curled up in her blue flannel bed in front of the roaring fire. Rex chuckles, his chest vibrating beneath me.

After I come out of my food coma, I go to the closet and get Rex's gifts. I hesitate, then leave the second one in the closet for later.

"You go first," Rex says when I join him on the couch. I'm suddenly really nervous that my brilliant gift isn't actually brilliant after all.

"Okay," I say, hesitating, "but you might not like it."

"Okay," Rex says very seriously. "Well, if I don't like it I can pretty much guarantee that I'll still like you a whole lot."

I roll my eyes and shove the box at him, the wrapping this garish, 1970s-looking gold and green deer print that I found at Mr. Zoo's. Rex untapes the paper and folds it neatly. He takes the lid off the box and holds up the thing on top. It's a Christmas tree ornament of a dog that looks a lot like Marilyn.

"It's to remember the night we first met," I say, my cheeks burning at how sentimental this is. "I know it's cheesy, but—"

Rex kisses me.

"Shut up," he says. He strokes my cheek. "It's great."

He dangles the ornament in front of Marilyn, who merely lifts one ear and opens one eye, decides nothing that's going on is worth her attention in the slightest, and snuffles back to sleep, turning to toast her other side equally in front of the fire.

Then Rex lifts a bunch of tissue paper out of the box and pulls out another, oddly shaped package wrapped in the same paper. I hold my breath as he struggles with my terrible wrapping job, looking at his face because I want to see his initial, unguarded reaction.

Rex's mouth falls open.

"Oh my god," he says, lifting out the vintage Marilyn Monroe ornaments. There's one of her with her white dress blowing up from the scene in *The Seven Year Itch*, one surrounded by paste diamonds and feathers from *Diamonds Are a Girl's Best Friend*, and one that's shaped like a regular ornament but has Norma Jean on one side and Marilyn on the other. Then he lifts out the last ornament. It's of Humphrey Bogart in *Casablanca*.

"The *Casablanca* one isn't vintage," I say. "I just thought you might like it."

"How did you...?"

"I found them online. Are they—do you like them?"

Rex's finger looks huge tracing the tiny figure in the white dress. When he looks up at me, there are tears in his eyes.

"They're just like the ones my mom had," he says, pulling me to him and crushing me against his chest. "Thank you."

He makes a big deal out of making me help him hang the ornaments on the tree. When we sit down again, he hands me his present. It's wrapped perfectly, in thick silver paper, and it smells like wood shavings.

I tear off the paper and inside is a carved wooden box attached to an ornament hook. The box is three or four inches square and is made of several different kinds of wood.

"Great minds," Rex murmurs. He's gotten me an ornament as well.

"Did you make this?" I ask. "It's beautiful." Rex nods.

"I got the idea at Ginger's. Looking at that puzzle box. I really liked that and I thought maybe I could make one. Turns out they're harder than I thought," he adds, sounding nervous. "Even a simple one." His hands are clasped in his lap.

"Um, you have to open it," he says.

I fiddle with the box, pulling on the corners and pushing the middle, then vice versa.

"Um...."

"Oh, you have to—" Rex points to a side piece and I slide it over. It takes me a minute—Jesus, this is an easy one?—but I finally hear a pop and it slides open.

"Ha!" I say, inordinately pleased with myself. Then I look inside.

It's a key.

I look up at Rex, whose face is open, vulnerable and hopeful.

"I thought maybe you'd want to move in. Here. With me," he says softly. It's his shy voice. The voice he uses with strangers when he's nervous. I look down at the box again. I pick up the key. It's on a simple wooden keychain cut into the shape of Michigan. It weighs nothing in my palm, but it feels like the heaviest thing I've ever held.

"But," I say, my mind racing. "But what if—what about the job? What if I get the job? We haven't even talked about it and I—"

"Move in with me," Rex says again, his voice resonant once more. "Live with me. Here, for now. Then, wherever. As long as you're with me, I won't care where we live."

I swallow hard.

"You'd leave here? With me. But what about—" I gesture around us to the cabin Rex worked so hard to build. To the place he created out of grief and fear and desperation; the place that became a home.

I'm squeezing the key so tight I can feel its teeth cutting into my palm.

"Baby," Rex says, putting warm hands on my shoulders, "I can build something else. Something just for us." His eyes never leave mine. "I came here because I didn't have anywhere else to go. Didn't have anyone. And now.... As long as I'm with you, I'll be home."

My eyes flood with tears.

Home.

I never felt at home in my father's house. The apartments I've lived in since then have been crap. Just places to crash. Ginger's apartment has been a home away from home—as close as I thought I might ever get to a place that feels right. That feels like home. Then I met Rex and, even that first night, when I thought I'd never see him again, something about him called out to something deep inside me. I love this cabin, these woods, but it's not this place that feels like home. It's Rex.

He's looking at me, eyes tracking mine. I can see the moment he thinks I'm about to say no and it almost breaks my heart. I nod quickly, my mouth getting twisted around all the things I mean to say. So I just launch myself forward and hug him as tight as I can, arms around his neck and legs around his waist. Rex's hugs feel like being wrapped in the warmest blanket.

We stay like that for a while, just holding each other, until I relax my grip and my fist that was clenching the key unfurls, revealing a perfect indentation of Michigan in my palm.

FINALLY, I haul myself off the couch to go to the bathroom. I catch a glimpse of myself in the mirror and my expression is unfamiliar. I look younger. Happy in a way I never have. I can't help but think of the first time I saw myself in this mirror, Rex behind me, the night we met. I shake my head, thinking that if I'd told myself that night that I would be living in this cabin, I would probably have drowned myself in the shower laughing.

On the way back to the living room, my phone buzzes with a text. At first I don't believe it can really be from Colin because there's not a profanity or an insult in sight.

I'm okay, it says. *Can't talk yet. Merry Christmas.*

"Holy shit," I say. "It's a Christmas miracle."

"What?" Rex asks, and while he seems relieved Colin's all right, he doesn't seem overly impressed with the message.

"Seriously," I explain, following Rex into the kitchen, "this is unprecedented. This could be the only nonaggressive Colin text the archives will ever see."

Rex pulls out a tray of gingerbread that's been warming in the oven.

"Oh my god," I groan. "That smells so good; what are you trying to do to me?" Rex waggles his eyebrows and wraps his arms around me from behind, kissing my hair.

"Daniel," he murmurs in my ear, making me shiver. "Say it again."

"What?"

"That you're really going to move in with me."

I turn in his arms, marveling again, as always, at how big and solid he is, how warm.

"I'm really going to move in," I say, grinning. "I just wish I wasn't leaving tomorrow because I'll have to wait until I get back to actually do it."

Rex squeezes me, running his hand up and down my back. I breathe in his smell.

"I'm gonna miss you when I'm in Philly," I say.

Rex lifts me easily, dropping me on the counter and barely missing the gingerbread. He steps between my knees and kisses me deeply.

"We have time," he says. He's looking at me so steadily. I can tell he doesn't just mean time when I get back from Philly.

"Oh, I almost forgot. I have one more present for you," I say. I jump down from the counter and grab it from the closet. Rex is back on the couch and I hand the gift to him, leaning over the back of the couch. He hefts it in his hand and gives me a strange look, then undoes the paper. Inside is my worn copy of *The Secret History*.

He looks at the book uncertainly, then opens it and looks at the text.

"I—Daniel," he says regretfully. "No. It's your favorite book; I don't want to ruin it with my shit reading. The print's so small and it's long and—"

I shake my head, climbing onto the couch with him.

"I thought, if you want, I could read it to you."

Rex looks sheepish.

"Yeah? I tried to order the audiobook after we met that night in the woods," he says.

I can feel a tightening in my groin just thinking about that night. Rex's powerful body pushing me against that tree. Then it resolves into a warm feeling in my stomach at the thought that Rex went to that much trouble when I thought he wasn't even interested in me.

"I didn't know what it was, but I thought any book you loved that much had to be worth reading. I only saw the author's last name—only read it, I mean. I asked at the library, but they didn't have it."

I brush his hair back and smile at him.

"So, what do you think? I've never really read out loud to anyone before, so I don't know if I'll be any good at it, but...."

"You have such a sweet voice, baby," Rex says, nuzzling my throat. "I think you'll be good at it." He kisses my ear. "Can we start now?" His voice is eager.

I nod, feeling almost drunk with contentment.

"One sec," he says, and a minute later he's back with a huge piece of gingerbread and some wine.

He sits back on the couch and I lean back against his chest, cradling the worn paperback. From this vantage point I can see the whole living room. The Christmas tree with our new ornaments gleaming among the green branches. The lights twinkling. The crackling fire and the snow falling softly outside, covering anything dirty or broken or sad with a thick blanket of clean, pure white.

It smells like wood smoke and cedar and Rex and gingerbread and, as I open my favorite book, adding the dusty smell of worn paper to the mix, I find I'm almost too choked up to read.

As if he senses how overwhelmed I feel, Rex tightens his arms around me.

"You okay?" he asks, his hand splaying across my chest. I nod, but can't quite get the words out.

"It's...." I look around us, then back at him. "It's... perfect."

"Too good to be true?" Rex asks, stroking my hair away from my face.

"No," I tell him. "Just good."

Epilogue

December

GINGER'S SHOP window looks like some kind of insane Victorian-era Chanukah circus exploded in a burst of needles and lace. Blue and white velvet ribbon tacked up with tattoo needles spells out "Tattoo Bitch" in scrolling cursive. The Bud Light can angels hover in the corners of the window and old tattoo machines are stacked on top of each other to make a metal tree. Everything is dusted with blue and silver glitter. It actually looks kind of awesome.

"Yaaaay!" Ginger calls as I step into the shop. "It's Chanukah!"

"Well, technically, Chanukah's over, but—"

"Shut up. Chanukah is never over. The oil will burn for *eternity*!"

Good thing no one's in the shop because Ginger is clearly in giddy mode. I can't help but grin into her hair as she launches herself at me for a hug.

"Okay, you can tell me everything while we go get the food."

I stow my bags behind the counter and Ginger leads me back to the door, her elbow linked in mine.

"Everything about what?"

"Everything about how you look stupid happy."

She squeezes my elbow in the crook of her arm and grins at me.

"Huh. So do you," I tell her. "I hope we don't get hit by a bus to even it all out."

"Pff. On South Street? As *if* the traffic ever moves fast enough for that to kill us. Golden Empress?"

"Of course."

As we get our takeout, Ginger tells me about going to Christopher's parents' house for dinner and how she made a mostly good impression until she accidentally laughed in his dad's face when he said he loved Neil Diamond because she thought he was kidding.

I tell Ginger what Virginia said about the Temple job and about Rex asking me to move in with him. What I don't tell her much about is that Rex and I talked a lot about the future last night. About our options. About how he'd feel leaving Holiday. I don't tell her that last night, when we went to bed, I put the key to Rex's cabin—our cabin, now, I guess—on the bedside table so I could see it until I drifted off. Or that, when I fell asleep in Rex's arms, his big hands all over me, I felt certain that he would be there in the morning. That I wouldn't wake up to find that the world had disappeared.

While we eat, Ginger plays Christmas music DJ, putting on everything from Scottish boy choirs to Scott Weiland's Christmas album. I practically choke to death on a mouthful of sweet and sour chicken when I crack up at a YouTube parody of a Time Life CD commercial featuring A Very Eddie Vedder Christmas in which some genius has manipulated Pearl Jam songs into the form of Christmas carols. Finally, she puts on *The Nightmare Before Christmas*, which is her favorite Chanukah movie because she says it's obvious that Jack Skellington—a skinny outsider who tries to gain access to Christmas by studying it—is a metaphor for Jewish kids growing up and trying to figure out what the big deal about Christmas is.

"So, you got the text from Colin, but you haven't heard from him since then?" Ginger asks as Jack discovers the portal to Christmas Town.

"No." I didn't really expect to, either. Mostly, I think the only reason he sent me that text was because he was afraid that if I didn't hear from him I might tell Brian and Sam what I saw at dad's funeral.

"What did the guy look like? The one at the cemetery?"

"I didn't get much of a look at him. Big. Like, Rex big. Maybe bigger. Dark hair, dark eyes. I don't know, man. He looked kinda hot, I guess. Mostly I just noticed he was, like, crazy still. He didn't react to anything that happened. Didn't step in and fight. Didn't try to help Colin when we were fighting. Rex pulled me off him, but this guy just stood there. It was weird, actually. He didn't even say anything, but…."

"But?"

"But not like he didn't care. I mean, when I walked in he was… *holding* Colin. Like, cradling him. Gently. Colin was sobbing and this guy definitely cared. It was more like… maybe he knew what was going on? Like, knew what was at stake for Colin and didn't want to intrude or something. Fuck, I don't know."

"They care about each other, then, right? I mean for Colin to have this guy at your dad's funeral—"

"Yeah, I know. I guess so? Ugh, I still can't wrap my mind around it. I'm going to try and find Colin tomorrow and see if I can talk to him."

Ginger flops upside down on the couch, her hair trailing the carpet, staring at her little Chanukah tree. It's wrapped in white twinkle lights and hung with hundreds of stars cut out of blue paint chips from the hardware store. Every shade of blue you can imagine, from the palest baby blue to the deepest navy. It's beautiful.

"Do you think Colin's a top or a bottom?" she muses.

"Dude, stop! He's my brother."

"Well, I'm just saying. Do you think he likes—"

"Jesus, Ginge, seriously. No. I refuse."

"Is it wrong that I think Colin's kind of hot now that I know he's gay? And tortured."

"You are seriously fucked-up." I think about it for a second. "Okay, I would totally think that about someone who wasn't my brother."

"Okay, but just for one sec—you saw this guy. Can't you guess if he—"

"Presents! You want your presents?"

Ginger pouts, but it's well established that presents are a subject change that she'll allow.

We have a firm rule that we can't spend money on gifts and an equally firm one that all gifts can be regifted, recycled, or trashed without any concession to sentimentality. Ginger nearly always gives me a tattoo, so that rule mostly applies to my gifts, which I always used to find by picking through stuff that people left at the bar. They usually weren't great, but one banner year some girl left a red leather jacket and I'll never be able to top it. Even so, I'm pretty pleased about this year's gifts, especially since I didn't have the bar as a hunting ground. Luckily for me, Ginger loves the intersection of functionality and kitsch and, if I've learned anything since moving to Holiday, it's that almost all Michigan souvenirs live in that intersection.

I hand Ginger the lumpy packages that I wrapped in extra handouts from my classes.

"Oh, thank *god*," Ginger says, fanning herself as she accepts them. "I was getting seriously concerned that I wouldn't know how to structure my conclusion!"

"Don't worry. The other one's on thesis statements, so you'll have a well-balanced essay."

"The tart cherries!" Ginger examines the jar of tart cherry preserves topped with a square of red and white plaid cloth. "This does *not* look free, you cheater."

"Oh, it was free. The lady who owns one of the touristy shops near campus gave it to me." Ginger narrows her eyes. I suppose it's justified:

one year I did try and convince her that I'd gotten a sheet cake for free. To be fair, the week before, one of my friends had gotten a whole cake from a Trader Joe's dumpster. Still, since this one said "Happy Chanukah, you animal," with a picture of Animal from the Muppets done in frosting, it was a hard sell.

"She just handed it to you for no reason?"

"Um, well, no. Her daughter was in one of my classes and I, um, accidentally used the shop's sign as an example when I went off on a rant about unnecessary apostrophes...."

"Oh, jeez. What was her sign?"

"She seemed like a Capricorn."

Ginger swats me.

"It's called Nifty Things, and the big sign is fine, but then in the window there are two signs and one says Nifty Thing apostrophe *s* and the other says Nifty Things apostrophe. Anyway, I guess my student told her mom and her mom got the signs fixed. Then, one day when I was walking past the shop, she just popped out of the front door like she'd seen me coming and gave me those preserves."

"Creepy."

"*So* creepy. Dude, seriously, half the shit that happens in Holiday would seem like something out of a horror movie if there was scary music playing in the background. Or a David Lynch movie."

"If it had happened in Philly, that lady would've come out of her shop with a baseball bat."

"Right? Rex says I'm pathologically negative because I'm afraid if I admit that things are good, then I have to be scared they'll go away, so I just make myself expect the worst. Even if it's a quaint old couple with chainsaws at a Christmas tree farm."

"Uuuummm, that sounds... accurate? Wait, a quaint old couple with a chainsaw like in that fucked-up movie?"

"Yes, *thank* you."

Ginger sighs and slumps onto the floor.

"I like him."

"Who?"

"Duh, Rex. I think he's great for you."

"Well, I liked Christopher too."

"Obviously."

I slide onto the floor next to her and push the other gift into her lap.

"This one, I totally cheated on. It wasn't free and I won't pretend it was, but it's awesome and I have a job now, so deal with it."

"Ooh, babycakes, I love it when you're so forceful. Oh crap, that's awesome!" she says, tearing the paper off the novelty ice cube trays. "Let's make some right now."

In the kitchen, Ginger fills the little Michigans with water.

"Wait, I know what we have to do."

Ginger pulls coffee ice cream out of the freezer, the only food she can always be counted on to have in the house. She scoops some into a bowl and mushes it up until it's soft, then she packs it into the second ice cube tray, smoothing it into perfect little Michigan ice creams.

"Hang on," she says, rifling through her cabinets. "Ah ha!" She pulls a dusty box of toothpicks from the back of a cabinet and sticks one in the center of each ice cube. "Do you think I should put one in the upper peninsulas too?" she asks. "So they don't detach when we pop them out?"

"Um," I say, staring between Ginger and the ice cube trays. "Who the fuck *are* you right now?"

Ginger drops her gaze to the floor for a second and when she looks back up her expression is sheepish.

"Okay, so maybe I saw Christopher do something like this once." She rolls her eyes. "Okay, and *maybe* he's teaching me to cook a little bit."

I fake gasp and put my hand to my heart.

"Ginger Marie, as I live and breathe!" She flips me off. "Um, well, Rex may be trying to teach me to cook, too…."

"Oh god, what's to become of us? Domesticated!"

"It's just ice cream in an ice cube tray, Ginge, let's not get ahead of ourselves."

"Oh? And what culinary masterpieces have you achieved?"

"Uh. None. I made eggs that actually tasted like what I would imagine it feels like to die. Though I *did* somehow manage to infuse normal toast with such a strong scent of fire that I think it might be considered molecular gastronomy."

"Molecular what now?"

"Molecular gastronomy. I saw it on one of Rex's cooking shows. It's kind of awesome. It's like, they use dry ice and a bunch of other chemicals to make one food taste like or look like another. So, like, they could make something that looked like coffee ice cream, but then when you taste it, it's actually meat loaf or something."

"That's the grossest thing I've ever heard. Why would anyone want meat loaf when they could have coffee ice cream?"

"Um, I don't think I explained it well."

We put the ice cube trays in the freezer and drop back on the couch as Jack Skellington's minions are abducting Santa.

"God, Oogie Boogie has the sexiest voice," Ginger says, and I nod.

"Oh, hey, Rex wanted to get you a Chanukah present, but when I told him about the whole free thing—"

"Which you cheated on."

"Which I cheated on. Anyway, he says that if you want, he'll build you new shelves in the back of the shop if he's in Philly again. He says he noticed that yours were uneven."

"He was only downstairs for, like, two minutes."

"Dude, he's creepy observant. It's…." I shake my head, remembering how I reaped the benefits of Rex's incredible powers of observation last night. How he held me down and explored every inch of my body, watching my reactions and zeroing in on all the places that had me squirming until, after what felt like hours, I was trembling in his arms, every touch electrifying, begging for him to be inside me. I shiver and shake it off, but Ginger is watching me like she can see the film reel playing in my head. I clear my throat.

"Well, that's nice of him. Tell him I'll give him any tattoo he wants in exchange."

"Don't you dare!"

"What? Why?"

Because Rex is perfect as he is. Flawless. Because he's already a work of art. Because I don't want anyone touching him but me. Not even Ginger.

"Um, I just… like him as he is…."

"Wait, what do you mean *if* he's in Philly again? Why wouldn't he be?"

"His words. I think he just didn't want to assume."

"Why shouldn't he assume?"

"No, I mean, he should. I just. I don't know. Who knows what'll happen. If I'll get the Temple job; if Rex would actually move if I did get it."

"Didn't he say he would?"

"Yeah."

Ginger pulls out her phone and clicks around, giving me a very Ginger look.

"Hey, Rex," she says.

"What the hell, Ginge?"

"I'm going to need confirmation on something. Did you or did you not tell Daniel that you would move to Philadelphia with him if he gets the job at Temple?"

"Ginger!" I hiss.

"Uh-huh, that's what I thought. And did he or did he not agree to move in with you, whether or not that happens?"

"Ginger, give me the goddamn phone."

"Excellent. I'm so happy for you both."

"Ginger!"

"Hey, are my shelves really so crooked that you—"

I grab the phone from her and glare.

"Hi," I say. "Sorry. She just, um, called."

"Hi," Rex says, his warm voice growly over the phone.

"Um, what are you up to?" I ask. I can picture him, drinking a beer in front of the Food Network, Marilyn curled by the fire, our Christmas tree lit up. God, I already miss him and I haven't even been gone for twelve hours.

"And what are you wearing?" Ginger yells from the kitchen.

Rex chuckles softly.

"Actually," he says, and he sounds a little shy all of a sudden, "I was using your computer. I hope that's okay."

"Yeah, sure. What for?"

"I was looking at a slideshow of stuff to do in Philadelphia."

"Yeah?" There's a warm flutter behind my ribs.

"Mmhmm. And as for what I'm wearing, well. I'll leave that to your imagination."

I groan, Rex's words turning the warm flutter in my chest to a heat that dips considerably lower.

"Ooh, they're perfect!" Ginger calls from the kitchen.

"What are you guys up to?" Rex asks.

"Making Michigan-shaped ice cream thingies."

"Well, I'll let you get back to your Chanukah," Rex says seriously. I love that he respects how important my traditions with Ginger are.

"Okay. I... I miss you." My voice is almost a whisper. I don't know why I'm so self-conscious that Ginger might hear me.

"Hey, Daniel." Rex's voice is liquid heat. "I love you. I miss you too."

I can feel myself flushing. I'm not sure I'll ever get used to hearing those words in Rex's deep voice. They're like a brand, marking me, claiming me.

"I love you too," I say softly, hunching around the phone like I can direct the words more precisely to him.

"I'll see you in a few days, baby." I can practically see Rex's smile, tender and satisfied.

"Bye."

When I turn around, Ginger's standing in the doorway to the kitchen, her expression soft. She's licking an upper peninsula thoughtfully.

"So, what's your pleasure this year?" Her expression turns mischievous. "Maybe Rex's name on your ass? Ooh, or the cabin? I do a really good wood grain."

I flip her off and she grins, but I can't help but wonder how Rex would react if he pulled my pants down and saw his name scrawled across my ass in Ginger's gorgeous script.

I fumble through my jacket pockets and pull out my keys.

"I want this." I hand Ginger the wooden keychain in the shape of Michigan that Rex put the key to the cabin on. "And a little heart here." I point to where Holiday would be.

"Oh crap, babycakes, that's so good." She sounds awed. "Let me grab the stuff from downstairs."

It's a small piece, but it turns out beautifully. In the end, Ginger convinced me that we should add the chain and the key. It's so detailed and realistic that it looks like Rex just dropped the key on my chest.

"You're sure it's not too sappy that we put it over my heart?" I ask her, gazing down at it in awe.

"Too late, sucker," she says, but she's looking at the piece with satisfaction. She takes a picture with her phone. "No, I think it's perfect."

"It is perfect."

"Should I send Rex the picture?"

"No. I want to surprise him."

I stroke lightly over the key, glad that I'll take the slight ache of the needle with me tomorrow when I try and confront Colin.

I lean back and let my eyes go unfocused as I look at the Chanukah tree. It's a beautiful blur of green and blues. It's almost like I'm looking through the window at Rex's cabin—*our* cabin. Like it's early in the morning and I'm still half-asleep, Rex's warmth behind me, his face buried in my neck, and I'm looking out at the pine trees and blue sky. I can almost feel his arms around me, smell that mixture of cedar and pine and wood smoke that is Rex's alone.

I close my eyes and let my hand rest on my chest. I'm not sure what's going to happen in the next year. Whether I'll get the Temple job or not. Whether I'll stay in Holiday or move back to Philly. But, for the first time, the uncertainty isn't freaking me out. Because I know that Rex will be there—wherever there is. And now I can look down at this key anytime I want and see my connection to him. See my way home.

ROAN PARRISH grew up in Michigan and lives in Philadelphia, but is always a few minutes away from deciding to move. A former academic, she's used to writing things that no one reads. She still loves to geek out about books, movies, TV, and music—now, though, she's excited to be writing the kind of romantic, angsty stories that she loves to escape into. When not writing, she can usually be found cutting her friends' hair, wandering through whatever city she's in while listening to torch songs and melodic death metal, or cooking overly elaborate meals. One time she might or might not have baked a six-layer chocolate cake and then thrown it out the window in a fit of pique. She loves bonfires, winter beaches, minor chord harmonies, and cheese. But mostly cheese.

You can find her on her website or on twitter. Have questions/comments/pictures of octopi? Want to recommend a strong cheese or express a strong opinion? Drop her a line on e-mail. She'd love to hear from you.

Website: http://www.roanparrish.com
Twitter: @RoanParrish
E-mail: roanparrish@gmail.com

THE STORM BEFORE THE Calm

CATE ASHWOOD

http://www.dreamspinnerpress.com

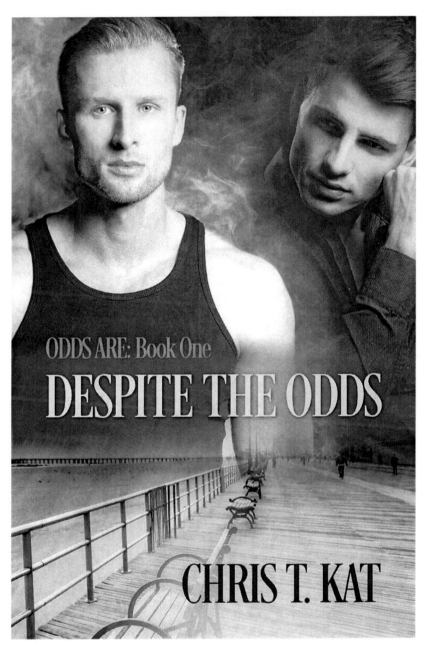

ODDS ARE: Book One

DESPITE THE ODDS

CHRIS T. KAT

http://www.dreamspinnerpress.com

SUKI FLEET

FALLING

http://www.dreamspinnerpress.com

FOR Mac

BRYNN STEIN

http://www.dreamspinnerpress.com

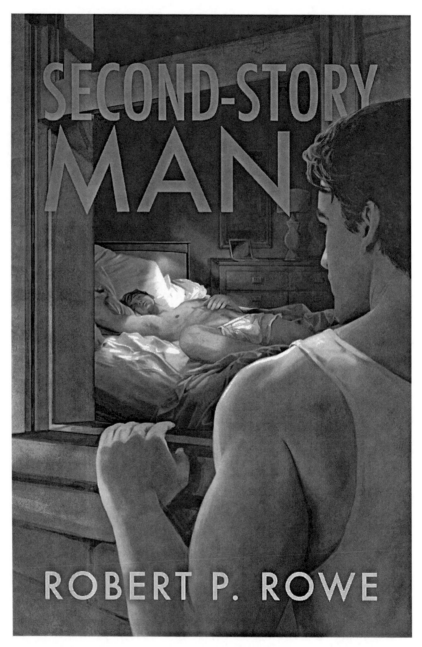

SECOND-STORY
MAN

ROBERT P. ROWE

http://www.dreamspinnerpress.com

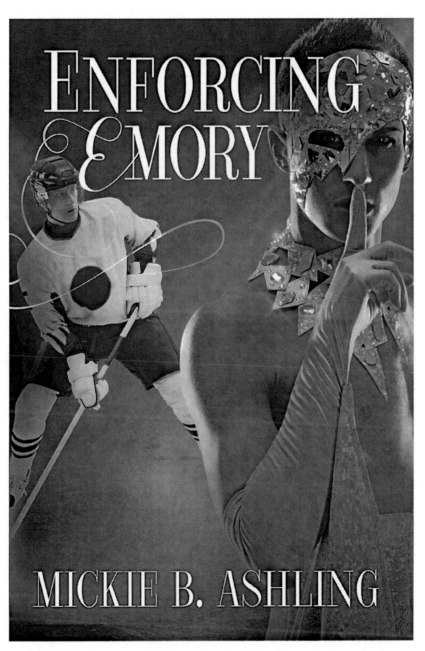

ENFORCING EMORY

MICKIE B. ASHLING

http://www.dreamspinnerpress.com

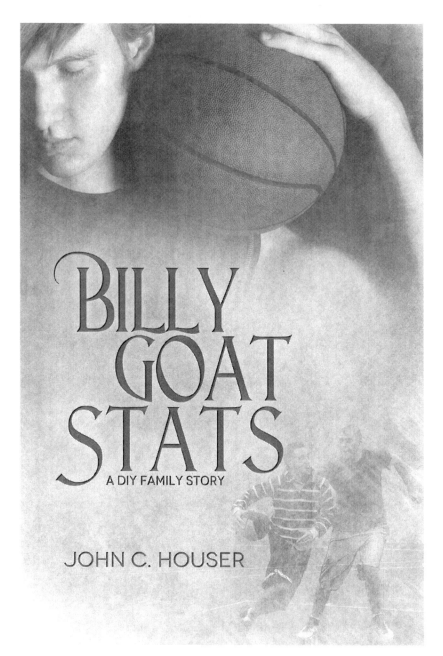

BILLY GOAT STATS

A DIY FAMILY STORY

JOHN C. HOUSER

http://www.dreamspinnerpress.com

The SHARED HARVEST

D.W. MARCHWELL

http://www.dreamspinnerpress.com